B

/20

'Kathryn Fox...
Cornwell will ad...

'Like Fox, her creator, ... of nature. *Blood Born* ... is a thriller that grips from first page to last' Kathy Reichs

'Author Fox displays the deft hand of a natural writer, whether she's weaving her break-neck plots, imparting fascinating medical and police procedural details or breathing life into her characters – both good and bad. What a compelling new talent!' Jeffery Deaver

'Voice, pace, suspense and detail – *Blood Born* has it all' Lee Child

'Brilliant and breathtaking ... Lock your doors and read this book' Linda Fairstein

'A fascinating novel about the real-life problem of leading sportsmen and sexual violence' *Sunday Times*

'Fans of Patricia Cornwell and Kathy Reichs and CSI will enjoy [this] new offering from doctor-turned-author Kathryn Fox ... It's tense, believable stuff' *Sun*

'Patricia Cornwell's forensic fantasies may have cooled, but Fox's morgue-talk promises to plug the gap with a crime debut that nicely marries the personal life of the sleuth with that of the murder victim' *Independent*

'Fox is stomach-churningly good' *Mail on Sunday*

'[This] forensic thriller . . . has just the right balance of pathological detail and tight plotting. Think *ER* meets *CSI* . . . Gripping from its very first page, it carries you breathlessly through its deftly plotted twists and turns' *Vogue* (Australia)

'Forensically speaking, *Malicious Intent* is top-notch in its genre' *Sunday Telegraph* (Sydney)

'A finely crafted novel' *Sydney Morning Herald*

'Watch out Patricia Cornwell' *Gold Coast Bulletin*

'*Malicious Intent* is . . . much better than anything Cornwell has written lately, and much superior to anything Reichs has ever written. Fox may be a medical practitioner, but she knows how to write decent prose, create sympathetic characters and pace a thriller, and she keeps the reader turning the pages. It's all very unsettling and deeply satisfying' *Australian Book Review*

'If you're into grisly forensic detail, as in the gore-spattered novels of Patricia Cornwell and Kathy Reichs, you'll love this' *Saga*

'Highly recommended reading' *Daily Telegraph* (Australia)

'With a chill factor that is enhanced by the reality of recent scandals in the sporting world, this compelling page-turner puts a stunning new talent firmly on the thriller map' *Daily Record*

About the Author

Kathryn Fox is a medical practitioner with a special interest in forensic medicine. *Cold Grave* is her sixth novel and her books have been translated into over a dozen languages.

Kathryn lives in Sydney and combines her passion for books and medicine by being the patron of a reading programme for remote and indigenous communities that promotes the links between literacy and health.

www.kathrynfox.com
www.twitter.com/kathrynfoxbooks
https://www.facebook.com/kathrynfoxauthor

Also by Kathryn Fox

Malicious Intent

Without Consent

Skin and Bone

Blood Born

Death Mask

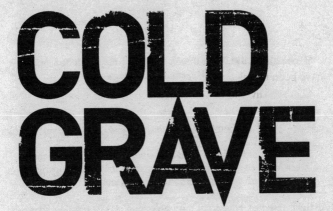

COLD GRAVE

KATHRYN FOX

HODDER

First published in Great Britain in 2012 by Hodder & Stoughton
An Hachette UK company

1

A CIP catalogue record for this title is available from the British Library.

B format ISBN 978 1 444 70953 7
A format ISBN ISBN 978 0 340 91911 8

Typeset in Plantin Light by Hewer Text UK Ltd, Edinburgh
Printed and bound by Clays Ltd, St Ives plc

Hodder & Stoughton policy is to use papers that are natural, renewable
and recyclable products and made from wood grown in sustainable
forests. The logging and manufacturing processes are expected to
conform to the environmental regulations of the country of origin.

Hodder & Stoughton Ltd
338 Euston Road
London NW1 3BH

www.hodder.co.uk

For all the victims on cruise ships and their families still searching for answers.

Ben peeled back the double bed sheet. 'Wake up, Mum! It's morning. Let's go swimming!'

Anya Crichton forced her eyelids to separate and saw her six year old standing over her, in rash vest and board shorts. From the sickly sweet smell, the globs smeared across his cheeks were sunscreen.

'Come on, MUM!'

Part of her was impressed that he had thought of the sun protection, but the rest wished he could have slept longer – the bedside clock read 6.15 a.m. First hint of sunlight and he was wide awake, ready for the new day's adventures.

She hauled herself up against the headboard and felt the vibration in the cabin. Despite a fitful night, she had escaped seasickness. For now. The last few days felt like a blur. Working in New York on an assault case involving the Jersey Bombers football team had been challenging but exhausting. The gift of a holiday on board the *Paradisio* with her son had been extravagant on the part of the Bombers' owner. Only thing was, he had included her former husband in the 'family' holiday.

Ben had begged for the three of them to be together and, for his sake, Anya and her ex-husband had reluctantly agreed to put aside their differences. Besides, it made sense for Martin, who had custody, to bring Ben from Australia to visit New York and see the Bombers play live. From there, the flights to Hawaii had been uneventful. Unfortunately at check-in, the two promised cabins had been unavailable, and they'd been allocated the same suite. At both their insistence, Martin was given a separate cabin on a lower deck.

Now Anya had Ben to herself for the first time in weeks.

'What about breakfast? Aren't you hungry? I bet they do fantastic pancakes.'

Hands on hips, Ben tilted his head. 'You never exercise or go in the water on a full stomach. We can eat *after*.' He moved his arms so his palms faced upward, emphasising the point. The gesture belonged to his grandfather.

Anya pressed the heel of her hand on her forehead. 'What was I thinking?' One lunge and Ben was squealing in her arms.

'How silly do you think I am?' she teased, exposing his belly with the threat of more tickles.

The scent of sunscreen filled the air. Suddenly the holiday felt real.

'You missed a tiny bit,' she joked, rubbing her hands all over Ben's face. He thought the action hilarious.

A knock on the door broke the moment.

'Dad!' He was off.

'I'll answer it. It could be anyone.' Anya scrambled to her feet.

Before she could stop him, Martin had entered and hauled their son into his arms.

Anyone would have thought the pair had been separated a lot longer than one night.

'Morning Annie.' He glanced at her oversized Tweety Bird T-shirt. 'Nice PJs. Didn't we give you that when Benny Boy was born?'

'It's still comfy.' It was all she could think to say. Truth was she wouldn't ever part with it because it reminded her of happier family times. Something in Martin's expression changed. He looked tired and drawn.

'What happened? Party too hard after dinner?' She regretted the tone as soon as the words came out.

He put Ben down. 'I don't have a hangover, if that's what you're suggesting. I was headed up for a jog, but if you'd like a lie-in? I can take—'

'Sorry, I didn't mean to . . .' She grabbed her swimsuit and overdress from the bottom drawer and headed for the bathroom. 'I'll just be a minute.'

By the time she reappeared, the curtains were drawn back, the balcony door was open and a brisk sea breeze drifted through the cabin. They had been sailing since leaving Honolulu the previous night and she had barely registered the movement. No nausea, no dizziness, no vomiting, unlike her earlier experiences with boats. Maybe the trip would be a new beginning; for her stomach at least, she thought.

'This is luxurious,' Martin announced, coming in from the balcony.

Anya felt guilty. 'What's yours like?'

'There's a picture of a porthole. From the sounds of it, I'm just above the crew's karaoke bar. Most of the rooms on the corridor are filled with guys in matching bowling shirts who aren't exactly considerate of anyone wanting sleep.'

That explained Martin's appearance.

Anya felt even guiltier. 'Maybe we should take turns here with Ben.'

He gave her a look that meant swapping cabins wasn't an option.

'If you were disturbed,' she said, 'chances are others were too. It might be worth saying something to the purser.'

'Hey look, Dad, this is where I sleep.' Ben had climbed the ladder and plonked himself on the bed that lowered from the ceiling, above the double-seater lounge. 'It goes away in the daytime.'

'Like a secret bed!' Martin pulled the sheet over Ben's

3

face. 'I think I will complain. Two weeks of what happened last night will do me in. We could stop by the main deck on the way up to the pool.'

Complete with room keys, sunscreen, hats and sunglasses, they headed to the birdcage lifts. At that time in the morning, Guest Services was quiet. Martin was greeted by a smiling purser with a Jamaican accent. Ben sat on a lounge chair nearby with his favourite book – *The A-Z of Animals*.'

'Last night,' Martin began, 'the noise on the corridor was louder than the crew singing karaoke below.'

'Sir, the crew are entitled to their downtime and, unfortunately, there is little I can do about that. Some passengers who sleep lightly find earplugs helpful. They may be purchased in the shop on deck four.'

The response took both Anya and Martin by surprise.

'Look,' Martin attempted. 'I'm into fun as much as the next guy, but last night deck one was out of control. A group of men were drinking outside the cabins and mucking around with fire-extinguishers.' His voice lowered, 'Some were naked and when I asked if they could keep it down, they became aggressive. To be honest, as a group, they're fairly intimidating. I get cutting loose, but not with families all around. There was even a nude couple in the corridor at one stage having sex.' He jabbed his finger into the desk. 'It's completely unacceptable. I don't want my son or anyone else's kids to have to see or hear that.'

Anya was surprised how annoyed Martin was. There was a time when he would have been the loud one in the corridor. He had been known to pull pranks at university, but they were harmless. Nothing like what he just described.

'Well, sir, we take safety on board very seriously and interfering with fire equipment is a breach of our regulations.'

Anya glanced at Martin. 'But nudity and intercourse in public areas isn't?'

4

The purser gave her a sympathetic look. 'Ma'am, it was our first night at sea. We find that people let off steam and have fun on vacation. It's why they sail with us. They usually settle down after a couple of nights.'

He handed across a couple of drink vouchers. 'We apologise for the inconvenience.' His smile revealed fluorescent white teeth.

'Is that it?' Martin was incredulous.

'I am only permitted to give you two vouchers.'

Martin breathed and his nostrils flared. 'What happens tonight?'

The Jamaican man tapped into a computer. 'I'll have a security guard patrol that deck. You have a great day now.'

At least that was something. Anya touched Martin's arm. Maybe the purser was right. It made sense that the first and last nights of a cruise would be the rowdiest. No one could keep up that pace for fourteen days.

'They'll be asleep by now. We could go play loud music outside their rooms.' Anya smiled, remembering the accommodation hall at university. A friend had once rewired the speaker system to play 'Too Many Times' early the next morning after a ball. The number of angry sore heads proved it had been effective.

'Maybe if you get seasick you could knock on one of their doors?' Martin said. 'You should have heard them carry on about a girl vomiting inside one of their rooms.'

Anya gestured for Ben and the trio caught the lift to the pool deck. Before Anya's towel hit the lounge chair, Ben had slid into the pool. Martin took the opportunity to go for a run on the deck above.

The sun had risen but had no heat in it. A fresh breeze caught Anya's hair as she pulled it back into a tie. Wisps at the side escaped and gusted about her face. Ben was already splashing in the pool and she imagined the holiday ahead

– nothing to do but lounge around and enjoy time with Ben. She had forgotten what it was like being outside. Her body seemed to crave every hint of energy the sun bestowed.

At this hour, only a handful of people were up and about. A cleaning crew swept the wooden decks and collected rubbish from the bins. Towels were already stacked in readiness for the day ahead.

'You coming in, Mum?'

Anya shed her sandals and lifted her dress over her head.

It had been a while since she had been in a swimsuit but, thankfully, her size and shape hadn't changed, just succumbed to some gravitational pull.

She sat on the side of the pool and dipped her feet in. The cool water was refreshing. If she wasn't fully awake, she soon would be. Ben dived under the surface and bobbed up like a dolphin. He had to be part-amphibian, she thought. For the moment they had the pool and quiet to themselves.

Anya closed her eyes to savour it. She missed Ben more than anyone knew and understood his desperate need to have both parents together sometimes. Just like she had wanted when her own parents divorced.

The peace was suddenly shattered.

'ANNIE!' Martin leant over the rail from the next level up. 'Emergency! Need you up here now! Ben, you stay there.'

Martin disappeared. He had been an intensive care nurse and his tone was enough to alarm her. Whatever it was, he didn't want Ben to see. 'Dad and I need you to sit on the lounger. Don't move anywhere, you're like a statue,' she said, pulling Ben out of the pool. 'If you go back in the water, there'll be no more swimming this trip. This is incredibly important, OK?'

Two elderly women in tracksuits saw the commotion and offered to sit with the boy.

Ben nodded and shivered. Anya wrapped a towel around his

6

shoulders and another over the goose bumps covering his legs. 'I'll be right up there,' she said, pointing to the balcony and throwing her dress on. Ben gave another understanding nod.

'Call out if you need me.' She thanked the women then rushed up the stairs, past a middle-aged man on his way down.

About ten feet along on the left, Martin was crouched at the open doors of a waist-high towel cabinet.

'There's no pulse. Help me lift her out.'

Anya couldn't immediately see a face but bare feet protruded from the door.

She took the legs and Martin carried the limp top half of the young woman. Long, wet black hair obscured the face. They gently lowered her onto the hard deck and Martin commenced mouth-to-mouth resuscitation. Anya began cardiac massage and the pair worked in synchronisation.

A passenger had attracted the attention of a cleaner who dropped his high pressure hose and ran over.

'This is a medical emergency; we need you to call for help.'

The panic on the cleaner's face showed he understood.

A minute later, an officer arrived with a first-aid kit. He took out a one-way breathing mask and introduced himself as William. Martin stepped away and used the back of his hand to wipe what looked like a small amount of vomit from his mouth.

'Please, not again,' William muttered, kneeling down beside the patient. He began blowing into the tube on top of the mask.

'Does anyone know what happened?' he managed in between breaths.

Anya continued the compressions, desperate for the patient to breathe. She paused to feel for a carotid pulse.

No pulse.

'Come on,' she urged, locking her hands together and

7

pressing on the chest with short sharp bursts. After each breath, William listened for any spontaneous sounds from the mouth.

'Med team's on the way.' Breath. 'Should be here any second.' Breath.

Anya was unsure who William was reassuring.

A woman in a crisp white officer's uniform squatted to their side, and unzipped a large backpack. A security man asked a small group of observers to step back.

'I'm Karen, senior nurse on board,' she puffed. 'What have we got?'

Martin spoke. 'Young woman. Feet were sticking out of that cupboard. When I found her, she wasn't breathing and had no pulse. We commenced CPR . . .' he checked his watch, 'four, no, five minutes ago.'

The nurse dropped to her knees and snapped on blue gloves.

Anya continued compressions, sweat beading on her forehead.

'She vomited and may have aspirated.' Martin wiped his mouth again, this time on the crook of one elbow.

'Reeks of alcohol. Do you have any medical training?' The backpack contained a small oxygen tank, which the nurse connected to a mask and bag. Working from the top of the girl's head, she extended the neck and placed a Guedel's airway over the tongue. With the mask in place, she held one little finger under the chin and the others on top. A few bursts of oxygen were delivered before she reached for the carotid with her other hand. Anya paused.

'My ex-wife's a doctor and I'm a trained ICU nurse.'

'In that case, can you grab me a sixteen-gauge cannula? And you may want to put on gloves and take over this end.'

Martin positioned his hands over the mask and continued to squeeze air into the girl's lungs.

8

With Anya on the right of the patient, the nurse moved to the left and extended the arm. 'Veins aren't good, but we'll give it a go.' She pulled the plastic sheath off the cannula with her teeth and pierced the skin. 'I'm in,' she announced. 'William, can you peel off some tape from the roll.'

The officer quickly obliged and the access vein was deftly secured.

'Do you have adrenalin, I mean epinephrine?' Anya had never understood why America used different terms from Britain and Australia for the same medication.

'And an automated defibrillator.' She held a mini-jet for Martin to see.

'One to ten thousand epinephrine.' Martin confirmed the dose.

While Martin and Anya continued their physical resuscitation, Karen injected the young woman's only hope of survival.

'You OK?' The nurse glanced at Anya who nodded and continued compressions, pausing only for Karen to cut off the young woman's blouse, revealing a flimsy bra. She slid it to waist level.

Anya looked up. A small group had formed and were watching, some even taking photos. 'Can we get anyone who isn't helping back,' she said loudly. 'Can you use towels to make a screen?'

This young woman deserved respect and privacy.

The nurse shouted orders to security and a wall of towels went up around them. She used a spare from nearby to wipe the chest.

'No piercings, no underwire. We're good to go.' Karen placed one gel pad on the right side, the other below the heart on the left. The machine charged and Anya knelt back and held her breath. The adrenalin had the chance to circulate. All eyes focused on the tiny screen.

'It's VF. Everyone clear.'

Anya felt relief. At least it was a rhythm that might be shocked back into a heartbeat.

The young body bucked with the electrical charge. Martin felt for a pulse and his shoulders tightened. 'No output.'

The monitor showed a flat line.

Anya resumed cardiac massage, with aching arms and cramping fingers. The physical effort was exhausting. But she was not giving up. 'What if she's diabetic and hypoglycaemic?'

'Could be, if she's been here all night.' Without hesitation, the nurse inserted a large pre-packaged syringe into the vein. 'Fifty mils of fifty percent dextrose going in.'

A tall olive-skinned man in white uniform arrived. He was unshaven, hair tousled.

'What happened?' His voice was gruff, and his accent eastern European.

The nurse filled him in.

'Give Narcan.' He remained standing, arms folded as if in judgement.

The antidote reversed any effects of narcotics, in case the patient had overdosed on codeine, heroin or morphine. It would not cause harm and could just save her life. The effect would be immediate. For the first time, Anya hoped illicit drugs were responsible.

The needle entered the cannula and the Narcan was injected. Nothing.

'Mum!' Anya heard Ben call for her and turned. He had slipped behind the towel screen and was crying, clutching one of the towels. 'I got scared. You didn't come back.'

Martin continued to squeeze oxygen into the lungs via the bag. 'Hey buddy, this lady's pretending to be asleep. Just like when we practise lifesaving on the beach.'

But it wasn't the scene that disturbed Ben; it was their

absence. Anya looked for someone to help. The women in tracksuits were nowhere in sight.

William was quickly at Ben's side. He turned him around and knelt down to his eye level. 'There's someone I know who would just love to play with you.'

He called over a female crew member who poked her head over the towels. She had a broad smile and introduced herself to Ben with an English accent.

After a word and a trip to the railing, William returned. Anya was relieved but the muscle fatigue and hand cramping were taking hold.

'One of our best kids' club counsellors is with your son. If you like, I can take over.'

By now, short of breath and strength waning, there was no argument. She slid to the side; hoping blood had circulated to the girl's brain with each press on her narrow chest.

Around a dozen staff stood guard and talked into phones, while peering over the towels. So much for privacy and dignity.

The ship's doctor knelt down and listened to the lungs. 'Air and fluid is in both sides. There is much congestion.'

Karen closed then opened her eyes. 'About to give more epinephrine, and then a diuretic.' Again, she presented the labels to Martin for verification while he kept up the rhythm of squeezing and relaxing the bag.

Within a minute, William was perspiring with his effort.

'We should open her chest,' the doctor announced.

Karen remained calm but assertive. 'We're not equipped for open heart surgery in the middle of the ocean. We can handle minor surgery but not that.'

Martin checked for a pulse then glanced up at Anya. The monitor still showed a flat line. Someone had to make a decision.

Karen noticed the exchange. 'How long?'

'Twenty-three minutes.' Martin had slipped back into his former role.

'What is the exact time?' The doctor demanded. He was about to stop the resuscitation and record time of death. Anya did not want to give up. The girl was young. She deserved every chance. So did her family. Especially on a cruise ship. Death was the last thing anyone expected on a family holiday.

'How about Flumazenil?' She blurted. It reversed the effect of benzodiazepines, like valium and rohypnol, a date-rape drug.

'It's a good idea,' Karen said. 'We might just get lucky. If not, we can honestly tell the family we tried everything we could.'

2

A little while later, Doctor Novak called the time of death. Karen peeled off her gloves. The team had exhausted themselves. The young body could not respond.

William received a call on his phone.

He ran his spare hand through his cowlicked fringe. 'A family's just reported a teenager missing. Apparently her bed wasn't slept in. Name is Lilly Chan.'

Karen sighed. 'That's the worst part of this job. Let's hope Wonder Boy over there handles it with a bit of sensitivity.'

It was one of the reasons Anya had chosen pathology as a profession. It meant being removed from breaking the initial bad news and not knowing the deceased personally. As a forensic physician, she now dealt with injuries in survivors, which could be traumatic, but was still preferable to breaking bad news to relatives.

The doctor sat on a chair nearby, scribbling notes on a small pad in between scratching his unshaven chin.

'Wonder Boy?' Anya asked.

'I shouldn't say that. He's from Croatia. Resumé is impressive. He was a military surgeon. His forte is cutting. People skills don't figure in his repertoire.'

Karen tucked an escaped part of her shirt back into her trousers. She was a solid woman, about five eight with broad shoulders, the type who could have been a swimmer in her youth. The roundish face and full cheeks made her age difficult to estimate, despite the absence of any make-up.

Martin stood, arms by his side, staring at the lifeless body on the deck. Anya noticed his hands were shaking. It had been a while since he had been involved in a cardiac arrest.

'How about you? What branch of medicine are you in? And please don't say psychiatry.'

'Pathology and forensic medicine. By the way, I'm Anya and this is Martin.'

A man dressed in a navy jumper and white trousers arrived. He bent over the body and began to take notes.

'That's David FitzHarris, Head of Security,' Karen explained.

Anya quietly asked if she could borrow the nurse's phone. 'Why?'

'The girl was in the cupboard, soaking wet. Someone put her there. For legal reasons someone should document where and how she was found.'

The possibility of a suspicious death didn't appear to have crossed the nurse's mind. She reached into her pocket and pulled out a smartphone. 'I'll pass them on with my report. Bosses are obsessive about paperwork, and everyone up the chain will have to be informed.'

Anya photographed the body, oxygen mask and defibrillator pads. The area around the young mouth had become paler, and lips a deep blue. Next she took images of the open cupboard and the dishevelled towels on the top.

'Ma'am, I'm afraid I'll need that phone.'

The head of security raised his gaze to meet Anya's. Ice blue eyes peered from beneath dark eyebrows, with an intensity that was designed to intimidate.

'It's OK, Fitz, this is the doctor who helped us in the resuscitation effort, and her ex-husband's an intensive care nurse. They were invaluable.'

The head of security used a rail to pull himself up to his full height of six foot or so before obscuring the lens with one hand. 'Ma'am, I still cannot allow you to take photographs.'

Karen sighed. 'She's a pathologist, Fitz, and it's my phone. For the report.' She leant back on her haunches and rummaged through the backpack. 'I'll need to get something to wash out Martin's mouth. We need to take some baseline bloods as well.'

Anya had almost forgotten. Any infection the girl had could have been transferred to Martin. Hepatitis, HIV and even ulcer-causing bacteria may have been transmitted during mouth-to-mouth breathing. It would be months before they knew whether Martin was completely clear of infection. Anya couldn't help but feel concerned.

'What about Ben?' Martin's hands still had a fine tremor.

William returned to the rail to check. 'He's smitten with Olivia, it seems. They're playing Uno and he seems to be winning. If you like, she can take him with her to the kids' club, and you can pick him up anytime. Gives you a chance to do what you have to.'

'He'd love that,' Martin said. Anya had to agree.

William disappeared down the stairs.

Karen's pager beeped. 'I have to get back to the medical centre. We can take those bloods and clean your mouth now if you like.' Martin obliged and followed her.

'A pathologist.' Fitz looked Anya up and down, as if to say she didn't look like one. 'I don't need to explain that we require complete discretion in this matter. For the sake of the family.'

Equal amounts of silver and brown were scattered throughout his short back and sides, a contrast to the dark eyebrows. The cut had the hallmark of former army, or police. The spare tyre around his middle suggested it had been a while since he had seen active duty.

'I appreciate that,' Anya said, 'but we also need to give as much information to the coroner as possible.'

He frowned and gestured toward the hot spa three metres to their right. 'Body's soaking wet. Are we looking at a drowning?'

'The problem is that Lilly was found inside the towel cupboard.' It seemed certain the girl would be identified as the missing Lilly Chan.

His frown released. 'A reasonable point.' He moved to the cupboard. Anya followed.

He curled his lip and covered his nose with a hand. 'Fermented vomit, smells like a big night.'

Anya took the best image of the regurgitated stomach contents. Digested alcohol was sickly sweet, one of the less offensive odours associated with death. 'It proves she was alive when she was put there.'

'Assuming it was her vomit.'

Anya was taken aback. Two people would never have fitted in that small space.

'Am just saying. Never assume in this business. Maybe she crawled inside.'

Fitz received a text on his phone. He took a deep breath. 'We need to move this along. There are over three thousand passengers on board looking for the good time they paid for. We need to clear this deck asap.'

Anya could not believe his priorities. A young woman had just died, and he was more concerned with partying passengers. 'If Lilly was so drunk that she crawled into a cupboard for shelter, would she have bothered lifting all the towels to the top? Surely she would have shovelled them out onto the deck, or covered herself, especially if she was cold and wet.'

He didn't answer the question. 'Any idea what time that might have been?'

'There was a heart rhythm, but no effective output when we found her. We were focused with saving her life, not calculating her core temperature.' Anya felt her face flush

16

with frustration, and anger that they had failed. Normally, death didn't bother her this much, but it was the last thing she had expected on a family cruise. No doubt Lilly's family thought the same.

'OK.' He lowered his voice. 'I understand this isn't easy, and you didn't sign up for this. But you have specialised expertise that can help. I've got limited resources and we're all under pressure to sort this mess out as quickly as possible. On a cruise ship, life goes on.' He sounded weary. 'I'm sorry I seemed rude. I'm David FitzHarris.'

'Karen mentioned that. I'm Anya. Crichton.'

His eyebrows arched. 'Then I'm pleased to meet you. Everyone calls me Fitz.'

Anya's focus turned to the dishevelled towels on top of the cupboard. The ones downstairs had all been cleared and replaced when they had arrived.

'What time were the towels changed? That may give some kind of window. Maybe the cleaners saw something.'

'I'll find out.' Fitz took notes. He moved closer, out of anyone's hearing range.

'Any suggestion of sexual assault?'

The thought had occurred to Anya when she suggested they try Flumazenil. Fitz's phone rang. This time he ignored it.

'Without an examination, it's impossible to say. Even then, it won't always be evident.'

Fitz moved back to Lilly and checked beneath the waist-band of her jeans. 'No underpants. We'll have to ask the family if going commando was her thing.'

Anya's heart sank. At least Doctor Novak wouldn't know to raise the issue when he broke the news to the family. That discussion would be difficult enough.

Very little of the scene made sense. The girl was fully dressed, and soaking wet, as if she had been placed in the spa. Anya moved back, bent down and examined the girl's fingers. She took some close-up images, then raised the hand to her nose.

'What is it?' Fitz approached.

'I can't smell chlorine.'

'That rules out the spa . . . and any of the pools.'

She'd been soaked in fresh water. It hadn't rained the preceding night.

'Are there surveillance cameras up here?'

FitzHarris shook his head. 'There used to be one with a view of the spas until some genius ordered a noticeboard in its place.' His phone rang again. This time he answered and listened before hanging up.

'Family are heading down to the medical centre to confirm the identity. Joggers and early risers are already out. We need to move her fast.'

A stretcher arrived with two crew members. There was little more Anya could do here now, and the small crowd around the towels had multiplied. Word, like infection, would spread quickly on a ship.

FitzHarris called over one of the security officers and they had a private word. Anya assumed he was leaving instructions about securing the scene.

'Hey!' A crew member pointed at a couple who had been snapping photos.

Anya shielded Lilly's body as best she could while it was transferred to the orange stretcher. She covered the girl with some clean towels, and gently draped another around her hair. Only a portion of her face was exposed, so she would be less identifiable if anyone knew her. From a distance, Lilly could have been sleeping.

FitzHarris ordered a clear path to the service elevators and he remained at Lilly's head. Anya noticed how he heavily favoured one leg. A permanent injury could explain why he worked on a cruise ship instead of on the front line of policing or military service.

Anya began to replace the unused backpack contents, and was joined again by William. 'Please stop.' He helped her up. 'I'll get someone to do that. You've done more than enough.'

Her own hands began to shake as her adrenalin levels dropped.

'How about I grab you a coffee? You look like you could do with one.'

William was right. She hadn't had breakfast and needed some sugar. 'My bag—'

He grabbed it from a locked cupboard adjacent to the towel receptacle. 'I brought it up when your son went to the kids' club. He's a good lad, by the way. They serve cookies, morning tea and other snacks down there so he's well looked after. My guess is, he'll never want to leave.'

A club with other children, games and biscuits would be Ben's idea of pure heaven. Anya had hoped to spend as much time as possible with him on this cruise, but for now she was glad he was occupied. It also gave her a chance to check on Martin once his blood samples had been taken.

They headed to the adults-only coffee club at the other end of the ship. William ordered and chose a table that was both outside and private. Most passengers were still sleeping or having breakfast. The water was calm and the sun had now appeared in its glory, warming Anya's skin.

'Thanks for helping. You were so . . . controlled . . . it made a difference to the rest of us. I know Karen appreciated it.'

Medical emergencies early in Anya's career had taught her never to show panic, no matter how she felt inside. As the doctor, other staff looked to her for instructions. If the person in charge panicked, the patient had little or no chance of surviving. Anya's apparent calm during the emergency belied her heart rate and fear of losing the girl.

'Looks can be deceiving.'

The warmth of the drink seemed to soothe every part of her. The breeze flicked strands of hair across her forehead. She appreciated the need to debrief. It was natural for people who had shared a traumatic experience.

'May I ask you a question, William?'

He blew on the coffee and tilted his head.

'When you arrived and saw Lilly, you said, "Please, not again".'

He straightened and his neck muscles tightened. 'I shouldn't have said that; it was unprofessional.'

He downed the rest of his coffee in record time and stood.

'Have there been any other young women?'

He checked his watch. 'It was a slip of the tongue. We always have injured people requiring attention. I'd love to stay and chat, but I'm afraid duty calls.'

He backed away and offered a salute. 'Thanks again for what you and your ex-husband did.'

Loose lips sink ships, Anya thought. If Lilly had been sexually assaulted, she may not have been the first.

Anya decided to go back to the towel cupboard and see if they had missed anything obvious. This time she had her own camera from her bag.

Arriving at the spa, she had to double-check she was in the right place. Instead of being cordoned off, the site was spotless. Towels had been removed and two couples were immersed in the bubbles, laughing and splashing.

A yellow sign cautioned people to take care because the surface was wet. The deck looked as if it had been cleaned with a high pressure hose, small patches of water were glistening in the sunlight.

Anya could barely believe it and felt her anger rise. All chances of finding any further evidence had just been washed away. There was something obscene about a girl losing her life here and people celebrating in the same place within the hour. There were ten decks of places people could go for entertainment and another spa on the opposite side of the pool. Even paying customers should be able to put up with the minor inconvenience of being down one spa for a few hours.

David FitzHarris had said life went on, but he was negligent in his duty if he allowed this to happen to a potential crime scene. Anya felt her face flush more. Maybe leaving his former employment had nothing to do with personal injury.

Someone had been involved in Lilly's death, intentional or otherwise, and any evidence of their presence had just been destroyed.

3

Anya peered around the open door. Martin sat on a treatment bed. Its base doubled as storage cupboards. Like everything else on the ship, no space was wasted. A wooden cabinet with lockable glass doors contained a myriad of medications, overhead cabinets contained equipment for minor surgical procedures, and an adjustable light was positioned above the treatment bed. Behind it, mounted on the wall, was a blood-pressure cuff and a suction bottle. Not built for comfort, the bed was two-thirds normal length and Martin's legs dangled over the side. A round bandaid was adhered to the inside of his elbow.

'Not exactly the morning we had planned.' He jiggled one leg, something he did when nervous.

Anya smiled and leant against the cabinet. 'In a way it was lucky you found her and that we were there to help.'

Even so, there was nothing lucky about what happened to Lilly.

'You know, I got tired of all the death and drama, but you've always been drawn to it.'

Anya stood upright, bracing herself for another argument about the effects of her work on their son. 'That's hardly fair—'

'Annie, wait.'

The leg stopped jiggling.

'This time I'm not blaming you.' He peeled off the Band Aid and revealed a small bruise. 'I went into automatic when

I saw her lying there. It was as if I'd never been away from nursing. I didn't even think about the risks.'

This was a side to Martin she had not seen for years. 'I'm sorry you got the . . .' she gestured around her mouth.

'I'm not. It was worth it if it meant saving that girl's life. You know what Ben means to us; she meant the same to her parents.'

Anya leant forward but the distant click of a door interrupted. It was soon followed by the sound of crying out in the corridor. Quiet sobs punctuated mumbled female voices; Lilly's family.

Martin looked to the door as the sounds faded. 'I was never any good at dealing with the relatives.'

'That isn't true. I remember the ninety-year-old woman who had a stroke one Christmas Eve and was unlikely to live.

'She and her husband had been inseparable for over sixty years. He'd been by her side for days, and a decision had to be made about whether to switch off the ventilator.'

'I remember.' Martin half-smiled. 'They desperately wanted kids, but it didn't happen for them. They were each other's world.'

'Even though treatment was pointless, you talked the doctors into keeping her alive until Boxing Day, so they had one last Christmas together. That was kind.'

Anya thought she saw his eyes glisten.

'He was so grateful for having the chance to say goodbye, his way.'

Karen knocked and pulled up a mobile stool. Her eyes were dark and she appeared drained. 'I'll send your bloods off. We can do some tests on board, but not all the HIV or Hepatitis antibodies.' She paused. 'If there are no questions, guess you're done.'

'How are you doing?' Martin asked her.

Karen cleared her throat. 'So far it's not your average

cruise. Our team has three nurses, but our second doctor had to disembark in Honolulu. His wife went into early labour, so we're a doctor down until Fiji.'

'Do you get a lot of deaths onboard?' Anya asked.

'I worked in Emergency for more years than I care to remember so I'm used to it. My husband and I loved water and planned to sail around the world when we retired. Died from a stroke eight years ago.' Karen lowered her hazel eyes. 'Since the kids were grown, I thought I'd see a bit of the world. We get a lot of passengers coming back for their twentieth or more cruise. The regulars become a bit like family. It's the young ones . . . they're the hardest. Enough moping. I've got some patients to check on, so better get moving.'

'Can we at least get you a tea, or coffee?' Anya offered. Her mother, a family doctor, often lamented the lack of opportunity to pause and refocus following an emergency.

Karen slapped both thighs and arose. 'I'm fine. Paco, our steward, looks after us pretty well. If I get desperate, I can always break into the jelly bean jar.' She took a deep breath. 'Thanks again for your help this morning.'

For this nurse, there would be no time to debrief or come to terms with what she had just dealt with. No time-out. The next patient had no need to know what had happened, and expected all of Karen's attention. Life went on.

As Martin and Anya left the medical centre, he paused. 'Annie, this is going to sound so callous, but I got the rush. You know, that adrenalin buzz when it's life and death and you can't afford to mess up?'

She knew exactly what he meant. It was what drew certain personalities to emergency medicine.

'I hardly even thought of Ben – saving that girl had to come first.'

This was a side to her former husband Anya hadn't seen for many years.

Leading up to and following the divorce, he had openly resented her dedication and commitment to work. What he hadn't ever appreciated was that when he gave up nursing, she had to work hard to support them. She had no choice.

Maybe Martin had begun to see things from her perspective.

He patted the crease of his elbow. 'It's eight o'clock. No wonder I'm starving.'

Heading to the lift, they caught sight of the backs of what she assumed was Lilly's family, accompanied by Doctor Novak.

Four women huddled together, arms around each other in comfort, heads lowered. One turned around and, despite the long hair curtaining part of her face, she could have been Lilly's twin. Anya and Martin stepped back, not wanting to intrude on their grief.

They took the next lift to deck nine and located a restaurant. Inside, a queue divided into two, one each side of a self-serve buffet. The sound of knives clinking on plates and animated conversation filled the area. A Filipino crew member handed each of them a melamine plate. The smell of bacon was too tempting to ignore. Anya had to admit she too was now hungry. Waffles with various syrups, eggs – scrambled and poached – ham off the bone, cooked beans, pastries, fruit and yoghurt all looked tempting. She chose small portions of fruit and drizzled maple syrup over a waffle.

Judging by the pile on Martin's plate, he was ravenous. She wondered if he had missed anything on offer. A server poured them each a coffee from the machine. Anya added a glass of water. They found an empty table inside, next to the windows.

As Martin began to eat, Anya glanced around. Most of the children devoured doughnuts and pastries, while the parents preferred the hot food. Cereal and fruit seemed the least popular. One frazzled mother tried to coerce a toddler to eat some egg, with little luck. The father was reading a magazine and seemed oblivious to his wife's plight. The child stuck his hands in some ketchup from the plate and smeared it over his shirt.

Martin pointed his knife in the family's direction. 'The husband thinks he's a hero for giving her a break, but he begrudges the expense. She wants to get away so he will spend some quality time with his son. Despite room cleaners and cooks, the mother'll stress because they're out of their normal routine. Junior's already fussy about food, and my guess is he won't sleep well, so Mum's in for a rough time.' He placed some egg and ham on his fork as the toddler began to scream. 'Dad thinks he'll get sex as thanks for the holiday, but not with Junior in the room and her all stressed out . . .'

Anya took a bite of fresh pineapple and stared at her former husband in disbelief.

'When did you develop that sort of insight?'

He grinned. 'You learn a lot as a stay-at-home father. Playgroups are a real eye-opener. You know how women like to vent at those things.'

Anya didn't know. Through no fault of her own, she had never been to one. She felt her resentment at the situation flare. More than anything, she had wanted to spend time with Ben, but part-time work wasn't feasible. When the magistrate awarded custody to Martin, the primary carer, she was shattered. The judge argued that Ben was better off with the stay-at-home parent, rather than a nanny. It also meant that Martin didn't have to work. He could surf and 'find himself' to his heart's content.

The irony was that Anya had been the reliable and responsible parent, but that made no difference in court. She had to work even more hours to pay for two homes.

Only Martin now had a girlfriend, which further complicated the situation.

She managed to suppress her anger though – she knew it was important to Ben that they got on and so far things had been going well.

'How's Nita? I didn't even ask how she felt about you coming away.'

A large man tried to squeeze past, accidentally bumping Anya's back. He held two plates stacked high with food.

'She thinks Ben should spend more time with you. And the time away from us will be good for her. She's been offered a job in London, and doesn't know if she'll take it.'

Anya paused, shocked. Ben had grown fond of Nita, and the relationship seemed mutual. She and Martin had been together for two years and, although not living with them, she was a frequent visitor to their home.

'Does Ben know?'

'I'm not that thoughtless,' Martin snapped.

Anya glanced at the nearby tables in case anyone else had heard.

Martin sighed. 'What I mean is, there's no sense upsetting him until we know for sure. This trip of yours couldn't have come at a better time, to be honest.' He stabbed a hash brown with the fork.

Anya wanted him to explain why, but experience had taught her probing would only irritate him. He would open up only if and when he was ready. At least she understood better why he had been so eager to come on the trip.

Four men in their twenties staggered in, looking as if they'd slept in their clothes. They walked past the food line and into the dining area, as if looking for something better.

'This boat is awesome!' one shouted and raised his arms as if expecting a chorus of agreement. Some of the diners laughed, others kept eating.

'Has anyone ever seen so many hot chicks after a good time?' Sunglasses were fixed to the friend's eyes. 'So where do they keep the champagne cocktails?'

'I don't feel so good,' the third one said. His shirt was clearly inside out. Without warning, he ran toward the exit, hand to his mouth. His friends laughed then disappeared out the balcony door.

'Were they the ones from your corridor?' Anya asked.

Martin shook his head. 'Sounds like it was a huge night all over. If this keeps up, it's going to be a very long fortnight.'

Anya felt sorry for him. Clearly, things weren't going well with his girlfriend, he had been kept awake and intimidated by other passengers, and by being a good Samaritan, had exposed himself to the risk of serious infection.

A group of young women, all wearing sunglasses, silently traipsed to the juice bar. They, too, looked like they'd been up all night.

'Maybe we're the odd ones out. Somewhere along the line, we must have got old,' Martin mused before consuming the last of his pancakes.

Anya disagreed. 'We just grew up. We had to. We've seen too many lives ruined by excess alcohol and stupidity, on what should have been a fun night out.'

'Casualty and the Saturday Night Specials.' He chewed and swallowed. 'You know, I used to begrudge having to work those shifts, plus Christmas and New Year because I didn't have a family back then. Truth was, I hated seeing lives destroyed by drunk drivers, senseless brawls and overdoses.'

'We were lucky. In our day, people used their fists, now young guys carry knives and guns.'

'I worry about Ben, Annie. How do we protect him?'

She had wondered the same thing. 'By encouraging other interests, like you're already doing. Swimming, sport, study, weekends away, holidays, like this one. And show by example. It's all we can do.'

'You're right.' He locked eyes and Anya felt an intensity she hadn't seen since they had separated. She wasn't sure how to respond so she looked away.

'Maybe you should head back to bed for a couple of hours and catch up on your sleep. You can use our cabin. I can check on Ben and—'

Martin finished the last morsel on his plate and patted his belly. 'After that meal, I should go for two runs, but a snooze does sound like a good idea. My cabin will be fine, but thanks for the offer.'

He stood and left, while Anya chose to stay and finish her water. From her reading, a few years ago, people would average a one-and-a-half-pound weight gain during a week-long cruise. Now, it was more like three times that amount. Judging by the amount of food, even on kids' plates, it was easy to see why.

A table nearby was cleared. Two women sat with their meals and a clean-shaven man in a gaudy shirt quickly homed in. The conversation was loud enough for everyone to hear.

'Hey ladies, fancy coming back to my cabin for a bit of one-on-one, or should I say, two-on-one?' He did a pelvic thrust and made a 'V' with his hands pointing to his crotch. A mother shielded her young daughter's ears and told her husband to hurry and finish his food.

'Come on.' He invited himself to a seat. 'You came here for a good time, I can make all your dreams come true, ladies.'

Anya found it difficult to believe that anyone would think a pick-up line like that would work.

One of the women giggled and covered her mouth. The other didn't appear impressed.

'Thanks, but we've got boyfriends back home.'

'So? Some of us have got wives, but it's cool. What happens on a cruise stays on the cruise, if you know what I mean.'

Within moments, the surrounding tables seemed to empty of families. There was something beyond annoying about the man's arrogance.

The two women excused themselves and left, despite vocal protests from the man. Anya saw him look her way, and decided it was a good time to check on Ben.

As she left the buffet area, William approached.

'Doctor Crichton, I'm really sorry to disturb you, but it's about the incident this morning. Our head of security has asked if you could meet him as soon as possible.' He leant closer. 'In the ship's morgue. Something about the body.'

4

FitzHarris greeted Anya at the morgue.

'Thanks for coming.' This time he shook her hand. 'Please understand that you're under no obligation to further assist in this matter.'

'If I can help, I will.'

FitzHarris nodded and led her into an area directly beneath the medical centre. The sudden change in temperature sent a shiver through her. 'How many bodies can be accommodated?'

'Most ships I've worked on can store three bodies, but this one has storage for six. I guess it's because of the sea crossing between Hawaii and Fiji. Normally the family would disembark at the next port and the body would be repatriated from there. Sometimes, people request their loved one be buried at sea. In that case, we can do a small service with the captain officiating. Obviously, it's something we wouldn't advertise.'

Anya wondered about the implications if a post-mortem was required. In this case, without a pathologist to confirm the exact cause of death, a death certificate could not be issued. Small ports couldn't always satisfy international travel requirements for a deceased person, let alone provide facilities and qualified staff for a post-mortem.

'What happens from here? Are police likely to come on board?'

'I've notified the captain, and he's liaising with head office. According to our procedures, they'll notify the Hawaiian coastguard who in turn contacts the FBI.' He scratched the back of his neck. 'I'm still waiting to hear back, normally they respond quicker than this.'

'So what are you asking me to do?'

'Doctor Novak took some bloods. We can test for basic things here but I thought you might be able to give us an expert opinion.' He walked over to a metal door and opened it. Dark hair was visible. He pulled four gloves from his hip pocket.

'You might want these.'

Anya took a pair. Due to the cold temperature, the powder on the latex made her cough.

Fitz slid out the metal drawer containing the body, and the stench of vomitus filled Anya's nostrils. This time, a white sheet covered Lilly to the neck.

'Would you agree there was alcohol on her shirt?'

'It was definitely present,' Anya said.

FitzHarris took notes. 'Apparently, the family swear blind she had never drunk before and never would. The sister spun some story about how Lilly couldn't sleep so snuck out to Centennial Garden at around 10.30 p.m. to read – wait for it . . . Shakespeare.' He rolled his eyes. 'If she was checking YouTube or texting, I might buy it. Wouldn't be the first time a kid from a good home went off the rails first chance they got.'

Anya examined Lilly's hands – they were fine-boned with long, sinewy fingers. The tips on the left were thickened and raised. She checked the other side. Those cushions were bluish and soft. Every nail was neatly trimmed and free of polish. None was broken or damaged, to suggest a struggle. 'Calluses are the result of repetitive stress and friction. The girl could have played a stringed instrument like the guitar. See the left hand?'

Fitz agreed. 'Any further thoughts on why she was so wet?'

They had already agreed she hadn't been in the spa or pools. 'There were men with high-pressure hoses cleaning near where she was found, and then *afterward* as well.' Anya emphasised the point about the destruction of evidence.

FitzHarris looked across, jaw clenched. 'Are you serious? I left specific instructions for my men to secure that scene.'

'Nothing was cordoned off. The deck's been cleaned and passengers were already back in the spa.'

His face hardened. It was unclear whether he was embarrassed at the incompetence of his staff or the fact that Anya knew before he did. He pulled off his gloves and stabbed a number on his mobile. 'I'll be right back.'

The door slammed in his wake and Anya moved closer to examine Lilly's arms. The skin was blemish free, and there were no track marks in the elbow creases. She was unlikely to have used intravenous drugs, or been injected with any. Anya noticed bruising on the insides of the girl's upper arms, which was unusual. The oval and round marks could have been caused by someone grabbing her around each arm – either holding her down or dragging her. They were unlikely to have been caused by bumping into something or day-to-day activities, even for a physically active teenager.

Anya moved some of the girl's hair to the side and smelt the subtle hint of apple shampoo. She gently examined Lilly's head, looking for obvious signs of trauma; no bruising, lacerations, lumps or fractures. No facial marks, no small haemorrhages and the whites of her eyes were clear. The one hint of imperfection was a small pimple on the left side of the slightly rounded chin.

A dark mark was present on the right side of the neck beneath the angle of the jaw. Anya leant in for a closer examination. The oval, blackened section of skin was 2.5 cm × 1.5 cm, the size of a thumb pressed heavily into the skin, just over the carotid artery. It could have been caused prior to her being found, or during the resuscitation attempt. Then again, teenagers were known to get hickeys in that spot. Anya ran her index finger over the mark. Just beneath the skin were tiny, raised lesions. She didn't remember seeing the bruise when they lifted Lilly out onto the deck. Then again, she had not had a good view of the girl's face during the resuscitation attempt.

She checked for other bruises on the front of the torso. There weren't any visible.

Both elbows had grazes over the joints, possibly caused by carpet burn.

FitzHarris banged open the door, slammed it and paced. His limp had become more defined.

'I ordered that idiot to seal off the area. Seems he thought that meant wash everything in sight. Is life so cheap to some people that they just clean up and act like nothing ever happened?'

Anya had wondered the same thing. 'How many security staff do you have on board?'

'Three, and the night duty manager's a woman I hand-selected. I didn't get to choose the others. They're just foisted on me. They know diddly squat about police work or security and just parade around in uniform flexing their muscles, checking out the women.'

He scratched his neck again and relaxed his shoulders. 'What do you think of that mark on her neck?'

Anya lifted the chin, studied it again, and listed the possible causes.

'So we don't have jack. Could be someone tried to strangle her, or hold her down, or not.'

Microscopic examination would provide more information as to how long the bruise had been present. 'It's worth taking a swab just in case it's a fingermark and there's any

36

DNA from skin cells or saliva from a hickey.' She didn't add that the water could have washed off any evidence; she hoped it may have been protected by the girl's curled-up posture in the cupboard.

The security officer pulled a swab from a plastic tackle box and handed it across. Anya wiped the skin and placed the swab back in its tube. FitzHarris quickly labelled it, noting the time, body location and Lilly's name. Anya repeated the procedure for the marks on the upper arms.

'Can you help roll her? I want to check the back.'

FitzHarris obliged and leant over to see what Anya described. 'There's grazing down her back. My guess is she was dragged on carpet.'

'Wouldn't have taken much effort. What is she? About a hundred pounds max?'

Any fibres left on deck would have been washed down the drain by now. The colour of the carpet may have at least narrowed down the areas of the ship in which she could have been.

They rolled Lilly gently onto her back again.

'I've put her clothes on a sheet to dry before I bag them. Maybe there'll be something there.'

FitzHarris seemed more familiar with forensic science than Anya had anticipated. Most people didn't think to dry specimens first; unaware that the moisture in clothes could interfere with DNA analysis.

Anya kept the top half of the sheet covering Lilly's body, and moved to the feet. 'Where did you work before this?' she asked, exposing the legs, to the tops of the thighs.

'Twenty years with the NYPD, eight of them in homicide.'

Finger-sized bruises bordered both knees and three fist-sized ones marked her inner thighs. Anya thought of Lilly's last few hours. 'Either she had incredibly rough sex or . . .'

'We're looking at rape and murder.' FitzHarris pulled more swabs from his kit.

Anya wiped separate cotton tips on the surface of each bruise. The chances of finding any physical evidence were slim, but she felt it was worth trying.

'I'll swab around the perineum, but I don't want to cause any more trauma. The pathologist who does the autopsy needs to see things as they are.'

'Appreciate what you're doing, helping us out.'

Anya pulled the sheet back down over the lower body and returned to the head. Opening the mouth, the acidic pungency of vomit quickly filled her nostrils again.

FitzHarris pulled a torch out of his kit and held it from behind Anya. She could detect mint on his breath as she gently eased open the girl's petite jaw and peered inside. There were no marks, dot haemorrhages or swelling to suggest choking or an allergic reaction. She spoke her observations out loud before swabbing the back of the throat for any ejaculate, again, not overly hopeful of a result.

'We're lucky to have someone with your reputation and experience on board.'

She quickly turned and banged the side of her head on the torch. 'What do you mean "reputation"?'

FitzHarris stepped back. 'I just meant . . . well, I saw your name on the passenger manifesto. You're world renowned.'

He switched off the torch with a guilty expression.

'Out of more than three thousand passengers, you happened to recognise my name?'

'What can I say? I'm a fan of the Jersey Bombers, and read about you being a whistleblower in the papers.'

She felt the heat rise in her face. Misinformation and ignorance caused more harm than fists and physical weapons. 'I don't know where you got your facts, but I've never been a "whistleblower". I investigated the veracity of a sexual assault claim, and advised Bombers' management on how to better educate players about what constitutes consent.'

FitzHarris threw up his hands. 'Didn't mean to get your back up. Sounds like I hit a real raw nerve.'

He had. When Anya was five her three-year-old sister had disappeared and suspicion had immediately fallen on their parents, then switched to Anya. The local community and media became obsessed with what had happened and regurgitated the family's most private details. Decades later, Anya still didn't trust the media, or any kind of intrusion.

Now she felt unsettled. She and her family were on holiday and FitzHarris claimed to have recognised her name on a list. But his eyes could not hold her gaze. As far as she was concerned, the conversation and her assistance were over.

'Is there anything else here to do?' she said, peeling off the gloves.

'Out of all the people on this ship, it's lucky that you and your ex both happened to be on the scene when Lilly was found. As you say, what are the chances?'

She didn't like whatever FitzHarris was insinuating.

Another of the security team entered.

'We're done,' FitzHarris's jaw tightened again.

Anya slid the drawer containing Lilly back into its place and closed the metal door. A small sink against the wall provided somewhere to wash her hands. She could feel the tension in the room, and wanted to be outside in the sea air again. She had done everything she could to help out. This was meant to be her holiday – a time to spend with Ben.

Heading for the kids' club, she began to regret being so defensive and rude. FitzHarris was most likely posturing to show he was in charge of the investigation. He could have researched her after the resuscitation attempt. In his position, Anya would have done the same.

Climbing the aft stairs, she thought of the bruises on the

39

fragile body and the drag marks on her back. If Lilly had been sexually assaulted, it had probably been on carpet. How she ended up wet, clothed and on the deck needed to be determined.

One thing was certain: whoever had assaulted Lilly was still on board. At least until the next port.

5

At the top of the stairwell leading to the kids' club a girl in black leggings and a sparkly top ran straight into Anya, almost knocking her off balance.

'Sorry!' She giggled and ran off. Another girl about the same size quickly followed but Anya managed to step clear.

The girls wouldn't have been more than ten years old and were roaming the ship without any sign of their parents.

As she approached a set of double doors, Anya heard laughing and music crescendo.

She felt like she'd entered another world. Behind a concierge desk and gates was a kids' paradise. For a moment it was unclear whether the barriers prevented children from escaping, or adults from interloping on the enjoyment. The open-plan area had everything a child would love. Toward the back wall, beanbags and miniature lounges faced a giant movie screen currently showing a cartoon. To the left, a kitchen contained a group of children with glass beakers. They were all wearing white coats and safety goggles. Ben was with two other boys, who couldn't seem to stand still. She thought he saw her and then looked away again.

'Can I help you?' Lori from Ireland, a small redhead with a freckled face, didn't look much older than eighteen. She smiled and her greenish eyes twinkled.

Sanitising hand gel was in a two-litre bottle on the desk.

'Hi, I'm Ben's mother. He's the one with curly hair over there.'

'You're little Aussie's mum. He's absolutely gorgeous. And so bright.' She pressed a button beneath the desk. 'Come on in, they're in the middle of making flubber.'

The gate clicked open, and Anya cleaned her hands. 'We hadn't planned on leaving him here during the cruise—'

Lori laughed. 'Good luck getting him out, he's having a grand time.'

'He wasn't shy?' Anya didn't get to see much of Ben at school, or interacting with other children.

Lori patted Anya's shoulder. 'Only when he first saw the place. Olivia brought him in and introduced him to some boys his age, and you would have thought they'd known each other for years. Been attached to each other ever since.'

The boys poured the contents of one beaker into another and cheered. They had successfully made slimy green gloop, and were taking turns putting their hands in it. Seeing Ben so happy and sociable was a joy.

'Aussie,' Lori called. 'Your mother's here to see you.'

Ben's shoulders rounded and he scuffed toward them, hands in short pockets.

'Do I have to go, Mum? I only just got here. We're having macaroni and cheese for lunch, and we're just about to start the Olympics. I'm representing Australia! Please can I stay? Pleeeasse?' He looked like a puppy on a greeting card.

Anya felt torn. She had imagined spending lots of time with Ben on this holiday, but perhaps she was being selfish. Childhood should be full of fun and, as an only child, Ben often missed out on company his own age.

'He's more than welcome to stay. We're open until eleven this evening.'

'There's no way you're staying here until then.' The doe-eyed look on her son's face made her regret sounding so stern. This was supposed to be a holiday. 'How about I come back around four and see how you feel?'

42

'Yay, thanks Mum.' He threw his arms around her waist and whispered, 'Love you.'

She squeezed him back. 'Likewise. Be good and have a great time.'

He was off. A game of Simon Says had begun near the cones.

Lori explained that parents were given pagers, and if the children wanted to be collected, the staff would call. She also wrote down the number of the club and asked Anya to fill out a medical background form, and give permission for excursions to the water slide and up to the sports deck.

'We also need a password, so you or Ben's father can sign him out.'

Anya thought of the two girls who had run past her on the stairs. 'I just passed a couple of kids outside.'

'Oh, if they're ten or older, parents can give consent for them to sign themselves out.'

'Kids that young just come and go as they please?' Anya thought of her own childhood. She and her brother were never allowed to ride bikes because they might get out of their mother's sight. They weren't allowed to meet friends or go for walks without an adult. Although it was understand-able, they had felt stifled and controlled.

Lori became serious. 'I wouldn't let any child of mine do it. But people assume ships are safe.' She leant closer. 'You should be very proud of your boy; he has the most beautiful manners. Just between us, that's a rarity these days.'

With no way of Ben leaving the club without her or Martin present, she had no qualms about letting him stay. From what she could see, the counsellors were experienced and adept at handling scores of children at once.

Anya headed back to her cabin for a long hot soak in the shower.

Inside, she clicked the deadlock and kicked off her sandals

before depositing the pager on the bedside table. The cleaning staff had already changed the linen and cleaned the entire cabin. The bunk bed was back in its recess in the ceiling. Appreciating the tidiness and lingering lemon scent, she slid back the balcony door and let the ocean breeze in. The sheer layer of curtains billowed in and out, like white sails. On the balcony, the weather was perfect, despite the occasional clump of grey clouds in the distance. Small white peaks periodically punctuated the smooth waves.

For the first time she felt like she was on holidays. No work to rush off to, no reports to prepare. Even more importantly, no seasickness. She contemplated what to do and picked up the daily activities sheet and a hardback book placed on the coffee table. On offer that day were Broadway dance classes, a lecture on the history of Hawaii, latest release movies in the theatrette, cooking lessons with the pastry chef, a tour of the kitchens, and a fine art auction in the atrium. While at sea, the casino opened at nine am, the shops at ten, and bingo ran throughout the day and evening. A top deck dance party began at ten and continued until midnight. The art auction piqued her curiosity. It was also the perfect opportunity to explore the ship, at her own pace. She sat on the lounge and flicked through the hardback. Glossy, coloured images of the ship-building process were scattered among astounding figures and facts about the *Paradisio*.

She turned to an article on the owners of the cruise line. Sven Anderson was a third generation shipping magnate, whose family originated from Sweden but moved to America to follow their dreams. The story talked about the business and a family photo showed a number of adults and teenagers grouped behind a ruddy-faced man in his sixties. The caption described two sons from his first marriage, the teenagers seemed to be from a second, and a young girl to his third wife, the daughter of a Russian oligarch. Anya wondered how the family managed Christmas. Having one child in a split family was challenging enough.

She put down the book, peeled off her dress followed by the one-piece swimsuit, and dropped them on the nautical-themed bedspread. The shower was anything but spacious and, for once, she was grateful for her thin body and long limbs. Some of the passengers would struggle to fit through the narrow doorway. Space was at a premium, but the stream was hot and strong. The morning's resuscitation attempt and visit to the morgue didn't easily wash away. She couldn't purge the image of Lilly's grieving family from her mind.

As water cascaded down her hair and back, her thoughts drifted back to that day in winter at the local football game. The day Miriam disappeared. Despite the weather, her mother decided they should have a picnic during the game. The two sisters were rugged up, in mittens, matching scarves and beanies as they devoured leftover pineapple chicken drumsticks with bread fresh from the bakery. Then a whistle blew and their mother told Anya to look after Miriam. Someone was injured and needed help. With that, the local doctor grabbed her bag and rushed onto the field.

Miriam quickly became restless and wanted their mother, just like Ben had wanted Anya this morning at the pool. To cheer her up and warm themselves, Anya suggested a race to the goal line. Miriam loved to run and quickly took chase. Anya heard her little sister call her name, but was too focused on reaching the white line to turn around. When she swung around to claim victory, her sister was nowhere in sight.

Now in the shower, the realisation hit her like a punch to her abdomen. Just like her mother, Anya had left her child to attend an emergency. She had assumed the ship was safe but now she knew anything could have happened. Ben could have been taken. Or worse. The thought made her want to throw up. She slumped against the wall and buckled over.

She pictured Lilly's bruised body. Is that what had happened to Miriam? For the first time in ages, she cried: for her sister, her family, and all the Lilly Chans.

With wrinkled fingertips, she eventually turned off the taps.

Stepping out of the shower and towel-drying her hair, she tried to push images of death from her mind. She was here to relax and enjoy some time with Ben. Once dressed, she stood on the balcony with arms stretched across the railing. Dark clouds had collected in the sky, but the wind and patches of the sun injected body into her fine, clean hair. The shorter layers flicked about her face and the breeze massaged the rest. As a child she had always imagined this was what unconditional freedom felt like.

She heard a sound inside and startled.

'Sorry, ma'am. I knocked but no one answered. My name is Junta; I am your cabin steward. I brought you some more fresh towels and some bottled water.'

The woman was the same height as her but with wide hips, highlighted by a belt for the navy trousers pulled in tight at the waist. The striped polo shirt stretched over her substantial chest. She smiled, like so many other staff members, with dazzling white teeth. Her skin was dark and her cheeks scarred by past acne.

'Thank you, Junta. I'm Anya.'

The badge beneath Junta's name read Jamaica. Judging by the speed with which the cabin had been cleaned, Anya assumed staff worked in pairs, and was curious about who to tip at the end of the cruise. 'Do you work with anyone else?'

Junta placed the towels on the bed. 'No, ma'am, we work alone so we have to work hard. But I have only three weeks to go. Then I return home to my family.'

'How long have you been away?'

'Eight months now. My baby girl turned two last week.'

She busied herself straightening a crease from the corner of the bed. 'I gonna be home with my baby.' She beamed.

Anya knew that could not have been easy. Eight months was a third of the daughter's life so far.

Junta quickly glanced around the room, and nodded, satisfied. 'You have a great day. And if you need anything, you call big old Junta.'

'Thanks again for the towels.'

Anya admired Junta's dedication and self-sacrifice and couldn't help feeling as if she should be more conscious of the state in which she and Ben left the cabin. She picked up her key. She was sure she had deadlocked the door when she came in, so how had Junta got inside? She must have been mistaken.

She headed to the internet cafe to check her emails. On the way, she heard lilting violin music coming from the library. She stopped and listened to what sounded like a CD. Halfway through the piece, a woman screamed 'Stop!'. The room fell silent.

Anya stepped inside the doorway.

A young teenage girl stood, eyes downcast.

'You will fail if you do not pay attention to the fingering. That was careless. Sloppy! Do it again!'

Anya could barely believe what the older Chinese woman was saying to her pupil. Then she recognised the pair. They had entered the lift with the ship's doctor. They were members of Lilly's family. The older woman turned around and stopped when she saw Anya.

'This is a private rehearsal,' she said in a husky tone. 'Please leave us.'

Anya regretted interrupting. 'I don't mean to disturb. There was shouting—'

'My daughter Jasmine. She has much work to do.' Puffy tissue encased the mother's brown eyes. The woman tugged

47

on a silk neck scarf, turned to her daughter and sighed. 'I suppose it is time for a break. Bad practice is worse than no practice.' After collecting a canvas bag and stuffing it with folders of sheet music, she added, 'Lilly would have wanted you to practise. But not like this.'

Jasmine stood motionless until her mother had gone. After that, she folded herself into a chair, violin and bow still in her hands.

Anya stepped closer, trying to process what had just happened. Lilly's family had known of her death for less than a few hours yet her mother was forcing another child to practise the violin. It didn't make sense. Grief affected everyone differently, but this was an extreme response, with or without denial.

'Are you all right?'

The girl looked up, through a mane of black hair. 'Things are never going to be all right again.'

Part of Anya wanted to tell Jasmine she should be with her family, another thought she was better away from her mother for the moment. Anya knew that nothing anyone could say would ease the pain they were all feeling.

'I heard you playing. You have a real gift.' Anya pointed to another lounge chair. 'May I?'

The teenager stayed motionless, almost catatonic. Anya dragged the chair a few feet closer and sat.

'I'm so sorry about Lilly.' The words sounded empty, despite her sincerity.

The girl had a puzzled expression. 'Does everyone on the ship—'

'No. I'm a doctor and I happened to be there. I promise you, we did everything possible.'

'I saw you outside the medical centre. We had just been told. My mother, she had to . . .'

Anya gently nodded. The words didn't need to be said.

Identifying the body of a child was something no parent should ever have to do.

The girl sat forward. 'Please don't judge her by what you just saw. She's trying to do what's right.'

'It may not be the right time to practise, if your heart isn't in it.'

'I insisted we come back here. Lilly and I found this place not long after coming on board, and thought it would be a great place to rehearse.' She gazed around. 'Lilly loves books. She reads everything.'

It was easy to see why the library was appealing. A gold spiral staircase in the centre led to another gallery. There had to be two storeys of bookshelves with only a few empty spaces. The only spare piece of wall was covered with a large painted portrait of the ruddy-faced man Anya had read about, Sven Anderson.

Jasmine stood, placed the violin on the chair and moved to one set of shelves. Stretching, she reached up and pulled down a paperback with a tattered spine.

'She put this here yesterday.'

Anya rose and moved closer. *To Kill A Mockingbird*. It had been one of her own favourites, one she returned to every few years.

'Lilly loves this, but thought it should be shared. We counted how many shelves high and how far across, so if we ever come back, we would know if it's been moved. There's a note for whoever takes it.' The young woman shook her head and took a deep breath as tears welled. 'It seems so stupid now. It was our version of putting a message in a bottle. Lilly hoped we would find it again some day, either here or in a second-hand bookshop somewhere in the world.' Jasmine's voice quavered as her long slender fingers loosened their grip.

Anya stepped closer and extended a hand to take the

book. 'May I?' The inscription read: If you love the story as much as I do, pass this book on and rewards will come to you. Lilly Chan, aged 16, *Paradisio*.

The handwriting was printed, with circles instead of dots on top of the letter 'i'.

'I have an audition in Vienna next month for a scholarship. Lilly is a cellist.' The sister gave a part smile. 'Except she's rebellious and only practises for three hours a day. She prefers books.'

Regular playing explained the calluses on the fingertips of Lilly's left hand. Three hours every day sounded impressive, but apparently not to Jasmine and her mother.

'What does your father say?'

'He says children should have fun, but he's American and grew up with eight brothers and sisters. They used to go out and play after breakfast until dinner. He lives in Hawaii.' Her eyes brightened. 'We've just been there for a week. When our parents divorced, our older sister chose to live with him. We miss her so much but Mother says she's a bad influence, with her Western ways.'

She paused. 'Who's going to tell them? They are so close to Lilly.'

'Probably your mother.'

Silence hung heavily.

Anya tried to distract Jasmine. 'What about your mother? Where was she born?'

'In China. Her parents farmed and did anything they could to earn money. They worked day and night to give her an education. It was my mother's duty to do everything they ever asked. While other kids played, she studied and now she is head of radiology at Angel Bay Hospital in Hong Kong. Since we were visiting Hawaii, our father paid for this cruise. He thought we would love it and have a break from our routine. Mother thought this was frivolous but gave in to our father this one time . . . She believes we are Chinese, which is why she wants us to be known by her family name. Our friends see us as more American, but we are neither.'

This family wasn't divided just by divorce, Anya thought, but also by culture.

'It isn't easy being half of anything. Chinese people have a saying about success. They believe the third generation destroys what the first two have built.'

Anya thought of the number of moguls whose offspring destroyed the business within two generations. 'Westerners say the same thing, usually about wealth.'

'Then you understand. She is afraid that Lilly and I will waste our lives and dishonour our grandparents. She has many rules and expectations. My father made her promise to give us more freedom on this holiday. Even so, music must be practised at least four hours a day. When we are not playing music, we are supposed to study.' Jasmine smiled. 'Well, Mother is often too busy working so we are not *always* studying . . . She sounds hard, but without her discipline, I would never be auditioning in Europe.'

Jasmine bent over beside the chair and opened the violin case, removed a block of rosin, and slid it back and forward along the horsehair on the bow.

'Do you ever get tired of working so hard?'

'Mother doesn't believe in wasteful activities. She says anyone can do one hour of music or study. Every hour after that gets harder, but that's what makes you the best. There is no such thing as a holiday from practice. The hands, mind and instrument need to work every day. Besides, when you become good at something, it becomes easier and more enjoyable.'

It was true to an extent, Anya thought, but the practice and study schedule left no time for socialising with peers, movies, and things that would become topics of conversation in years to come. With no focus on social skills and empathy, she had seen the lack of compassion doctors and lawyers could show, and this upbringing did nothing to encourage imagination or lateral thinking. Being a good doctor required infinitely more than rote learning and diagnostic skills. Finding common interests with others was important. Some knowledge of popular culture was a significant part of that.

'You said your sister has a rebellious streak?' It seemed kinder to discuss Lilly in the present tense.

Jasmine lowered herself to her knees and sat back onto her feet. 'Let's say she doesn't like all the rules. She fights Mother every day. They argue and shout at each other over the tiniest things. It started as soon as she was born. I remember even though I am only two years older. If Lilly didn't want to do something, she would refuse, kick and throw things. But Mother would not give in.'

Anya sat back on the chair, book still in hand. In some ways, the family situation was similar to her own. Being the older sister by two years, she was compliant and fitted in with the routine; in particular, her mother's work as a solo doctor and her father's legal practice. Then came Miriam, full of personality, headstrong and stubborn. It was the first time Anya had ever seen a tantrum.

Jasmine stared at her bow. 'Lilly was almost uncontrollable and used to hate the violin. She was left-handed and would hold it in the wrong hand, which drove Mother crazy until Lilly discovered the cello. She fell in love with it. I may have more prizes, but she has more natural talent. You should hear her play.' Jasmine's almond eyes widened. She dropped the rosin in her lap and her hand opened as if projecting the music. 'If you shut your eyes you can hear it sing, cry. She can even make it dance.'

No one would ever hear that again. Anya decided to do everything possible to find out what had happened to Lilly.

She knew exactly how the questions would haunt Jasmine and her family for the rest of their lives otherwise.

Jasmine's fingers closed at the end of the bow. 'That probably sounds strange.'

'Not to me, I know exactly what you mean.'

After a prolonged silence, Jasmine straightened, positioned her violin and closed her eyes.

The first few bars sounded familiar. A few more and the tune was obvious, 'Feed the Birds' from *Mary Poppins*. A tear escaped, down Jasmine's cheek, onto the chin rest, as she played the final note.

She wiped the cheek on her shoulder. 'That was Lilly's favourite movie when we were little. She wanted the bird lady to come and live with us. That way, she thought we could have the birds as pets but they'd still be free.'

Anya pulled a clean tissue from her pocket and passed it across. Jasmine flicked a strand of hair from her face. It had the same apple scent Anya had noticed on Lilly.

'How could this happen? I don't understand.'

Anya wished she had the answers. If Jasmine wanted to keep talking, she would listen. As inadequate as that felt, it was the most anyone could do.

'That's something the people in charge are trying to work out.' She paused and sat forward. 'Is it possible Lilly met someone on board?'

Jasmine shook her head. 'No way, she would have told me.'

There was another moment's silence.

'Mother will be back soon.' The violin was returned to its case.

Anya handed the book back and stood. 'Thank you for playing. It was beautiful.'

Jasmine clutched the bow to her chest. 'I'm glad you were with Lilly when . . .' The fragile voice faltered. 'She'd like you.'

In a way Anya was glad she had been there. Lilly Chan sounded like a remarkable young woman. Anya half-smiled and glanced around at all the spines on the shelves.

'May I ask one thing? Did Lilly choose anything from here to read?'

Jasmine nodded. 'Typical Lilly. She couldn't believe her luck finding a copy: *Romeo and Juliet*. She loved the romance and cried when the lovers died.'

6

That afternoon, the kids' club pager bleeped. Anya rang and was asked to head straight to the medical centre. There was an emergency. The Irish counsellor was quick to reassure her that Ben was fine but that's all she knew. Anya hurried and once inside the main doors, followed the screaming. It sent the hairs on the back of her neck to attention. It had to be Martin. She pushed open the treatment room door.

Doctor Novak glared in her direction. 'Out!'

'I called her.' Karen managed above the wailing of a dark-haired man. 'We need all the help we can get.'

Anya felt relief flood through her. Martin was OK.

A younger woman with a copper-coloured ponytail and green-rimmed glasses held a large surgical pad in its half-open pack for Karen. With blood-stained gloves, the senior nurse reached over and collected it, maintaining sterility.

'We're going to need a lot more,' she instructed. 'Rachel, there's another box on the top shelf.' She gestured with her head toward the glass-door cabinet.

In contrast to the junior nurse's crisp, white uniform and skirt, Karen's was saturated with blood across her belly and hips.

The man writhed, face down on the treatment bed. Tourniquets were tied just below his dark blue trousers, which had been cut at mid-thigh level. Karen placed the pads on top of the ones already there, compressing the backs of the knees. The man screamed at the contact.

'Can you do anaesthetic?' the doctor snapped.

Anya was taken aback. She had only ever assisted in anaesthetics as a medical student. 'What happened?'

The patient screamed again.

Rachel handed her some gloves and a plastic apron, which she slipped on.

'Carlos is a crew member. From Colombia.' Karen flicked her head to remove hair from the middle of her forehead. 'Shot in the backs of both knees.'

Anya's eyes widened. Shot? On a cruise? That explained the severe pain. Kneecapping was one of the cruellest acts; more painful than being shot in the chest and it generally caused long-term damage.

Doctor Novak repositioned the overhead light before collecting packets from a cupboard. Each parcel had a strip of black tape on the outside, proof it had been sterilised in an autoclave.

Karen had said Doctor Novak was a military surgeon. Anya's heart picked up pace.

'You're not thinking of . . .' She didn't want to alarm anyone else in the room, especially the patient. 'Dissecting?'

The whites of Karen's eyes flared. 'We can't. We have to stabilise him until we can get a medical team for an airlift.' She looked to Anya for support. 'There's a helipad on the top deck.'

'You're not talking of amputation?' Rachel said, sounding shocked. 'We can't do that.'

Dark red blood leached through the pads in Karen's hands. The patient panted faster.

Anya hated to think how much pain he must be in.

Another officer knocked and entered the room, perspiring. He caught sight of the blood and colour drained from his face. He half-turned away from the patient and swallowed hard.

'I've spoken to the captain. We won't be in helicopter

56

range for at least eighteen hours, and we're sailing into bad weather.'

That meant there was no guarantee a helicopter could land even if they were in range.

Doctor Novak spoke first. 'He will not survive unless we amputate. Better to live with no legs than die.'

Carlos began to flail again. As he turned his head, his dark, desperate eyes met Anya's. He grabbed her wrist with all his strength.

'*Please*. Help!'

Twisting, she tried to loosen his grip and bent down to his face. 'We're doing everything we can.' He released her wrist and Anya placed a hand on his forehead.

'Help . . .' He murmured something else.

Anya tried to understand as Karen and Novak kept up a rapid dialogue of instructions.

'Her,' he whispered again.

Anya bent down to better hear among the chaos.

'Stop him.'

'It's all right,' Anya answered, 'we'll look after you.'

'Is he refusing treatment?' Rachel pulled the stethoscope plugs from her ears after checking Carlos's blood pressure again.

'There will be plenty of time for naming the shooter once we are finished.' Novak was matter-of-fact.

'He's frightened, and doesn't understand what's going on,' Anya said. 'If you can stem the blood loss and get a stable BP, that could buy enough time to get him to a major treatment centre.'

Carlos had one intravenous cannula and a bag of saline dripping through it.

Doctor Novak may have been good at amputating legs in a war zone, but they owed it to Carlos to try to save both legs. Another pair of experienced hands would help. She asked the officer to page Martin Hegarty, a trained intensive care nurse. He exited the room in record time.

'What pain relief has he had?'

'Total twenty milligrams morphine,' Karen said. 'Didn't touch him.'

'We need to act now.' Novak seemed intent on operating.

Anya had to think quickly. 'Do you have X-ray facilities?'

'Already done,' Novak announced. 'There, on the screen.'

Anya examined the computerised images. Her heart sank. The first showed a shattered base of the right femur, where the thigh became the top of the knee. The left hadn't fared much better. Carlos needed both vascular and orthopaedic surgeons on hand to have the best chance of keeping either leg.

Rachel checked the blood pressure. 'It's dropping, eighty over sixty. Pulse rate's one-forty.'

He had lost a lot of blood. 'Do you have any O negative?'

The nurses shook their heads.

'We can put out a call for blood donors and do a transfusion, but it's not a simple process,' Karen explained.

'That will take too much time,' Doctor Novak replied. 'BP is already compromising the kidneys.'

'What if we give more analgesia? He should stop moving around, then we can push fluids.' Anya turned to Rachel. 'Can you take over from Karen?'

The younger nurse obliged.

Karen quickly changed her gloves and checked the cannula site. 'It's tissued.'

Anya could see the swelling in Carlos's forearm. The fluid was no longer going into his circulation.

Karen put a tourniquet on his other arm and tapped a vein in the back of his hand. Carlos was still flailing about and it was like trying to hit a moving target. Karen's hands began to shake.

Martin bowled in and quickly assessed the scene. 'If you like, I'll have a go at that.' He sidled beside Karen and she seemed relieved to hand over the task.

Anya was impressed at how calm Martin appeared, despite the chaos in the room. Karen locked the elbow straight and held it firmly to minimise Carlos's movement.

'Eureka.' Martin secured the access point. 'Just like riding a bike. Good thing I kept the old registration up.'

Karen breathed a sigh of relief as she reconnected the saline and it flowed, unimpeded. 'I owe you two dinner.'

Doctor Novak seemed to ignore everyone in the room, including his patient. He had already set up a surgical tray with scalpels, clamps and suture equipment. 'Give another ten milligrams morphine, two milligrams at a time,' he ordered.

Carlos drifted into unconsciousness. Anya placed prongs in his nostrils and turned on the oxygen supply attached to the wall. A rubber cap placed on his left index finger connected to a monitor on the wall and registered his pulse rate and oxygen saturation. The monitor beeped . . . 118 . . . 112 . . . 108 . . . Anya rechecked the blood pressure. 'One hundred over eighty.'

'The bleeding's slowing,' Rachel declared.

'Don't know what all the fuss was about.' Martin smiled.

Doctor Novak studied the monitor, as if in disbelief.

David FitzHarris arrived with a man of around six foot four, fit, with wavy blond hair and pale eyes, and four gold bars on white epaulettes. Judging by the way the room fell silent, he was superior in rank.

Hands behind his back, he surveyed the scene. 'What is the situation?'

'Gunshot to both knees,' Novak stated. 'Close range.'

Anya kept an eye on the vital signs. 'He's stable for the moment, but . . .'

'Captain Burghoff,' FitzHarris interrupted, 'this is Doctor

Crichton, and Mr Hegarty, who were invaluable this morning.'

'Ah, yes.' He bowed his head. 'We are grateful for your assistance, then and now. How long before the patient needs specialised hospital treatment?' Captain Burghoff checked the clock on the wall and immediately moved to the X-ray images on the screen, hands still firmly at his back.

Anya studied them again, from behind his shoulder. There was no need to explain what they showed. The femurs were damaged far beyond pinning or plating, even by the most experienced surgeons with every facility available. She knew they had only bought a short amount of time. The tourniquets could not remain on for hours without compromising circulation to the good tissue in the legs. Loosening them could result in the release of deadly amounts of potassium, the same thing that killed crush victims if they were lifted out too quickly.

Doctor Novak had begun to scrub. 'If I operate, he should be stable until Bora Bora.'

That was five days away, Anya thought.

'Do you have an anaesthetic protocol?' Martin asked, as if reading Anya's mind.

Karen answered. 'Propafol. It's attached to the portable ventilator under the bed. Number two on the picture.'

All equipment had been photographed and placed on the walls. It meant that, if necessary, non-trained personnel could assist. It also removed language barriers in emergencies. In medicine, pictures were universal.

Martin scanned the laminated document. 'I've used this type of ventilator before, transporting ICU patients. The protocol's pretty straightforward, but . . .'

Captain Berghoff nodded. 'If we turn back to Hawaii at full speed, we are at least sixteen hours from range for a medical evacuation. Either way, we are headed into severe storms.' He paused, and surveyed the blood on the floor and on Karen's clothes. 'I suggest you do what you can.'

There was little choice if emergency care was so far away. Anya made her mind up. 'I'll intubate and monitor the anaesthetic.'

'What about patient consent?' Rachel's voice sounded half an octave higher. 'He's had morphine.'

'He was not rational with the pain,' Doctor Novak snapped. 'He will have time to discuss more surgeries once he is at hospital. Now, we save his life.'

'I give you all the authority and indemnity to do whatever procedures are necessary,' the captain announced.

The issue had not occurred to Anya. International waters were a medico-legal minefield if anything went wrong with the surgery.

'Thank you,' she said. 'Doctor Novak is right. There's no other option. We're going to have to do a bilateral amputation.'

Martin and Karen had already begun to roll the patient onto his back. He had gone quiet after the last dose of morphine.

Reluctantly, she moved to the head of the bed and placed the rubber mask on Carlos's face. Martin prepared the anaesthetic agent. Anya would intubate once Carlos was fully asleep.

Suddenly, his body tensed and the fear returned to his eyes. She removed the mask and bent down to reassure him.

'Kill her . . . Stop . . . him.'

7

At the bar on the pool deck, Anya ordered a lemon, lime and bitters and thought about Carlos's words. The shooting could have had something to do with what he knew about Lilly Chan. Then again, he could have just heard about her death and been hallucinating with the morphine.

Anya took a sip of her drink. She was too tired for anything stronger and wanted to rehydrate. Years ago she had learnt that dealing with stress through alcohol was counterproductive. It only temporarily numbed emotions, which would predictably erupt later, at the most inopportune time.

Martin joined her. 'Well, Ben's in the middle of pirate night and begged to stay. I didn't have the heart or energy to argue.'

Anya was glad. Martin deserved to unwind after the horrors of the day, particularly as it had been so long since he had dealt with patients or handled an emergency. He had been confident and purposeful during the procedure with Carlos, but now he looked weary.

The sea breeze was nippy, but the fresh air on her skin was refreshing. Thankfully, the deck was still quiet and relatively private. An entertainment crew was preparing lights and a disc jockey was setting up his equipment under a small rotunda. Many of the passengers were still divided between the second dinner sitting and one of the theatrical shows.

Somewhere onboard was a gunman. Possibly the same person who had been involved with Lilly's death. She looked

63

around at the other people on deck. It was unnerving. Any one of them could be a killer. But when she rationalised it, this ship was like a town, with a population in the thousands. Shootings tended to be crimes of passion, drug or gang related, so the shooter didn't stray far from their usual home. Carlos was not randomly shot. He had been targeted for a specific reason, possibly even racial.

'I don't think anyone's planning on shooting us tonight,' Martin said, catching her look.

Anya smiled. 'No.'

In reality, whoever left Lilly Chan to die was far more dangerous. When Carlos was conscious, he could be questioned. Maybe he knew what had happened to Lilly, and who was involved.

Karen arrived and requested a mango mocktail, which sounded more exotic with her southern American accent. With their drinks, they headed for a quiet table behind the dance floor. 'God, what a day.' The nurse slumped into a chair and kicked off her sandals. She had changed into a nondescript pale shirt and jeans after showering Carlos's blood from her skin while Anya and Doctor Novak sewed up the wounds. Her short hair was wavy when wet, which made her look younger than her years.

'I'm used to occasional emergencies onboard, but nothing like today. I've seen old people die in their beds. It's the way some of them want to go.' She pushed the straw to the side and sipped from the glass. 'Who would believe the cost of constantly travelling on cruises is comparable to buying into a nursing home?'

'I know where I'd rather be,' Martin announced. 'No pureed food or unidentifiable slops for five o'clock dinner.'

'The cruise lines are starting to clamp down on it. Too much of a drain on the small medical teams. Did you know the line employs older men to dance with the widows who travel alone? They're a significant part of the entertainment. We have one widow who's a regular livewire – she's eighty-four and can samba with the twenty year olds. The sixty-year-old escorts can't keep up with her.'

Anya laughed. She could see her own grandmother being like that. She twisted the ring on her right middle finger, which had once belonged to her favoured Nanna.

'Never underestimate an octogenarian with dancing shoes,' Martin quipped.

'That will be me in a few years,' Karen said, only she was not smiling. 'Atlanta, Georgia, doesn't have the same feel I'm afraid. Unfortunately, Carlos's days on ships are over. And that poor girl from this morning . . . I need to check the blood results after this. With everything that happened this afternoon, I haven't had a chance.' She took a bigger sip of the mocktail. 'You know, some of the crew are saying this cruise is cursed. There's a rumour that not one, but two albatrosses have flown around the ship. Superstition says that one albatross means that the ship will be dogged by misfortune. Two of them have the older crew members really rattled . . .'

They were still days from port.

Anya asked Karen, 'Who will notify Carlos's family?'

'Thankfully, not Doctor Sensitive.' The nurse stared into the distance. 'Head office will do that. These men are away from home for up to a year. They're in close quarters with people who often don't speak the same language as them or share the same basic beliefs. Hundreds of years of ethnic pride and tribal fighting aren't easy to leave onshore. Guess I shouldn't give Novak such a hard time. Who knows what he's had to live through.'

'Is ethnic fighting something you see much of?' Martin probed.

'Well, it isn't surprising when you combine long hours,

alcohol and confined spaces for lengthy periods. Anyone caught fighting is automatically sent home from the next port. Guess you have to give credit to the staff that relatively few incidents occur.'

Anya thought that there might also be a wide variation in what constituted appropriate sexual behaviour and treatment of women. In certain cultures, men could feel entitled to sex, and in close quarters, there was a greater chance of incidents between crew. A crew member could have been with Lilly last night.

The barman delivered a plate of antipasto, french fries and fresh bread. Martin tore open a bread roll and filled it with french fries. 'Sounds like a tough life working onboard. Why do it?'

'Money. It's why most people are here. Earn money, see the world.'

Not to get shot and lose both legs, Anya thought. 'What happens at the end of all those months?'

'We go back to where we came from and rest. If we're good at our jobs, and stay out of trouble, we're offered another contract. Officers tend to work three months on, then have a couple off, but crew can do eight to ten months before getting a break. Still, most of our guys keep coming back year after year.'

'Is the money really worth it?' Martin asked.

'Tips can make it lucrative. And they're an incentive to work harder for the guests.'

Anya was curious, 'What happens if the passengers refuse to tip?'

'That's the crunch. If the cabins are half empty, or if the guests don't have the great time they imagined, tips don't get paid. Other passengers spend up big on board, get the bill at the end and can't afford to tip. It's hospitality, so it's unpredictable.'

Martin seemed fascinated. 'How easy is it to stay in touch with family?'

'Easy, but it isn't cheap. This cruise line blocks Skype or video-chatting because of the massive downloads involved. I write out all my emails in a Word document, then cut and paste them. Saves a mint on internet charges. I'm lucky the medical centre has twenty-four-hour access to anywhere in the world. The rest of the crew have to line up for hours just to get online.'

Martin pursued the point. 'Surely the company can spring for calls home?'

'Would you want to be paying international calls for four-teen hundred crew members a day? I don't blame them; they're trying to run a business.'

It had to be difficult. Anya thought of Junta and her baby in Jamaica. 'But it's not as if the staff have a choice being so far from home.'

'This is the thing. They do.' She sat forward. 'Working on a cruise ship is a way out of poverty, and gives the next generation a better life. We all want that for our kids. Carlos probably lined up for days to get the chance to work here. There are hundreds who would take his place like –' she snapped her fingers '– that. For him it was the opportunity of a lifetime. A few years on cruise ships would have paid for his home, and probably the education of his children.'

Martin sipped his beer. 'If there are hundreds of able-bodied employees wanting to take his place . . .'

The three sat in silence while the DJ played a 1970s medley.

Passengers had begun to filter up to the deck. Some women were dressed in full-length ball gowns, and a number of men wore dinner suits. 'Why would you come on holiday to dress up like a penguin when you probably wear suits to work?'

Anya imagined it was the women's preference. With few formal occasions, this was the chance to dress up and feel glamorous. Martin preferred casual at every opportunity.

Karen laughed. 'You Aussies are so laidback. These guys get two weeks off a year and make the most of every minute.'

A toddler waddled past in a tiny three-piece suit and slipped. A girl of around ten, in full make-up, maxi dress and heels, picked him up.

Karen's phone rang as she finished off her drink. 'Excuse me, I have to get this. And it's about time you two had some fun,' she said.

'Let's get this party started!' the DJ enthused. Bruce Springsteen's 'Dancing in the Dark' pumped through the speakers. A group of middle-aged women squealed like teenagers and ran onto the dance floor. Their men stayed behind. Anya found herself tapping her fingers to the beat while Martin bobbed in time. There was nothing more they could do for Carlos and it was supposed to be a holiday. The last thing she wanted was for Martin to accuse her of being a wet blanket. He always thought she spent too much time working.

'This takes me back,' he said. 'Remember when we first met?'

Anya smiled. 'There was a lot of good music back then.'

The opening bars to 'Footloose' played.

'You used to love this.' Martin extended a hand. 'Shall we?'

Anya wasn't really in the mood. She wanted to pick Ben up from the club and go to bed. 'I'd only embarrass you. All arms and legs. Remember?'

'Maybe you could teach me the praying mantis moves.' With a cheeky grin, he grabbed her hand and led the way to the dance floor.

Anya didn't have the energy to argue. She assumed one song would satisfy him, and then they could get Ben and go back to their cabins. The women on the dance floor cheered when they saw a man had joined them. Slowly, other men took the plunge. The mood was infectious, and Anya forgot her fatigue and self-consciousness by the time 'I'm So Excited' came on, followed by ABBA's 'Does Your Mother Know'. Martin spun her in and out, and they laughed when she squashed his toes. After a lively set, the DJ changed tone and played a Michael Bublé ballad. Women dragged partners to the floor, and Martin slipped his right arm around Anya's waist and held his left out. She was perspiring and her heart was pumping, but it felt good to forget the day's events for a few minutes. She placed her right hand in his and her left on his shoulder.

'I didn't know you could dance like this,' she managed.

He had an impish expression. 'Annie, I've changed a lot since our divorce. And . . .' He spun her around the floor. Her feet followed blindly. 'I have a lot of new tricks!' He finished the move with a dip.

She looked up at him and saw a different man. Martin had changed. He was more responsible and thoughtful. He had grown up a lot in the last four or so years.

A blinding white light went off. One of the ship's photographers had flashed in their direction.

Karen suddenly stood alongside them. Anya lifted herself upright.

'Can we speak?'

Anya straightened her shirt and wiped her hands on her jeans.

They followed Karen back to the table.

'Sorry to interrupt, but I wanted you to know. The blood tests on our dead girl from this morning are through. She had a low blood alcohol level, but she also had a significant amount of GHB in her blood.'

Anya stiffened. 'The date-rape drug.'

'It's also a recreational drug used by people to increase their libido. Silly girl was drinking under-age, so she's already done something illegal. It's not a big stretch to think she either brought it on board or voluntarily took GHB when it was offered.'

Karen sounded as if she was trying to convince herself.

From what Jasmine had said, Lilly was rebellious but not reckless.

'It would also have been easy for someone to spike her drink.' Despite common misconceptions, a girl who drank alcohol wasn't necessarily out for sex. 'If her blood alcohol was low, but GHB levels were high, it could have been added to her drink. She may not have been capable of consenting to anything.' The bruise on her neck still bothered Anya. It was highly suggestive of her being held down or choked.

Martin looked around. 'Seems like a fair few women are looking for holiday hook-ups. I've been hit on a few times already. Not that I'm interested,' he stressed. 'It's pretty scary to think that any of these guys could drug a woman that easily.'

A chorus went up on the dance floor. A number of men were hooting and hollering. One lifted a woman up and over his head. Her dress had flipped up, revealing skimpy underwear beneath, which led to more cheers. Another man stripped off his shirt, then trousers.

Bystanders clicked photos on their phones, as if it was part of the entertainment. To Anya, the women appeared uncomfortable. Another tried to get her friend down, but was lifted up and passed around in the process.

A female security officer approached the centre of the group. The two women were lowered to the ground, and quickly retreated to a table near where Anya and Martin were sitting. It looked as if the men were telling the guard to lighten up.

'Does she need backup?' Martin asked Karen.

'This happens all the time. There's not much she can do apart from ask him to put his clothes back on.' Karen rubbed her eyes. 'Company policy is to let people have fun on their holiday. If a fight breaks out, all security can do is let it play out. And we'll patch them up in the infirmary later.' She shrugged. 'I'd better go relieve Rachel. Thanks again for all your help. We couldn't have got through today without you.'

Martin watched the floor show. Anya knew he would step in if the men harassed the guard. She turned to the two women the group had treated like human parcels. They looked shaken, so she approached them.

'Are you two okay?'

'Bloody pricks. They've been hassling us from the moment we got on board. Guess their mums never told them "No".'

The young woman was trembling as she reached for the compact in her purse. *Emma* was engraved on the lid.

Anya knelt down beside one of the chairs. 'Did they hurt you?'

'It was just a bit scary when the big one threatened to throw me over the side if I didn't show him if I was wearing underwear. I mean, I know he was joking ... I guess I overreacted.'

'One of them offered me a hundred bucks to take my underwear off and dance with him.'

The dispute with the security officer continued on the dance floor, albeit more quietly now.

Emma added, 'After what happened to that girl, Bec and I are too scared to piss anyone off.'

Anya felt her pulse quicken. 'What do you mean?'

The two women exchanged quick glances. 'You don't know?' They moved closer. 'A woman died last night. We heard some guys were talking about a "chinger" who choked

71

on her vomit. The woman who told us said they thought it was hilarious.'

Anya felt bile rise in her gullet. 'Do you know who those men were?'

It was possible a group of men had been with Lilly. Finding them and proving they had drugs on board was one thing. Proving they gave them to an unwilling Lilly, raped her and left her for dead was something else.

Anya had to find FitzHarris straightaway.

8

After giving Martin the pass key to her cabin so he could put Ben to bed, Anya went to the customer relations desk and paged FitzHarris. She felt queasy, and wondered whether it was exhaustion or the movement of the ship. The massive chandelier in the centre of the atrium seemed to swing a little.

FitzHarris lumbered along with a strained expression. 'I was about to find you,' he said. 'I know it's a big ask, but would you mind looking at the scene where Carlos was shot? At the moment I have over a thousand suspects and not much to go on. Blood spatter may give us a better idea as to what happened.'

Her earlier irritation with the security head had subsided. He was merely doing his job, in difficult circumstances. She would have preferred to have been tucked up in bed, but she wanted to find out what had happened to Lilly, and Carlos could have known something. 'Sure, but there's something else you need to know.' She filled him in on the GHB in Lilly's blood and the men bragging about an Asian woman choking on her own vomit.

FitzHarris ran his large hand over his face. He offered Anya a seat near the porthole windows, and dragged another chair close.

'Men are bragging about a girl who wasn't even the legal age to drink?' He shook his head. 'Most people think the police are clever. Truth is, crims are just dumber.' He pulled a pen and notebook from his top pocket. 'Can the women identify them? Do you know who they are?'

'I'm not sure. I've seen a fair number of people out for a good time.'

FitzHarris chewed his bottom lip. 'Any in particular flying above the radar?'

Anya thought of the corridor above the crew's bar. 'Martin complained this morning because a group on his corridor had spent the first night messing with fire-extinguishers and being incredibly loud and obnoxious to anyone trying to sleep. One couple were having sex on the floor outside his room.'

'I haven't seen any complaints.'

'It seems the issue of the fire-extinguisher was the purser's only concern.'

FitzHarris looked up to the ceiling and shook his head again. 'Sometimes in this business, we forget what's normal behaviour. It's not just the passengers who leave their brains and sense of decency on shore. It's what you get for promoting all fun and no responsibility. I'll look into it.'

'If Lilly had her drink spiked with GHB, someone had to bring it on board. It's unlikely they only brought enough for one dose . . .'

'Do you know the women's names? I'll need to talk to them.'

'All I can tell you is Bec and Emma. They were up at the disco.' Anya described their appearances.

FitzHarris pulled himself to his feet. 'It's happy hour in the crew club, so we should go over Carlos's cabin now. This time it had better be still sealed off.'

'Any word on his condition?'

'In this business, no news is good news. Karen will let us know if there's a change.'

A waiter holding a large cardboard box waited until they'd moved, then placed a pile of sick bags in their place.

'We're heading for rough conditions.' FitzHarris commented.

Anya resisted the urge to grab one, just in case. Martin had always said seasickness was mind over matter. She followed FitzHarris down the corridor to an etched-glass partition. Behind it was a service lift. Inside, a man in a blue apron carried a skinned sheep carcass on his shoulder. A svelte woman dressed in a sequinned bikini and fish-net tights stood next to a man in a headless bear suit. Once the doors opened again, the decor altered dramatically. The patterned carpet, art prints and music were replaced with grey metal and a constant hum. As they stepped out, the heat hit Anya like a heavy cloth.

Metal floors were painted blue-grey, scratched and streaked black from traffic. Exposed studs were the only embellishment on white walls. Even so, nothing could temper the claustrophobic feel. Pipes ran along the already low ceilings. The whole area smelt of diesel and something else Anya couldn't pinpoint.

FitzHarris led the way along a vast corridor.

'Some call this the I-95. It's the main route from one end of the ship to the other. Mind you, sometimes it's more congested than the Jersey Turnpike.'

'Where's the I-95?' Anya assumed it was a freeway.

FitzHarris was already beginning to perspire, moisture spreading from beneath his armpits. 'It's the immigration form crew members have to fill in before they can enter a US port.'

He led the way down a set of steep narrow stairs, the type men slid down in submarines – more ladder rungs than steps. Seeing the floor beneath her feet was unnerving, but Anya did her best not to make that known. The security officer seemed to have no problem engineering his way, despite his size.

A small forklift laden with toilet paper rumbled toward them.

A blue-covered arm extended across her chest and yanked her out of its way. It belonged to an Hispanic man in overalls. Anya stepped back to the wall as the forklift forged on.

'If that door closes, you get chopped in half.'

Anya stepped back into the corridor a little confused. What door? The Samaritan was already on his way.

She looked down and noticed a hydraulic system connected a red lever to the floor. She'd been standing in a doorway – red paint on the floor showed the area not to obstruct.

'The metal's a foot thick,' FitzHarris explained. 'Designed to waterproof this section in an emergency. Once it's activated, nothing can stop it closing. Kind of like those screens in banks.' He took her by the elbow as another forklift charged past. 'Saw a guy crushed once trying to climb a bank counter. Wasn't pretty.'

Anya decided to defer to the crew's instructions without hesitation.

'First I'll show you where Carlos was shot. Get your opinion on the forensic side of things,' FitzHarris said quietly. 'We can talk upstairs later. You'll find everything down here has ears.'

As they walked, the sound of Calypso music pulsed louder. They passed a room with a naked man spread out on the grey floor playing a video game. Four beds each had a curtain for 'privacy'. She wondered what happened to people who worked nights and had to sleep in the day.

Outside a door in a nook off a side corridor stood one of the security men, a camera slung around his neck, arms folded. This time he did appear intimidating. A strip of hazard tape stretched the width of the door.

FitzHarris didn't need to speak for the guard to move away. Discarding one end of the tape before opening the door with an electronic pass key, he reached inside to switch on the light. The release of incubated cigarette smoke stung

Anya's eyes and throat. The cabin had two bunk beds, vertical lockers on top of each other, and a computer-sized flatscreen TV attached to the wall. The entire floor area would not have been wide enough for two people to pass. She stepped over the metal lip of the door and covered her mouth and nose with one hand.

What immediately struck her was how hot the cabin was, as if even less air circulated here than in the already stifling corridor. The overwhelming scent of body odour made her take shallow breaths. The absence of a window or natural light gave the cabin the feel of solitary confinement, not worker accommodation.

She stepped forward toward the narrow space which was the back wall. Blood spatters fanned out at knee level. About two feet in front of the wall were blood smears on the floor with footprints through them.

'What do you think?' FitzHarris asked.

Judging by a vertical blood smear, Carlos had been standing facing the wall when the first shot was fired. She tried to step around the dried stains on the floor. 'I think he was here to begin with.' The central ceiling light was not bright enough to see detail.

'Don't suppose you have that torch with you?'

FitzHarris pulled a small LED torch from his trouser pocket and held it over her shoulder.

'There are small fragments of bone embedded in the wall.' Anya pointed to an area about ten centimetres square. 'This is definitely where he was hit first. There's the bullet. It's embedded pretty deep by the looks of it. You'll have to be careful when you get it out.'

'Not a lot of point, to be honest.'

Anya turned and looked up. 'Excuse me?'

'My guess is our shooter tossed the gun overboard before Carlos even made it to help.'

'Maybe he, or she, still needs it for their own protection?'

FitzHarris did not look convinced. 'I've organised a cabin search of the crew anyway. So. If he was shot there . . .'

'The impact pushed him to the wall.' She examined the smears. 'It looks like Carlos tried to crawl to the door with the shooter still in the room.' From where she squatted, Anya could see photos of a family on the wall. Five children – three boys and two girls – surrounded an attractive woman with a shy smile. The lower bed belonged to Carlos.

She stood and straightened her back.

'With the space this tight, the shooter had to be straddling him as he struggled. They weren't in a hurry to finish the job.'

It could have taken minutes. She remembered the plea in the Colombian's eyes. The shooter would have seen the same thing.

'Whoever did this is callous and took their time.' She pictured the scene. 'Carlos wasn't meant to be killed. He was made to stand facing away from the gunman. A shot to the head would have been easy – clean – and Carlos wouldn't have been able to talk.' She bent down and saw the small hole in the floor; the second bullet. 'The knees were the target all along.'

FitzHarris rubbed his leg. 'We need to find out whether this was payback or a warning to others on board.'

'Shooting one leg would have achieved the same result. Carlos earned his living on his feet. This is vindictive.'

'I agree. He's either seen something he shouldn't or he's involved with gangs or drugs, or some other smuggling operation.'

'He's unlikely to tell us now,' Anya said. 'Whoever did this is powerful enough to know he won't talk.'

'Or he still has something they want,' FitzHarris suggested.

Anya shook her head. 'Kneecapping was a specialty of the various Mafia and IRA. They'd often use it as a calling card.

Taking out the kneecap from behind is incredibly painful. After that, the victims are too terrified to talk.'

Working in England she had seen victims of the IRA as young as fourteen who would forever struggle to walk, even if their legs could be saved.

'Maybe he was doing the horizontal cha-cha with someone else's woman. On a ship with 1400 crew away from home for months at a time that pretty much narrows it down.'

'Where was the room mate when it happened?'

'Let's find out.' FitzHarris checked his watch. 'Feeding time.'

They left the cabin and he replaced the seal across the door. 'No one gets in or out. No one!'

'Yes, boss.' The guard re-crossed his arms.

Down a long, seemingly endless corridor, they turned a corner into the crew mess.

The place could have been the United Nations. Anya was struck by the female crew – it was as if they had been hand-picked from a Miss Universe contest. A perfectly proportioned woman of around six foot with shoulder-length blonde hair and pale blue eyes carried a plate of fruit to a table with five other people. The three seated Asian women had bowls of white rice and soup. A fair-haired man was occupied by his plate of fish and potatoes.

Supplying halal and kosher foods, while catering to very different cultural tastes, would have been challenging. Anya's mouth watered at the buffet's aromas. They could have been standing in a Hong Kong market, instead of a ship.

The cacophony of chatter and different language intonations made it difficult to hear FitzHarris.

'I don't see him. Let's try the bar.'

Back out down the corridor and around yet another corner, they passed a mess half-filled with officers. There were no queues and the area was much quieter.

Further on the stench of stale alcohol filled their nostrils. They entered a smoke-filled haze that was the crew bar. The area was double the size of an average living room, crammed with plastic tables and occupied chairs. In one corner, a small man belted out 'We are the Champions' at a karaoke machine. No one paid him attention. A series of screens on an opposite wall showed various sports games, one a soccer match with two African teams playing. A cheer went up from one table at a goal. A group of men crowded around controls to a video game displayed on another screen. At a table against the wall, a group of men focused all their attention on a game of cards, despite a porno film playing on one of the screens.

'Any of these card sharks could fleece a newcomer of a month's pay in one sitting,' Fitz commented. 'Rumour has it Carlos is a pretty slick player.'

It wouldn't be the first time someone was shot over a gambling-related debt.

'Maybe he got caught cheating,' Anya suggested.

Within a closed community like this one, that would have been the ultimate betrayal. His injuries would have been a warning to any other potential scammers.

Fitz nodded. 'Not what my sources tell me, but let's go rattle some cages.'

A metal door led to a balcony. Outside, a dozen workers were smoking, some in quiet conversation. The waves were no longer calm. The swell was at least six metres and the air was damp. Away from the light, a couple were engaged in a passionate embrace, oblivious to those around them. Closing the balcony door did little to block out the inside noise. Anya realised they had to be directly below Martin's internal cabin; little wonder he had trouble sleeping.

FitzHarris approached the couple and tapped the man on the shoulder.

'Bruno, I want a word.'

The man moved one arm from his partner's backside and gestured for FitzHarris and Anya to leave.

'Bruno Vanii, we need to talk to you about Carlos's shooting.'

The man seemed to freeze and suddenly put distance between himself and the woman. 'You should go,' he told her. 'We will catch up later.' She shrugged her shoulders, grabbed a half-empty glass and staggered back inside. Anya couldn't help but notice the large diamond pendant around her neck. It seemed like perhaps some crew members were well paid.

Bruno turned to FitzHarris with wide, dark eyes. Average height but stocky, a short-sleeved pale blue shirt fit snugly around his biceps.

'I can't help you.'

'Maybe you know more than you realise.'

Two giggling women with glasses and cigarettes appeared from the door. They stopped when they saw the head of security, and headed back to the bar. The others on the balcony quickly joined them inside.

Bruno's eyes darted to the door and back. 'I know nothing. Carlos and I, we work different times.' Bruno pulled a cigar from a pack in the pocket of his khaki shorts and offered them each one.

Anya shook her head but FitzHarris accepted. The Italian snipped off the tips and handed one across. He lit FitzHarris's first, with a gold engraved lighter.

'How long you been with the company?' FitzHarris took a few quick puffs and looked out to sea.

Bruno did the same. 'Five years.'

'Clean record of service?'

'Of course, I mind my own business and do my job.' He glanced sideways at Anya. 'You did not introduce your attractive friend.'

'You're right, I didn't.' FitzHarris took another puff before admiring the cigar. 'You spent two years in the military.'

Bruno's eyes darted back to the door again. 'Ah, yes, in national service.'

Anya noticed the carotid artery in his neck pulsate faster. 'Where were you when Carlos was shot? It was four o'clock this afternoon.'

'After I finish work, I go back to my cabin for a towel to shower. One of your men was already outside. You can check with my supervisor.'

'We'll do that. So where will you spend tonight?'

Bruno drew in on his cigar and let out a slow, deep breath. 'A lady friend, she makes me . . . welcome. I would give you her name, but you understand . . .' He glanced at Anya. 'I am a gentleman.'

'You mean she's married, like you.' FitzHarris didn't miss a beat.

Bruno tapped his temple with his cigar hand and grinned, showing a gap in his middle front teeth. 'Ah, I can see we . . . understand each other.'

Anya felt sorry for the poor wife back home. Her husband was shameless. She wondered if Carlos had the same attitude, or if his family meant more to him. 'Did Carlos understand how much of a gentleman you are?'

Bruno waved his cigar to the side. 'With him it was all about work and going back home.'

Fitz puffed away. 'Did you know his wife has cancer?'

Anya hoped to see even the smallest amount of sympathy from the cabin mate.

He merely looked out to sea. 'We all have problems. On a ship, it pays not to get involved in other people's business.'

'Well, you might want to follow your own rule there. That woman you were just with, I hear she's a favourite of the captain.'

Bruno swallowed hard. 'She was drunk and upset. I was just . . . how you say . . . comforting her.'

'Yeah, we get it. You're a real prince.'

FitzHarris leant as close to Bruno as possible, as if the pair were sharing something very private.

Anya stepped to the side but could still hear despite the music from inside and the ocean wind. The view was now clear to anyone watching from inside the bar.

'Listen here, your roommate got shot and has had both legs cut off above the knee. You may be involved, or those bullets could have been meant for you. Maybe you banged the wrong woman. Maybe you passed on a little gonorrhoea, or syphilis. For all we know, Carlos was protecting you.'

Bruno's eyes darted back and forth, and again toward the door. Beads of perspiration appeared on his forehead and above his lips. Suddenly, he cared what had happened to his crew mate.

'You think so? Then I want protection.'

FitzHarris sighed. 'Sorry, I don't get involved in other people's business, unless they can help me out.'

It was as if the cogs in the Italian's brain were spinning, trying to think who he could have done the wrong thing by. There was clearly a long list.

'I don't know who shot him,' he said finally, sounding desperate.

The security officer slapped him on the back as if congratulating him. 'Then I wish you good luck. If there's anything you can think of, just call.' FitzHarris blocked Anya, just as what had to be a ten-metre wave lashed the side of the ship, showering the men's backs.

'There's something,' the Italian ventured. 'When can I get the rest of my things?'

FitzHarris opened the door for Anya and peeled off his jacket. This time, there was silence as they re-entered the bar.

All eyes were on them as they made their way back to the corridor.

'Right, let's go check out some trash.'

Out of anyone else's earshot, Anya stopped him. 'You wanted everyone to think he told us something.'

'An uncooperative witness interview is over in a lot less time than that, and the crew knows it. I had to make them think their code of silence was broken.'

'So you just marked him as an informant.'

'Nah. He doesn't know anything, and I think the shooter knows that too. Won't hurt to make him suffer and maybe pull his pecker in for a couple of days. But it might make one of the others nervous enough to talk.'

Anya had to respect FitzHarris's interrogation technique. 'And that bit about the girl being the captain's favourite?'

'Common knowledge. He has a few, but it varies from day to day. Did you see that diamond around her neck? It's career suicide for anyone messing with one of those women.' He smiled. 'We've just poured some boiling water down the ant hole. Now we sit back and see what comes scrambling out.'

9

Anya and FitzHarris headed back to the I-95.

'If you don't mind, I'd like to check out Carlos's work area.'

Anya had no objection despite her calves and thighs beginning to ache. By now Ben should be asleep, and she was curious about the inner workings of the ship. Her earlier exhaustion had been replaced by a new energy and she was keen to find out the truth about Lilly.

She stopped to adjust her shoe, this time careful to move to the side and avoid another forklift truck. It whirred past them, along with a beep from the driver. The hum and vibrations from the engines and vehicles were magnified in the grey steel corridor.

'You OK?' Fitz asked.

'I must be more unfit than I realised.'

'It's been a long day, and we've covered a lot of ground. Most of the workers here don't bother with gyms. Just doing their jobs can mean walking or running up to ten miles a day. Have to say, some days I struggle.'

A pair of crew in white overalls passed by, the smell of foreign cigarettes lingering in their wake.

Further along, they entered a large area filled with hundreds of bags of rubbish contained in clear plastic bags. Anya suddenly became aware of the stench of decomposing food in the dense, warm air. Machines and large receptacles surrounded the three walls. The centre area was dominated by an open container, about two by one metres, situated on a metallic table.

'This is where Carlos worked,' Fitz announced, tossing bags aside to make a small path for them.

'Mr FitzHarris, we were expecting you to visit. Terrible news about Carlos. Terrible.'

'This is one of our sanitation engineers, Sergio Perez, aka Cockroach.'

Anya greeted the man, who had greasy black hair and pasty skin. His hands had the coarseness that came with years of physical labour.

Anya assumed the nickname stemmed from the fact that he worked with rubbish in the bowels of the ship.

'What can I do to help?'

A machine clanged and there was a loud sound – like a bucket full of glass being smashed. Anya instinctively covered her ears.

'*Un minuto*!' Cockroach bellowed and hit a large red button attached to the wall. A grinding noise halted the shattering.

'We are short of space, as you can see, and a man down. We had no choice but to extend the shifts for our workers.' He pointed at the bags of rubbish, which were piled to hip level. 'All bottles and broken glass have to be crushed. In a week, that is forty thousand bottles of beer, wine and spirits alone. You can smell. Yes?'

'How long are the normal shifts?' Anya asked.

'Twelve to fourteen hours. Now, sixteen hours; more if we are behind.'

No wonder Cockroach looked like he never saw sunlight, she thought. Working sixteen hours or more each day didn't provide enough time for eight hours sleep after taking into account eating, washing and contacting home. She looked at the large grinding machines and wondered about the occupational health and safety standards. Chronically tired workers were more likely to have accidents.

'How often do you get days off?'

Cockroach chuckled, folding his lips behind crooked, nicotine-stained teeth. 'On ship we work. At home we sleep.'

'I'll take it from here.' A man in fresh whites and fine-rimmed glasses entered the area. Cockroach nodded and returned to the glass grinder. 'I understand you're here to examine the area. I'm Jeremy Wise, the Environmental Officer.'

FitzHarris stood legs apart, arms folded. 'I need to get an idea of what our shooting victim did; get a better feel for maybe why he ended up on a stretcher.'

'There was no staff conflict or reason to think what happened was work-related. From what I see, this team works well together. Some of the Latinos can be pretty hot-headed, particularly when alcohol, money and women are concerned, as you probably know.'

He held a lens rim between his index finger and thumb and made a miniscule adjustment.

'Thanks for the heads up.' Fitz patted his shoulder. 'But it's a little more than a heated altercation when one of those involved has his legs shot off. I'm covering all bases.'

'If it helps, I can explain how things work here.'

'Please do,' Fitz said. 'Doctor Crichton's getting a grand tour.'

'The industry has worked very hard over the past decade toward reducing its environmental footprint. The *Paradisio* is unsurpassed in terms of her green credentials. We go above and beyond every industry standard and regulation.'

Cockroach had begun to hand-sort rubbish from a number of bags, separating plastics, paper, glass and tin into separate tubs. Another man soon joined him, then another. Together, they worked quickly, to the clanging and smashing from the machines.

'As you can see, anything and everything that can be recycled is separated on board. We have state-of-the-art facilities: shredders, compactors and baling equipment, and crushers – as you can see, and hear – which we use for glass, tin and aluminium.

He took them through an open doorway to another section. Compacted cans compressed into large cubes were stacked in rows along one wall, almost to the ceiling.

Anya couldn't help but notice that each cube had been wrapped tightly in plastic from an industrial roll. The wall of crushed cans was astounding, especially considering they had only been at sea a day. This was a garbage tip for the equivalent of a small town, compacted into a few rooms.

'What sort of a worker was Carlos?'

Wise readjusted his glasses again. 'He was a hard worker. Kept to himself as far as I can tell.'

'Did he have any beefs with any of your team?'

The compactor clunked into action and, a minute later, produced a bale of crushed metal cans. A worker from the other room entered with more tubs of aluminium, refilled the machine and removed the compressed block.

'Not that I know of. The crew come here to work and aren't paid to socialise. Most of our team are from South America and speak Portuguese or Spanish.'

'What about religious or cultural differences? Does everyone pull his weight?'

'Yes. Our Muslim crew are permitted time-out for prayers, just as smokers take their breaks. No one should feel as though they're working harder than anyone else. Carlos was a consistent worker. We keep meticulous logs and records, and I'd know if any of the shifts was doing less than their share.'

Up until now, Anya had not thought twice about where rubbish and refuse from the staterooms and decks ended up. 'How much rubbish is generated on the ship?'

'Each passenger can generate up to three and a half kilograms of waste per day. We have just over three thousand passengers this leg, which makes over eleven thousand kilograms every day this week.'

The figure was almost inconceivable. 'Is all of that sorted and kept down here?' She thought it would have needed an army to keep up with that amount of rubbish, and felt a twang of guilt about how much she had already contributed.

Wise stood straight. 'It includes food waste, which is macerated and incinerated. We incinerate a lot of the plastic and paper, storing the ash in a specially designed cold room. I'd show you, but it also contains hazardous waste: sewage sludge.'

'That's fine,' Fitz commented, as he wandered around the room. 'I don't need to see and smell shit to know it's there.' He was examining the notes pinned to walls and machines, and the safety signs that were written in multiple languages. He then turned his attention to some of the bags and sorted materials.

'What happens to the sewage?' Anya hated to think how much passengers and crew produced, and where that was stored.

'On average, we process over a million litres of what we call black water – sewage and medical waste – every week. We have the most advanced water treatment systems available, which satisfy every environmental protection agency and marine standard.'

Wise sounded like a poster boy for the industry, proud of his role. Anya suspected he had not been in the job all that long.

'Where's black water stored?'

'That's the beauty of it. It's so clean that legally we're permitted to discharge it within three miles of shore, but we prefer to release it more than twelve miles out, to be sure.' He grinned, as if expecting praise.

Anya responded courteously. 'I had no idea the ships were so progressive in waste management.'

'Well, Doctor, we pride ourselves on protecting the oceans we sail in. If you're interested, I can tell you about the other innovations in my office. The ship is quite masterful.'

Anya looked at FitzHarris. He waved a hand. 'Go on, it is fascinating and a real eye-opener. I just have to ask Cockroach one last question and I'll be right with you.'

She felt set up. Fitz just wanted her to distract Wise so he could search and ask questions unimpeded. Ordinarily, she might not have minded, but a wave of exhaustion had hit her and the events of the day were catching up.

'Shall we?'

'I only have a few minutes before I have to collect my son from the kids' club,' she lied.

'This won't take long.' He led the way to his office. Every piece of paper was in perfectly aligned piles. A pen and pencil were placed horizontally, equidistant from the papers on either side.

Wise retrieved a well-worn spiral bound report. 'As you can see,' he flicked to a colour picture of a smooth hull, 'this hull is especially designed with non-toxic materials. It's like Teflon for ships. With reduced resistance, fuel efficiency has gone up dramatically. *And*,' he emphasised, 'sea life is repelled. No barnacles, no accidental transfer of organisms to other environments.' He admired the image. 'It really is marvellous. Maintenance is minimal, as you can imagine.'

From the enthusiasm, Anya would have thought Wise had a role in its design, but she suspected he would have mentioned it if he had.

Wise continued to rattle off an array of facts and figures, while Anya politely listened, willing FitzHarris back with every passing minute. They had navigated so many corners and turns, she had no idea how to find her way out, and suspected that asking Jeremy Wise would ensure a longer tour, via all of the ship's environmental aspects.

Finally a knock on the door heralded FitzHarris's return. 'Sorry, Jeremy, but I have to get the good doctor back to her son.' He winked. 'Maybe you should do lunch and you can fill her in on all the other advancements.'

Wise raised his eyebrows. 'I'll give you my direct number. Please call and I'll make a point of making time.'

'Thanks,' Anya managed, flicking a glare at Fitz, which only he was privy to. 'I'll check with my family.'

They left and headed back to the I-95, dodging the night run of heavy vehicles. Like an underground society, workers continued while those above partied or slept.

Out of range, FitzHarris pealed into hearty laughter. 'You should have seen your face when I mentioned lunch.'

Anya buckled over, gasping as her stomach muscles contracted with laughter. After a day of dealing with death and trauma, the slightest thing could set her off; it was impossible to explain to anyone else what was so funny. Thankfully, FitzHarris was the same.

They slumped against the wall for a couple of minutes before regaining self-control. Any animosity Anya had felt toward FitzHarris earlier in the day at the morgue was long forgotten.

FitzHarris wiped one eye. 'Maybe I should suggest dinner and a tour of the Teflon hull . . .'

They erupted again. Fitz folded at the waist, hands bracing his knees, to odd looks from the crew carting rubbish to and from the recycling centre.

For a few brief moments, all thoughts and images of Lilly and Carlos faded from Anya's mind.

By the time Anya returned to her cabin, she had regained control, grateful for the endorphin release she and FitzHarris had shared.

Ben had been struggling to stay awake until she returned. 'This was the best day ever.' He clutched his toy rabbit and yawned. One eyelid and its surrounds still had traces of smudged black paint, remnants of a makeshift eye patch. Anya reached up and stroked his soft blond mop. Within a minute, breathing deeply, he was fast asleep. Like so many young children, he vacillated between full speed and complete shutdown. She watched him resting peacefully after his fulfilling day of exciting adventures.

'Sweet dreams,' she whispered.

'He loves you a lot,' Martin said from the balcony. 'You're a good mother.'

Anya watched his face to see if he were mocking her. Instead, he smiled. It was the first time he had complimented her parenting. Normally, he derided how she spent more time at work than with the family.

She joined him outside. The breeze had picked up and it released pieces of hair from her ponytail.

He unscrewed a bottle of water and presented it over his forearm, as someone would a fine wine. 'Excellent vintage. Can I tempt you?'

Anya smiled as he poured two glasses and gave her one. They clinked. It was the first time in a while that they'd been in unison. She had to admit that they had worked well together today, in difficult circumstances. It reminded her of the Martin she had loved a long time ago.

For a brief moment, it felt as if the craziness of the world had stopped and for once they were a normal family.

'You know, Annie, it always amazed me how calm you are in a crisis. And how much you care about people.'

The cold water felt good in her dry throat. 'I thought it annoyed you. How I couldn't switch off.'

Martin shoved a hand in his jeans pocket. 'Well, I might have grown up a bit since then. Being a parent does that, you know.'

He really was an adult version of their son – curls, expressions, dimples and all.

'You're doing an incredible job with Ben. Sounds like he was a hit with the club counsellors.'

He looked out to sea. 'He can't wait to go back in the morning. But I said we'd have to ask you.'

Anya flicked his shoulder. 'Great, make me the bad guy if I say no.'

Martin became serious. 'I figured that security guy might want your advice tomorrow and it might even come in handy if anything goes wrong with our gunshot patient.' He put the glass down on the white plastic table. 'I get that you can't turn your back on these people.'

Anya thought of Jasmine Chan and the promise she'd made to herself to find out more about Lilly. She wanted to spend more time with Ben too though – she hardly ever had the chance to be with him all day.

They sat in silence as the wind whipped around them. Dark clouds buried the moonlight. The sound of the ship hitting waves became louder. The storm the captain had forewarned them about was starting to hit.

'Better batten down the hatches,' Martin finally said. He

stood and let Anya return to the room first. 'It could get rough out there, but the way the stabilisers are on this ship, we'll be unlikely to feel it.' She felt a little queasy but his words were comforting.

He closed and locked the sliding door before making sure the curtains were pulled shut. Within seconds, rain pounded the balcony.

She showed him to the door.

He patted a shirt pocket for his room key and yawned. 'I'll be off to bed then.'

Just like Ben, Martin's energy had expired.

'Will I see you in the morning for breakfast?' he asked.

She glanced at their son. 'Let's see what time sleepy boy wakes up.'

Martin grinned and headed out the door. 'Sleep well, and do me a favour: deadlock the door when I go. Whoever did that to Lilly is still out there.'

'Night.' She closed the door and clicked the bolt. She changed into an oversized T-shirt and curled up under the covers. Using the remote control, she scanned the television channels and stopped at one highlighting the facilities on board, which quickly drifted into the visual equivalent of white noise. The sound of rain outside and furniture scraping on the deck above filtered into the background.

Her mind replayed the day's events. Martin finding Lilly, her body in the morgue, FitzHarris referring to Anya as a whistleblower. Her thoughts drifted to Carlos. She sat up and checked the phone. No messages.

There was a knock at the door. Martin must have forgotten something. She climbed out quietly, not wanting to disturb Ben, and pulled on jeans. Without a peephole, she had no option but to open the door. Standing outside was a female officer carrying a large brown envelope. Anya's first thought was that Carlos's condition had deteriorated.

'Ma'am, I apologise for the interruption. This was left at reception and I was asked to deliver it to you asap.'

Her badge read Nuala, Florida.

'Thanks.' Anya accepted the envelope.

The woman glanced at both sides of the corridor. She seemed to be waiting for something from Anya.

'Do you need a response?'

'No, ma'am, it can surely wait until morning. Once again, apologies for disturbing you so late.' Nuala smiled broadly and headed down the corridor.

After closing and re-locking the door, Anya opened the envelope by the light of the television. It contained a number of pages with headings:

Anderson Cruise Lines – the Ocean's Richest Pirates
Flags of Convenience
Third World Wages
Corporate Tax Evasion
Eco Vandalism
Raping and Pillaging is their business

Each title was followed by two pages of websites and references. At the bottom, an unsigned handwritten message immediately drew her attention.

'Where you are guaranteed to get away with rape and murder . . . Trust no one.'

A burst of air from the air-conditioner made her startle. She sat on the bed and clicked on the bedside light. Ben didn't stir as she closed the curtain partitioning her bed from the lounge area. Re-reading the note, it seemed like someone had a major gripe against the company.

She wondered if Nuala was handing them out to all the passengers. Feeling exhausted, she removed her jeans and climbed beneath the covers. It was late and her eyelids were heavy. She clicked off the light. The handwritten message repeated in her mind. 'Guaranteed to get away with rape and murder.' Gut instinct told her the note wasn't random. It had to be from someone who knew about Lilly, and maybe even Carlos.

Was it a warning? Or could it be a threat? Nuala would be long gone by now. She listened to Ben's heavy breathing, before collecting her laptop and logging on to the internet.

She began with the term, 'Flag of Convenience'. Comprehensive definitions explained how many large corporations, like cruise lines, were registered in Panama, Liberia and Bermuda – known tax havens – despite conducting most of their business in and around the US, with American owners and managers.

A quick search for *Paradisio* found it had been registered in Panama, along with Anderson Cruise Lines. Sports stars were well-known for seeking havens like Bermuda and Monaco to avoid paying tax, so it made sense that companies would do the same. One of the references took her to a website that contained articles on the cruise industry. By registering offshore, Anderson avoided paying US company tax, and was immune from labour laws and most US regulations, including minimum wages.

Anya shoved a pillow behind her back. She had long forgotten how late it was. Minimum wages in America were shockingly low, it seemed. Someone working two to three jobs could still be below the poverty level. In Australia, tips, superannuation and holiday pay were factored into minimum wages. If the cruise lines were paying below even basic rates, they were no better than sweat shops. Fixed terms of employment meant companies avoided paying for leave, or medical care for families. What was to stop the company lowering the pay rates with subsequent contracts? Karen had said even low pay was better than what crew members could earn in their own countries.

The 'fun cruise' suddenly took on a new dimension.

From the smiles on the faces of the crew, it hardly seemed possible.

Anya thought of the subclass down below she had seen that night, and the large number of staff from developing countries living and working like Cockroach in the garbage disposal area.

Eight to ten months of living in cramped, hot conditions with no daylight would be a challenge for anyone, especially so far from your family. The air-conditioner spluttered again, and Anya felt a pang of guilt. She was free to control the temperature in her cabin. The workers on the decks below appeared to have no power over their lives while on board. They weren't even given sufficient time to sleep.

Rain pelted the balcony and windows, and Anya pulled the covers up higher. She typed in 'wages, housekeeper' and 'cruise ship'. The results showed an abundance of agencies advertising for staff, and the job descriptions read like holiday brochures where crew could visit the world's most famous cities and enjoy five-star facilities. She wondered how many places Cockroach and Carlos had actually seen.

The recruiting companies listed were based in the Philippines, Indonesia, India and the Caribbean. Searching for blogs by employees was more difficult. It was as if a code of silence existed among former workers.

She typed in 'cruise ship workers union'. No result. Out of frustration, she tried the catchphrase 'United Nations of crew'. This led to the Anderson company website.

'We pride ourselves on being a non-discriminatory, welcoming, international family. To ensure we employ people from every possible country, we hand-select our staff from all parts of the globe, to give our passengers a truly multinational experience.' As an example, various countries – again, developing countries – were listed along with the percentage of staff representing each area. She looked down the list. India, twelve percent; Malaysia, six percent; China, eleven percent; Costa Rica, five percent; Philippines, fourteen percent. The percentages seemed low given the recruiting companies were based in areas of high unemployment and poor education.

Anya unscrewed the lid on the bottled water by her bed, and wondered if there was an absence of unions because the company had a ceiling on the numbers from each nation. That would ensure every employee belonged to a minority group. With the exhausting working hours, they would not have time, energy or even the multi-language skills required to organise a union.

Passengers were totally oblivious to what went on out of their sight.

She took a few sips of water and listened to Ben mumbling in his sleep before resettling. The bedside clock glowed 2 a.m. The humming of the cabin was becoming hypnotic.

Anya did one last search: Anderson company profits.

The annual report described the company as four times the size of McDonald's, the fast food doyen. Only McDonald's paid taxes. It took her a moment to process the comparison. Cruising was far bigger business than Anya had ever imagined.

Despite record profits, crew welfare didn't seem to be a company priority.

She wondered if investigations into drugs, sexual assault and shootings were.

The contents of the envelope played on her mind.

Trust no one.

Five hours later, she woke up with Ben snuggled close beside her, his hair tousled. He had climbed in around four o'clock when the storm had intensified. She stretched her free arm and bumped the headboard. Ben stirred and buried his head deeper into her shoulder before opening his bleary eyes.

'Is it morning yet?'

She swept the fringe from his forehead. 'Yep, you had a pretty good sleep.'

He sat upright and stretched his arms. 'Is kids' club open?'

Anya's heart sank a little. She had hoped to spend the whole trip with her son, but he obviously loved the activities and interaction with other children. It seemed selfish to spoil his fun.

'I thought we could have breakfast with your dad before you go anywhere.'

Ben launched himself onto the floor, slipped out of his pyjamas and pulled a clean pair of underwear from the drawer. 'Is he coming?'

Anya laughed. 'Yesterday all you wanted to do was swim in the pool. And hey, don't leave those on the floor.'

He picked up the discarded clothes and shoved them into a drawer before removing a blue T-shirt and green elastic-waisted shorts. 'Should we get Dad?'

He was already fully charged and energetic.

'Can you please slow down, I haven't had a shower or even woken up properly yet, or had a hug.'

'Maaahhhaaahhhaarrrmmm!'

Children had a knack of inserting multiple syllables into a three letter name, making Mum sound like a profanity. He jumped onto the bed and threw his arms around her. She lingered as he twirled a piece of her hair around his finger.

'I won't be long.' She climbed out of bed. 'And I don't want you answering the door to anyone except your father.'

'Uh huh, can I please watch TV?'

Anya had no objections as she headed for the shower. Washing more of yesterday away felt good, and with the storm still lashing the balcony, a couple of hours in the kids' club would be fun for Ben. Then they could all go and see a movie or do any number of onboard activities.

By the time she had towel-dried her hair and used a spare to wrap around herself, Martin had arrived and he and Ben were sitting on the couch watching cartoons. Self-conscious in only a towel, Anya excused herself as she collected clean underwear, a polo shirt and jeans from her drawer.

'Don't mind me, I've seen it all before, you know,' Martin ribbed.

Anya returned to the bathroom to dress.

When she emerged, they had switched off the television and were ready to eat. Anya collected the papers Nuala had delivered and placed them in the side pocket of her carry-on bag.

They headed out, greeting Junta at her supply cart in the corridor. The room steward looked Martin up and down and winked at Anya.

'Good morning,' she said in her lyrical voice.

Anya returned the greeting, then spoke quietly. 'May I ask you a personal question?'

'Is something wrong in your cabin?'

'No, everything's perfect.' Anya felt awkward but continued anyway. 'Without tips, can I ask how much you are paid by the company?'

Junta looked up and down the corridor. 'About fifty American dollars each month, so I do a good job, Miss Anya?'

'Outstanding,' Anya declared.

''Cause I need to look after my family.'

'You're the best housekeeper I've ever seen,' Martin added.

Junta grinned a toothy smile. 'You and your family have a great day now.'

'Thanks, we will.' Martin winked.

He was in a surprisingly good mood, Anya thought.

At breakfast, they opted for the restaurant to avoid the queues at the buffet. The maître d' was named Ivan, from Bulgaria, and had a kind, but serious face.

Dressed in a blue and gold vest, with matching bow tie, he escorted them to their table, next to a well-dressed elderly couple.

'How do you say thank you in your language?' Ben asked as he took his seat.

Ivan squatted down to Ben's height.

'In Bulgaria, we say bwa-go-daria.'

Ben's eyes widened. He repeated the line, once alone and the second time with Ivan, whose face glowed when he smiled this time. Ivan headed back to greet more guests, with a lightened step.

The table servers hung back until Ivan had left. They introduced themselves as Iketut from Indonesia, and Kujan from Sri Lanka. Kujan handed each of them a menu while Iketut filled their glasses with water and offered juice, tea and coffee. Ben was on a roll. He asked the Indonesian and Sri Lankan words for thanks, and practised them a few times quietly under his breath.

'You have a great little man there.' The man from the next table commented. 'You should be very proud.'

His wife gave him a scolding look. 'Leave them in peace. It's their family time.'

'We're from Australia,' Ben announced. 'Where do you live?'

'California,' the old man smiled through a perfectly trimmed silver moustache. 'Would you like me to help with that . . . you've got a little something in your ear.'

Ben flicked both sides of his head. The man stood, unbuttoned his jacket and placed the linen napkin back on his table. He stepped across and reached out to Ben's ear. A shiny quarter appeared in his hand, which he held in front of Ben's face. 'Now you should hear your parents a lot better.'

Martin laughed. Ben sat with his mouth gaping. Anya loved that in a world full of digital toys, a simple illusion could still be captivating.

'Wow! How did you do that?'

The gentleman brushed the side of his nose. 'Trade secret.'

'Can you teach me?'

The man patted his Santa-like belly. 'I'm afraid there's a magician's code and only true magicians can learn the way.'

'Robert. Leave the child alone,' his wife muttered, while continuing to read the day's planner. 'You haven't finished your fruit bran.'

He stepped back to his table. 'I'll leave you to enjoy your breakfast.'

Ben felt his other ear, in case there were more coins hiding there, while Martin ordered bacon, eggs, sausages and toast for them both.

After choosing eggs Benedict with smoked salmon, Anya placed the napkin on her lap. 'Full breakfast? You are in a good mood.'

Martin's eyes seemed to shine. He leant forward. 'Yesterday changed me. What really matters seems so much clearer. Anyway . . . I have fantastic news!'

Anya felt a sudden heaviness in her chest. Had her former husband proposed to his girlfriend overnight? Ben, who would have a stepmother, seemed preoccupied with the colouring page and pencils that Iketut had delivered with their still water.

'The purser rang this morning and apologised for the fiasco with our cabins. In appreciation for all our help ... drum roll if you please ... they're upgrading us to a three-bedroom suite!'

That captured Ben's attention. 'Are we all going to be living together?'

Anya felt her chest lighten. They would be closer but have their own privacy as well. And she didn't have to worry about a stepmother just yet.

'No, mate, but we're being moved to one of the fanciest cabins on the ship. There's a bedroom for each of us. We'll even have our own butler!'

'Yay!' Ben reached across and high-fived his father.

As they ate, it was apparent how many of the serving crew were Filipino, Indian or Indonesian. They smiled and greeted passengers, but it felt as if there was an underlying tension in the room. Then again, Anya could have been imagining it given what she had learnt last night. She wondered how many of the crew were toward the end of a long contract.

With a full stomach and feeling sluggish, Anya began to regret her choice of such a fat-laden breakfast. Kujan cleared the plates and Iketut reappeared with a fruit smoothie that she hadn't ordered.

'For you, ma'am.' He bent over so no one else could hear. 'We heard Carlos is hurt but no one will say how bad.' The waiter's forehead glistened with perspiration.

'I'm sorry, but I can't comment. Maybe you should ask your supervisor.'

Obviously, the ship's telegraph did not relay everything

that happened on board. Anya had assumed Carlos's family would have been notified by the doctor. Iketut had a similar pleading look to the one that Carlos had shown. He wasn't asking if the shooter's identity was known and she thought there was a tear forming in his eye.

'His wife is in hospital in Bogotá.' He lowered his voice even further. 'Breast cancer. If he does not call, she will know something is wrong. We don't know what to do.'

Her heart went out to Iketut, and Carlos for his home situation. She carefully considered her response.

'All I know is that when I left last night, he was unconscious in a serious, but stable condition.' It was a way of saying a lot without giving anything away. She hadn't disclosed whether Carlos had been conscious at all, or what may have happened overnight. 'You didn't hear it from me, OK?'

Iketut wiped his forehead. 'Thank you, ma'am, may God shine on your beautiful family. Carlos is a good man. Our room is across the corridor from him. He is like our brother.'

His reaction seemed genuine. She wondered if he would be as happy if he knew Carlos had lost both legs.

As they left the table, Ben thanked the waiters in Indonesian and Sri Lankan, which brought a smile to their faces. Iketut moved quickly to Kujan, and a grin unfolded across Kujan's face at the news.

Anya caught up to Ben and Martin.

'Hey Dad, when do we move to the fancy cabin?'

'We can go right now. I have the key.'

They took the lift to the eighth deck and followed Martin to the end of a port-side corridor. Inside, they all gasped. The suite had two levels joined by a staircase. On the lower area, a glass dining table with eight chairs was positioned near a kitchenette that fitted beneath the stairs. The remaining area contained two leather lounge suites facing a large screen TV mounted on the wall. Adjacent, a baby grand piano stood in the centre of an area surrounded by bookshelves filled with pottery and hardbacks. A bathroom with two sinks was also included on the lower floor. Three loft-style bedrooms looked out over the main area.

Ben didn't hesitate to run up the stairs.

'Wow! Which is mine?'

Anya and Martin followed. Sliding doors offered privacy for each room. The design was modern and filled with natural light from the extensive ocean views.

'This is yours, take your pick of beds,' Martin said.

Ben chose the twin to the left. His bag was already at the foot of the other.

Both Anya and Martin's bags were in the queen-size room at the end.

'They moved our things?'

'That's the other great news,' Martin declared. 'They've been doing it all for us, while we had brekkie.'

'My laptop and papers were in the safe.'

'Annie, relax. I gave them permission to open the safes. They thought of everything. Check your carry-on.'

Anya wasn't sure it was a good thing if someone had access to their passports and valuables. She pulled the bag onto the bed and unzipped it. Inside were two passports, travel documents, her laptop, and Australian dollars. Everything of value that had been inside the safe.

She checked the side pocket. The information Nuala had given her was gone.

12

After they'd unpacked, Ben had begged to spend time in the kids' club. Neither Anya nor Martin had the heart to refuse. Martin happily took him there for a couple of hours and decided to spend that time in the gym and games room, to give Anya some time to herself.

FitzHarris sat at his desk amid a mess of paperwork. He had a five o'clock shadow and looked like he'd been up all night. The room was the size of Carlos's cabin and contained a filing cabinet, desk, two phones and a computer. There was barely enough space for the second chair.

'What can I do you for?' His eyes opened wide, a change from the forehead crease. 'How're the new accommodation?'

'Amazing. The view, all of it. Thank you for organising the move. It was a kind gesture and means Ben can see a little more of both of us.'

Fitz's cheeks ruddied a little.

'Yeah, well. Did everything get moved over okay?'

Anya wondered why he would specifically ask that.

'Yes – even the contents of the safe . . . I did have some papers in the side pocket of my carry-on bag that were misplaced, or lost.'

The crease returned to his forehead. He picked up a pen. 'Anything valuable?'

'No, but they were private.' Anya watched for any recognition, or surprise. His face was unreadable. This man could be a poker champion.

'Can you replace them?'

'Probably. It's nothing. I only mentioned it because you asked.'

'Junta's one of our stalwarts. No thieving on her shifts. Sometimes we get guests claiming to have lost thousands of dollars worth of jewellery, just so they can claim on insurance. I can't tell you the number of times ten thousand dollars in cash is allegedly "stolen" from a safe. Sure we get some light-fingered crew members but if they get caught, they're out. Usually, with questioning, it turns out the ten grand never existed.'

Anya suspected he was far too busy to go through her papers and had no reason to.

'Trust no one' was making her paranoid.

'You know,' FitzHarris began, 'all those years in the force taught me one thing when interviewing a witness or a perp. It's what people don't tell you that sometimes says the most.'

'Is this off the record?'

'If you want it to be.' He gestured to the empty seat.

Anya took off her wind jacket and placed it across her lap. 'An employee delivered an envelope to my room last night.'

Fitz stood and moved around to Anya's side of the table. He crossed his arms and leant back against the desk.

'Go on.'

Anya suspected Fitz thought this made it easier for interviewees to consider him 'on their side'. Only, with his imposing size, their side suddenly felt crowded. She preferred the barrier of the desk. She folded her own arms and tucked her ankles beneath her chair.

'The envelope she gave me contained references to websites. Nothing I couldn't have found on the internet myself.'

'Did you catch her name?'

Anya was loathe to disclose the officer's identity. What if

she was merely doing her job and had no idea about the documents?

'So this woman comes to your cabin at night. Either she's just an unsuspecting courier, or she wanted to connect with you. Otherwise, why not slide the information under your door in the night?'

He had a point. Although, an anonymous package might make Anya defensive and suspicious. There was nothing on the envelope to instruct hand delivery. All it had was her name and cabin number.

'What do you mean by connect?'

He lifted one hand. 'We care about a cause if we have a personal connection to someone involved. It sounds like she could have some axe to grind and her visit obviously caught your interest. You say it's nothing you couldn't get off the net, but you kept the stuff instead of throwing it out.'

Fitz was good, she thought, although she didn't like the way he made it sound as if she had been played.

He added, 'She didn't just happen to come across one of only two passengers who happened to be there to help out with Lilly and Carlos. You were her target. Or did Martin get a visit as well?'

'Not that I know of.'

The woman's uniform looked genuine, as did the badge. Someone went to a lot of trouble, and risked being caught, just to give her information that was readily available. It seemed more than a little coincidental that all their other belongings had been moved to the new suite, but the envelope and its contents had been discarded. She could not imagine Junta doing anything to compromise her job or only means of supporting her family.

'What sort of uniform was she wearing? I assume—'

'Yes. Officer's.'

'What colour epaulettes?'

Anya thought back. 'Black.'

'Then she was deck crew. If they're caught passing on company information or harassing guests with their own agendas . . .' He breathed out. 'I'm just saying, no one should be violating your privacy at night. Someone wants you to push their cart, and I don't want to see you being used.'

Fitz was more than astute. Documents wouldn't mean the same coming from a room steward or someone in overalls.

Anya wondered if she had underestimated him. He was making her feel foolish for having brought up the missing envelope.

'OK, humour me. Give me a first name and I'll tell you if it belongs to an officer. If it fits, I'll drop it. We're still off the record, remember?'

'Fine. Her badge said Nuala.'

Fitz returned to his chair and tapped away on his keyboard. A few minutes later, his left eye was squinting again.

'No officer with that name. If a badge is lost, it costs eighty dollars to replace. Sometimes staff use each other's badges to save paying the money.'

He typed some more and, from where she sat, Anya could see his eyes darting from side to side across the screen. His frown deepened.

'Not one crew member with that name. I'll go back a bit further, in case it's an old badge passed on as a spare.'

Anya held her breath.

'There used to be a Nuala. Cabin steward, she finished her contract two years ago and didn't renew. Your Nuala isn't who she claims to be.'

The anonymous woman could have been someone with a personal gripe against the company, but if she was pretending to be crew and knew her way around the ship, she could easily gain the trust of passengers. That concerned Anya, particularly in terms of children on board. She thought about Ben at the kids' club.

'We've got a significant problem if someone's impersonating an officer. But just in case one of our officers has lost her badge . . . It's an offence, but much less of a crime.' He tapped away some more.

Maybe she was actually an officer, Anya thought, but chose not to reveal herself for fear of recriminations if her superiors found out she had been giving potentially damaging company information to passengers.

'Would you recognise her again? Off the record. You don't have to tell me which one she is if you find her.'

Anya was sure she could identify the woman.

'All right then, there are fifteen female officers who would wear that white uniform.'

Fitz pulled up the dossiers on his computer, one at a time. Anya moved around to look at each photograph. She studied them all. No one resembled the woman she had met, even accounting for changes in hairstyle and colour.

'I can't show you the passengers' mugshots, confidentiality and all that. Besides there are thousands of them on the system. If you run into her again, will you let me know?'

Anya agreed to call him as soon as she saw the mystery woman again. She wondered how Nuala had known what cabin to knock on that night. She must have had access to passenger lists, or had followed Anya to the cabin. Either way, it proved she had been targeted.

'It doesn't make sense.' Fitz picked up a pen, clicking it once, twice and again as he spoke. 'We're in the middle of the ocean. No one can get on or off the ship. In the dead of night, some stranger hands you an envelope. Reminds me of a Hitchcock movie.'

Anya immediately thought of *The Birds* and the sailors' albatross superstition. 'You think I imagined it?' Face flushed with irritation, she turned to leave. 'Sorry to have wasted your time.'

FitzHarris tilted his head and sighed. 'Wait. I didn't mean it like that. I'm getting a lot of heat from above on the death and Carlos's shooting. If news gets out, we could have mass panic on board.' He discarded the pen and rubbed his eyes. 'There's an old saying on the sea: "You're only ever two square meals short of anarchy". The medical team tell me it's almost unheard of to fill every hospital bed, but we managed within hours of setting sail. Somehow, I got a feeling we're not over the worst of it. A power failure, a viral breakout, or any other incident and we could just get to anarchy stage. God help us if that happens.'

'There is something else you should know, this time on the record.'

He rubbed one eye. 'What's that?'

'Carlos may have some information on what happened to Lilly Chan. He said "Kill her. Stop him" just before the surgery.'

FitzHarris's face became pale as he moved to open the door. 'He would have heard the ship's gossip. The guy's a father. Add in the heavy-duty drugs you gave him . . .'

'You're right,' Anya lied.

Carlos did have a cocktail of drugs in his veins, but he was desperate to tell her something. He could have pleaded for his legs, or named the shooter. Instead, he had begged for whoever harmed Lilly to be stopped from doing it again.

FitzHarris's expression belied what he was saying about Carlos being delirious. Either he was out of his depth, or he didn't want a connection made between the shooting and Lilly's death. Anya had to tread carefully. Trust no one, the note had said.

13

Alone, Anya admired the two-storey view of the ocean. White-tipped waves competed for space and height and rain curtained as far as she could see. The water in the pool on the outside deck sloshed and slapped over the edge. She still hadn't felt seasick.

The beauty and power of nature astounded her. She wondered how many people were up and about to appreciate it. Her mind was still turning about what Carlos had uttered and FitzHarris's reaction. The two women, Bec and Emma, claimed some men were bragging about an Asian woman dying. Hearsay meant nothing unless one of the men admitted to what had happened.

Female passengers like Bec and Emma deserved to feel safe on board. Whether they were looking for love, casual sex or just fun, made no difference. How many other women had been intimidated or harassed? How many other people had those men bragged to about Lilly? David FitzHarris had limited resources until the FBI arrived to take over.

FitzHarris would have had a long night. There were drunken groups to contend with, not to mention a shooting victim to protect and question after the anaesthetic wore off, and Lilly's death to investigate.

Anya decided to clear her head with a walk, this time under shelter. She collected a sick bag from under the sink and folded it into her wind-jacket pocket – just in case.

The cruise brochures advertised the beauty of nature, the

ocean, islands, different cultures and people; yet the ship was focused on drawing people inward. Malls, bars and casinos pulled people to the ship's centre, away from any natural light, sounds or sights. Cabins that overlooked the city-like promenade seemed as popular as those with an ocean view. This was a floating fishbowl; a mobile Las Vegas. Alcohol and gambling had to be profitable for the company.

Anya explored the undercover mall. At first glance, the number of designer stores seemed odd. Like her, many passengers would shop regularly at outlets and discount department stores and not even consider buying designer labels. Along the retail strip, expensive brands lured passengers with windows featuring gold and crystal displays, and the offers of specials during days at sea. 'You deserve it' was the theme.

Not coincidentally, bars and brasseries peppered the 'district', so patrons had to pass shops on their way back to their cabins. Families could indulge in three courses three times a day without worrying about the cost. It was easy to see how everything took on an artificial value.

Like house mice, cleaners worked quickly and quietly, while the majority of passengers were still asleep or having a leisurely breakfast.

Three decks above, the equivalent of sideshow alley included hot dog stands, carnival games and a video arcade. Toward the aft, was a sign that said 'Centennial Garden'. Anya followed the path to an oasis of greenery. Despite the rain, mist sprinklers sprayed ferns, flowers and greenery. She picked up an umbrella from a stand at the entrance and opened it. It felt good to be away from all the noise and chaos. She bent down and smelt the leaves of a rose plant. Planted alongside were impatiens, petunias and daisies. Wooden garden chairs provided privacy and sanctuary for those wanting to enjoy the quiet. Cold air filtered through the area and sent a chill through her.

Meandering along the path, Anya saw a figure lying motionless on an undercover bench, beneath what looked like pool towels. Her pulse rate accelerated and she caught her breath.

'Hello, are you all right?'

No answer.

To her relief, the towels moved and a mop of dark hair appeared. The young woman's eyes were swollen and her clothes crumpled.

'Jasmine? What are you doing here?'

Lilly's sister sat up and pulled the towels around her shoulders. 'They locked us out of our cabin last night.'

Anya sat beside her. 'Who did? Why?'

'The purser said it was a crime scene. We don't understand. What's happening?' Jasmine buried her head in Anya's shoulder and sobbed.

Anya imagined the cabin had been sealed off because of the drugs in Lilly's bloodstream. Someone had ordered the room to be searched and, if security were busy, it would have been relegated to another time. How could the management be so incompetent? The family had lost Lilly, and now they were being mistreated.

'Your cabin isn't a crime scene, but Lilly had a bruise on her neck.'

Jasmine looked up, her eyes drawn and hollow. 'I know.'

Anya sat back. 'You knew about that?'

Jasmine nodded.

'How did she get it?'

'It's a hickey.'

If the bruise was from consensual behaviour it made a big difference to suspicions about how Lilly had died.

'You said she didn't have a boyfriend.'

Jasmine's fine-boned fingers pushed her hair behind her ear. 'She didn't. It's a violin hickey,' she explained. 'Most people think you hold it up with your arm, but it sits on your collarbone and the lower part of your jaw keeps it in place. Every student knows you're supposed to be able to hold it there with no hands. Sometimes, a player gets a hickey. Look.' Jasmine pushed her hair back to reveal a similar but smaller mark on her neck.

Anya was still confused. Lilly had calluses on the pads of the fingers on her left hand.

'You said she couldn't play the violin so took up the cello.'

Jasmine shook her head. 'I meant she couldn't play the violin with her right hand. A while ago, she found one for left-handed players. She has been teaching herself to play since. She's very good, although the cello is her love. Because the violin is so small, she brought it in her luggage. It's in our cabin.'

Anya hadn't considered a violin bruise, because she had assumed the cello was Lilly's only instrument. The girl had not been strangled or choked. In one sense, it was a relief she hadn't suffered that way, but there were still no answers as to how she got to the deck, and why she was so wet. Or what caused the bruises to her legs and arms.

'Where is the rest of your family?'

'My mother has been busy calling people and making . . . arrangements for Lilly. My cousin slept in my aunt's bed. I went to the library but people were playing cards in there. I just wanted to be alone.'

Anya felt nauseated. She, Martin and Ben had been moved to a luxurious suite, yet the Chan family had been kicked out of their own beds. Lilly might not even have brought the GHB onboard, someone could have spiked her drink.

'Come with me,' Anya gestured. 'We need to get you warm.'

Anya took Jasmine back to their suite and ordered room service. Coffee, hot chocolate, cereal, toast, eggs and fruit

118

would do for a start. She collected a clean long-sleeved shirt and some leggings from her room and laid out a towel.

'My son and his father aren't due back for at least an hour. You can have a shower here if you like, or just change for now. It's up to you. I have to go out for a short while, but I'll be back. Before you do anything else, please contact your mother and let her know you're okay. I'll be back as soon as I can. You're safe here. Just lock the door. The butler will bring the food.'

Anya left the suite and headed straight back to David FitzHarris's office. She didn't care if he was busy or not.

'Forgot something?'

'How the hell could you kick that family out of their cabin? Without any of their belongings and nowhere else to sleep?' Anya stood, hands flat on the desk. 'They have every right to sue—'

'Whoa, hold on.' FitzHarris rose, hands open. 'I have no idea what you're talking about.'

'The Chan family. Someone ordered Lilly's room be sealed as a crime scene, which left the family literally out in the cold!'

'Shit!' He looked up at the ceiling and sat back down. 'They were supposed to *move* the family.'

'I just found Lilly's sister sleeping in the park section, freezing.'

FitzHarris's shoulders slumped. Dark rings around his eyes made him look drawn.

'Where is she now?'

'Back in our new suite. Her mother is apparently sharing a bed in her aunt's cabin. They could have been moved to the ones we vacated. You know, we didn't ask for an upgrade.'

'Yeah well, someone was trying to say thanks.' The colour in FitzHarris's cheeks deepened.

Anya moved a pile of memos from the spare chair and placed them on a corner of the table before sitting.

FitzHarris dropped back into his chair. 'Those cabins could already be assigned to passengers coming on board in Fiji in a few days time.' He picked up his phone and punched in a number. After a stilted conversation in which he said little apart from stating the accommodation problem, he slammed the handset down.

'I'm told a liaison officer will board in Fiji and her job is to take care of the family until they get back home. In the meantime, you may have saved the company a lawsuit.'

'These people are grieving half a world away from home, and have no idea why Lilly died. I don't care about litigation—'

'I know.' He rubbed his temples. 'I'm just grateful you were there to find her, and she was safe.'

'There are other cabins you could be searching,' Anya commented.

FitzHarris riffled through some papers and pulled out his notebook. 'Those men you mentioned. I haven't had the chance to find any of them yet. But if they're using drugs, they'll be kicked off at the next port.'

Anya sat forward. 'Wait. That's it? They just get put off the boat? What about the police? They'll need to interview them.'

FitzHarris's elbow was now on the desk and he rested his forehead on a hand. 'I've been interviewing crew about the shooting half the night. The rest of the time, I've been on the phone trying to get outside help. We don't know what time Lilly Chan was given the drugs, and we'd need to pinpoint exactly where we were at the time to ascertain whose jurisdiction we were in.'

Anya had been under the impression that the FBI would send agents. 'Didn't you inform the Hawaiian coastguard, who involved the FBI? A young girl died in suspicious circumstances, and time is going to destroy what little evidence there may be.'

He let out a deep sigh. 'The Chans are travelling on Chinese passports; the daughters were born in Hong Kong. Chan is the mother's name, only the father is a US citizen. The most we have to prove suspicious death is that bruise on her neck.'

'About that . . .' Anya moved back in the seat. 'The sister confirmed that she had the bruise before boarding. It's from the violin rubbing against her skin while she plays.'

FitzHarris placed his left hand near his shoulder. 'Isn't it on the wrong side?'

'Not for a left-handed violin.'

The words hung for a moment.

'So she's an overdose as far as we know. Even if we find out who gave her the drug, all they have to do is say she took it voluntarily and no one's left to argue any different. If Lilly had survived, it would just have been her word against his. Shit, ODs are a dime a dozen, and we both know sometimes the first-timers are the ones who luck out.'

'But if Lilly was a US citizen the FBI would be more likely to investigate? We set sail from the US. This ship is full of American passengers, some of whom are implicated in a suspicious death.'

Anya felt her face redden and the back of her neck began to itch. How could police involvement be selective? Investigators in a country didn't get to choose what crimes they took on. Were passengers informed that there were different standards of protection depending on which country they came from? That it was easier to get away with killing a non-American on a ship? The cruise line owed every passenger the same duty of care, or should disclose otherwise.

'It's not just her nationality. For US citizens, there still has to be something more than "he said, she said" for the FBI to become involved. The neck bruise was the most suspicious finding. And now you say it had nothing to do with her death.'

Anya couldn't believe they were going to do nothing. 'What about the carpet burns on her back and the other bruises?'

'I'm guessing a number of women on board have marks like those. Alcohol increases the desire and can make performance pretty awkward. They aren't enough.'

'Then what about Carlos? How does Colombia stand with the FBI?'

The expression on FitzHarris's face gave her the answer. He ripped a page from his notebook, scrunched it up and aimed for the bin. 'My hands are tied.'

She summarised, to make sure she understood. 'So the shooter gets away with ruining Carlos's life and is perfectly free to carry on shooting whomever he wants. The only proviso is that he limits himself to foreign nationals. Anyone gets to drug and rape with impunity, so long as he picks on women with non-US passports.'

'I don't like it any better than you do. Interpol hasn't even got back to me. I've managed homicide investigations, but you need the proper equipment and trained manpower. When I took this job I was led to believe that I had more resources and investigative powers. We've got an LRAD on board, for Pete's sake.'

Anya raised her eyebrows. 'A what?'

'An anti-terrorist Long Range Acoustic Device. It channels sound into a narrow beam, kind of like a flashlight does with light. It's been used on pirates. The sound is painful to humans and, when directed at them, they have no alternative but to flee.'

'So pirates are discouraged, but if they walk on via the

gangway to rape and pillage passengers and staff, it's business as usual.' Anya's voice rose with frustration.

After a prolonged silence, FitzHarris conceded, 'One of the reasons crimes are committed is because criminals think they'll get away with them. All I can do here is offload the offender at the nearest port.'

'Some disincentive.'

He ignored the comment. 'If Carlos's shooter is an employee, and I assume that's likely, given where he was shot—'

'Maybe whoever shot Carlos and harmed Lilly is already aware of your lack of powers. But what if they're not? There may be a chance of catching them out.'

FitzHarris studied Anya's face. 'Go on, I'm listening.'

14

FitzHarris appeared keen to catch the men involved in Lilly's death and made a call to someone he said might be able to help. He sat upright when his office door opened.

'Is this *Groundhog Day*?' A thirty-ish woman in deck whites entered. 'You look like—'

'Laura! Company . . .' FitzHarris sneaked a look at the front of his long-sleeved shirt – the same shirt Anya had seen him in yesterday – to the woman's amusement.

'Thought we might need some nourishment.' Laura wheeled in a two-tiered trolley stocked with sweets and fruit, an urn, mugs, teabags, instant coffee and a jug of milk. She parked near the back wall, which was the only bit of floor space left.

FitzHarris's stomach rumbled.

'Laura Zississ.' She extended her hand. 'From IT.'

Anya shook her hand.

'This is Doctor Crichton.' FitzHarris looked over the trolley. 'Are we trying to impress the good doctor?'

'Just something I whipped up at no notice.' Laura pretended to buff a red nail. She had long black hair tied in a plait, and brown eyes with long lashes. The uniform and skirt flattered her petite shape. Judging by the paleness of her face and arms, Anya imagined she spent most of her time inside an office.

'Hey, I read about your work with the Jersey Bombers. Didn't used to be a fan until I saw what you did with them. Did you see they romped home by twenty points yesterday?'

Anya was glad the Bombers were doing well and had attracted more female devotees.

Fitz wasted no time helping himself to a coffee. He bent down to plug in the urn's cord, but faltered. His right leg seemed stiff.

'I'll get that.' Laura moved in and completed the task.

'Surveillance is her hobby.' FitzHarris gestured to Laura. 'She's normally bogged down in office work, but I'm hopeful she'll be able to help us pin down where Lilly Chan spent her last hours.' He rattled the spoon around the mug and returned to his seat. 'Help yourself.'

'I'm fine, thanks. May I use your phone?' Anya dialled the cabin. Jasmine had already showered and was resting on the lounge.

Fitz filled Laura in on Lilly's suspicious death, her drug and alcohol results and how some unknown men had supposedly bragged about being with Lilly Chan the night before she died.

Laura grabbed a croissant and sat on the corner of the desk closest to FitzHarris. 'Do you know what deck they're on, if they booked in as a group or individually?'

'So far, it's unsubstantiated hearsay. No names or descriptions.'

Laura didn't seem perturbed. 'Anywhere you want me to start?'

'Her sister said she went to Centennial Garden to read, about ten thirty that night,' Anya said.

'Right. I'll start with her room key charges.'

FitzHarris vacated his chair and Laura slipped past into position. She quickly piled papers to the side, cleared access to the keyboard, and re-adjusted the chair and screen height. She was clearly efficient. Within a minute, she had accessed the records.

'OK. At seventeen-fifteen there was a gift-shop purchase

with her room key. Eighteen dollars. Lip balm and a travel journal. There's nothing near Centennial Garden, and there are loads of clothes shops along that mall.'

'What woman or girl doesn't go crazy with a charge card? That's why they use room keys for all the extras. Saves having cash on board, to reduce crime,' FitzHarris said with a mouth full of cake, seemingly oblivious to the irony of his comment. 'Is that it for the night?'

'Hold your horses, Fitz.' Laura looked up. 'You can't rush my kind of art. You've got a little frosting on your . . .' She pointed to her top lip.

FitzHarris wiped his mouth with the back of his hand.

Laura turned the screen so Anya could see. 'Nothing until twenty three oh three. There were six drinks put on her room card at the one time in the Stag bar, up on the pool deck. It's an open disco. Two white wines and four beers apparently signed for by Lilly Chan.'

That was the same bar she'd been at with Martin and Karen last night, Anya thought. 'Someone served an under-age girl that many drinks?'

'For a girl who didn't drink, that's a bucketload of alcohol,' FitzHarris announced. 'Maybe she wasn't the goody-two-shoes her sister made her out to be.'

Their mother may have allowed them some freedom, but she was strict. She would have definitely checked the bill before paying the balance at the end of the cruise. Either Lilly was rebelling and didn't care, or this was a mistake.

'Can you identify which staff member served her?'

Laura nodded. 'There's a code on every receipt. We collate them at the end of each cruise because the bar staff work on commission. There it is. He's one of our longer serving barmen.'

'Hopefully, he might remember who she was with.'

Laura continued to search. 'From the receipts, that was a

busy first night, but let me check something.' She typed away, while FitzHarris helped himself to a chocolate eclair, this time grabbing a napkin as well.

'There were twenty-eight separate transactions within five minutes of Lilly's.'

The office phone rang and Fitz answered it.

Anya took the opportunity to ask Laura, 'Do you think your superiors would approve free room-service meals for the family of the girl who died? They'll be either in their cabin or the suite my family is staying in.'

'I don't see why not. We only charge for room service because food is freely available on board around the clock. We do make exceptions if people are sick. I can't see this is any different.' She clicked away with a smile. 'William's made sure you won't be charged for room service on your account. I'll clear it for the Chan party as well.'

Anya already liked her.

FitzHarris slammed down the phone and grabbed a set of keys. 'I need to sort out the Chan cabin before I do anything else. Anya, is there any chance you could look at the CCTV footage of the bar at that time. It shouldn't take too long since we have an exact time she was there now.'

'Or when someone else used her room key.'

'Point taken. If you could identify Lilly Chan for Laura it would be a great help. If she wasn't there, I need to know who was.'

'Isn't Doctor Crichton on holiday?' Laura asked.

Piecing together the puzzle of what had happened to Lilly was a challenge Anya wanted to help with. Martin had definitely matured and had surprised her by acknowledging he understood why she felt the need to help if asked. Besides, Ben was enjoying kids' club so much she felt it would have been selfish to insist on spending time with him.

'Carbohydrate overload, bad weather and being stuck

inside watching surveillance TV . . . What about this isn't a holiday?'

'Leave you two to it.' FitzHarris half-smiled and headed out the door, closing it behind him.

Laura plugged in a series of codes. 'I'll pull up the footage. There's a camera opposite the bar, and another above it.' Anya, hungry again, bit into a bagel with cream cheese and smoked salmon.

Now they knew the exact time and date, the footage was surprisingly quick to locate.

'I've taken it back half an hour to see who is in the field of vision. I don't know what the girl looked like, so let me know the moment you see her.'

The camera was a wide angle, with a fish-eye view of the bar and dance floor in colour.

It didn't take long. 'There. Stop. The girl in the red top, blue jeans. Long black hair.'

Lilly appeared to the left of the screen with a book in her hand. She wore flat sandals and walked like a dancer, with straight posture and feet slightly pointed outward. It could have been Jasmine; the sisters were so much alike. At her side was a taller fair-haired girl, who looked around the same age, in an above knee-length fitted strapless dress and medium heels, with a small bag slung across her shoulder. The pair paused near the bar and disco area to watch the dancing. The blonde wore a hair band with something like a flower on top that caught the light.

Shortly after, the blonde pulled Lilly by one hand onto the dance floor. Lilly placed her book on the platform next to the DJ's station. The pair danced together, at first self-consciously, and then with less inhibition.

The time was 22.53. It wasn't long before they attracted male attention. The girls didn't seem too interested but two men stayed close. Anya noticed writing on the backs of the men's shirts. Suddenly, one man took Lilly's friend in his arms and spun her around, knocking another reveller over in the process. It was unclear whether the girl welcomed the lift or not.

Lilly tugged on the man's arm but he was already carrying her companion to the bar.

'Can you freeze that and magnify it at all?'

Laura obliged. 'These aren't exactly the latest cameras, so we'll lose quality. It looks like a four letter name. B . . . last letter R. It's hard to see if that's two Es. "BEER". How original. I've seen these guys. They all wear bowling shirts, only with different colours and names on the backs. They go where the young women are.'

'Toolies, we call them,' Anya said. 'Older men who hang around schoolies parties hoping to have sex with intoxicated girls.'

'Nice.' Laura plucked some pastry from the inside of a croissant. 'The food and beverages manager asked me to check out a group who caused a scene when they boarded in Honolulu. There are sixteen of them in total, but it sounds like five or six are the real troublemakers. They paid bottom dollar and they're taking advantage of the all you can eat. First they hit the buffet then they go to one of the restaurant sittings. What they paid for the cabins doesn't even cover the cost of their food.'

'That doesn't make good business sense, surely.'

'I used to work in accounting. The first sixty-five percent of cabins pay running costs. Profit comes from onboard spending. An empty cabin is a loss of potentially thousands of dollars. It's cheaper to upgrade someone and heavily discount the smaller cabins at the last minute to ensure bodies are in bunks. The return comes from what they spend on drinks, gambling, shopping and company excursions in port.'

'So bar staff work on commission as incentive to sell more drinks?'

Laura burrowed out more of the croissant. 'There's a high profit-margin on alcohol, it makes financial sense to reward staff who bring in the most money.'

Anya thought back to the flag of convenience. With the company registered offshore, anything brought on board in the US would be duty free. Alcohol would be bought cheaply and sold at premium prices. It was in the cruise line's best interest to promote a culture of drinking.

'What about the casinos?'

'Drinkers gamble more,' Laura said, matter-of-factly. 'It's why there are bars in there too, and why they only close for a couple of hours in the morning.'

No wonder the fares were cheap for groups. Discretional spending was how the company really made its money.

'What about responsible service of alcohol? Can the barman who supplied under-age drinkers be charged?'

'At sea, US drinking laws don't apply. We can sack staff who behave irresponsibly, but they can't be charged with a criminal act if they serve under-age passengers.'

The revelation stunned Anya. Lilly had no idea how vulnerable she was. Her focus returned to the screen. 'The second vowel's an "A"! That one says "BEAR".'

The video played again. Another man, in a blue shirt, put his arm around Lilly and steered her toward the bar. The clock said 22.58 pm. The first two letters of his name looked like a 'V' and 'A'.

Once on her feet again, the companion said something private to Lilly, who nodded. She was no longer standing confidently. One of the men pushed in at the bar and appeared to order drinks. Bear blocked the girls' path out. They were sandwiched between the two men. Bear wrapped an arm around each girl, securing their place, which gave

131

Anya a better view of the blonde. The girl reached into her bag and then said something to Lilly again, this time with open hands.

They seemed to disagree, then Lilly pulled something from her left front jean pocket and was shoved closer to the bar.

'She didn't order. Just got stuck with the bill,' Anya said. The barman had barely seen her. The men had ensured it.

Four bar staff faced a barrage of customers. Lilly had to squeeze between two patrons to sign the docket with an extended left hand. Her key was returned and she slid it into her back pocket. The first man appeared two minutes later with a tray of drinks and the girls were led to a crowded table. The man had short, fair hair and was slightly over-weight. Two of six men vacated their seats and the girls sat, steered into chairs on opposite sides of the table. Each had a wine placed in front of her. The men all drank beer and raised their glasses. Lilly picked hers up and seemed to look to her companion for guidance. At the group's urging, she took a sip before putting the drink down. Her companion drank half of hers quickly.

Once again, Lilly was dragged onto the dance floor, but this time by one of the other men, in yellow. For a brief moment, his back was in clear view: GENNY. The blonde was one step behind.

Anya felt a knot in her chest. The scene was one that played out every night, and could have been anywhere in the world. Only this time, Lilly had less than seven hours left to live.

15

Anya watched as Lilly was manhandled by the older men. She looked so vulnerable. If only someone – anyone – had intervened, she could still be alive. As a pathologist Anya was able to detach from the cases she worked on, but talking to Jasmine had given her an idea of the person Lilly was, and had hoped to be. Lilly had a womanly body and brilliant mind, but at sixteen she didn't have the wherewithal or confidence to handle the situation. Her friend didn't appear to be faring any better.

All but two of the men joined them on the dance floor, with breakdancing moves. Other passengers chose not to compete for the space.

The time was now 23.08 pm.

Lilly and her friend were surrounded by the group of older men. Her friend stumbled and fell to the floor. Bear lifted her up and carried her back to the chairs, where she drank the rest of her wine. She was now laughing and it looked as if she were enjoying the male attention.

Meanwhile, Lilly pushed her way back to the table, grabbed her companion's hand, but was summarily dismissed. Genny slid his arms around her waist and pulled her back to the dance floor, this time engaging in a ballroom hold. Within minutes he had Lilly smiling as he spun her in and out. Her hair fell freely around her shoulders and waist. She was graceful and attracted glances from men and women. Genny was suddenly in demand, as women offered themselves for a whirl around the floor. His friends continued to entertain Lilly who appeared to have lost her initial shyness. On the surface, this was a group of strangers on holiday enjoying the freedom and fun.

The clock ticked over: 23.42.

Fitz re-entered the office and shut the door behind him. He took up position, leaning against a filing cabinet.

Laura showed him some of the footage. He watched a while before commenting. 'See the way they block the girls at the bar? These guys work as a team. Not only do the women pay, the drinks are hidden from them. Not that we could ever prove it.'

They all seemed to have the same thought.

'Our bartenders are trained to put the glasses on the counter to pour, so the passengers see exactly what goes into them,' Laura explained.

'Your barman could have done that. The men still had the opportunity to spike the drinks with GHB.'

FitzHarris turned to Laura. 'Do we know anything about them?'

'It's their first time cruising with us. That's not to say they haven't sailed with other lines. They're loud, unruly and generally obnoxious, nothing out of the ordinary.'

Anya stood, and made herself a mug of strong, black tea.

'Where are their cabins?'

Laura tapped away again. 'Eight are scattered, but there are two four-berth cabins on deck one. Not adjacent, but on the same corridor.'

'That's the same deck where Martin stayed,' Anya said.

'You said he complained about antisocial behaviour that first night,' FitzHarris added. 'Let's see.' He glanced at the cabin numbers then back to a chart of the ship's layout on the wall. 'The same corridor.'

'Martin said one of them whinged that some woman had

vomited in his cabin. Do you keep records on special cleaning requests?'

'They keep a tight schedule,' Laura said, 'so most stewards document reasons why one cabin takes longer to service.'

'It may be a stretch, but if you could pinpoint the exact cabin, we might find out where Lilly was when she had sex.'

Laura moved her hollowed-out croissant to a napkin on one of the files. She quickly had the cabin number.

Fitz stood, hands on hips. 'There won't be any evidence left now. It's been cleaned a couple of times since then. We don't know where our dead girl spent the night but it's the best place to start.'

Laura typed again. 'Our big spending toolies splurged . . . eighty dollars.' Her eyes didn't leave the screen. 'They were cautioned by security for being drunk and obnoxious but they didn't spend much.' She checked the bills again. 'Lilly's six drinks wouldn't have gone far. They could have brought their own alcohol and drunk that first, I guess.'

'Or taken drugs to supplement the alcohol.' FitzHarris scratched his stubbly chin.

'We've had ecstasy brought on board, sometimes by teenage girls,' Laura added. 'They love it because they get smashed on one tablet, and it has fewer calories than alcohol. Risk your life for twenty dollars a pop? No thanks.'

Anya sipped her tea. Teenagers' underdeveloped frontal lobes meant risk assessment was not their best skill. She hoped Ben would never be that reckless with his life. When she was younger, there was pretty much only marijuana and alcohol readily available. Heroin was much less visible then. Now, there were far more deadly options for partygoers, and no end of people quick to profit from it. Carlos could have been shot for a drug-related reason. Heroin and cocaine were smuggler's gold. She wanted to know more.

'Did you find anything in the Chan cabin?'

'It was clean, apart from this. I found it in a bag with Lilly Chan's student ID inside.' On the small portion of available desk space, Fitz laid out a plastic sleeve containing a crumpled piece of paper. 'It's on a dining room docket.'

Anya and Laura looked closer.

In childlike print, were the words 'U r Goddess. Meet u port spa midnite.'

The love note was unsigned.

'I don't trust secret admirers,' FitzHarris said with disdain. 'They mess with minds.'

Laura disagreed. 'If I were sixteen, I'd probably think it was kind of romantic, like getting a valentine and busting to work out who sent it.'

In Anya's experience, secret admirers were more likely to be stalkers. Besides, there was nothing romantic about an older man propositioning a sixteen-year-old girl. It was also possible Lilly ignored the note and didn't intend to meet the man. What disturbed her most was that a shy girl with a domineering mother was a predator's dream victim. 'He may write like a ten year old, but he sounds confident. He doesn't ask. Instead he tells her where to be.'

FitzHarris collected a mini fruit flan from the trolley. 'Could be we're reading too much into this. Maybe he just plays percentages.'

Anya looked across at him.

'You know, some guys work on a one percent rule. If they ask a hundred girls to hook up and one says yes, they're doing well. And if he wants to meet at the spa, chances are any woman who turned up would be prepared to strip down to at least swimwear. He gets a good look before he decides whether or not to commit himself.'

'So.' Laura tilted her head and rested a hand under her chin. 'This is a form letter he sends out and then he sees if he's hit the jackpot?'

The flan disappeared whole. Fitz mumbled, 'Not my fault some men like to put it out there.'

The note may have been innocent or sinister. Without knowing who wrote it, they were back to the bowling shirts.

'Well, out of anywhere on this floating city, our anonymous admirer just happened to choose to meet at a place without CCTV monitors.' Anya didn't believe in coincidences. 'Let's go back to the nightclub. See where Lilly went after.'

Laura clicked away at the keyboard, alternating between camera views.

A marathon dance set finished with the girls returning to the table and reaching for their drinks. Lilly guzzled hers as if it was water. Her friend finished her own and chased it with another glass from the table.

Lilly moved back to the dance floor and wove her way between the revellers. At the DJ's station, she bent down and collected her book, stumbling forward as she rose. Yellow-shirted Genny was suddenly at her side. He slipped an arm around her waist and Lilly attempted to push him away. She was ready to go back to her cabin, it seemed. Genny let go and put both hands up in the air, surrendering.

Lilly took a few steps and toppled. Genny caught her and she appeared to laugh.

'Look.' Anya pointed to the screen. 'She's had one drink and it's as if he knows she won't be able to walk.'

Laura paused the image and turned the screen to Fitz, who was sitting opposite now, rubbing his extended right leg in between taking notes.

'They drugged that one drink, probably at the bar.' Anya let out a deep breath and thought of Jasmine and her family. 'All the women on board looking for a holiday romance and they go for an innocent sixteen year old.'

Laura flipped the screen part way around so the three of them had a view.

Captured clearly was Genny sliding his arm back and steering Lilly toward the door that she and her friend initially came out from. She could barely stand, let alone walk.

'Can you follow where they went from there?'

A camera caught them entering the lift. Genny led Lilly inside, pressed a button and stepped out of the lift, allowing the doors to close.

The video paused with Genny moving back, toward the stairs.

No one spoke for a moment. So far, they had no proof that Lilly had been drugged. The men would argue she had been drinking beforehand and the alcohol must have caught up with her. The footage didn't show her being forced. In the lift, Genny might have pressed the button for her floor.

'It'll take a few minutes to check the other levels.' Laura wrote down the time recorded on the bottom right of the screen.

Anya arched her back, stretching her sore shoulders.

Fitz picked a pen from a holder and rolled it between his fingers. 'There are cameras in most public areas and outside restrooms, but not on all the passenger corridors. And, before you ask, we don't have surveillance inside rooms either. We're not about to violate passengers' right to privacy.'

'What about Lilly's basic human rights? Who protected them?' Anya thought out loud.

Laura had likened the ship to a city, only most cities had ubiquitous video surveillance. In London, more than 10,000 cameras captured images of people and, although they had not necessarily reduced the crime rate, they had helped enormously in collecting information on crimes, victims and suspects. Complaints weren't concerned so much with privacy as the cost to taxpayers.

'Even if we did film everyone twenty-four seven, unless someone was watching every camera every minute, we couldn't stop things like this happening. This isn't Big Brother.' Fitz dropped the pen back into its container. 'I need to take a leak.' He left, closing the door behind him.

'Don't mind him,' Laura offered. 'His leg's probably giving him trouble. Once he takes something, he'll be fine again.'

Anya had noticed the limp had become more accentuated. 'What's wrong with his leg?'

'He's pretty private, but one night we had a few drinks and he got kind of morose. I asked why he'd given up homicide for a gig like this, unless he was running away from something.'

Anya was listening. She had wondered the same thing.

'Turns out he was retired early from the force. One night he got a call to a domestic. When he arrived, it was a blood-bath. The wife was on the kitchen floor. He got down to check her pulse and suddenly the husband jumped out from the pantry with a carving knife. The maniac stabbed Fitz in the stomach, arms and leg, before killing himself.' Her eyes darted back to the door. 'Please don't let on you know.'

'I won't.' Anya had seen too many wives killed by partners. For police, a domestic dispute was the most dangerous call-out to attend. The situation sounded horrific, and would no doubt have left far more permanent scars than just the physical ones on Fitz. Maybe something positive came out of it. 'Do you know what happened to the wife?'

Laura bit her top lip. 'Apparently she was already dead when he got there. The police found the body of a two year old in the bedroom, only Fitz thinks that if he hadn't let his guard down, the boy could have been saved.'

Without knowing the details, Anya doubted it. Whether the father was psychotic or in an uncontrolled rage, a child that small was unlikely to have survived a frenzied attack with a carving knife.

A printer–fax beeped in the back left corner of the room.

Anya checked the machine. 'A fax is coming through. Where does Fitz keep the spare paper?'

Laura wheeled back to a cupboard and handed Anya a wad before returning to her task.

Anya filled the tray and the printer resumed. She waited to check there was no jam and saw the name of the sender.

'It looks important. Something from Mats Anderson.'

Laura clicked away, continuing with her search. 'His father had prostate surgery and is due out of hospital soon so Mats is taking every opportunity to throw his weight around. Personally, I think the younger brother, Lars, is the pick of them all. He's an environmentalist and wants the company to be more innovative. For Mats and the old man, it's all about money and cutting costs every possible chance.'

The fax completed. Anya glanced at it, and caught sight of her name. She checked Laura wasn't watching and read the message.

David, you must keep a lid on this. Do whatever it takes. Shares in the company are in freefall. We cannot afford any negative publicity. Keep me informed of every detail. Suzanne Wist is on her way. Brief her immediately on arrival. If family sues, we countersue. Drugs, whatever you think is useful.

Until then, keep Chans happy. Offer discount trips, champagne, the usual.

And watch Crichton. She could cause trouble.

More than ever, our image is everything.

If all goes well, you will be rewarded for your efforts.

Anya took a sharp breath and glanced at Laura who was still occupied at the computer. She wondered if she was also party to Anderson's instructions.

'I didn't think anyone sent faxes anymore. Why not just email?'

Laura pulled up some more views of cameras and didn't glance up. 'Employees and hackers have been known to leak emails, and phones can be hacked for messages. The Andersons have always been paranoid about privacy. Guess they think faxing a letter is safer. Sounds like Fitz just made it to the inner circle. We mere mortals aren't blessed with faxes from on high.'

The door opened again and Anya quickly moved away from the printer.

FitzHarris limped back in. 'Got anything yet?'

'Lilly didn't get out on her floor,' Laura announced. 'I'm trying the others . . . Nothing deck nine. Not on eight. Not seven . . .'

Anya studied FitzHarris. He often wore a navy windbreaker, even when the weather didn't warrant it. He was probably hiding the scars on his arms. He hadn't been kicked out of the force, but he was in the pocket of at least one of the Andersons. It wasn't in his or the company's interest to discover the truth, unless it made Lilly Chan look irresponsible. The anonymous information Anya received could well have been a warning about a personal threat.

Watch Crichton. Anderson's words chilled her. He was paying security to cover up a crime and make any scandal disappear. FitzHarris wasn't really interested in finding out the truth, he was keeping an eye on her. At least when Carlos reached Fiji, local police would have to be notified of a patient with gunshot wounds, even if the FBI claimed it wasn't in their jurisdiction. Anya's mind raced. This investigation was a farce, but if Laura were an unknowing participant, she could actually help identify whoever was last with Lilly. With her present, FitzHarris could not deny the findings.

'Got her.' Laura announced. 'She left the lift alone on deck one and headed to the starboard corridor.'

FitzHarris moved to a layout of the ship on the wall. 'What cabin numbers are along there?'

'Cabins 1074 to 1090.'

Anya realised it was the corridor Martin's cabin had been on. She felt the hairs on her neck rise.

Martin had spoken about a couple having sex in the corridor. He could have unknowingly seen Lilly being assaulted.

16

Laura continued searching, looking for another sighting of Lilly near the lifts. Anya doubted the girl could have managed stairs without assistance, and they weren't monitored anyway.

Anya checked the time and phoned her cabin. FitzHarris had put her on speakerphone as the handset was close to Laura.

Martin answered.

'How's Jasmine doing?'

'She's somewhere between shock and denial. Right now, Ben's chatting away about everything.' He spoke more quietly. 'Annie, seeing Lilly was bad enough. What happened to the family last night was criminal.'

Anya glanced up at FitzHarris, who looked away.

'I agree. That's why I came straight to FitzHarris's office. Their cabin's open again now. Also a liaison officer will meet them in Fiji.'

Anya now suspected the woman mentioned in the fax was not a customer liaison person, but a company lawyer determined to avert legal action.

'Thanks, Annie, they're lucky to have you on their side.'

There was noticeable relief in Martin's voice. He had really been affected by what had happened.

'The CCTV footage shows Lilly got off the lift on deck one and headed along a corridor. The same one your cabin was on.'

There was a moment's silence. 'God, you mean I could have been there and maybe done something?'

Anya rubbed her forehead. 'We don't know for sure she was there all night. It looks like she was drugged and went down in the lift – alone. Anyone could have grabbed her as soon as she was out of camera range, even a crew member.'

Martin remained quiet.

Anya knew how he'd be feeling – like he could have done something more. She felt the same way herself. They could both do with a break. 'I'll come back to the suite now.'

'Listen, Annie, we're fine here. In fact, Ben's just plonked himself at the piano next to Jasmine.' He paused. 'If you can help out more, I think you should. Just as long as you're safe. You've got more experience with this sort of thing than anyone and FitzHarris comes across as a dunderhead.'

Anya shrank into her seat a little. 'Did I mention we're on speakerphone?'

'Morning, Mr Hegarty.' FitzHarris spoke flatly.

Laura smirked. 'Just call him Columbo.'

'I'm guessing that's not the worst thing he's been called in his time . . . Seriously, Anya. Please do what you can – but be careful. I'll organise something special to do later on.'

'You're on.'

Fitz ended the call. 'Dunderhead?'

Laura kept her head down at the computer and Anya just raised her eyebrows. She wasn't sure what to think of FitzHarris right now.

'Well, considering I'm incompetent, would you be interested in accompanying me to deck one? I want to knock on those cabin doors and rattle some chains. Would be handy to have an independent witness in case they claim harassment.'

Anya thought about what Martin had said. The Chans needed to know the truth about what had happened to Lilly, whether FitzHarris and Mats Anderson wanted her to find it or not.

'I'll be your witness.'

Martin had been in cabin 1088, toward one end of the section of corridor that dog-legged and continued. In his hand, FitzHarris held a list of cabins occupied by males. Sandwiched between two of the groups was a family of four, and two single women from South Dakota.

Martin's location could have been worse. From what Laura had explained, these were the cheapest cabins. Guests spent more time out of them than in.

FitzHarris knocked on the first number he had.

Initially there was no response. After more persistent knocking, a male voice called out, 'Get lost!'

'I don't think so, buddy.' Fitz pulled up the sleeves of his jacket and Anya caught sight of the scarring on his forearms. They were classic defence injuries, and some cuts had been deep. She averted her gaze before he noticed her looking.

'Geez. Can't you read? *Do not disturb.*'

Fitz's knuckles whitened as he thumped harder and louder. 'Security. Open up.'

This time, it didn't take long for the door to open.

'Who the—'

'Watch your mouth, we have a lady present.' FitzHarris gestured toward the guest's Bugs Bunny boxer shorts. 'I'm more an Elmer Fudd man, myself,' he announced. The comment clearly caught the man off guard. Anya chose to wait in the doorway.

'Your name is?' FitzHarris's tone was intimidating.

'Brian. Peterson.' The man scratched his bare chest and yawned. 'Look, what's this about?' His hair separated into about four different directions, defying gravity.

145

Anya could see why these cabins were the lowest priced. Instead of a window, the wall was painted with an imitation porthole. Four bunk beds, two on each side, left little room in between. The room stank of bad breath, body odour and stale alcohol. A small dressing table was soiled with half-eaten pizza slices and shot glasses. Dirty clothes covered most of the small area of carpet. Three of the beds were dishevelled. The top left bunk had not been slept in.

'Maid hasn't been yet,' Peterson said. 'I'd offer you a seat but I don't want visitors.'

'That's too bad.' Fitz pulled up the covers and sat on the lower bed nearest him. 'I need to ask you some questions.' He looked around. 'Nice place you got here.'

'Can we cut the wisecracks? I need to take a piss.'

Peterson headed to the small bathroom, not bothering to close the door. He urinated what sounded like litres into the bowl, and didn't flush. Nor did he wash his hands. He came out and flopped into the other lower bunk, hands behind his head.

Fitz was more patient than Anya would have thought. 'There was a complaint about some activities during the first night on board.'

'What? We made a little noise, blew off some steam. Big deal. You people need to get a life.'

'Sir, we take safety on board very seriously. I believe emergency equipment was mishandled.'

'You've got to be kidding.'

'I never joke about safety. This is a significant breach of regulations and cannot be ignored, I'm afraid. So I need to ask. Did you interfere with any of the safety equipment on board?'

Anya watched, holding the door open with her back. She couldn't read FitzHarris, or where he was going. Lilly could have been assaulted in this very room. She chose to stay

146

silent. His unusual interview technique with Carlos's room mate had seemed effective the previous night.

'Man, this is a joke. What happens if I did touch some-thing? What are you going to do? Make me walk the plank?' He laughed and then coughed a smoker's hack.

Fitz just stared back, which seemed to unnerve his interviewee.

'Jeez, lighten up.' He reached for a glass and pulled a piece of melted cheese from its side, flicking it back on the floor. He gulped the contents.

Anya hoped his head ached with a hangover. This man had little respect for authority, or women, it seemed. The maid would risk her job trying to clean this place each day in the allocated time. No one should have to clean this pigsty but the men themselves.

'Which one are you?' Fitz changed tack.

'What?'

'Nickname. The shirts.'

'They always get people talking.' The man grinned and reached down for a chocolate-coloured shirt. He held up the back. 'I'm Taurus. The bull.'

Fitz raised an eyebrow. 'Powerful. So bull boy, what am I going to find if I search this place for drugs?'

Peterson went to stand up and hit his head on the top bunk with a loud thud. 'Shit! You have no right to touch any of our stuff,' he mumbled, rubbing his head.

If he didn't have a headache before, Anya thought, he did now.

Fitz stood and picked up a pair of trousers from the floor with the tip of his thumb and forefinger, as if they were contaminated. 'I have the right to search anyone, anywhere, anytime. No such things as search warrants on board a ship.'

Peterson's face lightened a shade.

'I'm guessing you boys like a bit of fun. Only trouble is, if

I find anything in here now, I'm going to have to hold you responsible. I'm afraid that means you'll be kicked off the ship. No refunds and a lifetime ban from the cruise line. Once I leave this room, it's out of my hands.'

'Hey man, I don't want any trouble.' Peterson vigorously rubbed his head. 'I don't have anything heavy, just a little weed. I'll show you.' He opened a drawer. The only thing in it was a sock. 'Look,' he said, pulling it half inside out.

Fitz leant forward. 'Yep, that's marijuana.'

'Hey, watch this.' Peterson headed back to the bathroom, door still open, Fitz right behind.

'See, it's all gone.' The toilet flushed.

Fitz rubbed his chin. 'I could overlook that, but I'd be very disappointed if you had anything else in here.'

'Man, that's all, I swear.' Peterson opened the drawers, and the wardrobe. 'You can look for yourself, but I swear that's all.'

Anya believed him.

'I believe you.' Fitz patted him on the back and turned to leave.

'One more thing, Brian.'

'Yes, sir?'

'Did you hang out with a woman named Lilly?' Fitz held his hand at his chin level. 'About yea high, long black hair.'

'The scrawny Asian chick. Yeah, she was at the disco, I think, the first night.'

'Well, I'm afraid there's another problem.'

'Man,' he rubbed both hands through his hair. 'You've got to be kidding. What the hell did she say?'

Fitz sucked air in through his teeth. 'Sorry, buddy, but I have to investigate.'

'Everyone was out for a good time that night, chicks can't say yes then say no later, if you know what I mean.'

Anya felt her pulse race. On the surveillance tape, Lilly

148

looked like she was in no position to say no. Which meant she was in no position to consent either with whoever had sex with her.

'By the way, if your name means bull, what's Genny mean?'

'Genitalia. He's a player and "Human Tripod" wouldn't fit. Women would kill to have sex with him.'

'Well, I gotta disagree with you there. You see, that sixteen-year-old Asian chick, as you call her . . . Her real name is Lilly Chan.'

'So we weren't into formal introductions. Arrest us.'

'Funny you should say that, 'cause I might have to.'

'I just got rid of the stuff!'

'Yeah, well, we got a bigger problem. Lilly Chan died after drinking with you and your friends at the disco. She had a drug in her system that happens to be used by date-rapists. Considering your admission to owning recreational drugs, you just became a person of interest in a homicide investigation.'

Peterson's face ashened. 'The one you're talking about was up at the disco, dancing. We all saw her, then she left. I didn't see her after that. You can ask the others, they'll say the same thing.'

Anya couldn't believe what FitzHarris had just done. She knew that before they moved to the next room, Peterson would have phoned and warned the others. The chances of finding out the truth just disappeared.

17

Anya thought about going to the captain and informing him of what she knew so far. But what if he worked for Mats Anderson too? She decided to hold off. For now.

She left FitzHarris and headed back to the suite. He said he wanted to interview Doctor Chan, and find out more about Lilly's history. She wanted to ask Martin more about the woman he saw naked in the corridor. She also needed to get away from FitzHarris before she said something she regretted.

Back inside, Jasmine was still at the grand piano with Ben. His attention span was remarkable, as was Jasmine's under the circumstances. She was teaching him to play a simple version of 'Für Elise'.

Anya bent down and stroked the back of her son's hair.

'Jasmine taught me.' He beamed and played again. 'Watch this.' They played together. This obviously took more concentration, judging by the way he held his tongue out to the side of his mouth.

'He's very musical,' Jasmine commented.

'Please keep going, it's wonderful.'

Martin was in the kitchenette and beckoned Anya over. 'How's Carlos?'

'Apparently he's still unconscious, so can't be interviewed yet.' She wondered if the ongoing sedation was ordered by Mats Anderson or FitzHarris. 'His body's been through a significant trauma with the shooting, surgery, and he's at risk of infection.'

'Maybe it's a good thing he doesn't know yet.' Martin sidled past her to the coffee pot and lifted it. 'Like one?'

Anya sat at the smoky glass table. 'Thanks.'

'It's not the best brew, but it beats going out for a latte in the rain.'

He placed the cup on a coaster and helped himself to one.

Anya looked out at the deck and beyond. FitzHarris had been ordered to sabotage the investigation, while keeping an eye on her. She wanted to confront him, but knew it was better to do as her father would say, 'Keep your powder dry until you absolutely need it.' The swell had increased. Water from the pool swished over the edge as wind buffeted the closed umbrellas. Lounge chairs were stacked in piles. Giant drops of rain pelted the floor-to-ceiling windows in rushes. They eased for a few moments then rallied again.

Jasmine played Ben the beginning phrases of 'The Entertainer' by Scott Joplin, and he looked mesmerised. Anya wasn't sure if it was the music or the pianist he liked more.

With the pair distracted, Anya could speak quietly but more freely. 'Lilly was last seen by one of those men in the bowling shirts. He wore a yellow shirt with "Genny" written on the back.'

'I had a run-in with him that first night when I asked them to turn the music down. I thought he was going to thump me, until the guy in green stepped in and gave him another drink.'

'There's something I need to ask.' Anya shot a look at Ben and Jasmine. They were engrossed in the piano tune. 'You mentioned there was a couple having sex in the corridor. Could that have been Lilly?'

Martin stared into the mug, trying to recall. 'No, way. That woman had blonde hair.'

'Did you see this Genny in his room or in the corridor?'

'It was outside. I remember, 'cause he came out and

closed the door. He had a towel around his waist, but he still came out.'

Anya took a slow sip. Genny may not have wanted anyone to see who or what was going on inside. 'We think Lilly might have been in there sometime around midnight. Four men – including Genny, whatever his real name is are registered.'

Martin covered his eyes. 'Look, Annie, if I'd known they were hurting her inside that cabin . . .'

Anya rested a hand on his arm. 'Unless she screamed for help, how could you possibly have known?'

'She was just a child. You saw how small she was. I'd only have to have seen her to realise something was wrong.'

Maybe someone else on the corridor had seen, or heard something, Anya thought. There was a family and another party in adjacent rooms. Surely someone could give them a clue.

The doorbell to the suite rang and Ben jumped up from the piano stool. 'I'll get it.'

'No!' Anya was swiftly at his side. 'You shouldn't answer the door to anyone but one of us.' Even if he could reach, there was no peephole.

'Yes, Mum.' He still wanted to see who was there.

David FitzHarris stood behind the woman Anya had met in the library. Doctor Chan looked tired and drawn. Relief spread across her face when she saw Jasmine. The pair exchanged words in Cantonese as Jasmine hugged her mother, who stepped back and lifted up the hem of the over-sized top her daughter wore.

'Mother, I was cold and wet and Anya kindly gave me this to change into.'

The woman shot a glance at the other man in the room, who stood by the table.

'This is Martin, and their son, Ben,' FitzHarris said. 'This family has been very kind. More than you know.'

Anya watched for a hardness in his expression, but his tone sounded sincere. He was very good at playing people – until now.

'Thank you for looking after my daughter. I had some important . . . I had to make many calls back to home. Come, Jasmine.'

'I was hoping we could have a conversation, in private,' FitzHarris said to Doctor Chan. 'Here's a good place, if you don't mind.'

Martin collected his and Ben's jackets and headed out the door. 'If you'll excuse us, we have a speed date at the kids' club. We'll take the long way round and stay dry,' he reassured Anya as they headed out.

Ben turned back. 'Bye Jasmine, thanks for teaching me the piano.'

'Maybe we can do it again some time.'

He ran and hugged his new friend tightly.

It was the first time Anya had seen Jasmine smile. Her face came to life and exuded warmth.

FitzHarris led Doctor Chan to the kitchen table.

He sat at one end, Anya at the other. Mother and daughter sat side by side.

FitzHarris cleared his throat. 'I cannot apologise enough for the inconvenience you were put through last night. It's no excuse, but again, I am deeply sorry and our staff will do everything to make it up to you.'

I'll bet, Anya thought, with the tawdry bribes you've been instructed to offer.

He cleared his throat. 'I'm here with some information about how Lilly died.'

Jasmine reached for her mother's hand.

'A blood test showed she had a small amount of alcohol and something else in her body. It's a drug called GHB.'

'What is it for?' Doctor Chan asked. 'I give the girls

vitamins and sometimes they take medicine for a headache. Aspirin, that is all. They are healthy girls, as you can see.'

'It's not a medication, Ma'am. It is what's called a recreational drug.'

Anya explained, 'Gamma-Hyroxybutyric acid. It can be used to treat narcolepsy, but it is more often abused.'

Doctor Chan's eyes squinted. 'My daughter was taking drugs? Is that what she snuck out for?' She let go of Jasmine's hand. 'You knew this? Are you taking it too?'

'No, Mother. Of course not. There's no way either of us would take anything like that.'

'Did your older sister give them to you?' Doctor Chan pushed back her chair and stood. 'I know she smokes. You can smell it on her. That is why I keep you away from her bad influence. I always tell you. Nothing good can come of Western ways.' She turned her back to the table and stopped. She took a few deep breaths. 'I don't want to hear any more.'

'Ma'am, I mean Doctor Chan, I'm afraid you need to. We don't think Lilly willingly took the drug. It's possible someone put it in her drink.'

Doctor Chan turned back and stabbed a finger on the tabletop. 'Alcohol, drugs, there is no difference. I warned the girls this could happen.'

'Doctor Chan,' Anya tried. 'It seems as though Lilly was at the disco, dancing with another girl who has blonde hair and wore a hair band with a sequined piece on top.'

Jasmine looked between Fitz and Anya. 'It sounds like the girl from the table near us in the restaurant. Kandy, I think her name is. She's with her parents and said hello that first dinner.'

'I remember. She was rude to her father. No respect. Chinese children would never speak to a parent like that.'

'Come on, Mother, you know that's not true. You and Lilly say the most awful things to each other. You fight all the time.' Her eyes became misty. 'I hate it.'

155

Doctor Chan slowly took her seat. 'We argue, that is all. Lilly refuses to practise and I yell at her until she does. It is the way we are.' She corrected, 'We were . . .' She looked at Anya. 'One minute we argued, then we would make up.'

'Lilly hated the fights. She was sick of being made to play music. She wanted a different life. One with freedom and fun, like our sister has.' Jasmine's voice trailed off. 'She hated what you did to us.'

'Do you think I like it?' Doctor Chan's voice became shrill. 'Do you know how hard it is for me? I work hard at the hospital but my daughters mean everything. Who will dream for you if I don't? Western mothers go out with friends, they enjoy themselves. Instead, I come home and make sure you practise.'

'Lilly hated it.'

'It is not my role to be popular. I do it because I am your mother.'

Jasmine suddenly excused herself and ran to the bathroom. The others sat in silence. Fitz stood.

'I don't know about you, but I could use a tea. Anyone mind if I make a pot?'

'That's a great idea. I'll go see if Jasmine would like something.' Anya headed to the downstairs bathroom and gently tapped on the door. 'Are you okay?'

The door opened a small amount. 'Everything's wrong. I just had an accident.'

It took a moment for Anya to realise. 'You mean you got your period?'

Jasmine nodded. 'It's come again. It's supposed to have finished. I'm so sorry, I think I've ruined your leggings.'

Anya moved into the bathroom. 'It's not a problem. Hang on a minute and I'll be back.' She headed upstairs to her room and pulled out her toiletries bag. Inside she kept sanitary products for emergencies, which she took back down, along with another change of clothes.

156

'It can happen with stress so don't even think about it,' Anya said gently, placing the clothes over the sink. Jasmine folded into her arms, gently sobbing, holding the bag the whole while.

'We'll have you fixed up in no time. No one has to know.'

'Thank you,' Jasmine pulled away and wiped her eyes with the sleeve of the top. 'I gave Lilly my last pad before she went out that night. She'd run out.'

Anya's mind whirred. 'You and Lilly had your periods at the same time?' Girls and women living in the same house often menstruated together, even if they were unrelated. For some reason, the cycles of women living in close contact frequently aligned.

Jasmine nodded with a puzzled expression.

'So she was wearing underwear that night?'

'Of course!' Jasmine's eyes darted between each of Anya's and her mouth trembled. 'What are you saying?'

She dropped the toiletries bag, suddenly aware of the implication.

18

After the Chans had returned to their cabin, FitzHarris arranged a meeting with Kandy and her parents in the Porpoise Club.

'Thanks again for meeting us,' Fitz said. 'We really appreciate you taking time out from your vacation.'

Mr and Mrs Ratzenberg sat opposite at the table. Their daughter was dressed in black slim jeans and a long buttoned shirt. A thick layer of foundation attempted to obscure a row of pimples on her cheeks and chin line.

FitzHarris had asked Anya to sit in on the interview, with the hope that Kandy would relate better to her, particularly, given the sensitive nature of what they had to discuss. He would have preferred to have spoken with the girl away from her parents, but at sea there was little choice.

The father was a large man, not only in height but mass. The back of the chair tilted with the weight of his axe-handle shoulders. His wife wore a red-and-white striped top with red jeans. She could not have been more than five foot two. It always amazed Anya how such giant men were attracted to tiny women, and vice versa. In terms of offspring, the genetic combination was ideal.

'This is Doctor Crichton, who is assisting me with enquiries.'

The family nodded politely.

'What's this about? Does it have something to do with that girl who died? The one from the table near ours?'

Anya watched Kandy, who blinked and looked at the floor in response to the comment.

'We don't know anything. Our Kandy said hello to her, but she didn't say much. We tried being neighbourly but the mother wasn't sociable.'

Mrs Ratzenberg explained, 'I guess they just preferred to be together. Kandy asked if the girls wanted to come to the teen club, but they said they weren't allowed. Something about study and practice.'

'Lilly Chan was sixteen years old.' Fitz passed across an enlarged photocopy of her ID image.

The parents sat forward and looked. The husband slipped his hand into one of his wife's.

'The poor family. Do you know what happened?'

'We're looking into a number of possibilities, and trying to piece together her last few hours. We were hoping Kandy might be able to help us out.'

The girl startled. 'Why me?'

'You might have seen her later that night.'

Kandy began twisting a section of hair around her index finger, then releasing it.

'I went to check out the teen club after dinner, watched a show, then I took a walk before bed.'

Mr Ratzenberg nodded. 'She was in bed when we came back from the nightclub, which was around one am, I think.'

His wife concurred.

Fitz took notes as the father watched. From what Anya had seen, there was little chance of anyone deciphering the security officer's handwriting.

'Did you happen to see Lilly at all after dinner?'

'Yeah, I saw her in the garden and she said we should check out the ship together. We went up on the deck to see the stars. There was a disco playing all this old-time music.' The hair twirling continued. 'We had a couple of dances then we went to get a drink of water. That's when she left, without even saying goodbye. So I went back to the cabin.'

There was no mention of the men.

'Did you two meet anyone else up there?'

The hair was wrapped in a tighter coil. 'Some men tried to get us to dance with them, and offered us drinks.'

'Did you accept?'

The hair bounced free. 'Of course not. I'm only fifteen. These men were old.'

'You're sure that's what happened?'

Mr Ratzenberg sat forward. 'What are you implying? If that's what Kandy says, it's what happened. Look, we came to help but if you're going to question Kandy as if she's a criminal.' He placed his enormous hands on the table, causing it to shift.

Anya spoke calmly. 'No one is suggesting anything. But it's very important to get as many details as possible. Someone knows what happened in those last few hours of Lilly's life, and the family is in so much pain. You can imagine how hard this has been for them. Not knowing is even worse.'

Mrs Ratzenberg patted her husband's hand. 'Of course we understand. Losing a child is every parent's worst nightmare. We couldn't bear to think if anything happened to Kandy. She's our miracle child. We didn't think I could carry a child to term, but God answered our prayers.'

She reached over and put her arm around Kandy's shoulders. 'Darling, is there anything else you remember that might be helpful? Something Lilly might have said about where she was going? Or something you saw, you don't think was important, but could be?'

'No, that's all.'

Fitz had one more question, it seemed. 'There were six alcoholic drinks purchased on Lilly's electronic cabin card. Do you know who they were for, or why she bought so many?'

All attention was on the teenager.

'No! I'm not allowed to drink. I don't know anything about that.' She began to bite her bottom lip. 'I can't believe she's dead. She told me she had a big fight with her mother that day and wouldn't follow all the stupid rules anymore. She wanted to live with her Dad in Hawaii.'

Kandy put her face into her mother's shoulder and cried.

'I'm not one to judge,' the father began. 'But children from broken homes need to be carefully watched. You know they are at more risk of doing drugs and having teenage pregnancies. I think buying those drinks tells you a lot. That mother should have kept a better eye on her children. I'll bet this wasn't the first time the girl went wild.'

'Frank, now isn't the time.'

He pushed the chair back and stood. 'No, I'm fed up with all this blaming society for a kid's wild behaviour. I'm telling you. It all starts in the home. Everything comes down to the parents. You look at the mother and you'll find all the answers you need.'

19

Later that afternoon, Martin decided to read so Anya took Ben to the cinema to watch a pirate movie, followed by dinner in the 1950s-style diner. Still not worn out, Ben begged to play Uno back at the suite. Martin joined them and they played until nine. Ben protested about going to bed, but was asleep within minutes of Anya stroking his hair.

Anya went back downstairs to discuss Mats Anderson's fax with Martin. She poured them each a glass of wine and the phone rang. It was Martin's girlfriend, and he seemed suddenly uncomfortable. Anya took the wine upstairs and closed the screen to her room to give them privacy. The afternoon with Ben had been special, and then the three of them had laughed and been silly during the card game, with Martin continually forgetting the rules. Or so he wanted Ben to think. Martin had been more relaxed than she'd seen him in a long time, but became awkward once he knew who was on the phone. She wondered whether there was more to him coming on the trip than he had let on. After an hour, tiredness overcame her and she slept.

The following morning, she woke up to the smell of toast and eggs. Ben carried a glass of juice up the stairs, his tongue sticking out with concentration. In the glass was a purple parasol.

'Morning, Mum, it's breakfast in bed time.'

Martin carried a room-service tray with poached eggs, toast and roasted tomatoes, with a frangipani as garnish. 'We could lie and say we made it ourselves, but . . .'

Anya sat up, touched by the gesture.

'I'm not allowed to carry hot drinks. Dad says you have to come downstairs for that.'

'Fair enough, this is so wonderful and considerate. Thank you, both of you.' She placed the flower behind her right ear and Ben beamed. 'Anybody like some?'

'We didn't want to wake you so had ours downstairs,' Martin explained before leaving the room.

Anya buttered some toast, took a bite, then offered one to Ben, who didn't hesitate to finish the piece. It was funny, she thought, how someone else's food always tasted better to him.

'Can we see Jasmine today? She's a really good piano player.'

'Tell you what. If I see her, I'll ask if she can come over here. Instead, would you like to spend a couple of hours in the kids' club, like yesterday?'

He kissed her cheek and slid off the bed. She could hear him thumping down the stairs. 'Dad, Mum says I can go to kids' club!'

Anya sat back. If the world ended at the cabin door, she would be happy.

After breakfast, Anya dressed and dropped Ben at the club, before heading to the medical centre. The waiting room was clean, white and had fresh flowers placed on the wooden coffee table. Lights were off, and the place was quiet. Just behind her through the door came Rachel, the junior nurse, in uniform, keys in hand. Her shoulder-length hair was slicked back into a ponytail. A full fringe covered the top of now blue-rimmed glasses.

'If you're looking for Karen, she isn't here. Clinic's between ten and twelve, then again from five 'til seven every day.'

'That's fine. I was hoping to see how Carlos is.'

'Oh.' The young nurse switched on the main lights and placed the collection of keys on her belt loop. 'He's slept pretty much the whole time since the surgery. He became febrile overnight. Doctor Novak stayed with him while anti-biotics took effect.'

Rachel's shoes squeaked on the lino floor while the keys jingled as she headed off to check on the patients.

Anya decided to wait and see what Carlos's condition was now. She kept thinking about the desperate way he'd looked at her. What did he know? She sat on one of the lounges and glanced through the magazines on the table. Beside the fresh flowers she found a print-out of the morning's news.

'Terrorist attack kills twenty-one: two missing, presumed dead.' The headline was like so many others, but something in the first paragraph caught Anya's eye.

'Tributes pouring in from around the world for shipping magnate Sven Anderson and his family.'

Anderson. The owner of the *Paradisio*.

She sat up and read on.

Anderson's yacht was destroyed by a tender filled with explosives. At this point, police weren't ruling out the possi-bility of a terrorist suicide bomber. According to unnamed sources, Sven Anderson had left hospital and travelled to Greece, where his super-yacht was moored for his eldest son Mats' fortieth birthday. It is believed Mats was on his way to the boat by helicopter and was two miles away when the explo-sion took place. A salvage operation has been launched to recover the bodies. It is believed Sven Anderson's second son from his first marriage Lars, died along with Simon, twenty-five, and Julie, twenty-three, from the second marriage. Police sources say that, due to the size of the explosion, it is likely everyone on board died instantly. Sven Anderson's daughter, Liesl, two, and her mother, Svetlana, a Russian socialite who became Anderson's third wife three years ago, were believed to be on the island estate at the time. It is not known if they had planned to attend the birthday celebrations.

The tragedy was compared to the misfortunes that

afflicted other rich and famous families – the Gettys, Kennedys, and the list went on. Something to make the masses happy to think that wealth and tragedy went hand in hand.

Anya felt for the family. Sven and Lars Anderson dead. Mats Anderson still alive.

So far, no terrorist group had claimed responsibility, but several theories were aired. Mats had supposedly gone out with the daughter of a wealthy politician from Pakistan and became embroiled in a scandal when he was photographed with two prostitutes at a nightclub. Extremist Muslims could have targeted the family, who represented all the indulgences and excesses of capitalism.

If it were a terrorist attack, Anya wondered if any of the cruise ships were potential targets. Thousands of people in the middle of the ocean were far easier to bring down than a plane. She tried to block the thought.

Reading on, it seemed Sven Anderson had bought up almost sixty percent of the competition in the cruise line industry. Further reports described him as a savvy business leader who wielded considerable power in Washington. There were some suggestions that early in his career he had sold arms to the Israelis and Palestinians. An investigation was ongoing.

It would hardly be a surprise if the man had made hordes of enemies over the years.

His Russian widow was quoted as saying that her husband, 'had travelled with a bodyguard' after receiving death threats from fanatical environmentalists, angered by the pollution they claimed cruise ships left in their wake. The story described Anderson as a pioneer in environmental policy and a visionary in protecting pristine territories.

Anya thought about what Laura had said yesterday about Lars being more of an environmentalist than Mats, who wanted to cut costs. Perhaps it wasn't just lucky that Mats wasn't onboard.

Rhythmic squeaking and jingling approached.

'Doctor Novak's changing the dressings so I didn't disturb him.'

The nurse studied Anya. 'Why are you here again?'

'I just wanted to know how Carlos was. I was at the surgery.'

'I know that.'

It seemed Novak wasn't the only one with a curt bedside manner.

'Flowers are pretty,' Anya tried to engage Rachel to find out anything more about Carlos.

'Paco, our steward does the flowers and prints the latest news for us. It isn't rocket science. I told you Karen wasn't in until later.'

'Busy night?' Maybe Rachel was more comfortable talking about clinical subjects.

The nurse bent down and straightened the magazines, checking the clock on the wall.

'The usual. A forty year old going through the DTs in the crew ward, a demented passenger with pneumonia who tried to punch a steward. He's on IV antibiotics, and restrained for his own safety. Each one had to be specialled.'

Anya knew that meant one-on-one, intensive nursing care. The team's resources must be stretched to the limit.

'Add to that a Colles' fracture, two sprained ankles and an anaphylactic reaction.'

'Is the person with anaphylaxis all right?'

'It's not uncommon. We carry EpiPens at all times. Karen was nearby when it happened.'

A Filipino man arrived through the main door with a room-service trolley. Rachel hurried over to hold the door open.

'Coffee for the others, and for you, water for your special tea. Careful, it is very, very hot.'

'Doctor's busy but will be out shortly, Paco.'

The smell of barista-made coffee was too tempting for Anya to ignore. He offered her a cup, which she gratefully accepted. The late nights and fitful sleep had her energy levels lower than normal.

'Miss Rachel.' He handed the nurse a mug with a tea bag. Steam wafted from its surface.

Paco disappeared and Rachel sat at the opposite end of the lounge from Anya. 'We don't get pathologists down here.'

'You've had some difficult circumstances.'

Rachel clutched her mug with both hands, blinked slowly and took a sip. Her shoulders sank back into the lounge.

'The terrorist attack on Sven Anderson's yacht may cause some anxiety among guests.'

'What?' Rachel sat up and reached across to read the print-out. 'Oh my God, where? Was anyone else—' The mug tilted and the black tea poured over her lap. She squealed and leapt to her feet. 'It's burning!'

Anya stood. 'Where do you keep ice?'

'In the consulting rooms.' Rachel's green eyes watered as she quickly followed Anya to the nearest room.

Anya closed the door. Rachel had already kicked off her shoes, pulled up her skirt and was peeling down her stockings. 'Icepacks are in the bar fridge, over there in the corner.' She grimaced.

Pain was a good thing, Anya thought. The boiling water hadn't burnt through Rachel's nerve endings. She located two large icepacks and wrapped each in paper towels from the dispenser on the wall.

The nurse had positioned herself on the bed. Anya took a quick glance and saw diffuse redness, with blisters already forming on her top and inner thighs. One blister was at least five by five centimetres. Some of the pantyhose nylon had melted into the skin.

'This may hurt, but it's the best way to limit the damage.'

Rachel winced as the packs touched her exposed skin. 'I can't believe it.'

Karen knocked and entered. 'I heard a squeal. What happened?' She looked at Rachel's legs and shook her head, with a motherly expression. 'Oh Rach. We're in smoother waters. You get through storms and do this to yourself now?'

Rachel began to cry. 'I just want to be alone.'

Karen nodded. 'We'll let you be, just promise you'll keep those icepacks in place until I get back.'

Anya followed Karen out and closed the door behind them.

'We can't afford for her to be off-duty for too long. Clinic's going to be busy enough with follow-ups, let alone new patients.'

'Is there anything I can do?'

'Good heavens, you've done enough.' Karen placed a hand on Anya's elbow. 'I'm about to relieve Doctor Novak while he has a break.'

'I just wanted to see how Carlos was doing.'

A shout rang out, followed by screaming. The voice was male.

Karen sprinted toward the noise, closely followed by Anya.

Inside the treatment room, Carlos was upright, hands clawing at the bedsheets. 'Help me! I can't feel my legs!'

Novak had a hand over one eye. 'He woke and started punching.'

Anya moved closer to the bed and Carlos lunged at her, wrapping his fingers tightly around her wrist. 'My legs!' He wailed.

Karen rushed to the cupboard and pulled out a vial of valium, which she showed Novak before drawing the content into a fresh needle and syringe.

While distracted by Anya, five milligrams of valium entered

Carlos's vein via the drip. Before it had a chance to circulate, his release on her arm had loosened. She gently moved her hand into his. With her other, she stroked his short dark hair and spoke calmly, before the benzodiazepine took full effect.

'You were badly hurt and lost a lot of blood. To save your life, and get you safely back home to your wife and kids, you had to have an operation.'

Mention of his family seemed to help. His breathing slowed. 'My legs?'

'Your knees were shattered by the bullets. You would have died if we didn't amputate.'

Carlos's eyes remained fixed on hers. It was difficult to know if the small dose of valium eased his tension, or that being told what had happened made him less afraid. Anya wanted to ask him what he knew about Lilly, but now wasn't the time. He needed to calm down.

'It's important you stay in bed until we get to port.'

'My wife . . .'

'Your friends, Kujan and Iketut, have been in touch with her. Your kids need you more than ever.' She didn't mention head office notifying his family.

He pulled Anya closer and glanced at the others and back. Karen recapped the syringe and placed it in a kidney dish by the bedside before dragging Novak over to the sink. 'Let's have a look at that eye.'

'There are some things I need you to get. For my wife.'

Anya imagined Carlos had been away from home for so long to earn enough to support the family and help his wife's medical bills. Every cent counted, and American dollars were worth far more than local currency.

He was barely whispering. 'My jacket . . . And my flowers.'

The hand slipped out of hers, back into the bed as he drifted into sleep.

20

FitzHarris entered the treatment room just after Carlos lost consciousness.

Anya stepped outside and waited. It wasn't long before he returned.

'Did Carlos tell you who shot him?'

Anya sighed. 'No, he wanted me to get something for his wife – a jacket and some flowers? It doesn't make a lot of sense.'

He rubbed his chin. 'I'm thinking this has to be drug-related. The silence from the crew is deafening; there's no way this was over a woman or gambling debt. And the fact they didn't kill him seems to suggest there's something still at stake . . . If Carlos isn't using . . .'

'Then he could have been dealing, or smuggling.' Anya wondered why FitzHarris would mention drugs again in front of her. It was not the best way to bury the shooting, unless Carlos was being made out to be a villain. Maybe the proceeds or drugs were inside the jacket, or somehow hidden in a bouquet. Perhaps the shooter was trying to find them too.

'Can you walk with me while we talk?'

Anya wanted to know what was so important about Carlos's jacket, and whether it was somehow related to Lilly's death. With Martin busy in the gym, and with Ben at kids' club, she had the chance to find out. She could also see how FitzHarris planned to 'keep a lid' on the investigations. They stepped outside the medical centre and moved toward the passenger lifts.

FitzHarris had managed to nick his neck shaving. A small amount of blood stained the top of his collar. Dark bags around his eyes seem to be spreading.

'Did you get *any* sleep last night?'

They headed aft along the corridor toward the lift.

'Laura asked the same thing. Don't suppose you heard, but the head of this cruise line and three of his kids were murdered on the family yacht outside of one of the Greek islands. Head office has told us to be on the alert for anything or anyone suspicious. They think terrorists are targeting anything or anyone connected to the family. We're supposed to be alarmed without letting the passengers know.'

'I'm a passenger, here with my child, if you remember.'

'Sorry, it's just that it feels like you're one of us now. Guess forewarned is forearmed, as they say. If you hear a safety drill, you'll know it's the real deal so get your family to your muster station as soon as possible.'

Somehow, that didn't engender confidence.

A man appeared from behind, wearing clean, white overalls.

'Hey Fitz, good to see you.'

'Alessandro, our Chief Engineer, meet Doctor Anya Crichton.'

'Alessandro is Italian for Alexander, as in "the Great".' The engineer kissed Anya's hand. 'The pleasure is all mine.'

'We're discussing the bombing,' FitzHarris commented. Anya slid her hand from his grip as the lift arrived.

'Terrible business.' The engineer scowled and got in the lift with them. 'At least one son survived.'

'Mats, wasn't it?' Anya fished. 'Did either of you deal directly with Anderson or his children?'

'The old man is very hands-on and visits every ship at

least once a year. The sons I know only by reputation,' Alessandro volunteered.

FitzHarris added, 'The father took over when the company was going under and turned it around. He wasn't about to relinquish control.'

He evaded the question, and obviously didn't want Anya to know he was in the 'inner circle' as Laura had mentioned.

They got out on deck one, passing guests covered up with jumpers and jackets. Others wandered around in summer outfits, seemingly happy to stay inside. No one appeared distressed or in a particular hurry. It was holidays as usual, barring the stormy weather.

FitzHarris stepped away to make a call.

Anya waited until she and the engineer were out of earshot. 'Has anyone claimed responsibility?'

'Not yet,' Alessandro said, 'but the police have their suspicions. Sources say the bomb was a homemade incendiary device – gun powder and nitroglycerin. A speedboat was controlled offshore by remote. When it hit the yacht, the nitro probably ignited a fuse and . . . Kaboomza! They are still collecting pieces of bodies and wreckage.'

Someone was serious about killing the family.

'Before you ask . . .' Fitz rejoined them. 'They're looking at groups of environmentalists who've been to Congress lobbying for changes to the industry. Old man Anderson is probably the most recognisable face in cruise lines.'

It was early to assume a lobby group was responsible just because they had an issue with the cruise industry. This was not the first terrorist attack in Greece, and would not be the last. Blockades, boycotts and public shaming of offending companies were more the pattern of environmental activists. Besides, there was no quicker way to destroy a cause than to murder a family.

Then again, some extremists had no logic behind their

actions. 'Was anyone aware of threats? I mean, were you warned something could happen?' Anya remembered Fitz mentioning the anti-terrorist long range acoustic device.

'There have been a couple of serious attacks on cruise ships by pirates, which is one of the reasons I took this job. After 9/11, I was involved in developing some of NYPD's counter-terrorism protocols.'

He didn't mention the knife attack or his injuries.

'Some passages around Indonesia and Africa are overrun with pirates,' Alessandro said. 'They're organised, well armed and high tech. A while back, there was an attack on a ship smaller than this one by a couple of pirate speedboats. They fired machine guns and RPGs – rocket-propelled grenades – at the vessel. One of the unexploded RPGs got stuck in the wall of a cabin. Can you imagine waking up to that kind of room service?'

Anya preferred not to.

'Anyway,' FitzHarris continued, 'the LRAD was the only thing that could repel them. Luckily none of the passengers were seriously hurt, but I can't say the same for the crew. And there was another time . . .'

Anya wondered if she really wanted to know this much information. She held up her hands. 'It's okay, I get the picture.' So much for the *Love Boat* concept of cruising. 'I still don't understand why anyone would target Anderson, when they could hijack one of his ships. That would have done a lot more damage to the cruise industry.'

'I agree,' Fitz said. 'But who knows? It's common knowledge Sven and Mats aren't the nicest guys to do business with. Could be any number of nut jobs, but there's an environmental group that claims the cruise industry is responsible for up to a quarter of all ocean pollution.'

'What they don't acknowledge,' Alessandro interrupted, 'is how much this company puts back into the environment. It supports numerous local economies, employs environmental officers, and complies with a strict code of conduct.'

Fitz slowed to pat his leg, as if willing it into better action. Again, Anya felt the enormity of the vessel. She had read statistics like it being longer than the Eiffel Tower on its side, but walking even a fraction of the length hit home. Her legs felt as if they had walked the equivalent of city blocks, and they had only just reached midship. It was easy to see how FitzHarris's job played havoc with his leg injury. By now, he was perspiring and taking shorter, sharper breaths.

His walkie-talkie crackled and he stopped to take the call, and maybe catch his breath.

'Fire. Where?'

Anya's heart raced. God, please let Ben be safe.

Fitz's eyes squinted as he listened. 'Go on.'

Alessandro dialled his own phone.

'Put Chef on.'

It was the kitchen, a world away from the kids' club. Anya doubted Fitz would have wasted time on an update if an emergency was in progress.

'Right. Fill in the report and have it on my desk by lunch. And take the restraints off the poor guy. He's sweating and nervous 'cause he thinks he'll be fired and sent home at the next port. And get the doc to see his hands. He needs treatment for those burns.'

Alessandro hung up. 'I'm needed up on the bridge. See you soon, I hope.'

FitzHarris checked his watch. 'We need to get a move on.'

Anya grabbed his arm. 'Excuse me? Fire?'

'It's nothing. A kitchen hand spilt oil on the hotplate, then tried to put out the flames with boiling water. Given the amount of fries served every day, it's a wonder it doesn't happen more often. One of my men restrained the kitchen hand because he looked guilty. See what I have to work with?

A terrorist alert then every incompetent kitchen hand is a saboteur.'

Anya was relieved it was under control. Clearly, the crew was on edge after hearing about the attack. It was still unclear where she and Fitz were headed. She had assumed they would return to Carlos's cabin but they were on the wrong level.

'Are you going to search the cabins of the other men in bowling shirts?'

'Not exactly.'

They turned another corridor dogleg and were back where they had been the day before. To the side of the corridor was a cleaning trolley, piled with sheets, soaps, shampoo and conditioner refills. One of the rooms had its door open. Inside, a Filipino man was finishing the corners on the bed and immediately responded to Fitz's tap.

She wondered what Fitz was playing at. Was this what Mats Anderson wanted him to do? Keep her occupied and always in sight?

'Ah, Mr FitzHarris, I have those things for you.' The man looked at Anya and back to Fitz.

'It's okay, she's with me.'

The man moved back to his trolley and collected two white bags from beneath the lowest shelf, with something written in black texta on each one. A third, larger one was handed over with a proud grin.

'This was on my cart while I cleaned that corridor, as you requested.'

'Excellent work, Testino. And you labelled them?'

In exchange for the larger bag, Fitz handed over what looked like fifty dollars in US currency. According to Junta that was a whole month's wages.

'Thank you very much. If there is *anything* else you need . . .'

'There was one thing. Can you check what room you had to clean vomit from after the first night at sea?'

'Ah, I remember. Room 1080.'

A middle-aged couple arrived behind them. The three moved to the wall to let them past. 'Good morning,' the steward slipped the money into his front pocket. 'If there is anything you need, please call me.'

'Thanks, Testino, but our room is perfect,' the wife answered and opened her door. 'And we love the bunny you made with the towels.'

With them back in their cabin, the steward turned back to Fitz. 'The guests were angry about the smell. Only it was not just vomit. Someone had gone to the toilet on the floor as well.'

Fitz clutched the bags tighter. 'Don't tell me they crapped on it.'

Testino's eyes widened. 'No, Mister, it was urine.'

'Dirty sons of . . .' Fitz took a sideways glance at Anya. 'Well, you're doing a great job, Testino, keep up the great work.'

Further along, the pair stopped at a locked storage room. Fitz opened it with his electronic pass key. It had shelves filled with toilet paper, soap and cleaning bottles marked 'carpet' and 'bathroom'.

Inside, Fitz opened the first bag. Marked 1087. It had come from Brian Peterson's shared room. The stench was foul. Fitz pulled on some gloves he'd retrieved from his jacket pocket. 'I'd offer you a pair, but I figure dead bodies and gore are more your style. Me, I'm a trash man. It's amazing how much you can tell from someone's garbage.' He pointed to a large green bag-dispenser. 'Would you do the honours?'

'I still don't see why you're bothering.' Anya peeled off a bag, and opened the top. 'If they had drugs in their cabin, they could have put them down the toilet, or in any of the thousands of bins on board. Or even overboard.'

'You're thinking like a smart perp. Look who we're dealing with. These guys are adolescent. Where does every teenager hide their secret stash? Their bedroom, even though that's the first place parents check. Peterson thinks we've already searched his room, remember?' He eyed the bounty. 'Testino bagged up every cabin's trash separately. So what's in the trolley's bag came from people putting it there in the corridor.'

Anya had to credit the idea, but was unsure how much information it would glean. Without a chain of evidence, it would be impossible to prove anything had come from the rooms of the men. This could all be a show for her benefit. His aim could have been to keep her close to discover exactly what she knew and planned to do with that information.

Fitz started with the largest bag, the one from the room steward's trolley. He rummaged through it. 'Most things bought before boarding would have been used and disposed of by now. Guests have unpacked, and don't have to carry handbags or wallets. Receipts fit into their cabin trash bins, and we know leftover food should, so . . .' He pulled out a small, blue velvet jewellery box and flipped it open. The ring container was empty.

'Okay. Someone's getting engaged. The ring's a surprise and he doesn't want the girl to know.'

'Or,' Anya thought from experience, 'she's bought herself a ring and is already wearing it. When he asks where it came from, she'll say, "What this old thing? I've had it for ages."'

'I'm going with my version. A woman would just hide the ring box under something else in the trash, or in the covered bin in the bathroom. Men never go there. Which is why a man put it in the trolley bin. He knows a woman might otherwise notice it.'

She had to admit he made another good point. Martin would never have looked in the rubbish bin, or laundry hamper, for that matter.

Fitz grinned. 'Hello. It's a water bottle, minus the label.' He grabbed a pen from his jacket pocket and lifted the bottle out, avoiding any chance of touching it further with his gloves.

Anya waited for the story behind this item.

'Okay, Doctor, what do you make of it?'

'It's an empty bottle. Someone refilled it after coming on board. Maybe they're environmentalists.' Anya could barely hide her sarcasm.

'It's a different shape from the ones used on the ship. So it has to have been brought on board. You can get cold drinks on all the activity decks, and anything but alcohol is free on tap.'

She looked at it. The label had been removed, or had fallen off over time.

'This is exactly the reason I asked Testino to collect their waste.'

Anya assumed he meant that the bottle had been placed there by one of the men. He asked her to pass him another plastic bag, to which he transferred the prize. 'I'd bet a month's salary this had GHB in it. And it should have at least some of our boys' fingerprints on it.'

If not Lilly's, she thought.

The next bag was from Genny's room, or Genitalia, as he was known. In the top were two used condoms.

'Either the human tripod and his buddies don't get much action, or they don't care for little raincoats,' Fitz deduced.

That meant there was a greater chance forensic technicians could find DNA on at least one of the samples she had collected from Lilly's body in the morgue, confirming one or more had sex with her before she died.

'What the—?' Fitz pulled out a series of half-chewed remnants of pizza and large numbers of crusts. 'Did you know that guests eat more than three hundred and fifty thousand pizzas every cruise? We just solved the mystery of where they go.' He ripped off the gloves. 'That's it for them.' He sounded disappointed.

'Let's see what Brian Peterson dumped after our visit.' He replaced the gloves with fresh ones. Anya remained skeptical as Fitz removed clumps of half-eaten pasta in what had been a cheesy, creamy sauce, stuck to receipts from onboard bottle shops along with the daily newsletter. It also contained a number of used condoms, coffee cups and an empty cigarette carton.

'And I thought I was unhealthy. Hang on . . .' He dug around for anything in the corners. 'There's something else.' After groping around, he held something small and blue, flicking off the creamy coating with the lip of the white bag. It was a one-gigabyte SD card in an eight-gigabyte container. 'Someone upgraded. It could be empty, but it's still worth a look.'

'Surely they wouldn't be so stupid as to throw away incriminating photos?' It seemed too obvious. Anya was starting to suspect FitzHarris was setting her up, or playing some kind of charade.

FitzHarris raised his eyebrows. 'You'd be surprised. Maybe one of them chucked it out in a drunken haze, or accidentally.' He started to put the card away.

Anya pulled out her phone to take photos of the evidence. The company may want to hide what happened, but she intended to do everything she could, for the Chans' sake. It irked her if FitzHarris was just wasting her time. Although, she thought, he didn't have to reach in and pull out the memory card. She would never have known it was there. Alternatively, he could have planted it there to make it appear he was conducting a proper investigation. Her mind raced with the possibilities.

'What are you doing?' FitzHarris snapped off his gloves.

'Documenting what you found. I'm supposed to be a witness, remember, so I might as well record the date, time and location of the find. That bottle, especially, could become important evidence, don't you think?'

'Sure. Given the FBI don't care and we're here on our own,' Fitz added.

21

With the rubbish sorted, FitzHarris asked Anya if she would accompany him back to the medical centre. He took a digital camera from the centre's office and explained that the staff used it to photograph unusual rashes and get second opinions from major medical centres. What he did not go into was how he knew exactly where to find the camera in the filing cabinet.

He removed the SD card from his trouser pocket and replaced it with the one from the camera. Scanning through, it was empty.

'We knew it was a long shot . . .' He didn't sound that upset. 'We've got nothing on those lowlifes to say they were even with Lilly on deck one. She could have slept anywhere. Laura's going through the footage trying to find when she resurfaced on the pool deck, but it could take her a while.'

He switched the cards back and threw the empty one from Peterson's cabin in the rubbish bin.

He unlocked the filing cabinet and retrieved a hessian sack and his forensic kitbag from the bottom drawer. Inside the sack was a black biker jacket.

'Out of everything in his cabin – family snaps, wages, souvenirs – this is all he wanted?'

Anya shrugged. It made no sense to her either. The leather on the sleeves and collar were cracking, suggesting it was cheap and could have been bought at a tourist market. The jacket was lined with polar-fleece material, and had a black hoodie attached from the inside. Printed in bright colours on the back were a skull, flowers and, of all things, a unicorn. Small, round rhinestones were embedded in the textured paint, a poor imitation of an Ed Hardy design.

FitzHarris led the way to a room she had not been in before, a far cry from the pathology labs she was used to. A centrifuge, spectrophotometer and blood gas machine sat amidst other high-tech equipment.

'Are the markings gang-related?'

'I thought of that.' FitzHarris laid the jacket, with the back fully exposed, on the glass benchtop and took some photos. 'None I've seen, and he doesn't have any tattoos to match.' A few images later, he added, 'I'll send these off to a friend who owes me a favour. If it's a gang, he's sure to know who we're dealing with.'

'Could something be hidden inside the lining?' Anya asked.

'I had it taken to X-ray in the baggage compartment. Nothing but a docket and handkerchiefs in the pockets. And this.'

He held up an empty, palm-sized, clear plastic bag with a press-seal.

'I'm guessing Carlos was dealing, and trod on the wrong toes.'

Anya wasn't sure if his choice of words was accidental or deliberate.

'We can test it in the puffer.'

Anya knew the machine from airports, as a mobile form of spectrometry. It could detect the presence of substances ranging from explosives and chemicals used to make bombs, to illegal drugs like cocaine, heroin and methamphetamine. Doctors needed to know what they were dealing with which made sense to have the machine in the medical centre. Even so, knowing about the GHB would not have helped Lilly. By the time she was found, it was too late to save her.

Fitz swabbed inside and outside the bag and placed the material square in the reader.

A few seconds later, it beeped.

'There must be a mistake. Let's check this thing's been calibrated recently.'

He pressed some buttons, then repeated the process.

Again, it beeped on completion.

Fitz scratched the side of his head. 'Negative. No PCP, meth, ecstasy, cocaine, hash or heroin. Nothing.'

The bag was clean. The machines were so sensitive that even the most minute trace should have been detected.

Without a word, Fitz headed out the door. Anya slipped off one earring and placed it in her jeans pocket just as he reappeared with a brown paper bag. 'These are the clothes he was wearing when he was shot. If he handed over his stash, there could be something on these.'

He swabbed almost all of the outside of the clothing. Over dried blood, and inside the pockets.

Once again, the reading was unequivocally negative.

'I don't get it. Why does he want the jacket? What's there we aren't seeing?' He paced the length of the room and back. 'This guy is in dire need of money for his wife and kids. Desperate people do desperate things. What the hell did he do to get himself shot? And where's the money?'

'The shooter or his cabin mate could have taken it.'

'I doubt that. Carlos must have something the shooter wants, otherwise why not just kill him? He has to have some money.'

'And he knows it's safe. But where on the ship would he hide money, knowing it was guaranteed not to be found?'

With the amount of cleaning and safety checks on board, he had to have trusted someone else implicitly, or had a brilliant hiding place.

'Apart from the jacket,' Anya remembered. 'He mentioned flowers.'

'All they found was a painting by someone I never heard of. If you ask me, a three year old could have done a better job. It's full of shiny lumps and glitter. One of my boys showed the fine-art auctioneer who assures me it's rubbish, not worth the cost of the canvas. If Carlos converted cash into something he thought would appreciate in value, he was ripped off.'

Anya wondered about other things he could have bought for investment. Something they could have missed.

'Where else has the ship been recently, while Carlos was on board?'

'Let's see,' he looked at the ceiling, trying to recall. 'Egypt, north of Africa, Mediterranean, India, the Baltic Sea before that, Mexico.'

Metals and jewellery should have shown up on X-ray. He had to buy something that was sellable and likely to maintain if not increase in value. The painting must have had sentimental value. Maybe one of his children did it after all.

'In the good old days, people sewed money into their clothing. But now, the metal strips on the bills show up on X-ray. The guy's paranoid about customs, the Colombian government, hell, he's even scared of the owners of the cruise line. He's not talking. If he has a stash, chances are he's leaving this ship without it.'

Anya wondered if anyone could blame the poor garbage sorter for not talking. Someone he probably knew shot him in both legs. Not to kill, but to maim. Whoever the shooter was, they were still on the ship and able to get to Carlos again. The shooting was a way of ensuring his silence. It had been highly effective.

Fitz walked into Carlos's room, with the jacket in the bag by his side. Carlos was awake again. 'Listen, you need a friend and, right now, me and Doctor Crichton are all you've got.'

Carlos gagged, then projected green bile across the room.

Anya grabbed a plastic bowl from near the sink and held it for him. Each of his fingers turned a bluish white, and began to shake. His arms quickly became mottled.

'What's happening? Is it a fit?'

Anya felt his clammy hand. 'Carlos, can you hear me?'

With a look of terror, he nodded.

'I think you have a temperature, which is why your body's shaking. It should settle in a minute. All right?'

He nodded again.

Karen arrived, with paracetamol. FitzHarris pulled out the jacket and Carlos visibly relaxed.

'Your painting's safe too,' Anya remarked and the rigors settled.

On the way out, she tugged on her empty earlobe indicating the missing earring.

'I'll check the testing room,' FitzHarris said.

Anya opted for the office, and plucked the memory card from the bin. She didn't know what she could do with it but it was the only possible evidence they had and she wouldn't just let FitzHarris dispose of it.

22

After meeting up at the suite, Anya, Ben and Martin chose one of the cafés for lunch. Outside the Four Clover pub they could hear a violinist playing Irish jigs inside. The music quickly piqued Ben's interest.

'Jasmine plays the violin. Is she here?'

'Not today, but you can tell her what you heard next time you see her.'

No detail was spared in the decor. The wood and glass fascia closely resembled a number of Irish pubs she had been to, complete with the harp logo of Guinness beer on the front doorstep. Inside it looked like St Patrick's Day, with green streamers and balloons. Wooden chairs and tables filled the place, broken up by dark wooden poles. Ben thought it was like something from a Harry Potter movie, but Martin corrected him with a story about how they had all lived in England and travelled to Ireland while he was a baby. Anya remembered the trip well. It had been one of their happiest times as a family. She stroked Ben's hair as he read most of the words on the menu and asked her to explain the dishes he didn't understand, like shepherd's pie, Irish stew, herb dumpling stew, and corned beef and cabbage. Predicatably, he asked for a hamburger with wedges from the children's menu.

'We know Ben had a fantastic time in kids' club, but how was Mum's morning?' Martin peered over his menu.

'I learnt some things, and saw the sick man in the hospital, who asked for some things from his cabin.'

A waitress delivered a paper placemat for Ben printed with activities, complete with colouring pencils. She took their orders and promised to be right back with drinks.

'Anything to explain why he got sick?'

'That's what's strange. All he wanted was a black leather jacket and a painting that's worthless, according to the art dealer on board.'

'Maybe he ate the paint,' Ben contemplated as he coloured in a pirate. 'Our teacher says we'll get sick if we eat it.'

Anya and Martin glanced at each other.

'They only X-rayed his legs,' Anya said, suddenly realising. Carlos could have swallowed the drugs in condoms. If he had, he could quickly become ill – a burst condom could be fatal. The tremors could be explained by a rush of cocaine or heroin through his system, but they had quickly settled with paracetamol.

'Fitz swabbed his clothes and possessions for medicines, but every test came back negative. We also went through some refuse, and found a memory card for a camera but it was blank.'

The violinist approached their table and began to play, 'Danny Boy'. The men behind the bar sang along and encouraged customers to join in. As the song ended, Ben had a lemonade, Martin had a beer and Anya had a small glass of house wine. The musician moved to another part of the restaurant playing 'When Irish Eyes Are Smiling'.

'Why would anyone throw out a blank card?'

'It was the size that automatically comes with a camera and can't store many images. It was inside a container for one with a lot more memory.'

'Still, I would have kept it as a backup. Do you think it was deleted or never used?'

'That's what I'd like to know.'

The waitress delivered their meals, and Ben's cheeseburger

filled up most of his plate. The wedges came in a large bowl. Anya reached across and grabbed one, to Ben's surprise. 'It's the tax you have to pay your parents.'

'You're so funny, Mummy,' he said with a giant grin.

Martin had the Irish stew and explained the contents to their son. Anya's corned beef and potatoes made her mouth water as she took a bite.

With Ben occupied by his lunch, Martin said, 'I once accidentally deleted some photos. I thought they were gone, but when I rang the camera shop they said if you haven't re-written over the files, the originals can be retrieved using a special software. It's still on my computer, in case it ever happens again.'

'Do you think you could try with this memory card?'

'Be happy to.'

They smiled at each other. It was unlikely they'd find anything, Anya thought, but at least they were trying to find out what happened to Lilly.

As they ate, the restaurant filled to capacity. It was obviously popular with passengers, especially in rainy, windy weather.

'Mum, Dad, can we go ice-skating this afternoon?'

'Don't see why not unless your mum has other ideas.'

'Ice-skating in the middle of the ocean. Why not?'

'Thanks, Mum.' He rewarded her with a long sideways hug.

'We need to have a short rest in the suite though, so your stomach can process all that food, and dig out some warm clothes. Mum and I have to look something up on the computer, then we can go skating.'

They left the restaurant and stayed undercover back to their luxurious accommodation. Once again Anya was glad they had moved cabins. It made life a lot easier for Ben, and Martin was proving to be good company.

Martin switched on his computer and she handed him the SD card. A movie Ben loved was playing, so he was happy to sit with Anya, snuggled up for a while.

It wasn't long before Martin had something.

'Annie, I think you need to see this.'

She excused herself from Ben and took a seat next to his father at the table.

A close-up image filled the screen. It was a profile view of a blonde woman performing oral sex, two hands holding the sides of her head. There was no ring on the man's exposed left hand. Dreading the idea of seeing Lilly in any of the shots, Anya pressed the arrow button. Two similar shots were taken from above. The next was a large hand cupping a small naked breast. There was a wedding ring on this hand. Neither male nor female face was in the frame. The final two images were of a naked woman lying on her back, head to the side with legs splayed open. Hair covered part of her face, but the hair band was unmistakable. The sequined embellishment glistened with the flash. This was Kandy Ratzenberg. Anya breathed out. The fifteen-year-old girl had been with Lilly earlier that evening and claimed she had gone to bed straight after. Either she lied or, because of drugs in her system, could not remember what had happened that night.

'She's the one I saw in the corridor having sex.' Martin sounded as if he were confessing to something. 'I had no idea she was so young or that she could have been under the influence of drugs.' He clicked the arrow again. 'There's one more.' This time, Brian Peterson was on his knees, posing with his tongue licking one of Kandy's exposed nipples. A number of exposed legs were captured in the background: an audience cheering Peterson on.

23

'I haven't played air hockey in years,' Anya said.

'I'm not good at sports so we could be as bad as each other.' Kandy sounded optimistic.

With Ben dozing on the lounge, Anya had decided to duck out and see if Kandy was in the teen club. Thankfully, she was there and not averse to talking. Although she had been initially wary when she'd first seen Anya the relaxed atmosphere of the teen club seemed to put her at ease. The club had a milkshake bar, tens of computers, a psychedelic music centre with egg-shaped chairs suspended from chains, and electronic sports games. A boy in a dark leather jacket with jet-black hair and skinny jeans slouched at a screen, collar turned up. He repeatedly flicked a long fringe from his eyes as he clicked away. It was like an adult-free fun parlour with high-tech devices.

Anya purchased two tokens and put the first into the machine. A bright red puck popped out from a dispenser at Kandy's end of the table.

The girl knocked the puck near her own goal. 'Are you some kind of psychologist?'

Anya held the small white mallet. 'Definitely not, I'm a forensic doctor.'

'Like in all those shows?' Kandy backhanded the puck. It ricocheted off the side and Anya trapped it against the back corner, before sliding it forward.

'Like that, only a bit different. Do you enjoy watching crime shows?'

'Uh huh.'

A rally of four hits ended with a goal and then the buzzer.

'I didn't plan that,' Kandy apologised for the goal.

Anya hit off this time. 'They're not very realistic. Pathologists and lab technicians don't really carry guns and arrest suspects.' Trying to block the puck, she managed an own goal.

'Serious? I thought it was a kind of cool job. I don't like science but the forensic stuff is interesting.'

Anya hit off again, this time the puck landed in the centre of Kandy's goal.

'Two to one.' Kandy twirled the plastic mallet in her hand. 'Why did you want to see me?'

'We didn't get a chance to speak privately last time.' Anya struck the puck. It rebounded multiple times along all sides before slowing in the centre.

'My dad can get pretty intense. It's like there's only one opinion in the world – his.' Kandy leant forward and thumped the puck.

Anya slid the mallet along the back wall, hoping to keep the rally going. 'I know a lot of people like that.'

'Am I in some kind of trouble?' A few hits later, Kandy scored again.

Anya took a moment's rest. She hadn't expected air hockey to be quite so active. 'Do you think you should be?'

Kandy clenched her teeth and took a breath, as if about to disclose something. Instead, she remained quiet.

Anya placed the mallet and puck on the table. 'Do you know there are security cameras on the ship, in the public areas?' She moved around to Kandy. 'There's footage of you, Lilly and the group of men at the disco. We know some of the drinks were for you.'

The teenager dropped the mallet and turned her back to the table. 'I only had one, or two. I promise. I thought they'd leave us alone if we had a drink with them. They wouldn't take no for an answer . . .'

'Did you go straight to your cabin when Lilly left?'

'I didn't feel well, like I was really giddy. I guess the alcohol went to my head. I told them I wanted to go to bed so one of them said he'd help take me.'

Anya took a guess. 'Was that the one in the yellow shirt? Goes by "Genny"? He helped Lilly to the lift earlier.'

Kandy watched a group of boys playing a racing game. 'Yeah.'

Anya pulled the camera from her pocket and stood by the girl's side. 'Someone took photos.'

'What's that got to do with—?' Kandy looked at the screen. Suddenly, her face flushed and the pulse in her neck beat frantically.

Anya clicked to the next image and held the screen a little closer. It seemed unkind and confronting, but Kandy needed to know what had happened. She was a victim as much as Lilly, only Kandy had survived. She could help Anya and the Chans find out what had really happened, and who was responsible.

The young girl's breaths became shorter and sharper. 'That . . . it could be anyone.'

Anya forwarded to another graphic photo, unmistakably Kandy, lying on the floor naked, legs splayed.

Kandy slid down the table leg onto the floor, clutching her knees to her chest.

'I said I wanted to go to my bed, but he took me to his cabin.' She began to shake. 'Oh my God, what if my parents see these? Please, you can't let that happen. You don't understand. I said I wouldn't go into his room, with all those other people in there. He said it was a party and Lilly was already having a good time. He opened the door and I saw her. She was having sex with one of them and the others were playing a drinking game, I think. I didn't know what to do. I felt sick and dizzy, and wanted to go home. I was tired, but Genny didn't care. I tried to stop him, but it was like a weird dream. I was on the floor and he was taking my clothes off and kissing me . . . after a while . . . it stopped hurting. I must have fallen asleep on the floor because I woke up really cold. Genny wasn't there so I got dressed as fast as I could and somehow made it back to the cabin before Mom and Dad.'

Anya listened. Both girls had been so vulnerable. In small amounts, GHB could increase sensuality, which was why some men thought it turned a woman into a nymphomaniac. Kandy had had a glass and a half of alcohol on the surveillance tape. Either way, the fifteen year old was intoxicated and in no position to consent.

'You know, there's this ad we got shown at school where girls drink and end up in bed with strangers then hate themselves in the morning. I never thought I'd be one of those girls.'

Anya crouched down next to her. 'Did any of the others touch you that night?' she asked gently.

She thought for a while. 'No. They were busy inside with Lilly, but she drank less than I did.'

'Did they offer you any drugs?'

'Oh my God! You think I took drugs as well?'

'No, that's not what I'm saying. Did the men offer you anything else to drink?'

Kandy thought back. 'They were passing a bottle of water around and someone had a bottle with a worm in it, but I didn't want any.'

The water could have had the GHB in it. It was colourless and odourless. They were probably drinking tequila as well.

'A test found a drug inside Lilly's body. One that is sometimes used as a date-rape drug.'

'They drugged her? Oh my God. I had no idea.'

'We suspect they may have put something into the drinks at the bar.'

Kandy held a hand to her mouth. 'I think I'm going to be sick.'

Outside the consulting room, Anya waited. Rachel, the junior nurse, appeared.

'How is she?'

'Karen's talking to her about infection and pregnancy risk. It's within five days, so emergency contraception is still an option. With a little luck, in this weather, her parents might just think she's seasick.'

As much as Anya believed Kandy should tell her parents, she had to respect the young woman's autonomy.

'She still doesn't want them involved?'

Rachel shook her head. 'Can you blame her? Not that it matters, once FitzHarris gets here, she won't have a choice.'

'Who called him? I assumed you were bound by confidentiality.'

Rachel glared at her. 'Not us – you're his sidekick.'

Anya resented the accusation and all it implied. 'I've been dragged into this. I'm just trying to help the Chans and make sure the company doesn't sweep Lilly's death away. I didn't ask Carlos to tell me anything. For your information, FitzHarris has no right to any medical or personal information about Kandy, unless she gives permission.'

Rachel put both hands up. 'Sorry, I just thought . . .'

Anya felt heat rise in her face and neck. 'I know what everyone thinks. I'm not working for FitzHarris, or anyone. I'm just trying to do what's right for the victims and their families.' This was supposed to be a holiday, and right now, she was disappointing her son. They would almost be finished ice-skating by now.

Rachel lowered her gaze and made sure no one was listening. 'You don't understand the way things work around here. Last time something like this happened, an "anonymous source" told the media that the woman who had been date-raped brought the drugs on board herself, and was supplying. Last I read, she dropped the lawsuit.'

Anya needed to know: 'Was FitzHarris involved?'

Rachel looked at her anew. 'He wasn't on that cruise, but the Andersons only employ people who are loyal and happy to do their bidding.'

'Even if innocent people get hurt?' Anya said, although she was hardly surprised.

Rachel leant closer. 'You wouldn't believe—'

Karen came out of the office and closed the door. Her shirt was only half-tucked in, and had a wet mark on the shoulder, no doubt where Kandy had cried. Rachel suddenly had to be somewhere else.

'I wish there was more we can do, but it's too late to test for GHB,' Karen said.

The window for testing had long passed. With a short half-life, it could only be detected in blood for two to eight hours following ingestion, and was only excreted for eight to twelve hours in urine. There was no way of proving it had ever been in her system. The CCTV showed her drinking alcohol at the disco. That in no way lessened the crime the men committed, but experience told Anya it could be used as a weapon to suggest she was a willing participant.

'I just double-checked. There's still only an eighty percent chance the morning-after-pill will be effective this far along. We're within the effective timeframe, so it's lucky she told you when she did. She's still adamant about keeping this from her parents, particularly her father.'

Anya thought back to his comments about blaming the parents for their children's poor behaviour and its consequences. No one could blame Kandy for wanting the assault kept secret. She would, though, need careful follow-up with a sexual assault counsellor. Whether or not Kandy would seek that after the cruise was another potential problem.

'Did you give her contacts for when she gets back home?' Anya assumed any good nurse would, but had to ask the question.

Karen nodded. 'That's the downside to this job. You can't guarantee or ensure follow-up. My guess is she'll try to deal with this herself, then have major issues down the road.' She touched Anya's arm. 'Does Fitz know?'

'No, and he's not going to. Our duty of care is to Kandy.'

Karen nodded.

FitzHarris was not aware Anya had the memory card, or that Martin had retrieved incriminating photos of the night Lilly died. If someone had taken pictures of Kandy in the corridor, it was likely Lilly had been photographed as well. That would prove the men had been with her that night. Anya just had to figure out a way to expose them *and* keep Kandy's secret.

24

Anya still felt guilty about missing ice-skating, but Martin had explained to Ben that his mum was sad for not being there, but had to look after a very sick patient. Reliving the moment through the photos that Martin had kindly taken seemed to make Ben happy. With their son peacefully asleep, Martin and Anya curled up on separate lounges to watch a classic movie. Martin had bought a bottle of wine, which they shared after a glass of sangria.

Rain lashed the windows and wind continued to buffet the secure umbrella canvases. The storm was nowhere near over.

'All that's missing are toasted marshmallows,' Martin remarked while the opening credits scrolled.

Anya was deep in thought.

'Penny for them?'

She sipped her drink, not wanting to discuss how emotionally drained she felt, and how torn she was between being with Ben – who was happy, safe and healthy – and helping the Chan family get the answers they needed to grieve properly.

'I know you feel bad about not being able to spend time with Ben, but kids just want to know you're there if they need you. He's pretty independent, but you're his only mother, and he loves every minute you're together. He'll remember this trip for years.'

'I just see time slipping away, and I don't want him to think I was an absent mother.'

Martin thought for a moment. 'It's not natural for kids to

spend every minute with their parents. It's our job to prepare them for the world. Right now, he's exploring friendships at the kids' club. He's able to do his own thing, with a safety net, and us as backup. He's secure and knows how much we both love him. We both had parents who may have been physically there, but not emotionally available. Which do you think is more damaging to a child?'

Anya appreciated the comments, and felt the wine warm her veins.

They watched the first part of the movie as if they were in a cinema. Anya had to admit to enjoying the sanctuary of the suite, and appreciated Martin's ability to sit in comfortable silence. One thing she liked about him was that he didn't feel compelled to talk for the sake of it. They were far removed from the other passengers, in particular Brian Peterson, Genny and their friends. She thought of Kandy and wondered if she had the strength to tell her parents about the assault, or if she was suffering alone right now. For the moment, there was nothing else anyone could do to help.

'How's Nita?' Anya eventually broached.

'I'm not sure.' He traced the rim of his glass with a finger. 'We've decided to have a break.'

The revelation took her by complete surprise. 'I'm . . . um . . . sorry to hear that.'

'Are you?' Martin turned his gaze to her.

Anya struggled to come up with an honest answer. Since the cruise began, she was less sure about her feelings for Martin. In New York, she had a met a man, Ethan, and, while working together, thought they had a connection. They had only kissed, but the situation was complicated. So far he hadn't texted or emailed. She was beginning to suspect her feelings were unrequited, which added to her confusion about Martin. For the first time in years, he resembled the man she had fallen in love with.

'I—'

Banging on the door interrupted her thoughts. She hoped whoever it was would leave. The banging continued. 'I'll get it,' she reluctantly said.

Outside, Rachel, the nurse, stood soaked and shivering, clutching a black satchel. 'Please, help me.'

'Come in,' Anya urged. 'What happened?' Her first thought was of the bowling-shirt men.

Martin grabbed a fresh robe from the downstairs bathroom.

'I need your help. I don't know who else to trust.'

Anya took the robe and wrapped it around Rachel's shoulders, steering her to the lounge, where she sat, still trembling. It wasn't clear whether it was fear, shock, cold, or all three. She adjusted the thermostat on the wall.

'I'll get a hot drink.' Martin quickly went to boil the kettle.

'What were you doing outside in the storm?' Anya sat next to her.

'I've looked everywhere. My room mate hasn't been back to the cabin since last night. Something's wrong. I just know it.'

Martin and Anya exchanged glances.

'Have you told security?' Anya asked.

Rachel grabbed Anya's wrists. Her hands were chilled and red with the cold.

'I can't. You can't tell anyone. You have to promise me.'

Ben staggered to the railing, rubbing both eyes. 'Is it morning?'

Martin headed for the stairs. 'No, everything's fine. You go back to bed, and have a good sleep.' He sounded convincing enough.

Ben yawned and obliged.

'If someone is missing, we have to notify security, the captain. In this storm . . .' Anya stopped herself. There was no need to say out loud what she was thinking.

Rachel pulled her hands back and hugged herself with crossed arms, her chin and lower jaw vibrating with cold.

'We can't. Carlos was shot, then Lars Anderson and his family were killed. I'm scared. Really afraid something terrible's happened.'

Carlos was probably shot because of drugs. The Anderson family was supposedly killed by extremists. Lilly Chan's death was possibly an accidental overdose. There could be a simple explanation for Rachel's cabin mate staying out. Earlier Rachel had accused Anya of being Fitz's sidekick and now she seemed to trust her implicitly. The nurse was irrational and showing signs of paranoia. Anya thought back to the way she had reacted to the leg burns. She had been more upset than you would expect for a professional, although sleep deprivation and increased responsibilities were enough to make anyone more fragile than usual.

'Sometimes bad things just go in runs. It doesn't mean they're all connected.' Anya decided the best person to call was Karen. She may be able to help calm Rachel down. She may even know her medical history. If Martin could distract Rachel, she could call Karen on the upstairs phone.

'You don't understand. They are all linked. That's why Nuala is missing.'

Anya's attention snapped back to Rachel. 'Nuala? The woman who came to my room that night?'

Rachel nodded.

'I checked. There's no officer on board with that name. She's an imposter.'

'You have to understand. Nuala just wanted to help. She took a risk seeing you – if anyone found out . . .'

Anya did not appreciate why anyone would impersonate an officer, and lie to gain trust. Obviously, Rachel was involved in the deception.

Martin stepped forward. 'It sounds to me like you two are

scammers. Whatever it is you're up to, we don't want any part of it.'

'Look. I know how this must sound. We do want to help.' She lowered her gaze. 'Lilly isn't the first woman to die.'

Anya thought back to William when he first saw Lilly not breathing. He made the comment, 'not again'. When she asked him about it, he became evasive and suddenly had somewhere else to be. Rachel may be telling the truth.

'Other women have died on board?'

'The Chan girl is the only one since leaving Honolulu. But there were others before. They're just covered up, written off as suicides.'

Anya sat back. Even to her, it sounded far-fetched. Genny and his friends weren't serial killers, and Laura had said it was the men's first cruise with the Anderson line.

'The company's doing everything to help the Chans. There's a liaison officer boarding in Fiji and FitzHarris is investigating.'

'The liaison officer doesn't care about the Chans. It's really a lawyer in damage control. They'll offer them a free cruise, upgrade . . . anything to stop them from suing. If the family does go forward, they'll try to bankrupt them by dragging it out for as long as possible and ruining the girl's reputation. If that fails, they'll silence them with a confidential settlement. The last thing the company wants is the media involved.'

Anya had suspected the woman boarding in Fiji who Mats Anderson had mentioned in the fax was really a lawyer. Rachel was lucid, and knew what she was talking about.

Martin made a steaming cup of tea, which he placed on the coffee table. 'Sorry, I don't know how you have it, so I put some milk and sugar in.'

It was what his mother always did if someone was upset or had had a shock.

'Thanks.' Rachel picked up the cup with both hands.

'Why would they automatically sue? It's a criminal, not civil case.' Martin sat on the carpet, cross-legged.

Rachel was still shivering. Concerned more hot fluid could spill on the already burnt legs, Anya pulled a section of robe across the nurse's lap.

'FitzHarris may have told you he contacted the FBI and Interpol, but you can't trust him. He was recruited by Anderson himself and one thing the family demands is loyalty. It isn't in his own interest, or his bosses', to get the FBI involved.'

Anya thought of the speed with which the deck had been cleaned after Lilly's death. The power hoses had washed away any evidence, so passengers could continue having fun. Fitz seemed genuinely angry about it when he found out. Or, it could have been an act for her benefit. So could the impression he gave about trying to get on to Interpol. He said that foreign citizens were not protected by the same laws as US citizens so the FBI would not even be interested.

'The papers Nuala gave me . . . I put them in a bag, but they weren't in the luggage when we moved cabins.'

It had to have been an oversight. So many things were successfully packed up and moved to the new suite – passports, cash, credit cards. Junta would not have sacrificed her job to steal papers. It made no sense whatsoever that anyone was deliberately looking for them either. Fitz had organised the cabin move, but he could easily have saved himself the trouble and quietly searched the room when they were out. His master key meant he could access virtually anywhere on the ship.

'See? No one wants you to find out what really happens.'

'But what was in them was freely available on the net anyway.'

'That doesn't matter. Nuala started you thinking. It was

only a matter of time before you checked things for yourself and found out more.'

'Rachel has a point there,' Martin offered.

Anya had to admit she had become more involved in Lilly's investigation in part because of what had been in those papers. If Nuala had disappeared, it had to be reported. There would be a thorough search of the ship.

Martin looked perplexed. 'What I don't get is what Carlos has to do with it? He was shot gang-style. He had to be doing something dodgy on the side.'

'Nuala was paying him – for information.'

This was beginning to sound more plausible. Carlos could have been an informant and Nuala an undercover police officer.

Martin sat up. 'What sort of information?'

'I don't know, but he knew things about criminal activities.'

'Carlos worked in the recycling department.'

Anya had visited the area with Fitz and seen the ship's 'cockroaches' manually sorting the tons of rubbish into recyclable materials. She thought of how much information was present in Brian Peterson's garbage.

Martin frowned. 'How can you tell us about Nuala, but not say what she was paying Carlos for?'

Rachel clutched the robe more tightly. 'We barely see each other. When I'm in the cabin, she's out. And when I'm at work, she hides inside. She left me a cryptic note suggesting she had found out something big, but wanted to tell me in person.'

Martin stood. 'You're harbouring a stowaway?'

'It isn't like that,' Rachel's voice rose. 'There's no other way. She's on a blacklist so can't sail as a passenger.'

'How did you get her on board? Everyone needs photo ID and an electronic key to come on and off.'

'Lars Anderson organised it. And now he's dead. Don't

you see? Someone blew him up, for God's sake. Now Mishka is gone.'

Anya interrupted. 'Wait. Who's Mishka?'

Rachel took a deep breath. 'Her name isn't Nuala. She used that badge so you would listen to what she had to say. And in case you told anyone. Her real name is Mishka Valencia. She's my cousin.'

Anya felt a shiver down her spine. First Jasmine lost Lilly, now Rachel's cousin was missing. She had checked with FitzHarris. There was no staff member named Nuala on board. She felt her heart pound. Maybe she had alerted him to Mishka's presence. 'Where did she get the badge?'

'Nuala was a room steward a couple of years ago. I met her and we became friends. One night she came into the medical centre, hysterical. She told me one of the security officers had raped her. She was asleep and her door was deadlocked, but he let himself into her room. She woke up with him on top of her and couldn't fight him off.' Rachel lowered her eyes. 'I talked her into reporting it to our then head of security.'

Anya thought back to the day she met Junta. She was sure she had deadlocked the door. Clearly, cleaners and security could override the locks at any time. No one was really safe in their cabin.

'What happened after that?'

'I told her she could stay with me or that I'd sleep in one of the patient beds. Next morning, my bed was still made up. Nuala never got there.'

Rachel began to cry.

Martin passed a box of tissues to Rachel. 'Do you think she was murdered?'

Rachel looked up. 'There was no sign of her on board. There was a search but we were told she had jumped over-board. That she had made false allegations about the assault and felt guilty. The man who attacked her lied. He said they were having a relationship and he broke it off, so she wanted revenge. Her cabin was cleared out within hours.' The nurse reached into her pocket and opened her hand. In it was the name badge. 'She left it in the treatment room. It's all that's left of her. The family has nothing. They couldn't even bury the body.' She slipped the badge back into the pocket.

Anya sat closer. 'Is there a chance she did make it up, and maybe regretted it?'

'No. No way. You should have seen her injuries.' Rachel buried her face in her hands. 'It's my fault she's dead. I told her to report it.'

When FitzHarris checked employment records, he found a Nuala who had not renewed her contract. There was no mention of a death or a missing person. Either the records were incomplete, or he had lied about what had happened.

Now the woman who had paid Carlos for information, and worn Nuala's badge, was missing.

Somehow, Carlos must have seen or heard something that was worth killing for. She thought about his words before the anaesthetic. It was possible Lilly saw or heard something she should not have. *Kill her. Stop him.* Maybe he had seen what had happened to Lilly on that top deck.

Anya felt light-headed. Even in pain, Carlos was trying to disclose something important. Was he confessing something about Lilly's death? Or was someone else in danger? Someone like Mishka.

25

After getting Rachel dry and warm, Anya suggested they look for Mishka. Perhaps she had felt threatened and headed where it was safest: where crowds of people gathered. Martin had no idea what Mishka looked like so he stayed behind with Ben, who was deeply asleep.

'Be careful,' he said to Anya. He glanced at Rachel. 'You don't know what you're dealing with.'

For others on the ship, the evening had barely begun. Families strolled along the promenade, many slurping ice-creams as if it were a pier on a blistering summer's day. Anya had grabbed her waterproof jacket, and wrapped it around her waist. Pink, blue and green neon lights illuminated the shops on either side. Anya scanned every face that came toward them; in case it belonged to the woman she had met outside her cabin. Rachel was clearly doing the same.

'How are your legs?' Anya asked.

The burns had not yet had time to heal, but Rachel was walking well.

'Blisters are beginning to break. The dressings help.'

They stopped at the diner she and Ben had been to the other day. Done up like a 1950s soda shop, it had swivelling red seats at the counter, jukeboxes, and waitresses in poodle skirts, tight tops and matching scarves wrapped around high ponytails. Male staff manned the soda fountains.

Buddy Holly played over the speakers and guests occupied nearly every booth and seat. Anya and Rachel walked through to the back without seeing anyone they recognised. On their way out, a line of staff performed a hand-jive while passengers clapped and sang along.

Once outside the door, Anya asked Rachel what she thought about Mats Anderson.

'He'll be somewhere, still pulling the strings. He's been waiting to take over the business for years.' Rachel shook her now wavy hair. 'The police are saying it's some radical green group, but don't believe it.'

Anya had argued that same point with FitzHarris. She wanted to hear Rachel's reasoning. 'Why not?'

They moved along and into the next door, a general store.

'It wasn't well known, but Lars, the second son, was a strong supporter of the environment. I mean, I met him. He used to work on the ships and didn't tell anyone who he really was. Kind of like bosses going undercover.'

It was an ideal way to see how the business really ran.

They separated around the stands adorned with key rings, souvenir mugs, shirts and shorts. A number of women pored over a glass counter containing jewellery.

Rachel searched the faces of the other customers.

'He wasn't anything like his father or older brother. Lars wanted to make a difference. He believed the company could lead the way in clean technologies and renewable resources. He wanted the ships to become more self-sufficient.'

From what Anya had seen, the company utilised a lot of technology to recycle, and solar panels minimised electricity requirements. Behind a curtain change area, a pair of feet protruded, but they were more like a basketballer's in size than a woman's.

'Nothing here,' she said, joining Rachel at the exit. 'Self-sufficient in what way?'

'Have you seen the onboard park?'

It was where Anya had found Jasmine one morning. 'I've been through it.'

'There are thousands of plants that are nothing but ornamental. Each needs fertiliser. Lars had this vision of combining aquaponics and hydroponics to create an Eden Afloat.'

Where Anya came from, hydroponics were something used by people who grew marijuana crops indoors to evade the notice of the law. As a result, police monitored sales by hydroponic suppliers.

The pair waited to enter the main thoroughfare as a steady stream of people meandered along.

'Mishka thought it was a good idea too . . . She—'

Anya noticed Rachel's breathing accelerate with the mention of Mishka's name. She began to hyperventilate. A panic attack here would draw too much attention. Anya tried to distract her.

'Tell me, how does it all work?'

Rachel swallowed and tried to slow her breathing, just a little. 'It's simple.' Short breath. 'A fish tank the size of a wall.' Slightly longer breath. 'Isn't decoration. Water and fish droppings are pumped through hydroponic pipes.' Another, deeper breath. 'Bacteria in clay at the base of each root turn nitrogen into soluble plant food. By growing the plants vertically, you save loads of space.' Her breathing was becoming more controlled. 'One tomato tree can produce around thirty thousand tomatoes each year, which could be used to feed passengers.'

She sounded like a commercial for her cause, but had managed to control her panic. Still, Anya thought, the implications of one tree producing that much fruit were enormous, and not just for the boat. A cruise ship like that would attract worldwide attention for its innovation and progressiveness.

A parade of elderly people with walkers and wheelchairs passed.

'I've never heard of a "tomato tree".'

They continued their search along the boardwalk.

'Neither had I.'

Rachel was visibly calmer.

'There could be an orchard of them in the park. They'd provide shade, and save the company a fortune on food from ports. It wouldn't require a large block of land or a particular climate. And it wouldn't deplete food sources for the local communities.'

They picked up pace until the next shop. A glance in the window revealed a couple of men and a male assistant. The merchandise was scarves and ties.

Rachel continued, 'By keeping most of the plant off the ground, diseases and pests are non-existent.'

With the ship's number of balconies, and stories facing inward, the area for hydroponics was extensive. Anya wondered why no one else had thought of it.

Rachel needed to keep talking. Anya knew that people under extreme stress often reverted to what they knew best. A Christian might quote the Bible for solace. Environmentalism was Rachel's faith.

'Lars also wanted to invest in vacuum toilets. They reduce the amount of sewage per day. Did you know each week the ship produces enough to fill around ten swimming pools?'

Anya didn't feel like a lecture in sustainability, but the imagery of that many pools filled with human excrement was powerful. She thought of the small team in the waste centre trying to process it all. Judging by the number of people consuming hot dogs, fries, burgers and desserts, and probably on top of dinner, the figures began to seem reasonable.

They paused at a cart handing out french fries and studied the faces in line. 'You know how much cooking oil is used on board?'

Anya had no idea, but knew she was about to hear. Rachel

was like a religious zealot with two minutes to convert someone on their doorstep.

'It counts toward the grey water the ships produce. That includes water from the galley, laundry, showers, sinks and baths. Can you believe this ship alone makes enough to fill forty swimming pools every week? That's one million gallons.'

They moved on, passing an ice-cream cart, complete with server in red and white stripes. Each flavour was presented in a gallon container. A million of those filled by the grey water from just one ship in seven days, was mind-boggling.

'At the moment it's discarded, but Lars wanted to set up facilities in some of our ports for recycling. Used cooking oil can be turned into biodiesel, which releases less carbon dioxide than standard diesel. Every ton recycled equates to about ten thousand car miles. In a year, that's likely to be a hundred and eighty tons, or one point eight million car miles. That's like driving around the equator more than seventy times. Just from this company.'

The statistics were beginning to blur. Like Jeremy Wise, the environmental officer, Rachel had a penchant for numbers. Although, trying to encourage businesses to change their practices for the sake of the oceans and wildlife required facts and figures.

They continued to look at every face.

'Is the company taking up these initiatives?'

'Mats and his father refused. That's why Lars wanted us involved.'

Anya stopped and grabbed Rachel's arm. 'How? What were you and Carlos doing?'

The nurse took a staccato breath this time. 'Collecting evidence to prove the company was breaking laws. Lars was putting together a dossier. He threatened to release what we found to the media, in which case the company would be prosecuted. He was demanding control of waste and environmental management for the fleet and future invest-ment projects.'

The control part sounded reasonable, but the family may not have taken kindly to threats. Damaging the company would harm Lars's career aspirations too. The fax from Mats Anderson expressly said that image was everything.

'What did the family say?'

'Lars's father was starting to listen, but Mats was still opposed. They were supposed to discuss it on their yacht. The night Lars died.'

Anya began to wonder if it was more than luck that Mats Anderson had survived.

'Do you have a copy of the report?'

'Mish does, but I don't know where.' Rachel continued to pan the crowds as she spoke. 'There's no way she'd be hanging out here, knowing how worried I'd be.' Her eyes welled with tears. 'Something terrible's happened.'

'You said not many people knew Lars was a conserva-tionist. Maybe the group the police suspect attracted some extremists with something against the Andersons.'

Rachel shook her head. 'It's impossible. There's no way environmentalists killed them.'

She sounded convinced, as if she knew more than she let on.

'What makes you so sure?'

'It's all over the internet. The police think a group called ESOW are responsible.'

Anya had not heard of the group.

'The Institute for Environmental Sustainability and Oceanic Welfare is something Mish and I made up, so the media would take us seriously. We set up a website and started putting out press releases. Suddenly, top scientists were blogging with ways to save the oceans and it just took off. We registered the name in Liberia, like the cruise compa-nies. Only now, that makes us sound like the terrorists.'

26

Anya returned to the cabin, unsure what to do next. She needed to think about what Rachel had said about Lars Anderson's damning report. It was also possible that FitzHarris was being less than honest about police and FBI involvement in Lilly's death and Carlos's shooting. But how were they all connected, and what did FitzHarris actually know?

She regretted ever mentioning Nuala's name. It could have tipped him off that a stowaway was on board.

He had access to all the CCTVs and could have reviewed footage from the night she had described. Even though cameras didn't capture corridors off staterooms, it would not have been difficult to track where Mishka had come from or gone after. He would have known the deck number, at least.

Anya's head ached. What had Mishka paid Carlos for? And what had they both found out that was so dangerous?

There was still no evidence that Carlos had money, or drugs, or anything contraband that could have got him into trouble. Unless he passed that onto Mishka as evidence. If it wasn't in Rachel's cabin, Mishka had to have hidden it somewhere safe on board. Maybe the same place Carlos kept his money.

Neck and shoulders aching, she slid her key into the slot and opened the door. Inside, Martin was hunched on the lounge in front of the fire. In his lap was her computer. The sight caught her by surprise. She wondered if he'd seen any of her personal emails.

'Any luck?'

She shook her head and untied her jacket. 'What are you doing?'

'Annie, you have got to hear this.'

She flicked off her shoes by the door and joined him on the lounge. 'Rachel's telling the truth. A woman named Nuala McKenny went missing while at sea just over two years ago. The cruise line says they co-operated with police and that, according to staff who worked with her, Nuala was depressed over the break-up of a relationship. Suicide was the official cause of death. Blah, blah, blah, the cruise line regrets . . .'

It wouldn't have been the first suicide over lost love. Maybe she had an undiagnosed depression before that. 'Is there anything about the family's response?'

'They went public saying that Nuala was a happy, vibrant woman who had everything to live for. She was engaged to her high school sweetheart. The lovebirds had been together since they were twelve. The parents refused to believe she had been unfaithful. Last year they filed a wrongful death suit from Florida, and apparently there was a confidential settlement. Since then, I can't find any articles or comments on blogs. But Annie, you're not going to believe this. In four years alone, thirty-seven people have disappeared from cruise ships, never to be seen again.'

'How is that be possible?' If thirty-seven people had vanished, there would be an international furore. Surely.

Martin climbed over the back of the lounge and collected the bottle of wine. He refilled her glass from earlier in the evening and topped up his own.

'There are multiple investigations. A group has even lobbied US Congress for better laws and protection for passengers. There are a lot of people angry at the way cruise lines manage the disappearances.'

Anya knew too well that people went missing every day in cities. In Australia, someone went missing every fifteen minutes, but ninety-five percent were found within a short period of time. Millions of people cruised each year, with one main difference. In the middle of the ocean, there was only one place to go. It was the perfect place to commit murder, and sexual assault, it seemed.

The note Mishka had delivered when posing as Nuala had said you were guaranteed to get away with rape and murder.

That meant a lot of victims and their families would have felt denied of justice. All it took was one vigilante to kill the Andersons on that yacht. Maybe the police needed to look beyond environmentalists.

Martin climbed back over the lounge, and handed Anya her glass.

'A handful of those people disappeared on shore excursions. And some of the places cruises go have some dubious crime stats involving tourists. But the others . . . Here, let me show you.'

He pulled up a page from a victim's association. 'These are horrifying stories. Sometimes it's a couple who just vanish. Everything is left in the cabins. No sign of a struggle, they just disappear . . . into thin air. A disturbing number of the missing people are young women travelling alone. One husband says his wife didn't come back to the cabin after dinner, but people in nearby cabins heard them fighting earlier. She was never seen again.'

Domestic violence was so common, it was no surprise it occurred on holiday. In the dead of night, a body, or someone intoxicated or vulnerable, could be pushed over a railing or balcony without anyone knowing the truth. And if the body was never recovered, chances were charges would never be laid. Anya rubbed the back of her neck, wondering why Lilly was not thrown overboard.

Her idea of a happy family cruise was fast being shattered.

'And there's more. Do you know that the Anderson company doesn't pay US corporate tax? They function as if they're American but weasel out of tax.'

Anya knew cruise lines and ships were registered offshore. She had read that this company was multiple times the size of many iconic American businesses and could imagine the outcry if those companies were exempt from taxes.

'The way I see it,' Martin became more animated, 'they fall under "Shipping" and all its rules and subsidies. According to the *New York News*, the industry spends hundreds of millions of dollars each year lobbying Congress to keep their status and limit restrictions on all aspects of the business.'

Martin had always loved thrillers and conspiracy movies. He had a spark in his eyes.

Shipping was struggling. The fishermen back home were affected by climate changes, pollution and areas becoming fished out. Cruise ships were more like floating hotels, and subject to the same seasonal influences as the hospitality industry. Only, unlike normal resorts, they could maintain bookings by relocating to better weather. No one subsidised local restaurants or hotels when business was slow. But that's what the American people were, in effect, doing for the cruise lines.

If they were spending that much on lobbying it meant there was a lot more money at stake.

Anya's temples throbbed. Mishka was missing. Carlos had been shot. There was no proof that the bowling shirt men were the last to have seen Lilly Chan alive. She still could have seen or heard something, and been left for dead by the spa.

FitzHarris was watching Anya for Mats Anderson, who happened to be the only surviving heir, apart from his father's Russian bride and young daughter.

If Mishka was to be saved, someone had to find out what else FitzHarris was hiding.

27

Before breakfast Anya knocked on FitzHarris's door. There was no answer and the door was locked. She checked nearby offices and found Laura and the captain in a meeting with William and other staff. Captain Burghoff stood to attention when he saw Anya. 'Can we help you, Doctor?'

She contemplated telling him about Mishka's disappearance but hesitated. She would need evidence of a cover-up in FitzHarris's office if the captain was going to believe anything she had to say.

'Sorry to interrupt. I don't want to bother Fitz, but I think I left my camera in his office.'

Laura rolled her eyes. 'Good luck finding it under all the paper. Do you need to see him?'

'No, I just need to grab it,' Anya reassured her.

'He prefers old school security,' Laura explained, handing over a metal key. 'I need to stay here to document the minutes, but if you could drop it back when you're done . . .'

Anya thanked her before hurrying down the corridor.

She knocked for the second time in five minutes. No answer.

Slowly, she unlocked the door and turned the handle. Without hesitating, she entered and locked the door behind her, bending the key inside the lock. If FitzHarris returned, it would buy her time while he tried his own key.

She picked up the phone and rang reception asking to speak to Laura. They quickly transferred the call and it was diverted to voicemail. Perfect.

'Anya Crichton here, I'm locked inside Fitz's office. I don't know what happened, but the key is jammed inside the lock and won't budge.'

She hung up and surveyed the room. The paperwork seemed to have multiplied since her last visit. Boxes of files were stacked on the chairs. She checked the fax. Nothing in the tray. She riffled through a wad of papers; it appeared everything was ordered. The cumulative effect created the mess. Manuals on security systems, alarms and safety equipment were furthest away from his side of the desk.

A file titled 'Incident Reports' was positioned closest to his chair. It was thick, and contained workers' statements and medical notes. Documentation on Lilly Chan and Carlos were not in this folder.

She lifted a folder underneath, one marked 'Anderson', and opened it. In the corridor, the sound of a clunk stopped her. Someone was trying to open the door from the outside.

The phone rang, and she startled. It could be Laura ringing back. Lifting the receiver, she answered in a quiet voice.

'You're still there. This is why we did away with metal keys. A technician's on his way, but it could be half an hour before he arrives.'

'I think Fitz might be outside right now, trying to get in.'

'I better tell him before he kicks the door in. He's in just the mood to do it.'

Anya hung up, knowing she had a few minutes grace. She had not bargained on anyone kicking the door in, but assumed it was stronger than FitzHarris's legs.

Inside the Anderson file, in chronological order, were tens of faxes. All from Mats, the surviving son. The first came six months ago and was effusive in its flattery of FitzHarris. It mentioned his diligence and attention to detail and waved the carrot of a bonus if the cruises continued to run smoothly. It was as if Mats were courting him.

There were no replies from FitzHarris. The correspondence in the file was all one way. She closed it and replaced the Incidents file on top. In the process, she bumped into a full coffee cup, splashing some onto the top of a tattered blue folder to the left of the others. She tried the top drawer for something to wipe it with and pulled out a crumpled napkin. She dabbed the coffee mark and hoped he wouldn't notice, especially since there were other stains on the cover. This file wasn't labelled but was positioned as if he were working on it.

There was a *thump, thump* at the door.

'You have got to be kidding. You gave her the key?'

FitzHarris sounded livid. Laura's voice was muffled, but was followed by audible expletives from Fitz.

'Sorry about all the trouble, but I found my camera!' she shouted, and the others became quiet.

Anya looked inside the blue folder. A headshot photo of a toddler with a cheeky grin was attached to an autopsy report. For a moment she thought it was a cruise victim, but there were two other pictures and reports. The three deceased had the same surname.

The medical examiner's form deemed two deaths – the child and a woman – homicide. The adult male had been classed as a suicide. They all had lived in New York and died at the same address.

This had nothing to do with cruises. It was the family Laura had mentioned. The scene at which FitzHarris had been seriously injured.

Bang! Bang! The banging grew louder. This time, the handle was rattled.

From Anya's experience, deadlocks like the one on this door were designed so they could not be levered off or unscrewed. That meant the technician would have to drill through with multiple-sized bits to knock the pins out of place and disable the lock. That gave her enough time to search the office.

As if on cue, the first drill began.

Anya returned to the filing cabinet. So far there was nothing on Lilly or Carlos. She slid her hand beneath the suspended files and located an A4 envelope. It contained the boarding ID photos of her and Martin, along with a copy of their marriage certificate and date of divorce. Both of their work and home addresses were circled, along with a map of where Martin and Ben lived. It also contained the note that Nuala had delivered. The one supposedly misplaced when they had moved cabins.

She slid into Fitz's chair, feeling as if she'd been kicked in the chest. FitzHarris had gone through all her possessions. She felt violated. If the lock wasn't dismantled soon, she would try and kick it down herself.

Her mind tried to recall all of their conversations as her eyes fixed on the handwritten note.

Trust no one.

Palpitations pounded in her chest. Fear filled her. FitzHarris was working for Mats Anderson and being bribed to make problems go away, whatever that meant. He wasn't an investigator, he was a fixer.

She had alerted him to an imposter on board. Now Mishka was missing.

Anya wondered if he was paid enough to commit murder.

28

Ten minutes later, the technician drilled the final piece in it, from the other side.

By now, Anya was perspiring, wondering what to do next. Surely enough people on board had seen her and knew her by now to protect her. FitzHarris would ruin his set-up if he harmed her. Even so, she would email her friend Ethan Rye in New York as soon as she got to her computer.

The door opened, and Anya breathed a genuine sigh of relief. She wanted to get out into the corridor where she felt she could breathe properly.

'Are you all right?' Laura sounded concerned.

'Just got a little claustrophobic after the first few minutes.'

FitzHarris was not so kind. 'What the hell were you doing?' He scowled. 'Find what you wanted?'

Anya refused to meet his eyes. Instead, she pulled her camera from her pocket. The security officer grabbed it and immediately checked the pictures. There were none taken inside his office.

He took a slow deep breath out. 'You and I need to talk.' He ordered the technician to take a break and Laura scampered at his tone.

Anya wanted to flee too. 'We have nothing to say,' she said. 'I need to go be with my son.'

'And your *ex*-husband.'

Anya glared at him. 'You had no right to go through my things.'

'Inside. Now!'

Anya resisted, but he pushed her by the arm and kicked the door closed behind them. She looked around the room for something she could use as a weapon if he tried to attack her.

'Who are you really working for?' he almost spat as he scanned the room.

Anya pulled her arm free. 'Me? You can't be serious. I came on a holiday and you know it. Do you know the addresses and personal details of every passenger, or did we get special treatment?'

'Most passengers don't have their holidays paid for by a private investigator's company. And the reason people divorce is because they can't stand to be together. This friendly routine with your ex isn't fooling me. The charade ends now.'

Anya began to suspect FitzHarris was disturbed. 'You think this is an act?'

'Who are you working for?'

Suddenly, it made a little sense. FitzHarris had assumed she was a whistleblower from what he had read in the papers. Ethan Rye had bought the cruise tickets on behalf of the owner of the Jersey Bombers, so the bill was in the name of his private investigation company.

'You think I'm out to sabotage the company?' She almost laughed and some of her fear subsided.

'You tell me. It's a nice cover, the whole family thing.'

'You can check out Ethan Rye. He works for the Jersey Bombers, and is like a son to the owner. He handles all of the owner's private affairs, and this trip was a thankyou bonus for the work I did with them. Ring the Bombers, they'll verify it.'

FitzHarris squinted. 'And Martin?'

'He has custody of our son. We've begun to get along,

which is cheaper and far healthier for Ben than us fighting over access in the courts.'

Anya moved a box of files onto a spare bit of floor and sat in the chair. 'Why would I arrange for a visitor in the night to deliver me some cryptic message about not trusting anyone.'

'Maybe you have a mole in your organisation.'

'You are the mole in yours.' Anya fired back.

FitzHarris crossed his arms and widened his stance. 'What the hell is that supposed to mean?'

'You're working for Mats Anderson.' Anya stood up, reached over and pulled the file out from under the Incidents folder. 'You had no intention of investigating Lilly Chan's death or finding out who shot Carlos. That's why the FBI hasn't been in touch, or Interpol.'

FitzHarris rubbed his face with his hands. 'I've been busting my butt to get answers.' He moved over and slumped into his own chair. 'I'm hog-tied. Because these ships are registered offshore, they're foreign. What I told you is true. The FBI will only come on board to investigate a crime involving a US citizen. Right now, Lilly Chan wouldn't appeal to them even if she were American. There's nothing to prove she was murdered or sexually assaulted. *Nothing.*'

The man had a point.

A knock at the door interrupted them.

'Come in!' Fitz said, louder than necessary given the gaping hole in the door where the lock used to be.

Laura appeared with a clipboard, which she handed across. Anya suspected she was checking on both of them. FitzHarris flicked through a series of pages and initialled each one. The IT expert took back the clipboard and left.

Anya waited while FitzHarris dialled the switchboard. 'I want to speak to Lyle Buffet, from the Jersey Bombers, New Jersey.'

A few minutes passed and he was finally connected. The part of the conversation she could hear began with him asking if Buffet knew anything about Anya Crichton and where she went after leaving New York. FitzHarris covered his eyes with one hand, and listened to the person on the other end of the line, only contributing the occasional, 'Uh huh,' and 'Yes, sir.'

'Thank you, sir. Keep up all your great work.' He hung up and glanced back at Anya. 'He verified sending you on a cruise from Hawaii and how an Ethan Rye was supposed to organise it.'

Anya stood up to leave.

'We're not finished,' FitzHarris said calmly. 'If that woman came to your cabin uninvited, it could have been a warning or a threat.'

She had already considered that and decided to quiz him.

'You said Nuala failed to renew her contract.'

'I believe that's what I said.' His expression did not change. 'Have you seen her impostor again?'

'No, but I wondered why she would use Nuala's name.' She watched his face for any reaction.

'She found an old badge and dressed up for a laugh.' He changed the subject. 'It always amazes me how many women fall all over a man in uniform. The officers could be full-time Romeos if they took up all the offers they get.'

Before, he had seemed concerned about someone impersonating an officer. Anya decided to push him.

'It doesn't bother you anymore that a woman misrepresented herself as crew?'

'Of course it does. But what can I do? There are over three thousand passengers on board, one of whom is an amateur international lawyer. If we screened passengers for fantasies, we'd be out of business. Did she hurt anyone? No. You said she hasn't bothered you since.' He looked up, with hollow eyes. 'Excuse me if I have a few bigger fish to fry right now.'

He opened the top drawer and pulled out a mint, unwrapped it and popped it in his mouth.

'I think Nuala was a deliberate choice,' Anya began, 'because a Nuala McKenny reported a rape, then disappeared overboard.'

'Whoever you've been talking to is feeding you a line.'

'Just a minute.' Anya felt her anger rise. He was dismissing the rape. Maybe he had helped cover it up. 'I wanted to know why someone would use her name. I looked her up online. Just like anyone can.'

He stared at her, one eye squinting. 'Well, I heard differently. From what I read, she busts up with her boyfriend, makes some wild accusations then jumps overboard. A number of colleagues said she'd been depressed and her work wasn't up to scratch.'

Anya was convinced Rachel had told the truth. 'Which the family seemed to adamantly deny.'

'Since when does a grieving family ever stand up and say, yeah, we should have done more, we should have seen the signs, but we were too busy with our heads up our own backsides to notice.' With a lowered voice, he continued the aggression. 'Has it occurred to you that sometimes people don't want to be helped? Maybe you should spend less time sticking your nose into other people's business, and pay more attention to your own family.'

Anya couldn't believe his newfound arrogance. The back of her neck began to itch. She headed out the door, and he followed. Spinning on her heel, she pointed her index finger near his chest. 'Let's get something straight. You asked me for help and I've done everything I can, and more. Now you tell me to get lost.' She turned, not caring if anyone heard her. 'You're the one with his head up his arse. I hope you enjoy the view.' She took off down the corridor, fuming. He was a pig of a man. She didn't know why she hadn't seen it sooner. There was no way she could risk telling him about Mishka.

'Anya, wait!'

She ignored him and continued to the lift. He followed and made the lift just as the doors closed.

'I'm sorry. I was a jerk. You didn't deserve that.'

They rode in silence to the atrium floor. She headed aft and he kept pace.

As she stopped to end the conversation once and for all, a loud crash and shouting came through the side door of the restaurant.

'You did that on purpose. You broke my plates.'

'You should not have left them there.'

'You will pay for them.'

'No! I will not. If you were not so stupid. You were stealing my cutlery.'

Fitz pulled her by the arm. 'Come with me.' His limp was more pronounced this morning as he led her into the side door. The restaurant was preparing for yet another meal.

'They could come to blows over this one.' Fitz said, releasing his grip.

'Over a broken plate or two?'

He sighed. 'Wouldn't be the first time. Dining room staff have to pay for breakages and losses. That way they're a hell of a lot more careful. If they don't have enough for their service, they get blasted by the maître d'. Speaking of whom . . .'

The maître d' had already heard the commotion and was speeding toward the arguing staff.

'We'll let the boss handle this one.' Fitz pulled out a chair at the table closest to the door. 'Look, I'm apologising. I had no right to go off at you like that.'

Anya chose to remain standing.

A waiter passed and bumped Fitz's extended right leg. He winced and perspiration soaked his forehead.

'I'll get you some water.' Anya moved to a station with rows of water in jugs and filled a glass.

'Thanks.' He took a few large gulps and rubbed his leg, which seemed to provide some relief. He then gestured for her to join him at the table, which she did.

'People die every day in the city, some aren't found in their apartments for years. No one bats an eyelid.'

'Fitz, thirty-seven people disappeared without a trace from cruise ships alone in the last two years.'

'Yeah, well. You've already seen what alcohol, drugs and gambling can do. Some guy loses the family savings in the casino. A wife tries one more time to make the marriage work, then finds he has no intention of saving the relationship. Some have a fight and on the spur of the moment do something stupid. Some are simple accidents. Remember planking? Morons proved Darwin's theory by trying that one on balcony railings. In one case, a mental patient threw someone over the side. Do you think we should screen guests for stupidity, addictions and mental illness? That should cut down the problems. Oh yeah, and maybe ninety percent of the clientele.'

'Point taken. But Lilly Chan's death proves how difficult it is to investigate suspicious deaths on a ship.'

The salt shaker warranted his attention. 'Ships can be pretty goddamn lonely if things are going bad – and they're a pressure cooker when relationships get involved. How many cops and doctors have ended it all and everyone stands back scratching their heads wondering why? Sometimes there is no "why".' He sighed. 'All I'm saying is that for some reason, a cruise is supposed to be an escape from everything bad in people's lives. Well, guess what? There is no paradise. Problems and the past stick like shit to a baby blanket, wherever anyone goes.'

'Fine, but what if Nuala was raped? Was there a proper investigation?'

'I wasn't here, but when her colleagues said she was depressed and the crew member confirmed the relationship split, the investigation wrapped.'

'What about a rape kit?'

He sipped more water. 'Nothing in the file. If she reported a rape but wasn't prepared to be examined, it also suggests that she'd falsified the accusation. Who knows? If she had gone to the medical centre, maybe things would have been different.'

Anya went and filled a glass of water for herself, trying not to show what she was thinking. Rachel said she had seen Nuala's injuries in the examination room, and that they were consistent with a violent sexual assault. But the notes had vanished, just like Nuala. Someone had to have covered up or disposed of that evidence. Or someone in the company hierarchy did it for them.

'So it's just assumed she committed suicide.'

'Who knows what someone in that state of mind is thinking. Suicide is anything but rational.' He reached into his pocket and pulled out a small vial of pills. 'They say drowning is incredibly peaceful. There are worse ways to die.'

As a pathologist, Anya believed otherwise. 'I disagree. Drowning is horrific. Initially, the victims hold their breath until involuntary inspiration takes over. That means they gasp, filling their lungs with water. If the're lucky, they get laryngeal spasm as the cardiorespiratory system collapses. It's likely they swallow and vomit, aspirating the vomitus into their lungs. And this is all before they lose consciousness. Then they have a respiratory arrest and cardiac death occurs after a few more minutes. Drowning is anything but peaceful.'

'Yeah well, as fascinating as the lecture is, I have work to do.' He stood up and stumbled, his weight buckling. With a teeth-gritting moan, he hit the floor.

Anya tried to help, but he pushed her away. A waiter was greeted with the same response. He was like a sad drunk at the end of a big night, too proud to admit it.

Red-faced, he hauled himself up, back onto the chair and quickly downed two pills.

Anya asked the waiter to bring a sandwich. She appreciated FitzHarris had two major cases to investigate, but something else had him rattled. Today his behaviour was more belligerent and almost self-destructive, as if guilt was getting to him.

'How can you work for Mats Anderson?'

Blood engorged his face. Anya moved her chair back.

'You have no right to judge me. You don't know anything about me.'

'I know how your leg was injured. Did that jade you? After all your years of service, you were invalided out.'

'We're even then. I went through your personal things . . .'

Anya expected more anger, but he remained silent for a while as if debating whether or not to speak. Eventually, he reached into the inside pocket of his jacket and removed a photograph of a mother and a little boy.

'I was close by when I got the call about a domestic.'

He put the photo on the table and his hands gravitated toward the salt shaker. He studied the crystals inside, as if watching the scene again. With a flat tone, he began to speak. 'I walked in and saw her . . . Elise. She was on the floor in the kitchen. There was blood everywhere, like she had put up a hell of a fight. I knew straightaway she was dead, but her eyes just stared at me, begging for help. That was my fatal mistake.'

Anya swallowed, knowing what came next.

'I should have checked the rest of the house. Before I could react, the bastard husband came out of nowhere and stabbed me more times than I can remember. I tried to fend him off, but he caught me off guard. You see, I was on my knees with Elise.' The salt shaker rotated a couple more times. 'I blacked out. Guess he thought he'd killed me too so he cut his own throat.'

Eventually, Fitz looked up. 'Only thing is, there was a son. His name was Ricky. He was two years old with all this curly hair. A lot like your boy.' He took a deep breath and sucked air in through his teeth. 'Ricky was stabbed while he slept but could have been alive when I got there. Elise tried to protect him, but she didn't stand a chance.' His voice trailed off.

'Is this them in the photo?'

Fitz passed it across. 'It was the last one taken.'

Two faces grinned at the camera. The mother was pretty and looked so happy holding the little boy in her arms. He had a cheeky face.

'Ricky would have turned five today.' Fitz said, with a vacant expression. His face was gaunt and grey.

Anya blinked to prevent her own tears spilling. Crimes affected not just the victims and families, but everyone in their wake. That included the doctors who fought to save Fitz's life, the pathologists, crime scene technicians, and, obviously, the police.

By carrying their picture, Fitz was never going to forget. Or forgive himself for what he thought he did wrong. She had seen that all-consuming guilt many times before, especially in her own family. Anya fought back tears. Ricky would always be two years old. She hoped he hadn't suffered and had died quickly in his sleep.

A third person had been cut out of the frame, presumably the man who had killed them. She looked closely at the faces – the mother had a broad grin and dimpled chin. The expression was familiar. Suddenly, it became obvious.

FitzHarris had failed to disclose a crucial fact to Laura.

'Elise looks a lot like you,' Anya said.

'You think so? I thought she got her mother's brains and looks. Both of them hated me being a cop. They were convinced I'd get killed on the job one day. Ironic, huh? I've outlived them all.'

Anya passed back the photo, which Fitz studied again.

'Ricky was the spit of me as a kid.' He half-smiled. 'It drove Elise mad that he was just like his pop.'

The sandwich arrived, and FitzHarris devoured it, barely taking time to chew.

'There's something that's really bothering me about Lilly Chan. We can't prove she was with any of the bowling shirts when she died,' he said before swallowing.

Anya had not yet told him about the photos of Kandy, but without the girl's agreement to give a formal statement, there was nothing to link those men with Lilly.

'We've overlooked the secret admirer. The one who wrote that note and wanted to get her to the pool spa,' he continued. 'Gut feeling tells me we find him, we get the answers we've been looking for.'

29

Anya stood at the glass wall and watched the winds gust through the outside area, continuing to batter the folded umbrellas and rattling the chains that anchored the stacked chairs and lounges. Cords banged against the empty metal flagpoles in an irritating, syncopated rhythm. She felt emotionally wrung out after her time with Fitz and was almost relieved that Martin and Ben were still out at brunch together.

A worker in full wet-weather gear pushed against the wind to move a few feet forward around the pool, its contents were being displaced and replaced with more rain. The monotonous repetition was no longer hypnotic. For the first time, her stomach seemed to roll with the movement and she wanted to be anywhere but on the boat. A wave sloshed over the side, knocking the man to the deck. A second worker forced his way over to help. Hoods covered both crew's faces. More of the faceless staff who worked in third-class conditions on a first-class resort.

She thought of Mishka. In this weather, she could have easily lost her footing and slipped beneath a railing. With everyone inside avoiding the weather, no one would hear cries for help. The double insulated glass ensured it. Rachel had risked her own life searching for Mishka. Anya would have done the same if there was any chance of bringing Miriam back alive.

Trying to put herself in Mishka's shoes was not easy. Her

secret employer had just been murdered, and she and Rachel were accused of extortion and mass murder. And Carlos, her paid informant, had been shot. She had to be terrified. All of her support network, apart from Rachel, was gone.

She knew too well the pain Rachel was going through. Her father coped with Miriam's disappearance by convincing himself that his three year old had been murdered – quickly. She pictured their mother, setting the table at home tonight, like every other, in case Miriam found her way back home.

Wind howled outside and Anya shivered. Each new year brought hope that Miriam's tiny remains would be found, so they could all finally have some degree of peace. Up until now, that was all she had wanted. But David FitzHarris had proven that having bodies to bury did little to numb the pain.

Anya decided to see how Jasmine was doing. Ben had been begging to see her again to play some more piano. If she enjoyed the distraction, it could be good for both of them.

She flinched at the ring of the phone. Karen asked if she could come urgently to the medical centre. Rachel wasn't well.

Anya grabbed her jacket and room key, scribbled a note for Martin, and headed to the lifts. A few minutes later, she entered the medical centre through the double doors. An elderly lady sat in the waiting area with her arm in a sling. Karen was nowhere in sight.

Doctor Novak strolled out of one room holding up an X-ray.

'Excuse me, but can you tell me where Rachel and Karen are?'

'Neurotic passengers take up my day. Now I must deal with hysterical staff,' he scoffed. 'There.' He pointed to the third consulting room and turned his attention back to the film in his hand.

'Nasty humeral fracture, could need open reduction,' she

commented on the X-ray, just to be annoying, before knocking on the closed door.

Rachel sat in a chair, head between her legs, breathing into a brown paper bag.

Karen sat opposite, stroking her back. 'That's it, deep breaths. In, two, three, four; out, two, three, four.'

She saw Anya. 'We were dressing Carlos's wounds when it just came on. She felt palpitations and had a heart rate of two hundred and was struggling to breathe. She's never been like this before.'

'Hi Rachel, I came as fast as I could.' Anya turned to Karen. 'Did anything upset her? A phone call, patient or visitor from earlier?'

'We had the normal clinic: coughs, colds, Cockroach and the regular hypochondriacs. David FitzHarris dropped in for a coffee and a chat, to see how Carlos was doing. I stepped outside to see a woman who had fallen out of her wheel-chair.' She stood up. 'Rach, you're doing well. I'm just going out to see the X-ray, Anya will be here with you.' She looked up for confirmation.

'I'm here.' Anya sat and placed a finger on Rachel's wrist as the senior nurse left the room. 'Heart rate's pretty normal.'

Rachel looked up from the bag, mascara smeared around her eyes.

'FitzHarris knows.'

'About Mishka?'

'No, I mean . . . I don't know. He was asking me all these questions about Nuala McKenny.'

'What exactly?'

'He knew I was working on that sailing and wanted to know if she had come in to be seen, and what our protocol was for rape examinations.' Rachel took a deep breath. 'I told him she came in and that she wanted me to examine her, not the male doctor, and he got . . . I don't know . . . he started pacing, and getting angry. Then he said there was no medical record so maybe I wasn't remembering Nuala right. I got scared about what he wanted me to say, so I said it was years ago and I could have made a mistake.' She took a few, sharp breaths. 'He wouldn't let it go. He just kept asking me over and over again what happened that night. And whether Nuala and I were friends.'

'Slow breaths again.' Anya had told FitzHarris about the rape accusation but he hadn't necessarily connected the Nuala impostor with Rachel. 'Maybe he doesn't know anything about Mishka or the ESOW.'

'Then why did he say that if I was lying about anything, or knew more than I was letting on, he'd make sure I was charged with falsifying medical records and a whole heap of other things?'

Anya considered the logical sequence. 'He looked up the records and found out you worked the night she disappeared. It makes sense to ask you what you remember because there was no medical report that Nuala had been seen.'

'But I wrote one. It took hours because I didn't want to get it wrong. It was my first rape case.'

Anya suspected FitzHarris was upfront enough to confront Rachel directly about Mishka if he knew she existed. There was a chance he was putting pressure on Rachel to see if she'd crack about other things as well.

'I don't trust him.' The hyperventilation started again.

'Breathe slowly, in and out. You'll pass out if you don't.'

Anya was not sure if she should trust him either. He had been employed on the basis of his anti-terrorism experience. Someone was setting up ESOW to look like violent mass murderers. If the police were closing in on the members, FitzHarris could have been given information on Rachel. He knew she was trapped on board until the next port so he had time to catch her off guard. Like a cat toying with a terrified mouse.

Rachel reached around her neck and removed something silver from a chain. 'Can you look after this?'

Anya saw it was a key.

'Mishka told me to never give it to anyone, but I trust you. I can't risk FitzHarris or anyone from the company finding it.'

Anya listened for Karen's footsteps or voice. 'What does it unlock?'

'All I know is it was important. To Lars as well. We got paid extra for keeping what's in there safe.'

Karen tapped and entered. Anya slipped the key into her jacket.

'Rachel's feeling better,' she said. 'It sounds like a simple panic attack, but if you get it again, it might be an idea to have an ECG to exclude supraventricular tachycardia.'

'Sounds like a good plan to me. We're all a bit stressed and overtired, but not long 'til backup arrives in Fiji.'

Outside the room, Karen asked for a quiet word. 'Thanks for coming. She asked for you.'

'I'm happy to help.'

Karen didn't seem satisfied. 'Something's really bothering her. Has done since she burnt herself. And I can't help wondering if it has anything to do with the Anderson deaths.'

Anya wondered what she was getting at.

Karen raised her hands. 'I'm not prying, but I know she's not herself. I care a lot about Rachel, and if there is anything I can do to help . . . Anything, day or night, please call me. It could just be cabin fever, which affects all of us at times, but something tells me it's more than that.'

'Can I ask you something? What happens to all your medical reports and test results? Are they kept in paper form as well, or just on computer?'

'They're all on computer these days, have been for a few years now. Reports go to a number of places. Security, the hotel manager, the captain and head office. Everything gets double and triple checked. It's the bane of our life.' Karen added, 'Don't suppose you know why Fitz barged in here harassing my nurse?'

Anya shrugged. 'Who knows? I think he's having a pretty rough day though.'

The nurse gave a knowing nod. 'Someone should tell him that just because you have pain doesn't mean you have to be one. Before I forget, say hi to your gorgeous husband for me.'

'Ex-husband,' Anya replied.

'If you say so.' Karen was already on her way to the next patient.

30

Still in the medical centre, Anya asked if Rachel wanted her to stay while she rested. She was grateful, and gave Anya her internet logon code before she lay on the examination couch and closed her eyes. There were a few emails, all work-related. Some from her secretary, others from colleagues asking for second opinions on cases. Nothing personal.

Anya hadn't yet written to Ethan Rye to explain what she had learnt about Lilly, Carlos and Mats Anderson, in case anything happened to her. If someone was monitoring outgoing messages that could put her, Rachel and Carlos at further risk. Mats Anderson's contacts were wide-ranging and high-ranking. She decided against it.

Finding Mishka was the priority, if she was still on board. Rachel was terrified of being arrested at any moment. Anya looked up the latest headlines on the Anderson bombing. Thousands of entries were listed. It was big news on a number of fronts.

Paco knocked and entered with a coffee and plate of biscuits.

Anya thanked him.

'Have you heard the latest news?' He lowered his voice when he saw Rachel. 'The police know who killed Mr Anderson and his family.'

'Who did it?' Anya moved toward the door, trying not to disturb the sleeping nurse.

'I tell you. Some group calling themselves ESY, or

something like that. The police have proof and are about to arrest the bad guys.'

Anya's heart raced. 'Could it be ESOW?' How could the police have missed that it was funded by Lars Anderson?

Paco waved his hand. 'That's it, sorry, my English is not so good. They are hugging tree people, and murderers.'

The investigation would have to involve the FBI and CIA if it was considered terrorism against US citizens, and Interpol. With the resources at their disposal, they should have known about Lars's involvement.

Anya glanced at Rachel, whose hands twitched in her light sleep. Mishka's disappearance could have been part of the cousins' plan if they were discovered. She wondered if ESOW was a front for violent activism, and Rachel had been lying all along. For the moment, she would give Rachel the benefit of the doubt and do whatever it took to find whatever Carlos had been shot for.

Leaving the medical centre, Anya examined the key Rachel had entrusted her with. A two followed by a four, or what could have been a nine, had been scratched along the silver metal shaft. Attached to a lanyard, the only hint about where it came from was its size. Rooms and most access areas on board required electronic access.

There were locked cupboards near the fresh towel stands near the pools, but they were frequently accessed by staff.

Crew had cabinets in their cabins to store belongings, but they had much smaller keys. Nothing like this one.

Anya found it odd that Mishka was so secretive. She shared a cabin with Rachel, yet chose to hide all the information some-where else and keep all contents of the documents to herself. Rachel believed it had been for her own safety. It also meant that she couldn't let anything slip if someone like FitzHarris asked too many questions. Anya wondered if there was more to Mishka's reasoning. Perhaps she was up to something else.

Industrial espionage was worth a fortune. And the competition in the cruise industry was rampant. From what she had read, the attack on Anderson was designed to wipe out his empire. Despite owning only a third of company shares, the heirs held the majority of voting shares. Anderson and his brood had complete control. That could have upset other shareholders, or even executives who could never aspire to the top jobs without being part of the inner circle that was his family.

Suddenly, the company was without leadership and shares were plummeting, despite the immediate rush in bookings.

The vultures were already circling.

Anya slid the key away. She had been intending to go and see Jasmine. The Chans may want to be alone, but a change of scenery might do Jasmine some good. The least Anya could do was offer.

Turning the corner into their corridor, she stopped.

A teenage boy in black skinny jeans and black jacket, with black hair, scuffed along, hands in pockets. He stopped at the Chan's door, bent down and slid his fingers part way under the door.

Anya thought of the anonymous note Lilly had received.

The boy didn't wait for an answer. He stood and headed away with a quickened pace. Anya had seen him somewhere before but couldn't place it. She decided to follow him.

Around the next dogleg, he was stopped by two males. One in a lettered cardigan, another taller one in grey sweatshirt and pants.

'Hey, check out the geek.'

From their size, each could have been a footballer. The pimply complexions were definitely high school.

The boy in black tried to pass but his path was blocked with an outstretched arm.

One of them flicked the black jacket with the back of a hand.

'What are you supposed to be, ghoul boy?'

'That's original. Especially coming from someone with the brains of a goldfish.'

'What'd he say?' The pair moved closer.

'Impressive. Short-term memory less than three seconds.'

The teen in the cardigan pushed his sleeves up. 'Did this peewee just call us dumb?'

The taller one shoved the boy in black against the wall and held him by the lapels. His quarry went limp, and made no attempt to resist.

Anya was twenty feet away.

'You take that back, ghoul boy,' the boy in the sweatshirt threatened.

The boy in black flicked a long piece of hair from his eye. 'Fine, I take it back.' He held both arms up in surrender. 'You don't have the brains of a goldfish.'

'That's better.' The taller one released the hold and the boy in black straightened his jacket.

'Goldfish are *far* more intelligent.'

The one with a sweatshirt clenched a fist.

'What do you think you're doing?' Anya was within ten feet.

The pair turned and stepped back from the wall.

'Nothin', ma'am. We're just joshing with our friend here.'

There was a pause.

'Aren't we?'

The boy in black didn't respond.

'See you later, ghoul.' The taller one slapped his prey on the shoulder. Significantly harder than a friend would.

Anya waited until they moved on. 'Are you all right?'

He nodded. 'Evolution still has a way to go. Thanks.' He started to leave.

'I saw you try to put the note under the door.'

He froze.

248

'I stopped to tie my shoe.'

She glanced down at his feet. High-top sneakers, laces fashionably undone.

'I'm no fool and every bit as strong as those two, and possibly faster.' Anya sized him up – he could not have weighed more than fifty kilograms. 'I know what I saw.'

He frowned and pursed his lips. 'Wow. I'm sensing some serious hostility. And, maybe some unresolved issues with your father ... no ... it's your mother. Definitely your mother. You crave authority for some reason, and assert it well. Only. Wow.' He raised his eyebrows, with exaggerated surprise. 'May I say, those chakras would really benefit from some realignment.' He shoved his hands into his pockets and stepped back. 'I really hope you find peace.'

Anya was in no mood for a smart alec. This boy could have stalked Lilly and was now playing some sick game with the family. She stepped uncomfortably close, using her height to advantage.

'I'm sure I will. Right after I call the head of security.'

As he glanced up, she saw a flash of fear in his pale eyes. The hair had been dyed black, his eyebrows and lashes were much lighter. The freckles across his nose and cheeks were more orange than brown. He was all bluff and had to be around seventeen.

'Listen—' he began.

'No, you listen. Someone gave a young girl an anonymous note to meet up. Only thing was, she turned up at the place a few hours later. Dead. Now, it's a homicide investigation.'

'Whoa. Lady, you are totally insane. More than your chakras are out of whack.'

An elderly couple headed along the corridor toward them, the man had a walking frame.

'Excuse me,' the boy moved toward them. 'This woman's harassing me.'

'Why don't we go and check the Chans' cabin then, and see what you put under the door?'

He stopped and waved back to the couple. 'Just kidding. Nothing but a lovers' tiff.'

Anya couldn't believe his audacity. They waited for the pair to pass by.

'Fine. I put a note under the door. But there's no way I can go there with you.'

'Because you'll get caught?'

'No.' He flicked the hair, this time further covering his eyes. 'Because she doesn't know I exist.'

'That makes stalking her totally acceptable then. How did you know which cabin she was in? Did you follow her?'

'Hell no.' He shuddered. 'That'd be weird and kinda creepy.'

Anya wondered if he heard what he was actually saying. 'How then?'

He lowered his head and looked both ways. They were alone. 'Promise you won't tell?'

Anya remained silent. Her gut feeling told her he was harmless, but he had already proved he could worm his way out of trouble.

'I saw her at dinner. She was amazing. Like some kind of angel. Then she smiled at me, just as they were leaving. I didn't even know her name.'

'So . . .'

'I checked out the passenger list and found her there.'

He was lying. FitzHarris had said the list was confidential – he wouldn't even show it to her.

'Passengers can't access the list.'

'Maybe others can't. The security is old-school, too easy. It didn't take long before I pulled it up on the computer. The hard part was going through all those names. She's travelling with her mother, sister and I'm guessing cousin and aunt. They've got cabins next to each other.'

He had brazenly broken into the ship's computing system. He thought following the girls to their cabin would have been creepy, but stalking them online was somehow fine. Then she remembered where she'd seen him: in the teen club, hunched over a keyboard.

'You're a hacker. And a cyberstalker.'

'Whoa. That's harsh. I prefer to call it cracking. It's code-breaking and quite a prized skill, I might say. I'm a problem solver, not some cyberstalker.'

'What else did you find out?'

'She's an Aquarian. That's totally compatible, and she lives in Hong Kong. The tyranny of distance is not easily overcome.'

He may have been a con artist, but he was also a romantic, even if he did write love notes in texting shorthand.

Anya marched him back to the cabin, with the threat of security the alternative. As they approached, they could hear the violin. The music was sad and slow. The boy paused. 'Have you ever heard anything as moving? I knew you were making all that murder stuff up. Got to admit, it really had me going for a second.'

Only one person could be playing. 'Wait. Who did you write the first note for?'

'Jasmine. Who else?'

If he was so smitten with the older sister, he may not have noticed Lilly, who had collected the note by mistake.

'Where did you put the first note?'

'I saw her a second time practising in the library. Once I found the cabin number, I just asked the housekeeping lady to put it in her violin case.'

Now it made sense. He didn't know that both girls had violins. The housekeeper had put the note in Lilly's case by mistake and Lilly must have assumed it had been for her.

'Did you go up on deck to meet her?'

'I tried. I really tried. Dad had one of his attacks. He

served in Afghanistan and Iraq and has these screaming nightmares after a few drinks. That night he got wasted. It was worse than usual. By the time he calmed down, it was after two. Check with the nurse. Karen, I think that's her name. She came and gave him something so he could sleep.'

Anya would check. If the boy had pulled up the passenger files, it would have been possible to access the staff list as well.

'What's your father's name?'

'Wesley Meeks Senior. I'm the junior portion. Only I just go by Wes.'

If he had been able to go that night, he could have found Lilly and got her help.

'Wes, there's something you need to know. I'm a forensic physician. I wasn't lying about the homicide. Jasmine's sister was drugged and died up by the spa that first night.'

He suddenly looked even paler. The violin stopped. Anya knocked. A few moments later, Jasmine opened the door with a piece of paper in her hand. Anya turned to introduce Wesley. He had already gone.

31

Anya arrived back at the suite with Jasmine, who was happy to have a break from her cabin. Ben gave her a giant hug. Martin relayed a message from FitzHarris, who wanted Anya to meet him urgently in his office. She was unsure what to expect and wanted to spend time with Ben. She had promised they would go to cartooning classes later. Martin insisted she go and promised to take Ben if she wasn't back in time. Ben didn't seem to mind who he went with. He was infatuated with Jasmine and her musical ability.

A few minutes later, Anya was back in Fitz's office. The lock on the door had been replaced with an electronic coded version. Laura entered, carrying a laptop.

'You both need to see this. Fitz said there was no real evidence to say who had been with Lilly Chan, but I did some searching on social network sites and blogs to see if anything had been said about the cruise. These days, if someone makes a cheese sandwich, it's bound to be posted somewhere.'

Fitz rolled his eyes.

'Around two hundred passengers have posted so far.'

'Let me guess,' he said as he clicked the end of a pen. 'The usual whining about time taken to board, cost of alcohol, and size of the cabins. Oh yeah, and they want a refund 'cause it's raining.'

'Naturally. On the bright side, they all seem to like the food, although one blogger thinks the gluttony is a disgrace and suggests feeding Third World populations with lefto-vers.' She looked up. 'We can't get medical backup or police on board in the middle of the ocean, but we can fly food off? What goes on in some people's brains?'

That had been a mystery to Anya all her life. Now the internet had meant anyone with an opinion, no matter how bizarre, could spread it around like a contagious disease.

'Here's the post you want to look at though. It's by someone whose tag is "Hornycollegegirl". She, and I assume it is a female, brags about an orgy on the first night and how one girl had sex with *heaps of guys* then got so drunk she passed out and peed all over the floor. She says she took photos that were, quote, hilarious.'

Laura read out the post: '"I saw a blonde slut having sex in the corridor and got so horny, I could have fucked a doorknob. After this guy with a massive cock finished with this blonde chick, he saw me watching. Then he crawled on his knees and ripped down my thong and . . ." Well, she had sex with him. After that, she says it was the best night – ever.'

Anya was too appalled to speak. Someone had seen Kandy, a fifteen year old, drugged and raped, and saw Lilly raped by 'heaps of guys', and laughed about it.

FitzHarris clicked the pen on and off. 'Could be the one who wet herself was Lilly Chan, although Brian Peterson and the others all denied ever seeing Lilly anywhere but at the disco.' He slumped in his chair, elbows on the desk, face in his hands. 'Just when you think humans can't stoop any lower. What the hell happened to the sisterhood?'

Anya felt a tightening in her throat. 'The carpet soiling could have been a direct effect of the drugs, or Lilly could have had a seizure.' This blogger hadn't thought to check, or call for medical assistance. If she had, Lilly could still be alive. She still had a heart rhythm when Martin found her.

Fifteen minutes would have meant the difference between life and death.

'I feel sick thinking this person is still on board, clueless,' Laura paused. 'After that, there are more posts, mostly about who she's slept with since. She doesn't use names. She may not even know them.'

From over 3000 passengers, there was a witness to what happened that night. An anonymous one.

'Is it possible to identify her?'

'That's the challenge,' Laura replied.

'Can you trace who posted the entries?' Fitz sounded more like he was giving an order.

'It will take a lot of man-hours, and it depends on whether the social site gives us the private information. Normally, it takes a police warrant and lots of to-ing and fro-ing to get names and addresses of subscribers. Unless you know a good hacker.'

Anya and FitzHarris looked back at Laura.

'What? I don't hack. Seriously . . . Well, OK, maybe I aspired to be a white hacker in my college days, but I couldn't crack this site.'

Surprisingly, Anya knew just the person who might be able to help.

Anya knocked on the cabin number Karen had given her after she'd confirmed she had seen a war veteran that first night. If Wesley Meeks Jr wasn't here, Anya's next stop was the teen club, where she had first seen him at a computer.

It took a moment for anyone to answer. Then Wes appeared, in his trademark black T-shirt and jeans. Only this time, the shirt had an image of Humphrey Bogart and Ingrid Bergman from *Casablanca* across the chest. His face dropped when he saw Anya. He tried to block her entry. 'I'm kinda busy right now, maybe you can come back later.'

He was hiding something. For all she knew, he could have been in the process of hacking into the CIA or World Bank.

'Can we talk?'

'Wes!' A voice came from inside. 'I'm done.'

'No, I'm busy. I have to go.' He went to close the door, but Anya's foot was already in the way.

'I don't mind waiting. Do what you have to.'

Wes stared back, as if contemplating his next move.

'Son!'

He let out a breath and held the door open while she entered.

'Dad needs me.' Wes went into the bathroom and closed the door.

The cabin was larger than the original one she and Ben had shared. The linen, curtains and wall colours were the same. On the lounge sat a guitar with a broken string. A closed laptop computer was next to it.

The double bed was unmade, but the rest of the cabin was surprisingly sparse.

'Excuse me.' Wes appeared and headed for the wardrobe. From one of the drawers he pulled out a pair of boxer shorts, then a folded shirt and trousers, before returning to the bathroom.

Anya waited. Ten minutes later, the door opened again. Out came an older man in a wheelchair, clean shaven with wet, combed hair. He was missing an arm and a leg. She immediately regretted coming. Wes was obviously his father's only carer, no easy task for a teenage boy.

'Dad, this is the doctor I met. Remember I said she's happy to talk war stories with you. The stuff she's seen . . .'

'Not checking up on me are you?'

'Dad, she's Australian.'

Anya wondered why that seemed relevant.

'Well then, she's welcome here any time. Your soldiers are

some of the best I served with. You guys have been with us all the way. Afghanistan, Iraq.' He seemed to drift for a moment. 'Well, you wasted your time. I don't need no check-up.'

'I'm actually having computer troubles and your son very kindly offered to help.'

Wes raised an eyebrow.

'That's my boy.' The father beamed. 'He could do worse than being like that Bill Gates fella.'

'Maybe we can do this later,' Anya suggested.

'No, don't mind me,' Mr Meeks said. 'Wes should get out, maybe meet a nice girl his age.' He glanced at Anya. 'No offence.'

'None taken. I don't need him for long. And there are some very nice teenage girls on board.'

Wes blushed.

'Dad, you had a bad night. Are you sure?'

Mr Meeks reached up and patted his son. 'Hand me the remote for the TV and I'll be like a pig in poop, as the Aussies say.'

Anya smiled.

'Do you want me to take the walkie-talkie?'

Mr Meeks chuckled. 'You're gonna have to cut them apron strings sometime. Go on, give a man some peace.'

Wes collected the laptop and shoved it into a bag, which he slung over his shoulder. 'Thanks, Dad. I won't be long.'

Anya tried to imagine how difficult the situation was for both of them. The veteran needed full-time care, and assistance with even the most basic functions. Wes had a lot more to deal with than bullying and meeting girls he liked.

Neither spoke until they were near the stairwell.

'Computer trouble?' Wes slinked along, hair back over his eyes.

'In a way, yes. But the trouble isn't necessarily going to be mine.'

He stopped again, and Anya thought he might run. She touched his arm.

'Or yours. Don't worry. I'd like to put your skills to good use, and you could be helping Jasmine and her family in the process.'

'Doctor, something tells me this could be the beginning of a beautiful friendship.'

32

Back in the suite, Ben and Jasmine were playing "Chopsticks" at the piano. Like the first time, they were absorbed in each other's company. Wes watched them, his face reddening toward the end of the tune. It was introduction time, and Jasmine stood up to shake his hand. Ben offered a perfunctory 'Hi.'

'Slight change of plan, Ben,' Martin interrupted.

Their son's shoulders slumped. 'Dad—'

'How about we go out for hot dogs and bring some back?'

Ben's response took about a nanosecond. 'Yay!'

'Wes, you up for it?'

'I don't eat anything from an animal. Hot dogs are made from snouts, ears and blended-up organs from pigs, cows, turkey and chicken. Then they're stuffed inside animal intestines.'

'They're not really made of dogs, silly,' Ben announced. 'It's a frankfurt on a bun with ketchup and mustard.' He looked to his father for verification. 'And cheese. I like them with cheese. At home we only have them with tomato sauce, don't we Dad?'

'Too right.' Martin grinned. 'Guess Wes is more of a pizza man. And I'm thinking . . . vegetarian.' Anya followed them outside the door.

'That kid could suck life out of an active volcano. Come to think of it, reminds me of myself at that age.'

'Which part?' Anya mused. 'The dyed black hair in his

259

eyes, low-hung pants, illegally accessing private websites, breaking laws for a challenge, or aversion to mystery meats?'

'What's that famous quote – Bismarck, I think. "Laws are like sausages. It's better not to see them being made." Only I say, it's no reason not to get stuck into them either. Maybe we are alike after all.'

Anya went back inside. Wes was standing by the piano. 'Lush. This must have cost a mint.'

She wasn't sure if he meant the suite or the instrument. Jasmine sat quietly at the keys.

'Do you play?' Anya asked.

'Guitar is more my thing.'

'What sort of music?'

Jasmine was listening.

'My tastes are pretty eclectic. Renaissance, Baroque, Classical, Romantic. Occasionally Neo-Classical.'

Anya had to smile. That may have seemed like a broad range to the teen, but not to anyone else.

'What about you?' Wes asked Anya, obviously nervous about addressing Jasmine.

Her interests were in no way as refined as those of the teens in the room. They were both musicians, whereas she played for fun, dabbling in music she'd loved since childhood. 'Drums. Rock, jazz, pop. There weren't a lot of solos written for drums in the eighteenth century.'

Wes's eyes crinkled. Just a bit. 'You look more like a flute. Or oboe.'

Anya was not quite sure what that meant. 'Looks can be deceiving.'

Jasmine glanced up at her and smiled.

Wes pulled open the computer bag, and had a glint in his eyes. 'What do you want me to do?'

Anya unplugged her laptop and placed it on the table. Wes joined her while Jasmine began to play something classical.

'Jasmine's sister, Lilly, died after an overdose of a drug called GHB. Sometimes called liquid fantasy, some people think it improves sex drive. Unfortunately, it's used as a date-rape drug.'

'Holy shit.' He bit his lower lip. 'I've heard stories about it, but I've never taken anything like that. I promise.'

Anya believed him. He was only guilty of social ineptitude when it came to expressing himself to girls. 'We know that.'

'That stuff is insane. My dad got addicted to painkillers after the explosion. He was a medic, and his team was headed to some injured soldiers in Kāpisā. Only there was a roadside bomb. Dad was lucky. Two other guys got killed.'

That explained the injuries to Mr Meeks's right side, and the night terrors.

'I mean it wasn't his fault, the painkillers. But then he starting drinking pretty heavily. It wrecked our family. Man, I could never do that to someone I cared about, no matter how bad things got.'

Anya plugged in the power cord on the wall behind the table. 'You couldn't give anyone drugs, or take them yourself?'

'Either.'

That, Anya thought, was a large part of the problem they now faced. The men who had raped Lilly and Kandy had treated them like objects. The blogging girl seemed to view them the same way.

Anya typed in the address of the social site Laura had identified, but she couldn't access members without an account herself. 'Don't suppose you have an account?'

Wes glanced across. 'Only two because this site's more for old people.' He tapped away and located his own page.

Anya wondered how old he considered college students. 'We need to access someone's account to help find out who gave the GHB to Lilly. It's under the name of Hornycollegegirl.'

The hair was flicked from the eye. 'Seriously? Sure it's not a fifty-year-old man?'

The thought had not occurred to Anya. It could have been a man masquerading as a woman. 'I was told a search warrant was the only way to find out who she is.'

'In theory, you need a warrant to get neoprints and photoprints. They're profile information the networks keep to themselves. They're supposed to be inaccessible to anyone. None of us is supposed to be able to see our own.'

'Is there an easier and quicker way?'

Jasmine continued playing, seemingly lost in the music.

Wes was checking one of his own pages and seemed to be deleting entries. 'People are basically stupid. They use easy to remember passwords, like their birthdate, pet's name, kids' names. It's unbelievable. So what's Hornycollegegirl done, apart from being stuck in the 1970s?'

Anya didn't want him to see, or Jasmine to hear. She spoke quietly, 'She says she took photos of someone we think was Lilly Chan. Lilly had already been drugged and could have been unconscious.'

She didn't want Wes to know she had already seen some photos of Lilly's fifteen-year-old friend.

He closed his eyes. 'What a douche nozzle.' He glanced over at the piano. 'Does Jasmine know?'

'I'm not sure if the family's been told yet. I thought if we could stop the photos spreading . . .'

'You came to the right person.'

Part of Anya felt a little guilty about getting Wes involved, but unless something could be done to identify the College Girl, no one would be accountable for what had happened to Lilly.

'Wes, I want to take complete responsibility for this. You were never involved. Okay?'

He reached over to Anya's computer. 'Fine. I'll use yours

262

then. And what I'm doing is only illegal if I get caught. If he or she's as juvenile as they sound, I'll find them in no time.'

Anya had no idea how. With all the random permutations of numbers and letters, the chances of guessing a password, even using algorithms, should have been almost impossible. As far as she knew, that was the point of passwords – to stop others accessing personal information.

Obviously, Wesley Meeks Jr had other ideas.

33

Martin and Ben returned with a tray full of hot dogs, burgers, and slices of pizza. Judging by the sauce smear on Ben's face, he hadn't waited to eat.

'Wes,' Martin said, 'if you're anything like I used to be, you're always hungry. And I can assure you only vegetables were picked, chopped up and cooked in the making of this pizza.'

'Any fries?' Wes didn't look up from the computer.

'Do I look like a smorgasbord?'

Anya picked up the pizza and a plate of fries and placed them on the table next to Wesley. Martin could never help himself when fries were on offer. She dipped into a few herself.

'This place sure has amateurs running its security system.' Wes took a large bite of pizza and spoke with his mouth full. 'I'll leave them a message before Sydney.'

Martin stared.

'What? I'd make sure it's anonymous. Kind of like a public service.'

'As opposed to the police, knocking on your door for all your "good deeds".' Martin joined them at the table. 'If you can access the passenger lists, what about internet usage? Everyone has to sign up for an account and log in every time they use it, whether you use a personal computer or one of the public ones.'

'While I'm in, do you want to check yours before you settle the bill?'

Martin covered his ears. 'I'm not hearing this.'

Ben took a plate of fries to Jasmine, who joined him on the lounge.

'If you prefer, I can delete the whole account.' The teenager gave a wry grin.

Martin groaned. 'Of all the IT savvy people on board, we end up with Al Capone's accountant.'

Anya stretched her neck. 'If you can tell when the entries were posted, we could check the times against the logon information.'

'Or I can make small talk with College Girl and as soon as she posts, find out who's accessing the ship's internet at exactly that time. We can catch her with her pants down. Sorry. Poor choice of words there.' His face flushed again.

'Says you,' Martin said, under his breath, 'with your trousers halfway down your butt.'

The thought of being outsmarted by a teenager was obviously galling.

'Are you really married to him?' Wes asked.

Anya tried to suppress a laugh. 'Not anymore.'

'That figures.'

'Hello! I can hear you.' Martin bit into a hamburger.

'Do you want to know what College Girl or Guy looks like?'

'Why do you ask?' Anya was curious what else he could propose.

'Because we can snap whoever it is in the act.'

Wes had Martin and Anya's complete attention.

'All I have to do is write a virus that goes to all the computers on the network. The ones for passengers all have webcams for video calling.'

'How does sabotaging the network help?' Martin clearly disapproved.

Wes took a prolonged breath. 'Not all viruses are

destructive. You can write a programme to do whatever you like. Every computer has its own MAC address. No two are the same . . .'

He seemed to wait for them to finish the concept. Neither spoke.

'So . . . I get the webcam to switch on when anyone logs on to these sites. The camera takes a photo of the user right at that moment. I get the virus to send the MAC address and image to my email.'

'Isn't the MAC address numeric? How do you know where it is?' Anya wondered how they would find the woman – or man – on a ship this size, even with her photo. Sifting through thousands of passenger IDs was time-consuming and it would be easier to miss a woman, especially if she had a different hairstyle or was wearing a hat.

'It's simple. There are naming conventions for computers in offices and places like this. The IT manager has to be able to locate any one if there's a problem or complaint. All I do is get the unique name of that computer sent to my email with the other info. We should know straightaway what deck and part of the ship she's in.'

'And if it's on a personal computer?'

'Seriously. College Girl doesn't sound like the type to take a personal computer with her to a party. Isn't that what this cruise is supposed to be?'

'The kid makes a good point.' Martin almost sounded impressed.

Anya felt uncomfortable about what they were doing, but knew there were no other options. She glanced over at Jasmine talking with Ben on the lounge. They had good reason for doing it. 'You promise not to damage any of the computer systems or programmes?'

Wes was already tapping away. 'Trust me. I use my powers for good, not evil.'

'One thing,' Anya was still concerned. 'What if the virus gets found. You – or we – could be in a lot of trouble.'

For the first time, Wes smiled. The corners of his eyes upturned and his whole face changed. Dimples appeared in each cheek. He should do it more often, then girls like Jasmine would melt, Anya thought.

'You underestimate my powers. I can make the virus delete itself whenever we want. Every twelve hours, or every hour if you want. Then I pre-programme it to reinstall just before the deletion.'

'So by the time someone from IT notices, and works out what it is, it's gone again.' Anya didn't want to think of all the others like Wes, who may not be so civil-minded.

'There's no footprint. No way of ever tracing it.'

'You are a scary little dude,' Martin said. 'But you're growing on me.'

'In that case, you might want to change your email password. "Benjamin" is way too obvious.'

'Growing on me like tinea,' Martin clarified.

34

Jasmine returned to her mother. She and Anya had played cards and charades with Ben for a couple of hours, before he had begged to visit his friends in the club before dinner. Wes was still programming his virus. It would take at least an hour more, he said.

Anya changed into exercise gear and headed out. Wes seemed engrossed in his new challenge and she suspected he wouldn't move from the chair, or notice her absence. He had finished the pizza and fries and had a supply of fruit to last him until dinner.

The last thing she wanted was to exercise, but it was the best way to clear her head. Staying inside was becoming more claustrophobic, and the idea of getting blood pumping seemed the closest thing to escape for now.

The gym took up a large section at the aft, along with the spa and hairdressing facilities. Inside a gold-edged set of double doors, a water feature trickled away, and the sounds of the ocean drifted through speakers. Smiling staff in mint green asked her to fill in a disclaimer and medical form. After completing it, a young Scottish woman in a pantsuit showed her through to the change rooms and handed her a key on a toggle that could be worn around the neck.

On the key's tag, in bold white, was the letter 'S'. She was given a fresh towel to place on the exercise equipment and shown where bathrobes and spare towels were kept. Candles, smelling of lavender, flickered against the mirror as a flute and harp melody were piped overhead. The lockers were labelled by letter alone; 'S' was on the top row. To her disappointment, none had a number to correspond to twenty-four or twenty-nine, like the key Rachel had given her. From the size of it, it had to belong to a locker as well. Just not these ones.

'Do the men's lockers have letters as well?'

The woman nodded. 'Believe it or not, people want their lucky number, or the number one, so we find letters solve that problem.'

Another dead end.

Anya locked her room key and bag with change of clothes inside and followed the escort to the gym. It had a full view of the ocean, and the dark mass of clouds. Dance music pounded more loudly than necessary, especially since there were only a handful of people exercising.

Inside, a young trainer rubbed the shoulders of a woman in her sixties as she used the lateral pulldown machine. 'I can feel your arms strengthening with each repetition,' he proclaimed.

'Are staff always that hands-on?' Anya asked her guide. The last thing she wanted was to be touched while she exercised. The point was to be alone and in her own head and body space.

The woman rolled her eyes. 'He thinks he'll get a bigger tip if he schmoozes them. Mind you, that ring and watch were from *very* grateful clients, if you know what I mean.'

From what Anya could tell, the older woman was enjoying the personal attention.

She decided on the treadmill and gently accelerated the pace and incline. Within minutes she was pounding along to her favourite tracks on her mp3 player. A little while later a couple of men entered her peripheral vision, over at the weights. She recognised one. Brian Peterson. The other had been with Lilly at the disco. Brian saw her and said something to his friend, who stopped flexing and extending oversized biceps to see.

Anya pretended not to notice them and checked the time. Ten minutes more to make it worthwhile. Part of her wanted to leave and avoid being anywhere near these men. They bullied men and women, and felt powerful in a group. Brian Peterson had looked like he would pass out when David FitzHarris mentioned a murder investigation but showed none of that vulnerability now.

Peterson left the gym, and she felt some relief at there being only one man remaining. His friend began triceps extensions with mini barbells. By the time she had finished, Peterson was nowhere in sight. Perspiring and fatigued, she headed for the showers.

It was easy to see why people raved about spa treatments. The four-headed water stream massaged her thighs, head, shoulders and back, warming and relaxing her tired muscles. The tension in her neck seemed to dissolve as the events of the last few days replayed in her mind. First Lilly, then Carlos, Jasmine and her violin, Rachel and Mishka. And Nuala, who died under suspicious circumstances but was written off as a suicide. Now Mishka was missing and she had asked a seventeen year old to hack into the cruise computer system to find out who had taken compromising photos of Lilly.

So much for a holiday. At least Ben was enjoying himself. She thought about how Martin suddenly seemed interested in her work and hadn't harangued her about how much time she was spending helping the crew while on board. He was more insightful and understanding than ever. There was something he wasn't letting on about his relationship with Nita, but it had to be serious for him to have mentioned a break. Anya had to admit she was enjoying being with him, more than when they were married. Then again, she had felt the same about Ethan in New York and he hadn't been in touch since. She could have misjudged his intentions.

She forced herself to concentrate on the key Rachel had given her, and where it could lead. If they discovered the door it opened, there was a good chance they would find Mishka. The number two and four. Or was it two and nine? Somewhere on the ship had to be a door or locker marked twenty-four, or twenty-nine. But where?

She switched off the taps and wrapped herself in a thick, fluffy towel and picked up a spare. Bending at the waist and flipping her hair over, she towel-dried as much as possible and stepped into the slippers provided. With the key, she retrieved her belongings and quickly dressed back into jeans and a shirt. Mishka's key was in her jacket pocket. When the attendant finished restocking towels, Anya was alone and compared Mishka's key with the locker key. They were identical. Scanning the lockers was no help. There were twenty-four labelled 'A' to 'X'.

She decided to check locker 'X', the last one. The key slid inside the lock but didn't turn the mechanism. Frustrated, she shoved it back into her pocket. It was worth a try. Before leaving, she decided to blow-dry her hair with the dryer attached to the bench. Finger-combing her hair, as air blasted through her waves, she could see the lockers' reflection. They were configured in a block four high and six along. She switched off the dryer and turned around.

Reaching into her pocket, her fingers found the key again. What if Mishka was a chess player? This time she tried the locker that was two across and four down. It didn't fit. A pair of women entered and she waited while they discussed which restaurant they would try for dinner. Once they had changed into bathrobes, they left. Anya tried one more time. Four across and two down. The key slipped effortlessly into the 'J' lock. Anya held her breath and turned it to the right.

Click.

The door opened. She looked around. No one else was present.

Inside the locker was a pile of papers, five inches high. Some were stuffed inside bursting A4 envelopes. A number of CDs lay on top. She removed them and filled her backpack. Before closing it up again, she ran a hand around the inside walls. Stuck to the ceiling was a piece of paper, with a series of numbers on it. She carefully peeled it away and placed it on top of the other contents and zipped the bag up. The spa assistant entered with a woman in casual clothing, and showed her around the change room. Anya quickly locked the door again and shoved the key back in her pocket.

'Did you have a good workout?' the attendant enquired.

'Yes, thanks.' Anya headed for the exit.

Turning back into the corridor toward reception, she caught her breath. Blocking her path were five men, two dressed in bowling shirts.

35

'Excuse me,' Anya tried pushing through.

The men refused to let her pass.

'Well, well. If it isn't the lady who likes asking questions with the baboon from security.'

One pushed his shoulders back and pressed his chest against Anya's. 'Not getting any yourself so you turn into the fun police?'

The man beside him lowered his shorts and flopped out a circumcised penis. 'Maybe you want a bit of this for yourself.'

Anya refused to react. These men were cowards and unlikely to risk hurting her in a public place. From what she had seen, Brian Peterson wasn't brave on his own.

'A bit of free medical advice.' She squinted her eyes, as if straining for a view. 'That looks like early syphilis. Hope you haven't shared partners with anyone lately. And you should avoid sleeping with your wife until you're clear.'

The man bent forward, trying to study himself, then snapped his penis back in its pants. His face was flushed.

'The bitch just owned you.' One of his friends laughed.

'Shut up.' He retreated to the change rooms.

'Medical centre has a clinic,' Anya said to the others. 'You all might want to get checked.'

She swung the bag to her front, in part to protect the contents, but more to provide a barrier. She pushed forward.

'Not so fast.' The one with the biggest mouth held up an arm, blocking her path. He had been shown on the CCTV footage. Genny. The one who had assaulted Kandy on the corridor floor.

'Are you following us?'

Anya pushed harder. 'This may be a surprise, but you're not the centre of the universe.'

'Maybe she does want some action.'

'Looks pretty strung up to me.' Genny pushed her back and moved his face closer.

She could feel his tobacco breath on her face and tried not to gag. Still, she held his gaze.

'I think she needs one . . . good . . . FUCK.'

The others snickered. Anya kept eye contact and did not flinch.

'Problem is,' she began, 'I don't see any real men here. Just a bunch of pathetic, petrified adolescents who drug young girls because it's the only way any of them can get laid.' She stepped back. 'Does that mean you have to drug your wives and girlfriends, or wait until they are too drunk to refuse?'

Genny clenched his jaw and fist. 'Shut your mouth or I'll . . .'

Anya's pulse pounded in her temples. If he hit her now, he would be locked in the ship's brig until Fiji. She almost hoped he would.

'How about we phone shore and ask them?'

The veins in Genny's neck bulged and he swiftly lifted his elbow. Anya braced herself.

A trainer appeared from another door and Genny splayed his fingers, pretending to examine his nails.

'Everything OK here?' the trainer asked, biceps stretching short white sleeves.

Anya didn't stop to complain. On the way back to the suite, she detoured through the shopping village and back through the reception area, to make sure that if anyone was following her they wouldn't find out where she was staying.

She doubted any of them had the computer skills Wes Meeks had used to find Jasmine's cabin.

Inside, Martin was lying on the lounge reading a thriller. Wes didn't even look up. Anya went upstairs and put the files in her bedroom safe then headed back down.

'How's it going?'

'Still waiting for the programme to upload across the network. Shouldn't be long now. There's been another post to that page. Only this is from someone else. Night Rider 14.'

Anya moved over to see as Wes read aloud. '"You are one horny bitch. Let me know if you want me to . . ." Let's just say he offers to have sex with her again.'

Martin stopped reading and popped his head over the lounge. 'That could be anyone who knows her from before.'

Wes continued, 'A few minutes later someone else posted, "If there are no pics, it didn't happen."'

Anya looked at the page onscreen. Another 200 people had approved of College Girl's orgy comment. Anya couldn't believe how many people sat glued to computers reading this tripe, waiting for another instalment, instead of living their own lives.

'There's something else I thought you should know. It isn't good.'

Anya sighed. 'Did you and Martin have an argument?'

'Us? No way. Someone, sounds like a friend from school, set up a RIP site for Lilly Chan.'

That was one positive thing to come from social networking, the ability to post condolences from anywhere in the world. Although the ship felt like an alternate universe at times, they could still connect with the outside world.

'Why isn't it good?'

'Trolls are all over it.'

Anya had no idea what that meant, but remembered

reading *The Hobbit* while at school. In that, trolls turned to stone if they ventured into daylight. 'Which means . . .?'

'Trolls. They act like major league jerks on the net. They deliberately say disgusting things to bait fundies.'

'Fundies?'

'Up-tights. Trolls think it's funny to say controversial stuff. Sometimes they flame, and say offensive things about murder victims, or someone who died, just for fun. A lot of people on the RIP site are feeding the trolls by getting angry and telling them where to go.'

Martin joined the conversation. 'So the trolls go around vandalising tribute sites?'

''Cause there are more likely to be fundies there, and . . . well, because they can. Then other trolls find out and join the party.'

The whole notion was sickening. 'What sort of things are they posting about Lilly?'

'The usual. That she was a slut, bitch, or dog. They post stuff like she had sex with her father, then suddenly, all these Christians get on and say incest is a sin against God and she should burn in hell. Then her friends get upset and feed the trolls and it keeps going.'

It boggled Anya's mind how the tragic and sudden death of a teenage girl could be a source of amusement and cruelty. Worse, there were names for the behaviour, like it was a type of sport with players on different sides.

'Have you ever done it?' Martin asked Wes.

'Heck, no. These guys are sick. They think it's hilarious to make fun of people. I've had that all my life. Why would I do it to someone else?' He paused. 'I thought about getting into some bullies' sites, but that'd just be lowering myself to their level.'

Wes was proving himself to be mature and insightful. Anya hoped Jasmine and her family did not see the website.

'Can you take the site down, or at least delete the foul comments?'

He shook his head. 'Only the site owners can do that. Police are helpless. There are a lot of people who fight to protect the First Amendment and the right to free speech. It's what media moguls use to get away with trolling legally. Only they do it in papers and on TV.'

Anya wondered who cared about the rights of people who are libelled, tormented and devastated by cruelty disguised as amusement.

'Can you identify who's doing it, maybe report them to the school they come from?'

'Guarantee you, not one is a real name. One calls himself Mahariji Yumyum. Another goes by Banana Pie.'

He checked the screen again. 'Oh no. You are not going to like this. Someone just posted graphic pictures on the blog. It says they're of Lilly.' He turned the screen around. They were nude images of the sixteen year old lying on her back, head to the side, eyes closed. They were accompanied by the post, 'Asian chick wasted. Screwed her once. Didn't bother again.' There was also an image of a blonde, Kandy, performing oral sex on an unidentifiable man. 'Blonde bitch bigger tits and swallowed the load.'

Anya felt acid rise in her throat again. 'Is your programme working yet? Did you get the photo of whoever posted them?'

Wes checked his email. 'Sorry,' he sat back in the chair. 'This time he got lucky. Five minutes more and we would have had him on camera.'

Night Rider 14 was the name of the poster. It had to be one of the men who had seen Lilly in the cabin that night. Proving who was the challenge.

Martin moved around to the table, pulled out a chair and sat. 'You have got to catch these bastards. They can't . . .'

'Let's focus,' Anya suggested.

'Maybe I can get his email address using his password,' Wes said. 'Maybe he uses his real name for work or home.'

'Why would his password be any easier to work out than College Girl's?'

'He's used the number fourteen. He's probably born on the fourteenth, or lives at a number fourteen.'

'Couldn't he have a child who's fourteen? Or maybe it's his wife or girlfriend's birthday?'

Wes shot Anya a sympathetic look that made her feel simple.

'The age of a kid would change so he'd have to remember when he started the account. He also has a Smartface page. Judging from the detritus on it, he isn't the kinda guy who respects a woman enough to remember her birthday. Besides, if he had a girlfriend, why would he bother being such a perv? But what would I know?'

More than Anya had anticipated. Wesley Meeks was wiser than most people his age. She suspected caring for his father had made him grow up a lot more quickly. 'Logical thinking.'

He interlocked his fingers and stretched both arms at chest level. The knuckles cracked and Anya felt a shiver down her back.

'You still prefer I don't do anything illegal on your computer?'

'If there's another way . . .'

He returned to his laptop. 'You might want to powder your nose, as they say.'

Anya preferred to make a tea. Wes asked for white coffee and took a bite out of an apple. A few minutes later, he had a list of passengers whose birthdays fell on the fourteenth or had the number in their addresses.

There were almost 200 names on the list. Anya put her face in her hands. It was worse than a needle in a haystack.

'If I eliminate the women . . .'

'And what about anyone over seventy . . . or under sixteen,' Martin suggested.

Wes typed as if he had claws, and didn't once look at the keyboard. After the last keystroke, he lifted his hand in the air, like a concert pianist at the conclusion of a piece.

'That leaves us with . . . twelve.'

Anya's heart skipped. One teenage boy had already narrowed down the passengers who could have posted the pictures. 'Can you take out the ones travelling with families or women?'

The speed typing began again. Screens scrolled as he deleted the least likely candidates.

'When you do that, you're left with three. 'Leslie Rivers, on deck twelve. Brian Peterson and Gus Berry. They're both on deck one. In separate rooms.'

Anya could have hugged him. It wasn't a lot, but it was more than they had before. It was too much of a coincidence for Wes to have been wrong about the number fourteen being important.

'Can you check if any have Smartface pages in their own names?'

'Yeah, but you can use any name. Let's see who's friends with Night Rider.'

It sounded a reasonable, if slightly circuitous way, to find out if they were linked to the unidentified page.

'Surprise. No one is using their real name. Let's try something else.' Wes was in his element. 'These guys aren't smart. Night Rider doesn't have privacy settings.'

'Meaning?'

'Anyone can see his photos and posts. There's also some personal info.'

He went back to his own computer again.

Anya began to feel nervous, but thought of Kandy and

Lilly. Neither girl deserved the degradation these men had inflicted, and were continuing to inflict through the internet. There was enough consensual pornography people could access for free. This had to be about power and boasting, for friends.

'I have a thought,' Wes said. 'What if I start a new page, making out I'm a young woman. See if he becomes my friend.'

Anya didn't follow the logic.

'I get him talking about himself, where he is, what his real name is.'

'Isn't that entrapment?' Anya knew none of this would hold up in court, but if Wes managed to find out the identity of Night Rider, it could help them notify authorities. At the very least, Kandy was under-age.

Martin interrupted. 'I don't like it. These guys are intimidating. Wes, I'm concerned—'

'You sound like my grandmother. Trust me. These guys will never know who they're talking to.'

36

That evening in the central dining room, the mood was upbeat. The bowling shirts were already seated at two tables of eight, all in uniform. The maître d' led Anya, Martin and Ben through the central section, past the table with Genny and Peterson. The men began to howl and bark.

Anya took a deep breath and held Ben's hand. She was more concerned about Martin rising to the bait than what the men were doing. Trolls was a good word to describe them. Thankfully, Martin pretended to ignore them this time.

Karen was tending to an elderly passenger at one of the tables near the wall.

Anya detoured to say hello. 'Need any help?'

'Nah, our Mr Jonas had a giddy turn but promises to lay off the Scotch. At least until I'm out of sight.'

The elderly gentleman pouted like a sulky child. His similarly aged male companion nodded, beer in hand. 'No fool like an old fool, I always say.'

Karen stood and moved closer to Anya. 'Don't suppose you know anything about a mad rush we had this afternoon for genital checks? They were all convinced they had syphilis. One mentioned a doctor but it was all pretty vague.'

Anya coughed to stifle a laugh. 'Probably good that there's increased awareness out there.' She changed topic. 'How's Rachel?'

'She's managing, but her mind's definitely somewhere

else. Carlos is doing better, but Fitz is like a bear with a sore tooth. I wish I knew what was going on. Maybe I could help.'

'You know where I am if you need me,' was all Anya could think of to say.

Karen nodded and whispered, 'Likewise.'

Shouting on the other side of the room caught their attention. Anya saw the maître d' rush over. A woman stood and threw a plate of food in a man's face. It was Doctor Chan. The object of her throw was wearing a bowling shirt.

'You crazy bitch!'

Screaming, Lilly's mother punched him repeatedly with her fists. He tried to cover his head, but then Doctor Chan's sister launched into him as well. Karen headed over, a little more slowly than she could have. Jasmine was trying to calm her mother down. The rest of the room was silent, apart from laughter coming from the other bowling shirts. Four more waiters appeared and attempted to escort the Chans from the room.

Karen seemed to stop them. Jasmine noticed Anya and rushed over.

'Please help my mother. That man said he knew Lilly and said he was sorry she had died. Mom went crazy. She thinks he gave her the drugs and did unthinkable things to her. And now people are writing things about Lilly on the internet. What sort of monsters are they?'

Anya's heart sank. The Chans had seen the vandalised RIP site. They didn't deserve any of this.

She headed across with Jasmine, and the men began barking again. Waiters had physically separated the Chan women from the man they were assaulting. FitzHarris strolled along, after calm had been restored. Service to other tables quickly resumed.

'What happened here?' he demanded.

'Just a misunderstanding.' Karen had an arm around

Lilly's mother. 'The gentleman said something about knowing Doctor Chan's late daughter. No harm done.'

'No harm done!' Genny, the one who had physically threatened Anya, was quickly at his friend's side. 'That crazy bitch should be locked up. She threw a plate at my friend and started laying into him. Then her freaky lookalike joined in.'

FitzHarris glanced at the men, who stood a good foot and a half taller than the women they accused.

'And you're saying you boys couldn't defend yourselves against these petite, older ladies.'

Karen squeezed Doctor Chan's shoulder.

'She went nuts. Everyone in the room saw what happened. Ask anyone.'

The waiters and maître d' all had their heads down, going about their business. Animated conversation in the restaurant had resumed. Then Anya saw two familiar faces: Emma and Bec, the women from the disco who had been harangued and intimidated by some of the men on board. They were going around the room saying something to people at each table. Within a few minutes, the men were getting glares from other guests.

'Hey,' Genny shouted. 'Can I have your attention?'

The room fell quiet again, apart from some clanking of cutlery on plates.

'Can someone please tell this idiot how those women attacked my friend, totally unprovoked?'

No one spoke.

'This is bullshit. Everyone saw what happened.'

FitzHarris pulled a dining chair out for Doctor Chan's sister at her table. Karen did the same for Doctor Chan.

'This is bullshit.' Genny shouted to his friends, 'We're outta here.'

Sixteen men stood and exited the restaurant, all eyes on them.

Genny turned back to Anya and snarled. 'This isn't over.'

After their dramatic exit, one by one, the other passengers began to applaud.

'Are you OK?' Martin was at her side.

Anya nodded. When forced into the light, trolls did turn to stone, she realised.

After dinner, Jasmine and her family returned to their cabins and Anya and Martin took Ben to bed.

Inside their suite, Wes was still glued to his computer.

Anya suddenly thought of Mr Meeks, alone and unable to take care of himself. 'Won't your father be worried?'

'Nah, I called him and said I'm helping a doctor research a difficult case. That seemed to impress him. He's got room service, but I have to put him to bed soon. Hope you don't mind, but I ordered ice-cream. I would have gone myself, but I wouldn't have been able to get back in.'

Martin told Ben to go to the toilet and he'd help him with teeth in a minute. 'Any new postings?' he asked.

'Nothing helpful. I got ninety emails in the last hour, but nothing's been posted on Night Rider's site ... Wait a minute. This could be something.' He reloaded the page. 'He's just posted a comment about a crazy bitch mother.'

'That's got to be him!' Anya said.

Wes downloaded the email with the captured webcam image. Anya and Martin moved to the computer to see. The image slowly spread down the screen.

'What's he doing?' The image was a Caucasian man, with short brown hair, his hands across his forehead, shielding his face.

Wes stared at the image, disappointed. 'He's acting like he knows the camera is on.'

'How can he?' Martin asked.

Wes frantically typed away. 'Of course – a red light appears when the webcam is on. How could I be so stupid to miss that?'

'So you can't catch him?' Martin stood, hands on hips.

'I didn't say that.' Wes gave him an irritated look. 'Give me a minute to change the programme. Next time he's on, we'll get him for sure.'

'I'm ready,' Ben called from the downstairs bathroom. 'Can Mum help tonight?'

'Coming.' Anya was happy to do the bed routine. They finished teeth, washed some tomato sauce off his cheek and he was ready for pyjamas.

When they came out, Martin was missing.

'Where's Dad?' Ben asked.

Wes looked guilty. 'College Girl posted again. She's at a computer in a vestibule on deck seven. She's got brown hair extensions and googly eyes. You couldn't miss her.

'I told him we should contact head of security, but your ex thought she'd be gone by the time anyone got there. He said he'd act like he just bumped into her, find out her name, then come straight back.'

Martin was right about contacting FitzHarris. College Girl hadn't assaulted anyone, and was looking for hook-ups. Even though Martin was sensible, Anya felt concerned. What if one of the bowling men saw him? Genny had almost been violent to her, and she wouldn't put it past him to assault Martin if the odds were in his favour. She put Ben to bed and waited.

Ten minutes passed, then thirty more. Wes needed to go back to his room and be with his father. Reluctantly, he packed up his computer and its power cord. 'Do you want me to call if Night Rider logs on again?'

She thought about it. There was little they could do overnight, and she already knew what Brian Peterson and Genny looked like. The last thing she wanted to do was rush out to a computer where any number of those men could be.

'Let's wait until morning. In the meantime, we should all get some sleep. That means you too.'

Wes headed for the door.

'Thanks for everything you're doing.' She closed the door and checked her watch again.

It had been forty-five minutes. What was Martin doing? What had happened? If he wasn't back in fifteen minutes, she had to call David FitzHarris.

37

Anya heard laughing outside, then the buzz of the electronic key.

Martin had his arm around the shoulder of a young woman. She was giggling when she saw Anya.

'Who's she, Marty? I thought we were going to be alone.'

Anya's relief that Martin was okay was quickly replaced by irritation. She raised her eyebrows. Martin was just supposed to ask the woman at the computer her name. She could not believe he had brought this woman to their suite, where Ben slept. And she'd been worried enough to leave a message for FitzHarris to call her asap. 'If FitzHarris rings, I'll get it from upstairs.'

'Oh no,' her former husband lunged and reached out for her hand. 'I thought we could have a chat. Anya, this is Shelby. She's a college girl.' He emphasised each word.

'We have to talk quietly,' Anya urged. 'Our son is upstairs sleeping.'

'Marty, you're very naughty,' Shelby wagged a finger in his direction. 'You said there was a party. And you definitely didn't mention any wife.'

'Ex-wife,' they answered in unison.

'Well, this is awkward,' Shelby mumbled. 'I'm sensing you two have some issues . . . and I just remembered I have to meet someone for drinks.'

'The men who had the orgy on the first night?' Martin said. 'I was on the corridor and saw you that night, among other things.'

That seemed to temporarily sober her up. 'I'm getting a weird vibe. I'm just gonna go now.'

Anya tried appealing to her conscience. 'A teenage girl died that night. We think you saw her not long before and maybe took photos.'

Martin stepped to block the door.

Shelby's eyes darted from Martin to Anya. 'I don't know what you're talking about. I want to go.'

'Her name was Lilly Chan. She was Asian, with long black hair.'

'That's a stupid rumour,' Shelby said. 'That chick was just blind drunk.'

Anya gestured toward the lounge. 'Lilly was sixteen. She died in the early hours of the morning. We believe she and a friend had their drinks spiked with a date-rape drug. That means they were both sexually assaulted. Only someone gave Lilly far too much. Her heart and lungs failed.'

Shelby looked to Martin, as if hoping he would deny it, then back to Anya.

'I'm a forensic physician. Lilly's body is in the ship's morgue.' Anya sighed and sat on the lounge. 'I can arrange for you to go and see for yourself, if that's what it takes.'

The young woman slid down onto the lounge like an invertebrate. She buried her face in fingers with leopard-patterned nails. 'I thought she'd just passed out.'

Martin retreated to the kitchen to make coffee. Anya excused herself and followed him. 'Why did you bring her back here?' she demanded, trying not to raise her voice.

'What was I supposed to do? She propositioned me, and wouldn't tell me her name until I agreed to take her back to my room.'

The hour Martin was out, she had felt ill thinking he had put himself at risk.

'Don't tell me you were worried about me?' Martin grinned.

Anya felt an old frustration return. She glanced back at Shelby – she was still on the lounge looking shocked. 'This isn't funny. What if something –'

Martin took her by a hand. 'I love it when you care.'

She pulled her hand back. 'This isn't a joke.'

'I get that,' he retorted. 'This is so typical of you. Why is it all right for you to take risks? Look at how you went out looking for Mishka. I can't handle the forensic side, but I could do something here to help. Besides, I don't trust FitzHarris, and I don't think you do either. What choice did we have? Think about it.'

Anya hated to admit it, but he was right. He had successfully made contact with Shelby and coerced her into coming back for a private discussion.

There was a loud knock at the door. Without a word, Martin crossed the suite to answer it.

Anya listened to see if Ben stirred, and studied the girl. She was a student who liked to party and may have taken drugs herself. The image on the internet was far from the person on the lounge.

David FitzHarris walked into the room. 'Got your message. Didn't know you had company.'

Martin introduced Shelby to the head of security. The college girl became silent.

Anya explained. 'We saw a blog Shelby posted and think she saw Lilly Chan in a cabin with some of the bowling-shirt men, and may have taken some photos.'

FitzHarris placed his hands on hips. 'How?'

'Internet. You'd be amazed what your average Joe can find,' Martin quipped.

'You've got to believe me,' Shelby said, 'I had no idea anything was wrong with that girl. She was rolling on the floor, peeing, totally out of control. It was just like a frat party. Everyone was wasted.'

Anya tried to make it clear. 'Lilly could have been having seizures. That would explain why she became incontinent. By that stage, her lungs were filling with fluid and she was probably struggling to breathe. If she vomited, that could have gone into her lungs as well.'

'Oh my God,' Shelby covered her mouth with one hand.

FitzHarris moved over and sat opposite her. 'I need to ask. Did you see anyone attempt to help her, or give her anything?'

'Just water, I think. Some of the guys were trying to get her to come around so she'd leave.' Shelby seemed to struggle. 'It's a bit hazy but there is something I do remember. One of the guys went off his head about how she pissed on the carpet and how much she stank, and how she'd messed up their cabin.'

'Do you remember what he looked like?'

She reached into the evening bag in her lap. 'I know what you're going to think. At the time I thought he was funny.' She pulled out a smartphone. 'It was like he was Jim Carrey on speed.' She clicked a few buttons and held up the phone. 'Here he is.'

Martin disappeared and returned with coffees, along with a small carton of milk from the fridge. He sat cross-legged on the floor while Anya took the seat next to Shelby.

'May I?' she asked, and took the phone. The first frame was of the man who had exposed his penis at her outside the gym. He knelt beside a naked Lilly, looking down at her. All he had on was a pair of green socks. Other images were more candid. It was clear the men didn't realise the photos were being taken.

The memory card from Brian Peterson's room had only one face visible – his own. Shelby had not been so selective. A few shots along, Anya saw what she had hoped.

In one hand a man with a partly shaved head held a label-less clear plastic bottle with a clear fluid. In the other, he held

292

a blue lid tilted into Lilly's mouth. The bottle was the same shape as the one Anya and FitzHarris had found in the garbage. One that could not be purchased on board, and one that probably contained the GHB. This was not the act of someone trying to give a well person water. Lilly was lying flat on the floor. A few frames along, the same man was captured, straddled across Lilly's neck, trying to place an erect penis in her mouth. Then Anya saw the shot that confirmed Kandy's story. Genny's face was clearly visible, having sex with the fifteen year old. Kandy's eyes were closed, with both arms by her sides.

She scrolled through more photos. There were images of a naked Lilly, presumably taken from the doorway, and others in close-up. In one shot, there was frothing in the corner of Lilly's mouth, a sign of pulmonary oedema. Her lungs and heart had already begun to fail. There were two other pictures of the water bottle and lid, each with a different man holding the cap.

From the sequence, the more drowsy Lilly became, the more doses she was given. GHB was thought to improve sexual desire. The men had no idea what they were doing. Instead of making her aroused, they were overdosing her – repeatedly.

'I didn't know that girl was in trouble. I swear to God. I just thought she was drunk.' Tears began to flow down Shelby's cheeks, along with her heavy mascara and eyeliner. 'Give me the phone, I want to get rid of them.'

'They're evidence in a homicide investigation,' FitzHarris announced. Anya handed him the phone so he could see for himself. 'I'm going to have to download and document these. I'll need your last name in case I have to interview you again.'

'I'm so sorry. I didn't know she was in trouble. God, I was going to send those photos to one of the men who wanted to see what I'd taken.'

293

Lilly's death was tragic enough, without knowing that there were people who ridiculed and laughed at her as life drained from her small body. At any stage that night, if someone had called for medical assistance, Lilly would still be alive.

FitzHarris rubbed his chin. 'The blonde is only a fifteen-year-old girl. That's under-age according to Hawaiian law. Maybe now we can get the FBI to investigate a crime committed by US citizens against a US citizen.' He thought for a moment. 'One of the men in these photos asked you to email him the photos?'

Shelby nodded. 'He emailed me through the blog address but I don't know his name. Night Rider 14 is what he goes by.'

'Well did you?' FitzHarris pushed.

Shelby looked around as if pleading for support. 'You don't understand. I didn't know she was fifteen, or the other girl was drugged. I took them as a joke.'

'A joke you had to share with this man, you don't even know the name of,' FitzHarris snapped. 'Do you know what you have done to the dead girl's family, or the fifteen year old? What the hell is it with this generation? Do you ever think? Once photos are on the net, they are out there. Forever, for anyone to see.'

Shelby sobbed.

'It's not so funny now, is it?' FitzHarris could not hide his contempt.

'This isn't helping,' Martin interjected. 'The men are the ones who drugged and raped the girls. You need to talk to Night Rider, surely.'

Anya offered, 'We think we have narrowed it down to either Brian Peterson or Gus Berry from that floor.'

FitzHarris didn't ask what led them to that conclusion. 'Figures, the scumbags. I ran a swab from their bottle. Came out strongly positive for GHB.'

Unfortunately, Anya knew the photos could not prove Lilly was an unwilling participant in the drugs or sex. It was still their word and no one would be able to refute that. Even an eyewitness thought Lilly was consenting to what went on.

Shelby looked up with red eyes. 'Am I going to be charged with anything?'

'Negligent homicide, if I had my way.'

Anya sighed. 'This really isn't helping.' She placed a hand on the girl's back. Shelby lacked empathy and had behaved impulsively without giving a second thought to Lilly and Kandy, but had not wished them harm. Somehow, that was unlikely to be a consolation for the Chans.

The best Shelby could do now was minimise the damage she'd caused. 'What Shelby can do is take whatever she posted about Lilly down.'

The college girl looked up at Anya. 'I'll do anything.'

Within a minute, she had accessed her page. She gasped.

Anya was quickly by her side. 'What's wrong?'

'There are over three hundred comments on the last post.' She scrolled down. 'That bastard has put the photos on my page. People are tagging them and sharing them on all the other social network sites. He's even put one of me and him having sex.' She lowered her voice. 'Genny wasn't the only one I hooked up with that night.'

Anya glanced at the screen. 'At least we know which one Night Rider is. It isn't Brian Peterson, it's Gus Berry.'

FitzHarris stood and leant over Shelby's shoulder. 'Can you tell if he sent them to anyone else?'

'Give me a minute.' She typed and clicked.

'What do you know,' Fitz said. 'Looks like Peterson, and a number of our bowling boys, have been enjoying their handi-work all over again.'

38

Shelby returned to her cabin with a promise from FitzHarris that he would speak to her in the morning. The security chief asked Anya if she would accompany him to act as a witness when he approached Gus Berry, or Bear as his shirt boasted. Martin had no objections and was happy to read while Ben continued to sleep.

Anya had seen FitzHarris interrogate Carlos's room mate, and was curious about how he would attempt to get Night Rider to admit that he, and/or his friends, had sex with Lilly Chan before she died. After a few calls from Anya's suite, Fitz knew where to find Berry.

'He's in the casino, been spending up big. Could be just in the mood for an inquisition, given he's just dumped two thousand dollars.'

They headed out. The mood among the passengers was more buoyant as the storm seemed to have passed. Couples drifted in and out of the balcony doors, making the most of the improved weather.

FitzHarris held the elevator door open with one hand so an elderly gentleman could exit. They caught it up to the promenade deck. Anya had thought it crowded the other night, but now it seemed everyone had come out to walk, shop, eat late and gamble.

Neon lights enticed punters into the casino. Like the rest of the ship, the decor consisted of bright blues and pinks. It looked more like a fun parlour, with poker machines lining two walls, and a well-staffed bar with a number of waitresses carrying trays of drinks to customers. Tables offering roulette, blackjack and three-card poker were full. A crowd had gathered around the craps table.

'Over at the slots.' FitzHarris weaved his way through groups of people enjoying the atmosphere. Anya followed, but was blocked by a bearded man who asked her to kiss his dice before he threw.

'I've never been lucky,' she said, more interested in following FitzHarris. 'Excuse me.'

Gus Berry had his back to them when they arrived at his slot machine. His cologne could not disguise the fact that he was sweating. They watched him put fifty dollars in, then thump the screen when it ran out five spins later.

'Come on baby, this time,' he pleaded and deposited another twenty in US dollars.

'Looks like you're on a losing streak,' FitzHarris remarked.

'Yeah well, she's gonna pay out any minute,' he replied. 'Get lost and find your own machine.'

'We can wait,' FitzHarris said. 'We've got all night.'

Berry turned his head as bells and electronic music sounded, and coins cascaded from a slot machine on the other side of the room. Cheers went up, but not from Berry.

The scowl on his face had no hint of nervousness or fear. 'Why don't you arrest someone for jaywalking? Oh, that's right. You *can't*. Bull told us how you and your little girl Friday barged into his cabin. I've got nothing to say to you.'

'That's true, but I don't have to keep my mouth shut, Mr Night Rider 14.'

He laughed. 'You don't scare me. You're a freakin' joke. I'm outta here.' He guzzled the last of his beer and slid off the stool, stumbling on an ankle before correcting himself.

FitzHarris remained calm. 'Fine. I don't have the authority to charge you with murder, negligent homicide or even sex with a minor. You're right. Maybe you will get away with what you did to Lilly Chan and her friend that first night.'

'What we did to them? Man, they came on to us. And no one heard them complaining.'

He was talking loudly and casino patrons began to stare. Just like in the restaurant.

FitzHarris moved his face close to Berry's. 'You are going to pay for drugging and raping those girls. One way or another.'

Berry took a swing with his right hand and Fitz blocked it, then twisted the arm around Berry's back. 'You lot may think you're king of the world around here, but when you get back home, everyone's gonna know exactly what you are. A sex offender.'

Berry's face contorted in pain. 'Man, you're hurting me. You're a friggin' psycho.'

'Drank too much, nothing to see folks,' FitzHarris announced loudly. Gamblers went back to their business. Poker machines continued to play tunes.

'Do you know what paedophiles are, jackass?' He whispered into the man's ear as he pushed him toward the exit. 'The scum of the earth. They pedal porn to other sick bastards who get off screwing innocent children.'

'Can you get this maniac away from me?' Berry pleaded to Anya.

'He's making perfect sense.'

'Bitch! You're in this with him. My lawyer's gonna sue you both for everything you got.'

'That's a great idea. There'll be media, worldwide attention.' Fitz deferred to Anya. 'Which one do you think's my better side for when I get interviewed?'

'Definitely your left.' Anya stood, arms crossed. Fitz's theatre was growing entertaining. 'In fact, I can see you on all the major networks. You could even get offered a reality show.'

'Somebody?' Berry's arm was still pretzelled behind his back.

'We know it was you who put the nude photos of Lilly Chan on the web. And the blonde girl too.'

'Posting photos *isn't a crime*.' Berry enunciated as if talking to idiots.

Fitz released his arm and Berry rubbed it. The wrist was red, but unlikely to bruise.

'Yeah, it kind of is a crime. The blonde was fifteen. That's *fifteen*. In case you didn't know, that is *under-age*. My assistant is about to call the FBI to report you as a kiddie fiddler and child rapist. You're going to make new friends. The FBI will want to get to know you. First thing they'll do is say hi to your wife and kids while they go through your house with a warrant. Then there's your work . . .'

'You're full of shit.'

Fitz sucked air through his teeth. 'Poor boy's having trouble understanding,' he said to Anya. 'Let me make it really simple. Your name is gonna be on that sex-offenders' register *forever*. No more coaching your kid's football team or living near a school. And no court is going to give you custody of the kids when your wife leaves. Your neighbours will have to be notified. Look on the bright side. When you come out of the "big house" – that's *prison* – you're gonna be *fam-ous*.'

'You gotta believe me I had no idea that bitch was under-age. This is a mistake. What do I have to do to straighten things out? My father-in-law is loaded. Is that what this is about?'

'Did you just offer me a bribe, or were you accusing me of trying to extort money from your family?'

Anya cocked her head. 'I think the first one. Sounded more like a bribe to me.'

Berry's hair was becoming damp at the hairline, and his

face glistened in the glow from the neon casino sign. 'I didn't. I mean—'

'You are an even bigger dumbarse than I thought. This is about the law. Right and wrong. Justice. I want to know what happened to Lilly Chan. If you don't start talking, that call goes through to the FBI in five minutes.'

A pianist played in the club lounge. Berry rubbed one hand through his hair, then the other.

'Look, I never slept with her. Some of the other guys did. I pulled a stomach muscle in training and went to Brian's room to get some rest. But Genny and the others had no intention of getting any sleep that night. I get it on with some other chick. When I eventually made it back to our cabin there was this naked chinger sleeping on the floor, puke and piss all over the carpet. Then she makes this gross noise and goes all quiet. Genny said she didn't have a pulse. That's when everyone panicked. This dead naked chick in your cabin. We were shit-scared the drugs would be found, we'd be kicked off, and all our wives and girlfriends would find out.'

No one seemed remotely concerned about Lilly or her family. No one commenced CPR, even if she had lost a pulse. Anya was stunned that not once did they consider anyone but themselves.

'I said we should call for help, but Genny said it was too late. He reckoned no good could come of telling anyone about it. He said she was right into the fantasy and brought it on herself. She was already dead, but our lives could all be fucked up. That's when they decided to get rid of the body.'

'How did they plan to move a body through the ship and up onto deck?'

'It wasn't light yet. Everyone else was asleep. The place was deserted. Genny and Bull got her dressed, put a hoodie on her and held her upright, like she was drunk.'

Anya believed that's why they hadn't been flagged on the surveillance footage. Laura would have identified Lilly by her long black hair and red shirt. A hoodie would have covered them both.

'They said they tried to throw her over the side. Then she made some noise. They nearly wet themselves. Turns out she wasn't really dead. They said they tried to wake her up by throwing a leftover beer in her face. She moaned. They got one of the hoses the cleaners use and sprayed her with it.'

'You mean the high pressure ones?'

'That's what they said. The guy who put it there went off to do something else. When they saw him coming back, they shoved her into a cupboard and ran. They went to sleep and we all thought she'd be fine. Next thing we hear, she was dead.'

More bells went off and they could hear loud cheers from inside the casino. Someone had just won the jackpot.

'I have one more question,' Fitz calmly asked. 'How would you feel if someone did that to your little girl?'

Berry began to cry. At first softly, then uncontrollably.

Fitz shoved a hanky in his direction and led him away from the casino entrance. Berry took it and wiped his face.

'What happens now?' He sniffed.

'For one, I have to tell the Chan family. The authorities will take it from there.'

'I need to ask something.' Anya moved in front of him. 'Have you seen or heard of a woman – late twenties, long brown hair. Pretty, about five foot four. Nuala or Mishka?'

'There are a lot of girls on board who look like that. Name doesn't ring a bell.' Berry ran the hankie across the tip of his nose. 'Then again, Genny and Bull aren't big on finding out names.'

Anya could feel the heat of FitzHarris's stare but did not look at him.

'I need to get this guy's statement,' Fitz said. 'But I want to talk to you. Straight after.'

Anya walked away. Maybe Mishka's disappearance had nothing to do with ESOW. She could have been at the wrong place, wrong time and run into any of the bowling men. If they'd spiked her drink and something went wrong . . . They had already been in trouble because Lilly was found. If they had succeeded in throwing her overboard, there would be nothing to tie them to her. They may not have made that mistake a second time.

39

The following morning, with Ben happily spending the morning at the kids' club with his new friends, Anya returned to the suite and removed the contents from her bedroom safe.

Between Wesley and Martin locating College Girl, and FitzHarris interviewing Gus Berry, there had been no time to go through the papers Mishka had hidden. The night before, exhausted and drained, Anya had climbed into bed in her clothes, and woken up in time for breakfast.

She put the files into a pile on the floor downstairs, curled up on the lounge and began to read. Something in here had to explain what had happened to Mishka. A myriad of newspaper clippings had been stuffed into a folder. They might as well be where she started.

Martin appeared through the door, half wet and bare chested. Glancing up, she couldn't miss the six pack in front of her and didn't take her eyes off quickly enough. He patted his abdomen. 'The water is gorgeous.'

A towel was wrapped around his waist, over his board shorts. Or so she hoped.

'You should grab your suit and go in.' His hair was damp and the waves had shrunk it into soft fair curls. He inclined his head toward a shoulder and patted the outside ear. Something he always did after showers, surfing and swimming. It was then the other ear's turn. It used to irritate her, but for some reason, now, it was almost endearing.

'It's as if we passed through a weather warp. Not a cloud in the sky.' He wandered over and opened up the balcony doors. A gust of wind blew a number of papers across the floor. He turned back and chased the loose sheets, like he was after a moving chicken. 'What are these?'

Anya hadn't yet explained about Mishka's locker. She deliberately omitted the scene outside the change rooms with the men. Martin didn't need to hear any more about their behaviour. Besides, no one had harmed her.

'Why didn't you tell me? I would have helped.' His eyelids creased at a slight angle, as if he were wounded. 'But that's what you always do. You still haven't learnt that you don't have to go through all this on your own.'

In some ways, it hadn't occurred to Anya to enlist Martin's help. This felt like work and she functioned alone most of the time in her job.

'Annie, no one expects you to be a superwoman.' He slapped the papers on the coffee table. 'No one that is, except you.' He grabbed his novel and headed out to the balcony.

She hadn't even registered the change in weather until he'd mentioned it. On a cruise. On their holiday. Squeals, shouts and laughter drifted in through the open door. From the sounds, holidaymakers were making the most of the sun and warmth. She glanced out the massive windows – the sky was perfectly clear and a deep blue. Martin was right. In the latter part of their marriage, she had been so busy working to support the family, she had disconnected from the people in it.

Putting down the file, she walked out onto the balcony. The grey, rain and wind had been replaced with the vibrant colours of swimsuits and clothing. Families frolicked and fathers splashed with their children in the pools. She breathed in the fresh sea air.

'If you're interested, I'd love some help sorting through the information.'

'Honestly?'

She nodded.

'Where do you want me to start?'

Inside, she handed him a file. He lay on the floor, while she sat cross-legged on the lounge. To begin with, they each read in silence.

Not surprisingly, the news clippings and print-outs were about the cruise industry. A couple on holiday reported plastic bottles and cans being discharged from the back of a boat along the east coast of Canada. They were informed by crew that international maritime regulations permitted dumping of rubbish beyond twelve miles from the coast. There was a denial of any wrongdoing from the company spokesperson, and an investigation was looking into a faulty release lever on the ship.

'Do you mind if I put on some of my music? It's a compilation.' Martin switched on the CD unit and Dire Straits played. 'This reminds me a bit of when we were at university. Remember?'

Anya did. Back then, she had moved to the mainland from Tasmania and for the first time in her life felt free from public scrutiny and town gossip. Her sister's disappearance wasn't as well-known in Newcastle, so she was able to study in relative anonymity. Martin lived across from her in Edwards Hall, the college residence. She had liked him from the start, and he had seen her around the hospital when he did his nursing practicals. His humour and kindness to patients drew her in. That was years ago.

'Uh huh.' She kept reading.

'Do you remember going to that bowling club every Friday night?'

How could she forget? They could dance for hours to

songs that became anthems and the drinks were the cheapest around. Music by the Angels, the Hoodoo Gurus, along with Madonna and Michael Jackson – before he became androgynous. Twisted Sister's 'We're Not Gonna Take It' was guaranteed to bring everyone to their feet.

'And what about that awesome shaving-cream fight. The one that went for hours.'

'The one you started.' She smiled. It was difficult to forget. Half the residents became involved and the engineering students were masters at ambushes. It was the most fun Anya had ever had.

'Was it really you who moved the entire contents of that poor guy's room onto the oval?' She had never wanted to know before now.

Martin gave a sheepish grin. 'That poor guy pranked most of my friends, so you could say it was well deserved.'

The warden had tried to find the culprit. Until now, Anya had been unsure who was the brains behind the venture. Like magicians, practical jokers had a code of secrecy.

'You know, we enjoyed ourselves but it was harmless.' He returned to the floor, this time lying on his side, head resting on an elbow. 'Sure we drank a bit, but we didn't hurt anyone. I was sort of hoping this cruise would be a bit like that. But the world has changed – a lot.'

Anya had to agree. They had partied when they were younger but always knuckled down to study. At the end of a week, money would be short so they would play cards with their friends, pool what was left of the weekly food allowance and buy hot chips and white bread. Chip sandwiches washed down with gallons of water were filling and became a favourite treat.

'Or maybe we all had to grow up.'

'True.'

'Here's something interesting,' Martin looked up. 'A study

of a hundred ships in Alaskan waters found all but one sample of ship's effluent had faecal bacteria or total solids in violation of something called the Clean Water Act. This is scary stuff.'

'That explains why the environmentalists wanted action.' She recalled the conversation with Rachel about Lars Anderson's plans for the company.

'It sounds like the Alaskan authorities were pretty ticked off.' He flicked to the next page. 'Monitoring had been voluntary and the industry pretty much self-regulated until they made more stringent laws and started enforcing them.' He sat up. 'Listen to this, it sounds like ships are exempt from normal pollution and water laws. They are allowed to dump treated sewage less than three miles from shore and raw sewage just over three miles. Imagine if a hotel on the water did that? How many people have no idea they're swimming or surfing in turds?'

He pulled a face. 'If that isn't offensive enough,' he referred to the document, 'untreated sewage contains pathogenic bacteria, viruses, intestinal parasites and by-products that could contaminate fish and shellfish, potentially causing major disease outbreaks and devastation to those local industries.' He looked up. 'Oh yeah, and that doesn't include the harmful chemicals in faeces. Algae thrive on nitrogen and phosphorous. Deposits use up the oxygen in the water. That can kill off whole ecosystems, especially fish. You wouldn't want to be a fisherman in that wake.'

That was different from the version Jeremy Wise, the environmental officer, told.

'News clippings cite tens of millions of dollars in fines paid by cruise companies. It's probably cheaper to pay them than invest in technologies like advanced water treatment equipment to do the right thing,' Anya surmised.

'Mind you, from what this report says, the industry

reckons their sanitation devices produce drinking-quality water, but they don't even use it for washing on board because apparently it discolours the whites. I'm thinking marine life may not be so thrilled with what is pumped into its ecosystems.'

In the pile, by the lounge, there were water sample reports from a laboratory in California. Some of the samples were 10,000 times the limit for coliform bacteria. Others were up to 150,000 times higher. The majority were described as being dumped between two and three miles from shore.

'Carlos worked in the waste department,' Anya commented. 'Mishka could have been paying him for samples prior to the waste being jettisoned. Independent analyses show this company is consistently in serious violation of environmental standards.'

'Maybe this is the leverage that was going to be used by Lars Anderson.'

Rachel had been adamant that the information they were gathering was for Lars's report which he was using against his father and brother. Anya sifted through the pile and extracted the large envelope. The contents were the size of a manuscript. 'Taking Anderson Lines into the future.' By Lars Anderson. In the introduction, ESOW was acknowledged as the inspiration for making Anderson Cruise Lines the most innovative, energy-efficient company in the industry. A world leader. Just as Walt Disney had vision and embraced new technologies, it claimed, Anderson Cruise Lines could enhance their brand by use of clean energy and sustainable programmes.

'Someone,' Martin added, 'went to a lot of trouble to blow up the Andersons' yacht. Whoever that was sent a pretty powerful message to the family.'

Martin sipped from a bottle of water on the coffee table. Anya reached for hers, and he handed it across. She opened it and his bare torso caught her attention again.

Without thinking, she flicked the open bottle in his direction. He shook the water out of his hair. 'What the—'

Anya began to laugh and something compelled her to do it again. This time, Martin leapt from the chair, wrestled the bottle from her and poured some down the back of her shirt. Instead of resisting, she buckled over and laughed, harder than she had in a long time. Martin joined her. Once he relaxed, she snatched the bottle back and poured it down the back of his shorts.

'You are in so much trouble.' He picked her up from behind, trapping both arms by her sides. She wiggled, still laughing as he carried her inside to the downstairs bathroom. They could have been teenagers again.

'You asked for it, Annie.'

'You wouldn't.' She struggled. 'You were already wet,' she managed between chuckles. She was fully clothed. There was no escape. Seconds later they were in the shower cubicle with the water full blast.

She squealed with the cold shock. Martin had his arms around her, keeping her in position as her T-shirt and jeans became saturated. In a pitiful attempt at revenge, she tried to catch water in her hands and throw it in his direction. She turned and looked to see his reaction and felt his breath on her face. His eyes were wide and focused. It was the same look he used to get when they made love. She felt his warm hands slide to her hips, pulling her to him. When their lower bodies touched, it was electric.

'What are we doing?'

'Don't think, Annie.'

'This isn't . . .' He brushed her mouth with his. 'Supposed to happen,' she mumbled. Her mind was a jumble.

He kissed her gently and nuzzled her cheek. Water flowed around them. They paused, foreheads touching. She could feel her heart pounding as she met his mouth. At first tentatively, then passionately, savouring the chlorine on his lips. He peeled off her shirt and unclipped the back of her bra, sliding the straps off her shoulders, one at a time. His mouth caressed her neck, firing every nerve cell. She arched her back as his soft hands and mouth cupped her naked breasts. She gasped.

'What about protection?' He pulled back. She had bought condoms in New York. She grabbed one from the toiletries bag.

He pushed her gently against the wall and his fingers traced a line down her abdomen, circling above the tops of her jeans. Teasing. She kissed him harder and lowered his board shorts.

For the first time in years, she wanted to lose control.

40

After showering, Martin kissed her head.

'I'll leave you to dry off,' he said tenderly, and closed the door behind him.

She stared in the mirror, trying to understand what had just happened. They were away from everyone who knew them. Martin had broken up with Nita. They hadn't even had a chance to discuss how he felt about it. She combed the knots out of her hair. There was nothing binding her to Ethan Rye. He hadn't even emailed. Maybe it was just comforting sex for Martin. They had been reminiscing and were relaxed in each other's company. It had been natural, unforced, and she had forgotten how good it felt to be touched, and loved by a man. She wrapped herself in a towel and headed upstairs, her face still flushed and warm.

'Forever Young' played on the CD.

Once dressed, she headed back down. Martin was dressed in jeans and a polo shirt, standing at the table examining photos.

'We need to talk to Rachel. If someone got rid of Mishka, they could already know about the cousins' involvement in ESOW.'

Martin slipped on sneakers. Anya collected up the papers and placed them back in the bag. 'After you.' He held open the door. They took the elevator and followed the corridor along to the medical centre in an awkward silence.

'Hey you two. Good timing,' Karen said. 'We've just

ending a busy clinic with a poor old man passing away in his cabin.'

'What happened?' Anya wanted to know.

'He was eighty-eight, one of our regulars. Metastatic prostate cancer and pneumonia took hold. He refused treatment in the end. His wife was with him and it's what they wanted.'

Paco arrived with his trolley.

'Ah, the good coffee's here. Can I get you one?'

'Actually, we're looking for Rachel.'

Karen frowned and led them inside the reception area. 'I don't know what's going on. She's been a nervous wreck. Last night, I found her about to inject the wrong medication into Carlos's drip. There's a big difference between local anaesthetic and antibiotics. I had to fill out an incident report which has gone to security and the captain. It took FitzHarris less than an hour to storm down here and confine her to her cabin until further notice.'

Anya held the bag's contents tighter.

'What the hell is going on? Is she on drugs? And why am I being kept out of the loop? I am supposed to be responsible for my staff . . .'

'I'm sorry.' Her thoughts raced. Did FitzHarris lock Rachel in her cabin to protect patients, or for another reason? He could have assumed she was trying to harm Carlos, or maybe he had discovered her ties to ESOW. 'I can't answer why Fitz reacted the way he did.'

Karen touched her hand. 'I'm not asking for personal details and don't want to break any professional confidence. It's pretty clear, Rachel is in serious trouble.'

The nurse locked eyes with Anya, who clutched the bag of documents in both hands. She glanced at a frowning Martin, who nodded. 'We can't do this on our own.'

'Fine. Anything we tell you has to be in the strictest confidence.'

'I don't have a problem with that. Something tells me I need to brace myself.' She got three coffees from Paco's trolley and led the way into a consulting room. Before closing the door, she flipped a sign over: 'Consultation in Progress'.

Anya decided she had to trust Karen completely. Mishka's life could still depend on it. She sat in a consulting chair and told Karen all she knew about Rachel, Mishka, Nuala and the environmental group Lars Anderson had funded for the women.

Karen sat opposite Anya, listening intently. 'The poor thing is scared to death. No wonder. The police are talking about arrests in the Anderson bombing. That explains why FitzHarris was on the rampage.'

The phone rang and Karen excused herself to answer. 'She's standing right here,' she stammered, looking at Anya. 'That's impossible.'

Anya took the phone. FitzHarris was on the line. 'I want you all down in the morgue now!'

His tone disturbed her. 'Why? What's going on?'

'You'll see when you get here!'

Karen, Martin and Anya took the same lift the Chans had used when they went to identify Lilly's body.

The morgue door was open and FitzHarris barked into his phone, 'I'll call you back.' He hung up, perspiration under the arms of his shirt and on his brow.

'Something's turned up. The nurse brought the old man's body down here and opened up the second drawer. But guess what he found? It was already occupied.'

Lilly was in the top compartment. Anya wondered if Rachel's cousin had been hiding in the other drawer.

'Any idea who this is?' Fitz moved toward the drawer.

Anya took a breath. Karen and Martin kept their heads bowed.

He slid open the drawer and peeled off a covering sheet. A woman's body lay in front of them. Anya instantly recognised it.

'That's her,' she admitted. 'The woman who pretended to be Nuala. Her real name is Mishka.' Anya immediately thought of Rachel.

'You asked Gus Berry about a woman. I checked. There's no Mishka on the manifesto.' Fitz's eyebrows furrowed. 'Any chance you can explain to me how someone you happened to meet, who officially doesn't exist, just happens to turn up dead in the morgue?'

41

Anya handed Martin the document bag and moved over to the body. It was clad in a pair of navy overalls and the woman's brown hair was pulled into a short ponytail, most of it still within the elastic tie. The body was damp, and reeked like a stagnant pond.

'That's rancid.' Martin covered his mouth and nose. 'What is it?'

'That's what I want to know.' Fitz said. 'Karen, have you ever seen this woman?'

The senior nurse shook her head.

Anya stepped forward. 'Mishka Valencia was a member of the environmental group, ESOW.' It was possible Rachel had murdered her and the search had been an act. Maybe she had intended to kill Carlos by injecting anaesthetic. It would have eliminated both connections to her. They had assumed the shooter was a man, but there was no reason it couldn't be a woman. 'Rachel was hiding Mishka, in her own cabin. She said they were cousins.'

'And it didn't occur to you to mention any of this?' The vessels in his neck bulged.

'They were working for Lars Anderson. He put together a damning report on the environmental damage the company was doing. I didn't believe they had anything to do with the bombing of the boat. They were terrified that they'd been set up and had no idea by whom.' Anya realised how ridiculous it must have sounded. Maybe Rachel and Mishka had used Lars Anderson, and things had gone wrong.

'And you know all this because?' Fitz paced, hands on his hips.

'Lars Anderson wrote a report his father and brother were supposed to discuss the night the yacht was destroyed.'

Martin held the bag up for Fitz to see. He moved over, unzipped it and dug through the contents. 'It's full of papers.'

'They were hidden by Mishka in the change-room lockers at the spa.'

'Right. I want Martin and Karen upstairs. Wait for me in the medical centre. Do not go anywhere or call anyone. Unless there are any other bodies you've forgotten to mention before I phone Captain Burghoff?'

Before leaving, Karen located a couple of breathing masks, and handed plastic gowns and gloves to Anya and Fitz, which they put on. Her expression was solemn.

Martin brushed Anya's back. 'Will you be all right?'

Anya assured him. 'I want to know what happened as much as anyone. None of this makes any sense.'

They left and closed the door behind them.

'I can't tell you how angry I am,' FitzHarris announced.

'Don't bother. You have no right to be sanctimonious. I heard you've locked Rachel up. The way you intimidated her about the records from the night Nuala McKenny died was reprehensible. Why would I trust you?'

'I did what?' His nostrils flared and top lip narrowed. 'I intimidated her? That takes the cake. I was following up what you said, if you want the truth. I thought it was odd there was no documentation if there was in fact an alleged assault. Every move the medical team makes is recorded in triplicate. And those comments about Nuala's work being below par, one of them was signed after she disappeared. It was hand-written, but the date was pretty clear and had been changed.

Someone wanted to distort the circumstances around her death. The supervisor who signed the assessment suddenly got an all-expenses paid vacation in an "employee of the month" prize. Turns out it was the only month it was ever offered. More than a coincidence, I assume. I demanded Rachel tell me the truth about the assault.'

Anya felt an ache in her gut. She had misjudged FitzHarris. He had tried to do the right thing as much as she had. 'So, like me, you think the company will do anything to keep these cases from going public.'

He drew a deep breath. 'From what I can tell, in an alleged sexual assault involving a crew member, the accused is immediately flown back to his home country without ever being interviewed by police. By the time anyone decides to investigate, potential witnesses are long gone and crew have been moved on. They're instructed that they are under no obligation to leave their duties to answer police questions.'

He looked at the body. 'Any indicators as to how or when she died?'

Anya began with the face and neck. There were no ligature marks or bruises. Palpating the head, there was no obvious sign of fracture, laceration or bruising.

Anya moved the sheet down, exposing the hands. The fingertips had a typical 'washerwoman' appearance. 'She's been immersed in water, I'd estimate somewhere between twenty and fifty minutes.'

'How can you be sure?'

Anya lifted Mishka's hands. Unlike Lilly Chan, this woman had small, short fingers. A diamond solitaire in white gold sat on her right ring finger. 'She's been in water long enough for the fingertips to wrinkle, but not so long to affect the rest of the fingers and hands. It doesn't tell us, though, whether she was dead or alive when she entered the water.'

She eased the ring off and handed it to FitzHarris's gloved

hand. He held it to the light. 'It's engraved inside.' He bent down to his kitbag and removed a magnifying glass.

'There's an inscription. "In appreciation. L.A." Didn't you just say she was—'

'Working for Lars Anderson.' Rachel's story was adding up. She obviously had good reason to be worried about her wellbeing after the attack on the Andersons' yacht.

Anya pressed on the dead woman's chest. Pink frothy fluid erupted from the nose and mouth, bringing with it a foul smell.

Fitz stepped back. 'She is dead. I checked for a pulse.'

'It's haemorrhagic fluid from the lungs, and airways. We need a toxicology screen and full post-mortem. We could be looking at pulmonary oedema from another cause, but it's highly possible she drowned. Working out time of death's more difficult. It depends on the temperature of the water she was immersed in.'

'Does the goose flesh on her arms tell you anything?'

'The erector pilae muscles spasm as a result of rigor mortis, so no.' Anya pressed on the upper abdomen and more froth and liquid spilled out of the mouth and nose. 'There's fluid in her stomach as well. My first thoughts are that she drowned. So far, no defence injuries to suggest a struggle, either.'

Fitz shone a light over some of the fluid from the mouth. Something caught Anya's attention. She bent down to closer examine the nose. 'Can you hold the torch over the nose?'

He obliged.

'There's something tiny stuck to one of the hairs just inside the nostril. Can I borrow the magnifying glass?'

He handed it over.

'There's something in there. I'll need tweezers and a slide plate.'

The security officer ferreted through his box. 'These do?'

he handed her a pair of fine-tipped tweezers, as if they were a peace offering.

Anya felt comfortable again with him. They were working on the same side and had been all along, it seemed. At the very least, no other security officer would be so well-equipped in a morgue.

'You must have been a boy scout.' She tried to lighten the mood.

'Until fourteen. Dib, dib, dib,' he muttered and moved to the other side of the steel tray, where he held the slide and torch.

'I thought it moved, but that could have been the hair when the fluid gushed out. Whatever it is, it's hanging tight.'

She plucked the hair and lay it on the glass slide. With magnification and light, she could see it more clearly. 'It looks like a slater bug, only much, much smaller.'

Fitz stood up straight. 'Damn. On top of all this, are you going to tell me the ship's infested with some kind of bug?'

Anya didn't want to consider the possibility either. 'It's tiny, less than a millimetre.'

'Would a microscope help?'

Anya looked at his kitbag. 'Don't tell me you have one of those too.'

'Do you know how much those things cost? There's a digital one in the medical centre. If we can identify the damn thing, the sooner the better.'

He covered the body, slid it into the recess and closed the door while Anya removed the gloves and washed her hands.

On the way up in the lift, Anya carried the slide. Fitz leant against the lift wall, scratching his arm. 'This is turning into the cruise from hell. I can already see the headlines.'

'It might not be anything.' She changed the subject. 'If you knew Rachel was telling the truth about Nuala's assault, why did you put her under cabin arrest?'

'Someone wanted Carlos silenced. Karen caught her trying to inject the wrong drug. I had no choice but to protect Carlos for the time being. Rachel's a good nurse and shouldn't make mistakes like that. I ran a check and she's been a member of Green Speak, Citizens against Global Warming and other groups.'

'Do you really think Rachel tried to kill Carlos?' She thought back to Rachel's shock when it was decided to amputate his legs. Someone who wanted to harm him would not have been so keen to save his legs.

'I wouldn't have picked her for a killer, but I had one in the family for years and didn't know it. I'm not taking any chances.'

At least if she was confined to her room, Rachel was less likely to be killed by whoever harmed Mishka.

'Is she safely confined?'

'Housekeeping, the hotel manager, and security are the only ones with overriding keys. She won't starve, if that's what you're getting at.'

'Don't you mean universal keys?'

'No, we need to be able to override the deadlocks, in case passengers refuse to open up.'

'If deadlocks don't protect passengers, women sleeping assume they're safe but are still vulnerable to sexual assault. Nuala said she was assaulted by a security guard. He could have overriden her lock.'

'I take your point, but the system still has to function.'

They entered the medical centre.

'The microscope's in here.'

It was the same room she had been in once before with the blood gas and other high-tech machines.

Turning on the power, she placed the slide into position. The monitor screen glowed white. Anya navigated the slide until the creature came into view.

'There it is.'

It was a segmented invertebrate, with antennae at the head. At the posterior end were a number of round-shaped objects, and a filamentous trail behind the body.

'It's small enough to get in anywhere. Hell, if people are carrying it in their noses . . .' Fitz didn't finish the thought.

'It's female and fully grown. Those are eggs inside.' She pointed to the posterior end.

'What are we looking at? Mite, louse, bed bug?' Fitz scratched himself again.

Anya didn't think so. 'It's far too small. And it isn't an insect. I think it came from the water. If we can identify what sort of water it lives in, we might be able to narrow down where on the ship Mishka could have drowned.'

She took a digital picture and saved the file.

'Jeremy Wise, the environmental officer, has a science degree, specialising in microbiology, if that helps.'

'Can you get him here?'

FitzHarris was already making the call.

42

Jeremy studied the image on the medical centre microscope.

'This is brilliant,' he declared. 'Isn't she a wonder?'

That wasn't a word Anya normally associated with wriggling organisms.

'It's most definitely a crustacean. Do you have access to the internet up here?'

'Any of the consulting rooms, and the doctor and head nurse's office.'

Anya and FitzHarris followed him into Karen's room, where she was waiting with Martin.

When he saw Anya, Martin stood, hands in his denim pockets and raised his eyebrows.

'This is Jeremy Wise, the ship's environmental officer. He needs to look something up on the web.'

Karen vacated her chair and Jeremy enthusiastically took her place and logged in. 'Science is all about solving life's mysteries,' he said, adjusting his glasses.

He had no idea how relevant his comment was.

Martin took the opportunity to talk to FitzHarris.

'The police were pretty quick to blame that environmental group for bombing the Anderson family boat that happened to wipe out most of the heirs.'

Fitz crossed his arms. 'Your point?'

'Shouldn't every investigation begin with who is likely to benefit most from the deaths?'

'That would be Mats, the third wife and her kid. Old man

Anderson was worth a fortune. A couple of years ago when his new wife had a daughter, there was speculation as to how his estate would be divided when he eventually dropped off his perch. The other people to benefit would be his business competitors, along with everyone else he or the family rubbed up the wrong way.'

'Well,' Karen stood, arms folded. 'I know Rachel. She couldn't be involved in anything like terrorism. What would she possibly have to gain? She's terrified.'

'Of getting caught, or something else?'

Anya stepped forward. 'From what I can tell, it was public knowledge that the family convened on the yacht for family occasions. The media was already covering it because it was Mats' fortieth.'

'It's a lot of collateral damage for someone who was passionate about saving wildlife and the environment,' Karen argued.

'Fundamental right-to-lifers have no hesitation in killing doctors working in clinics,' Martin conceded.

Anya argued, 'Only Lars was demanding the company improve energy efficiency and work toward sustainability for ships.'

'You know this how?' Fitz demanded. 'Something else Rachel sprouted?'

Anya collected the bag from the floor and placed it on the examination couch. She located the copy of Lars's 400-page business plan and gave it to Fitz. 'This is what Mishka kept hidden, and was probably killed for.'

Karen moved over and began to flick through the papers.

'Narrowing it down . . .' Jeremy looked up, then down again. 'It's definitely a copepod.' He searched something else. 'I think this is it. *Porcellidium*. It looks like a miniature garden slater.'

'I don't care what it's called,' Fitz snapped, 'I just want to know if it's some kind of outbreak.'

Jeremy placed both hands on the table. 'I've never actually seen this species before. This female's carrying eggs so the breeding conditions have obviously been favourable.'

The word breeding caused Karen to cover her mouth. 'Are you saying we've got an infestation? The ship will have to be quarantined at the next port . . .'

'Before we go off half-baked, we need to be sure. Do you have any idea where it came from? Food supplies, wheat or rice?' Fitz pressed. 'The captain will be here any minute to see for himself.'

Jeremy sat back. 'It isn't like that. This isn't an insect. It's a crustacean. They occur in sea water.' He scrolled the screen. 'That's it! I've got it. This is a *Porcellidium ravanae*. They live on seaweed in rock pools. Looks like this one's only found off the coast of India.' He looked up, chest puffed. 'We can send it for confirmation ID, but that could take days.'

'Great. The woman dies in Indian waters then mysteriously turns up in our morgue. This is insane.' Fitz turned to Anya. 'Is it in any way possible the dead body has been on the ship for months? Frozen or otherwise?' He rubbed his forehead. 'Are you absolutely sure this is the woman you saw outside your cabin?'

Anya doubted the crustacean would have survived outside of water for long.

Jeremy interjected. 'I can't explain how it got onto your body, but I know where this one could have come from. The ship takes on and releases ballast water, depending on the onboard weight and sea conditions. Water got picked up on the Indian leg, and is still in the ballast tanks. The *Porcellidium* was probably going about its business on the water's surface in the tank.'

'That has to be where Mishka drowned, and inhaled the organism,' Anya said. 'She was collecting samples and having them analysed by outside laboratories. Maybe she slipped.'

'Or was pushed.' FitzHarris was already dialling the captain. 'Anya, I'm going to need you to come with me, it's still a possible crime scene.'

Karen placed her hand on Fitz's and laid some papers from Anya's bag on her desk. 'You might want to see this first.'

He hung up before being connected.

'They're logs of some kind. This one is signed by Carlos. The other is dated the same day, but the signature's different, so are the figures.'

'They're probably from different sections.' Jeremy looked closely. 'Wait. This can't be right. These are waste disposal logs, only there has to be an error on the date.'

'This one is unsigned,' Fitz noted. 'I can't read the other scrawl.'

'I don't have to,' Karen said. 'I'd know that handwriting anywhere. He comes into the clinic every couple of days.' She moved to her filing cabinet and pulled out a thick folder. 'Incident reports from the world's greatest hypochondriac. A scratch and he thinks he's dying from blood-poisoning and wants compassionate leave to sort out his affairs.' She passed a document to Fitz.

'You're right. It's identical.' He looked up. 'Who is it?'

'Sergio, or Cockroach. He works in the waste centre.'

Anya and FitzHarris had met him when they visited Carlos's workplace.

'So what do the two different logs mean?' Martin pressed. 'Is it a misprint, sloppy practice?'

Jeremy's face was pinker than before. 'We have to keep meticulous records. I countersign them every week. I always thought this was Carlos's writing.' He looked at the one signed by Cockroach. 'It goes into my in-tray at the end of every day.'

Martin stood over him. 'Are you signing off on the real or faked logs?'

'Why would I risk my job approving fraudulent records?'

'Money,' Martin said. 'If environmental rules aren't followed, the cruise line faces fines that run into millions of dollars. And you must save a packet by discharging rubbish and sewage into the ocean. Much lower disposal fees at the other end. Fudge the figures here, pocket the difference.'

'That's ridiculous,' Jeremy stammered. 'I don't even manage the budget, and I'm not on any commission. I get the same salary ever week, like any other officer.'

'You'll keep for now,' Fitz announced. 'Our first priority is to get to the ballast tanks before some clean freak destroys any more evidence.'

43

On the way to the ballast tanks, FitzHarris used his cell-phone to notify the captain of the crustacean and how they suspected it had got into the body. Anya accompanied him in silence. The most likely scenario was that Mishka Valencia had been collecting a sample of water and somehow fallen into the tank. The other was that she had been pushed. If someone was falsifying waste records, they had a lot to lose if caught. That could have been the reason for Carlos being shot, especially if he were selling the documents showing the real figures to Mishka.

They left the tourist-filled halls and entered the crew elevator, down below the I-95. The vibration from the engines was amplified, and the humming more intense than the deck above. The corridor was narrower than on other decks, and the heat suffocating.

Fitz's hair was damp and curled at the back of his neck.

'The captain said there are four large tanks down here. They fill and empty them according to needs. It's how this ship can handle forty-foot waves without a waiter tipping a glass. Well, normally anyway.'

The place seemed deserted. 'Not a lot of need for staff. They're only cleaned when empty so we could be in luck.'

They climbed over a tall lip into the first tank room. On the floor was a square metal latch door, half the size of an average desk.

'Can you lift it open?' he asked.

Anya hesitated for a moment. It would leave her in a vulnerable position. She could not trust anyone that much right now.

'All I want to do is see if you can move it. Mishka was roughly your size and weight.'

It made sense. Anya unbolted the latch and pulled. Once the initial resistance was broken, the task became easier. She lowered the hatch to the floor. The odour from the tank was foul.

'I've smelt some pretty disgusting things at crime scenes, but this takes the cake,' Fitz said, looking around. On the wall were reusable breathing masks.

Anya covered her mouth and then pulled on the mask Fitz gave her. After fitting his own, he released a flashlight mounted on the wall and switched it on, directing the beam of light inside the black hole. Anya knelt down, keeping her centre of gravity away from the hole as best she could. She could make out the rungs of a metal ladder.

Fitz moved the torch around, light reflecting off the water, roughly three feet below.

'If Mishka had tried to get a sample, she could have easily toppled forward when she reached.'

Fitz squatted, knees not making contact with the floor. He looked back to the door. 'Or if someone had seen her, it wouldn't have taken much to push her off balance. Someone that size would fall straight forward.'

Anya tried to visualise the situation. Bent over, it was possible Mishka could have fallen forward and hit her head on the wall, except Anya had found no signs of fracture or bruising in the examination. There hadn't been any signs of scratching to the fingers either to suggest she might have tried to climb out by the ladder rungs.

'But if she was turned around, and someone pushed, she'd go in backwards or in a half roll. Close the hatch and she's in pitch black. It would be easy to become disorientated. She might have never found the sides and the ladder rungs, despite being inches from them.'

'That could explain the absence of any head trauma,' Anya said.

'I heard about a guy dying once in one of these. He had no safety gear and they said he suffocated while treading water.'

Anya took the torch. 'There's rust everywhere. It's possible that's where the oxygen is used up. He could have dry-drowned: held his breath until his heart gave out, so he was dead before he could inhale any water.'

That didn't seem to be the case with Mishka.

Fitz examined the interior side of the hatch and the floor around them. 'No signs of a struggle here.'

Anya's head began to pound with the heat, noise and enclosed space.

Once back in the corridor, she ripped off the mask and took a few deep breaths.

'Let's try number two. It's further along.'

A worker stood to the side to let them pass. 'Where you off to?' Fitz spoke loud enough to be heard.

The man pulled a pack of cigarettes from his top pocket and popped one between his lips. He didn't stop for a discussion.

'If she did fall, or was pushed,' Anya said, 'that still doesn't explain how she ended up in the morgue.'

'Maybe it was an accident,' Fitz said, 'and they panicked.'

'Why not just throw the body overboard?'

Fitz looked up. 'It's a long way to a balcony from here. A lot of people might notice you. The morgue's closer.'

Inside the second room, a man in blue overalls was mopping the floor. He startled when he saw them, the ambient noise must have drowned out their footsteps.

His features were familiar. The greasy hair – Cockroach. Anya's pulse raced. He had a brush and was now on his hands and knees scrubbing the floor.

FitzHarris shouted, 'Mind if we take a look around?'

Cockroach slowly stood and dropped the brush into a bucket. The knees of his clothes were soaked, and he had leftover suds on his right hand.

'Can you move to the side?' Fitz ordered, with an outstretched arm. 'Stay there.'

This time he opened the hatch himself, eyes on Cockroach the entire time. As soon as he shone the light, Anya saw the string. FitzHarris moved between the worker and Anya as she bent down and cautiously lifted it with a finger. It was two metres long and tied to a small plastic jug.

Cockroach, now with hands in pockets, leant past FitzHarris for a view.

'Can you untie it carefully?' Fitz shouted. 'Could have prints on it.'

Anya bent down. Out of the corner of her eye, she saw Cockroach charge at FitzHarris, knocking him off balance. They wrestled, and Anya reached for the hatch door to close it. Cockroach broke free and kicked Fitz hard in his bad leg. Fitz screamed in pain. Anya moved to help him and was met with a gun in her face.

'Get up slowly,' Cockroach yelled. 'Or I shoot you and the pig.'

Heart drilling in her chest, Anya did as she was told. Cockroach snatched her hair and pulled her toward him.

He stuck the gun in her neck and shouted at Fitz. 'You.'

She felt the cold steel digging in and tried not to breathe or do anything to panic him.

'Get into the tank. Now! Or I blow her head off.'

Fitz had both hands up and slowly pulled himself toward the open hatch, his eyes on Anya.

Cockroach tightened his grip on her. 'I will shoot. Get in!'

Fitz manoeuvred himself into the opening and lowered himself down the ladder, still keeping his eyes on Anya. She hoped he had a plan. So far, she had nothing. The soles of her shoes were soft, not hard enough to ram down Cockroach's shin and force him to release his grip. All she had was the plastic jug and string in her hand.

The rest of the room was filled with vertical and horizontal white pipes with circular valves at eye level. One wall was full of lights, switches and computerised gadgets. She strained to see if there was an alarm button. Anything to alert others on the ship they were in trouble. Fitz's head disappeared out of sight.

'Let go of the woman,' a voice shouted.

Cockroach turned, Anya moving with him. Standing in the doorway was the chief engineer, Alessandro. The Italian who likened himself to Alexander the Great. He stepped toward them, arms outstretched. 'Put down the gun.'

'It's out of control,' Cockroach said, one clammy hand still holding her shoulder. The barrel of the gun moved to her temple.

'That's why I'm here. To fix everything,' Alessandro announced. 'Just trust me.' A pipe made a clunking sound, distracting Cockroach, and Alessandro pounced, wrestling the gun from Cockroach. Anya stepped away and took a deep breath. They were safe.

Alessandro slammed a wall button with his elbow as Anya moved to the hatch to help Fitz. Help was on its way.

Suddenly, the sound of gunfire ripped through her ears. She turned her head to see Cockroach on the floor, his body twitching. He had a hole in his chest spurting blood. Alessandro turned the gun in her direction.

'You. Inside.' He mouthed.

All Anya could hear was the echoing inside her head.

Calmly, Alessandro stepped forward and placed the gun against the back of her neck.

Anya had no doubt he was serious. She shouted, hoping the words were loud enough. 'He attacked you,' she lied. 'I saw it. You had no choice.'

The pressure on her neck increased. Anya slowly climbed down the ladder rungs. Fitz held out his hand. Before she lowered herself in, she flicked the open length of string onto the floor. If the hatch closed, it was the only thing that could point to them inside.

FitzHarris held the belt loop of her jeans as biting cold water enveloped her lower body.

Surging adrenalin could not prevent either of them shivering.

By waist level, the echoing in her ears had eased.

As long as the hatch door remained open they had a chance.

Fitz tightened his grip. 'If we can get him to come closer . . .'

'Someone had to hear the gunshot.'

The light cast a shadow on the lower half of Fitz's face.

'Too much engine noise . . .' He inhaled and coughed, shaking his head. 'The others could be in on it.'

She took some deep breaths. Diesel fumes were preferable to the fetid odours in the tank.

Fitz released his grip on her jeans and hauled himself higher. His injured leg couldn't take weight it seemed.

'We get one chance. Don't let go of the rail . . .'

Anya swallowed and nodded. She eased to the side of the ladder, fingers beginning to cramp. Letting go of the ladder meant almost certain drowning, especially if Alessandro closed the hatch.

'Wait!' they both pleaded.

No response.

'Hey! I have a diamond ring,' Anya bellowed. 'Worth thousands. Here on my hand.'

The Italian appeared above them, inches away from the opening.

'Show me.'

Anya flicked a glance at Fitz who blinked 'yes' with his eyes.

Clinging to the rail, she revealed her grandmother's engagement ring on her right hand.

'It's over a carat of diamonds,' she lied.

'Take it off. Then we talk.'

She retracted her hand. 'No, we need to make a deal first.' Her body shuddered in the cold.

He responded by aiming the gun directly at Fitz's head.

'Wait! I can't get it off. It's stuck.' She pulled again but it didn't budge. 'It won't go past the knuckle.'

Their captor glanced around then quickly moved from sight. Anya strained to hear if he had left. The hatch was still open.

'Maybe someone's coming.'

Fitz lifted himself higher. Alessandro reappeared, this time kneeling and peering down at them.

If he leans a bit more forward, they might be able to jerk him in to the tank, Anya realised.

'Give me your hand,' he ordered.

Fitz tensed, ready.

One chance. That's all they had.

Anya climbed three rungs.

'Closer,' Alessandro demanded.

Anya closed her eyes. Any higher meant she was blocking FitzHarris' path upwards. It all came down to her.

She slowly climbed two more rungs, then another and braced herself to pull with every ounce of strength she had.

With a swift move, Alessandro lunged forward and grabbed her hand, wrenching her arm with it.

337

Ripping pain tore through her shoulder. Her left hand lost contact with the rail. FitzHarris pushed upward and took her full body weight on his shoulders. Her ringed hand was splayed on the floor above, the metal rim of the hatch cutting into her lower arm.

From the throbbing, his knee was pressing her wrist.

She screamed at the sight of an axe held above his shoulder and desperately struggled to break free.

A sudden pull from behind launched her back first into the water, her head and feet following. The shock of cold forced her to draw breath, sucking water into her lungs. Kicking hard, she reached the surface and coughed uncontrollably to expel the vile fluid. Gasping, she lifted both hands. All fingers were still attached.

FitzHarris had saved her and was wrestling with the axe, still in Alessandro's hands. With the small amount of light, Anya propelled her way to the ladder. Before her legs could reach a rung, Fitz had taken a hit to the head and descended into the abyss. The last hint of light disappeared with a clunk.

'Fitz! Fitz!' She panicked. There was no sign of him. Nothing but abject darkness. Anya could barely breathe.

A small beam of light appeared from the water.

'I'm OK.' He was panting. 'Boy scout, remember?'

Relief filled her. The light from his pocket torch approached and Anya wrapped one elbow around the rail in order to reach out to him.

Within seconds he was back at her side, breathing heavily.

Another clunk, then a pump started up. The water began to slosh about them.

'What's happening?' It felt like a weight on her chest. Every breath was becoming more difficult.

'The tank's filling.' He held on to her arm with one leg on a lower rung. 'The water's rising fast. We don't have long.'

Above them, the sound of another shot rang out.

They both shouted for help, but the hatch remained closed.

'If the torch battery goes, we'll become disorientated. We need to get as high as possible.' Freeing his belt, he wrapped it around Anya's wrist and the metal rung, finishing with his own before fastening it tightly.

The water reached chest level. FitzHarris blessed himself with the free hand.

Anya's thoughts flashed to Ben. She didn't want him growing up without his mother.

She screamed for help again. And again. And again.

Nothing.

FitzHarris banged on the hatch with the torch and attempted to force the door. It was too heavy, even when they both pushed.

Anya tried not to waste oxygen.

The light shone on Fitz's watch. Five minutes had passed. The water was now up to their chins and their foreheads hit the inside of the hatch.

They didn't have long.

Anya thought of her parents, and the agony of outliving another child. They didn't deserve that. If only she told them more often that she loved them and shared Ben with them more.

Fitz banged frantically with the torch before the light vanished. They strained to keep their noses pressed against the tank ceiling.

'I'm sorry . . . I got you involved,' he said, taking a shallow breath before going limp by her side. With an arm around his shoulders, she tried in vain to keep his face above the water.

Exhausted, she thought of Martin's smile and the feel of his touch. He would give Ben a good life. Silent tears dissipated into the water. There was so much she wished she could have changed.

The tip of her nose touched the hatch. Lightheadedness and fatigue took hold. She closed her eyes, held her breath and prayed one last time.

In the distance, an expanding white light appeared, warm and comforting. A child skipped forward and Anya knew everything would be all right. She reached out to take Miriam's hand.

44

Anya awoke on her side and coughed out water. Someone held a mask on her face. She tried to rip it off and coughed again.

Karen's face came into focus. 'Breathe slowly, slowly. It's oxygen. You're safe now.'

Anya remembered the tank. The water up to their foreheads. Swallowing water, then blackness. 'Fitz!'

'He's okay.' Karen pressed Anya's shoulder back to the floor. 'You can't kill that old coot. He's breathing by himself, and responsive.'

Martin was on his knees tending to FitzHarris.

'Who—?' Anya struggled to speak.

'The captain. He saw the pump lights go on from the bridge controls and came to see what Fitz was doing taking on ballast. He found Cockroach dead and Alessandro, the chief engineer, had been shot in the arm. He's upstairs with the doctor now. If that string wasn't coming out of the hatch, no one would have found you in time.'

Anya breathed in, and out. The plastic smell of the mask was a godsend. She looked across at Martin, who reached for her hand.

'Alessandro . . . the chief engineer.'

'Don't worry,' Karen said. 'He's safe. Bullet went clean through. He was lucky.'

Anya's mind was beginning to blur. She pulled herself to her elbows.

'He told us what happened,' Karen explained. 'Cockroach pulled a gun on him and they fought. He had no idea you two were in the tank. If it wasn't for the sharp eye of the captain, you'd still be there.'

'He tried to kill us.'

'Yes, yes, we know. But he's dead now and you're safe. I want you to breathe deeply,' Karen said. 'You could have aspirated water.'

Anya coughed and coughed again. Suddenly, she gagged and the world went black.

Ben was asleep at her side when she woke in the hospital.

'You gave us a scare.' Martin stroked her hair.

Karen checked the intravenous drip and adjusted the dose on the tubing. 'Before you ask, Fitz is having a good sleep.'

'Alessandro shot Cockroach.'

'We know.'

Her mouth was dry, and she tried to lick her lips. 'Cockroach gave up the gun and Alessandro shot him.'

'Did you see it?' Martin asked.

'No.' Anya had her back to him at the time. 'I was trying to help Fitz out and heard the shot. Cockroach was on the ground.'

Martin and Karen exchanged glances.

'It sounds to me like he had no choice,' Karen replied. 'Cockroach lunged at him.'

'You don't understand.'

'Try and keep her calm,' Karen told Martin, and excused herself.

'Don't worry about anything now. All that matters is that you're safe, Annie.' He kissed her forehead and took her hand.

She glanced at Ben, who stirred. He opened his eyes, blinked, then went back to sleep.

'I need to talk to Fitz,' she said, and tried to sit up. 'He knows what happened.'

Martin held her by the shoulders. 'Karen just explained. He's out of it, and you're confused. You need to rest.'

'I need to wake him.'

'You can't.' Martin frowned. 'He aspirated a lot of water and dropped his oxygen saturation a little while ago. He's on a ventilator and may not make it.'

There was silence apart from the beep of the monitor.

'I'm sorry, Annie. All we can do now is wait.'

Anya fought the urge to sleep. Her body had the weight of lead, and refused to do what she wanted. Ben roused and asked to go to the toilet. Martin lifted him up.

'Can you please check on Fitz,' Anya managed.

'Sure. I'll get a snack for Ben too and be right back.'

The regular beat of her heart was hypnotic. Her lids became heavier and she began to drift off. The sound of the monitor faded.

She forced open her eyes and caught a glimpse of a blurred figure standing over her bed. At first she thought it was a bad dream, then she realised he was in the room. The equipment was switched off.

'You should have kept your mouth shut,' Alessandro said through gritted teeth. 'Cockroach panicked when he saw that nosy bitch and pushed her into the tank.'

Anya needed to buy time. Long enough for someone to walk into the room before he tried to hurt her.

'Why put her in the morgue?'

'What choice did I have? She was too big to jettison. You think I could move a body and throw it over the side without someone seeing? I had to hide it somewhere until port. The morgue's the only place that isn't manned around the clock.'

Anya glanced at the doorway. No one was there.

343

'Why shoot Carlos?' Her voice rasped from coughing and screaming for help.

'Carlos is paid handsomely to forge the records. Then I found out he was being paid by Lars Anderson to feed that woman the real figures. Cockroach shot him to warn others what happens to traitors.'

'But you didn't kill him.'

'I still needed to find all his money.' Alessandro smiled. 'If you don't mind, I'm tired and I need to get some sleep.'

Before she could call out, the pillow was over her face, pressing hard against her mouth and nose. With what little strength she had, she bucked and clawed at his powerful hands and struggled to fill her lungs. She reached out to her side for something – anything – to make him stop. Suddenly, the pressure released and the pillow was gone. She took a deep gasp.

Captain Burghoff stood at her bedside, holding a fire-extinguisher.

'Take some slow deep breaths. I'll buzz for the nurse.'

Karen ran in and assessed the scene. Once she saw Anya was all right, she moved to Alessandro on the floor.

'What on earth happened?' She felt for a pulse. 'He's breathing, but only just.'

'He tried to kill Doctor Crichton. I did what was necessary to subdue him, under the circumstances,' the captain replied, clearly in control.

'Why were you here?' Anya managed.

'To arrest him. Security are searching the centre now.'

'But how . . .'

'I suggest you rest your voice.' He placed the extinguisher on the floor and stood behind Karen.

She had pulled on gloves and was feeling Alessandro for fractures. Blood covered her gloves.

'I hit him on the right side, behind his ear.' The captain

turned back to Anya. 'I recognised Alessandro's handwriting on one of the fake logs your husband gave me. Alessandro had to be involved in falsifying the records. His gunshot wound was superficial, and Doctor Novak has confirmed it was self-inflicted.'

'If he needs a medical evacuation,' he addressed Karen, 'let me know asap. The Fijian authorities will be notified as soon as I am informed.'

The captain spoke with little emotion, even though he must have worked closely with Alessandro on the cruises.

Doctor Novak arrived and threw his hands in the air. 'What now?' He mumbled to himself as he grabbed dressings and equipment.

Karen didn't bother with details. 'Skull fracture, his coma score is three. He's opening his eyes and flexing to pain. I'm keeping pressure on the wound.'

Captain Burghoff wheeled a chair to Anya's side and sat down. 'You deserve to know why you were placed in that ballast. According to another crew member from the refuse centre, he and Carlos were paid to illegally dispose of waste – by Mats Anderson, the late owner's son. He communicated with them by a fax machine in Alessandro's office. The scheme on one ship alone saved the company millions of dollars over a year. We don't know how many other ships are involved, or where Carlos hid his money. That secret, both men are keeping.'

That meant the two competing brothers, Mats and Lars, were both paying Carlos.

The captain smiled at her and Anya could see why he had many 'favourites' among the crew. She remembered the woman with Carlos's room mate, the one with the diamond pendant.

The *Paradisio* had been to Africa and India during Carlos's contract. He could have made a similar purchase to the captain. 'Where are the world's cheapest places to buy diamonds?'

The captain raised his eyebrows. 'There are some markets in India that peddle what some believe are blood diamonds. They are the cheapest I have come across and the quality is excellent.'

'Why didn't I think of it before? No wonder Carlos wanted me to get the painting and the jacket.'

The captain gave her a quizzical look.

'Fitz didn't find anything when he X-rayed Carlos's jacket because glass and crystals are radioopaque but diamonds are radiolucent. Carlos used his money to buy diamonds and then hid them in plain view, on cheap items no one would want to steal. We just assumed they were rhinestones.'

'I can see why FitzHarris respects you so much,' Burghoff said.

'How is he doing?'

The captain pursed his lips. 'Fighting the breathing tube as of a few minutes ago.'

That was better news, he had to be making efforts to breath on his own. She had to know, though.

'Was FitzHarris in with the others?'

On the floor, Alessandro groaned and Doctor Novak snapped at him in something that sounded like Serbian.

The captain half-smiled. 'No, but he has kept a detailed file on Mats documenting everything he communicated. Times, dates, instructions, offers of payment. Thanks to FitzHarris, Mats Anderson can be charged with fraud and a number of corporate crimes.'

Anya felt relieved about Fitz's innocence.

'What about Rachel?'

'I'm afraid you can't see her. She is busy attending to her patient. FitzHarris requires twenty-four-hour care, you see.'

346

Anya took a moment to process what Burghoff had said. Rachel had been released.

'Ah, you would not have heard,' he said.

Two security men arrived with a plastic stretcher and lifted Alessandro onto it. Karen carried a drip and Doctor Novak gave instructions about how to load the patient. As quickly as they had appeared, the patient and medical team left for the emergency treatment room.

'Heard what?'

'I spoke to a contact who informs me the piping used on the tender to hold the explosives had old Russian markings, the type used by their mafia. Apparently, Sven Anderson was about to divorce his latest wife. Word is, there's no scorn like a Russian oligarch's little princess. Plus the added incentive of a multi-billion dollar industry. With the other Anderson heirs dead, or under arrest, Sven's wife assumes control.'

'What about Mats?' Anya cleared her sore throat. 'He could fight the charges.'

'Ah, but he still has to survive the Russian mafia.'

Anya had read that old man Anderson had married the oligarch's daughter to gain better access to Russian business. In the end, it had cost his family their lives.

Martin had been right. The first question in an investigation should always be who was most likely to benefit from the crime.

'So Rachel is free?'

'She will see you when she can.' The captain stood and placed the chair back by the desk. 'If you will excuse me, I have a ship to command.'

45

The following night, before arrival in Bora-Bora, the captain arranged a private dinner for Anya, Ben, Martin, and whoever else they wanted to invite.

Alessandro had been airlifted in advance and it looked like he would survive to face murder charges.

Wesley pushed his father's wheelchair into the dining room. The elder Meeks wore a tie and suit, one arm of which was pinned to his side. He nervously greeted everyone at the table. Wes had on a grey button-down shirt and black jeans, his hair swept off his face. He looked more handsome than usual. Karen wore a casual skirt and blouse, plus make-up. Rachel's glasses were purple-rimmed, and her top a cobalt blue.

Laura brought FitzHarris in a wheelchair. He had been extubated and demanded to be released from his hospital bed so he could attend.

Anya kissed him on the cheek. 'You've had a rough few days.'

He squeezed her hand. 'You and me both.'

Anya excused herself for a moment. Jasmine arrived, looking stunning in a turquoise, knee-length dress. Doctor Chan, Jasmine's aunt and cousins had chosen to stay in their cabin. Ben ran and launched himself at Jasmine. She flicked her loose hair over one shoulder and bent down to return the hug.

'How's your mother doing?'

'Better. We are getting on and she says I don't have to go

to the audition in Vienna if I'm not ready. There's always next year, she said.'

Anya felt relieved. Jasmine deserved to experience life and make friends, like other teenagers. 'She knows Wesley and I have been talking, and she doesn't seem to mind. I just have to tell her where I am and when I'll be back.'

The look between Wes and Jasmine said it all. Wesley's crush was requited. They were quickly involved in an animated discussion about music.

Laura interrupted. 'Wesley?' Both males looked up. 'I need to have a word to you about a virus we found on the computers. It was clever, and deletes itself. Only problem was, it slowed the system down. We had hundreds of complaints.'

The father turned to his son. 'Do you know anything about that?'

'Well . . .'

FitzHarris interjected. 'I asked Wes to do me a favour.' He winked at Anya. 'It was a way of testing the security of our system. And I have to say, there are improvements that can be made. Wes just needs to write up the last of his suggestions before I hand over the final report.' He looked across the table. 'Mr Meeks, you have a fine son there. I'd be happy to give him a reference any time.'

Wes stared at Fitz with a look of disbelief. His father beamed.

Anya smiled at FitzHarris, who was parked at her side.

'Without Wes,' he spoke quietly to her, 'we wouldn't have Shelby's statement or photos, or found out that Berry posted them online. I just got a message. The FBI are treating this as a paedophile ring. Seems the clowns who slept with Kandy and Lilly love to share dirty photos online. These ones are just the latest. Even if they get off on the drug and rape charges, they'll all be branded sex offenders. Kandy decided to come forward and wants the men charged.'

350

It may not have been the perfect outcome, but the men were being punished for what they did to Lilly and Kandy. Anya hoped the Ratzenbergs would be supportive of their daughter. It had taken a lot of courage for her to come forward. She also hoped the outcome would at least help Jasmine and her mother get some kind of closure.

After a dinner filled with amusing anecdotes about ship life, Martin and Anya took Ben to bed.

Something inside the suite was beeping intermittently. Martin rummaged under the lounge cushions and located his phone. 'It's a text.' He turned around to read it. Anya assumed it was from Nita, his now former girlfriend.

He sank into one of the chairs and ran a hand through his hair, not taking his eyes off the phone screen.

'Is everything all right?'

'No. I mean . . . I don't know.'

Anya sat forward. 'Has something happened?'

'It's Nita's mother. She says I have to call her straightaway. The old bird can't stand me so something must be wrong.'

Anya was unsure what to say. They were yet to discuss why they made love, or what it meant for their relationship.

'I won't be long, Annie. We really need to talk about us.' He excused himself to return the call.

To give him privacy, Anya grabbed her pashmina and headed out for a walk.

She left the suite and walked along the corridor. Couples – young and old – wandered arm in arm, hand in hand. How naive had she been? It was just sex she and Martin had. The artificial closeness from the trip was the cause. It had been fun while it lasted, but the holiday was ending. Life had to get back to normal, whatever that meant.

Feeling a chill, she pulled the shawl tighter and decided to visit the library one more time. Inside were Jasmine and Wes, holding hands.

'Anya,' Wes said. 'Can we ask your opinion?'

She ventured closer, feeling like an intruder.

'Lilly signed this book and wanted it put in here, but Jasmine's afraid to let it go. Just because someone isn't physically with you, doesn't mean you're really apart.'

He gently moved a piece of hair from her face. 'We may live in different places, but we'll still be together, I mean, we can still be . . . well we can . . . you know . . .'

The boy who had a quip for any situation was suddenly tongue-tied. Jasmine just looked at him admiringly.

'Anyway, what do you think? Should Jasmine keep it or leave it here for someone else to read?'

To Kill A Mockingbird. 'I think Jasmine can only do what's in her heart. All I know is some people think they can hang on to someone they've lost by keeping things from their time together. I prefer to think that memories and ongoing love, not possessions, keep them alive. In us.'

Jasmine bowed her head. 'Thank you.'

She stretched up and put the book back on the shelf, as Lilly had done.

'If it's ever meant to come back to us, it will,' she said.

Anya left with a tear in her eye.

Back in the suite, Martin was upstairs packing his things. Her heart skipped. She didn't want him to go.

He stopped when he saw her.

'Annie, I'm so sorry.'

'What happened in the shower shouldn't have,' she said quickly. 'It was crazy, and we just got carried away.'

He stepped toward her. 'Is that what you really believe?'

Unsure, Anya pulled away. She was too afraid to admit how much Martin meant to her, but he had made his choice. He had chosen Nita over her.

'Annie—'

'You don't have to worry about Ben.' She picked up a shirt

and began to fold it. 'I'll take good care of him. It'll give us some special time together.'

'Stop, please. You need to know why I have to go.'

He grabbed the shirt and sat on the edge of the bed.

He took a deep breath. 'About five years ago, Nita had a melanoma cut off her back.'

Anya sat down beside him. 'You never said.'

'It was before we even met. They thought they got it all,' he continued. 'But she's been feeling short of breath and went to a doctor. They did some tests and found a lesion on her lung.'

Anya could barely move. The prognosis for melanoma-spread was poor. Vaccinations and promising treatments were still being developed. 'I'm sorry.'

Martin leant forward and put his head in his hands. 'She was really upset, Annie.'

Anya thought of Nita – she had always liked her and she'd seemed like a strong woman. She didn't deserve this.

'She asked me to go back. She needs me to be there. I want to stay with you, Annie, but . . .'

Anya squeezed his hand. 'It's the right thing to do.' And she wanted more than anything to believe that.

They sat together in silence until daylight broke. The foghorn blasted as the ship came in to dock at Bora-Bora.

KATHRYN FOX

MALICIOUS INTENT

Dr Anya Crichton, a pathologist and forensic physician, finds that work is sparse for the only female freelancer in the field. Between paying child support, a mortgage and struggling to get her business off the ground, Anya can't yet afford to fight her ex-husband for custody of their three-year-old son, Ben.

When Anya is asked to look into the seemingly innocent suicide of a teenager, Anya notices similarities between the girl's death and several other cases she is working on with her friend and colleague, Detective Sergeant Kate Farrer. All the victims went missing for a period of time, only to be found dead of apparent suicide in most unusual circumstances.

As Anya delves deeper, the pathological findings point to the frightening possibility that the deaths are not only linked, but part of a sinister plot. Nothing can prepare her for the terrifying truth . . .

HODDER

KATHRYN FOX

BLOOD BORN

A teenager is found barely alive by the roadside, bleeding from her slit throat. The police can't even begin to imagine the horrors she has faced. For inside their house lies the girl's older sister: brutally tortured, raped and stabbed to death.

As the girl struggles for survival, forensic scientist Anya Crichton is brought in to examine the evidence, all of which points towards a well-known family of career criminals.

However, it soon becomes clear that they will stop at nothing to evade the law.

Even if others have to die.

HODDER

KATHRYN FOX

DEATH MASK

When the victim of a violent gang rape accuses five premier sportsmen of the attack, she has no idea that her suffering has only just begun . . .

It's a scandal that rocks a nation of sports fans. But, in spite of a huge amount of evidence, no one seems to believe her.

So when Dr Anya Crichton, a forensic expert in sexual assault, is asked to become involved by the team managers, she simply can't say no.

But as she investigates further, Anya realises that the scandals, violence and abuses run much deeper, and much further into the past than she could ever have imagined.

And it's down to her to find out exactly who's responsible.
Before it happens again.

HODDER

In the best books, the ending often comes as a shock.
Not just because of that one last twist in the tale,
but because you have been so absorbed in their world,
that coming back to the harsh light of reality is a jolt.

If that describes you now, then perhaps you should track down
some new leads, and find new suspense in other worlds.

Join us at www.hodder.co.uk, or follow us on
Twitter @hodderbooks, and you can tap in to a
community of fellow thrill-seekers.

Whether you want to find out more about this book,
or a particular author, watch trailers and interviews, have
the chance to win early limited editions, or simply browse
our expert readers' selection of the very best books,
we think you'll find what you're looking for.

And if you don't, that's the place to tell us what's missing.

We love what we do, and we'd love you to be part of it.

www.hodder.co.uk

 @hodderbooks

HodderBooks

 HodderBooks